KIDD BLACK

"The Beginning"

KIDD BLACK

"The Beginning"

by
Harvey Black and
Jonathan Levine

Laddin Press, LLC
Huntington Station, New York 11746

2011

ISBN 978-0-9839433-0-3
Library of Congress Control Number: 2011917512

Laddin Press, LLC
70 Cornehlsen Drive
Huntington Station, NY 11746-1133
e-mail: laddpr@verizon.net

Laddin Press edition November, 2011

Printed in the United States of America

Extra Special Thanks to:

My mother, Lillie Black, for reading to me and telling me stories as a child;

My father, Dr. Asher Black, for teaching me the importance of knowledge and morality;

My co-author, Jonathan Levine, for believing in me;

And last, but not least, my children, Sabrina Rose and Jared Diamond, for being my inspiration and just being fun.

With Love,
Harvey

To Viviane, my wife, my everything.

To Harv, thanks for asking me along for the ride.

Jonathan

PART ONE

1

KIDD BLACK adjusts his sunglasses and looks out over the steaming streets of Athens. His skin glistens like fine milk chocolate melting in the hot Greek sun. The Australian sitting across from him catches a glimpse of his ice blue eyes as Kidd says in an unmistakable American accent, "What a mess these Olympics are."

Nothing was moving. Just a lot of tourists wondering why they had come and a lot more Greeks waiting for the tourists to leave. The place was tense. The traffic jam wasn't helping either. But, tense or not, as far as he was concerned, things were looking good. Maybe the seven hundred seventy-five million dollar security budget was worth it after all. Cops are everywhere. On horses, bicycles, roller blades, even on foot.

An Australian accent pierces through the din of the cafe. "A mess? I like to think of it as organized chaos. After all, I helped put this show together. So, let's sit back and enjoy it. We're almost home."

The Australian shouts something to the waiter and reaches for his beer.

Kidd asks, "How come your Greek is so good?"

"Melbourne has the second largest population of Greeks in the world. One of them just happens to be my mother." He lifts his beer, smiles and says, "To my mother."

"Easy for you to be in a good mood. I just spent the last two weeks watching ping pong. I'd rather watch tiddlywinks."

"What can I tell you? We kept on picking up the words, 'ping pong,' and then we had some hard evidence linking Dalakos and ping pong."

After all these years, the name of Christopher Dalakos has a strange effect on Kidd. He's been after him for eighteen years and still doesn't know what he looks like. Doesn't even know if he really exists. Could be what they say is true: The legendary Dalakos is just that, a legend.

The American shakes off a cold shiver, adjusts his sunglasses and takes a sip of water. He shakes his head and mumbles, "Ping pong."

"Come on, Yank, watching ping pong couldn't have been that bad."

"Easy for you to say. You've been holed up at this cafe watching beautiful women walk by since the Opening Ceremony."

"You're not going to stick me in some hi-tech HQ. And there's no better spot than Syntagma Square. All roads might lead to Rome but in Athens they all start right here."

A yellow school bus inches by them. Kidd asks, "Another one? What is this, a school bus convention?"

"They've shipped in kids from every country of the world for the Closing Ceremony." The Australian looks satisfied as he says, "I've checked out every driver. All one hundred fifty-five of them."

The American looks at the children's faces. Every kid's dream. To come to the Olympics. Makes him wonder if he should've settled down and had a few of his own. He's quickly brought back to earth when he notices the bus driver has the harassed look of someone who's stuck in a traffic jam and running late.

A water tanker pulls up by their cafe. Everybody, including the Australian, notices it and starts laughing. Everyone that is, except the American.

"What's that all about?"

"That, my friend, is not something you see every day. That guy's wearing a Pongrati work shirt and driving a Pingoros truck."

Kidd says, "Yeah, real funny."

"They hate each other. Two villages that claim to have the purest water in the world. Three years ago, there was nitroglycerin found in the Pongrati wells. They accused Pingoros and there was almost a war. No kidding."

A bus driver yells something to a couple of cops who go out in the intersection and block traffic so the school buses can get through. After a lot of honking, traffic starts moving again. The people in the cafe taunt the water tank driver. He looks agitated.

The Australian adds, "He's Albanian. Probably doesn't speak a word of Greek."

A pretty blonde in a short skirt comes by and the Australian, along with most of the crowd, forgets the driver to watch her walk away.

Kidd doesn't even notice her. He's thinking, There's an Albanian driving the wrong truck. How is that possible? Can't read Greek. Got in the wrong truck? Which means somewhere there should be a Pingoros truck with a Pongrati driver.

Pon-grati and Pin-goros. Or maybe, PINGrati and PONGoros! Nitroglycerin. About as explosive as you can get!

Kidd Black, all six feet two of him, jumps to his feet. He looks up the hill and sees the truck starting to pick up speed as the traffic finally breaks. "Something's not right. Tell 'em to stop every Pingrati and Pongoros water tanker!"

Kidd runs towards the truck. The Australian doesn't hesitate. He picks up his phone and gets all of the forty thousand cops and soldiers in Athens looking for Pingrati and Pongoros water tankers.

Kidd runs up the street. Cops on horses and cops on bikes.

I'd rather crawl than ride a horse. I'm going with the bike.

He puts two fingers to the throat of the unsuspecting cop and knocks him off the bike. He jumps on and starts pedaling up the hill. He's trained all his life for this moment. Though there will be no cheering crowds, this is his Olympics.

The hill is the steepest in Athens. But, like a man possessed, he gains on the truck. He pulls up alongside it and grabs onto the spigot that opens the water. Balancing precariously with his other hand, he turns it and is almost knocked over by the strong smell of nitroglycerin.

Behind him he hears the unmistakable sound of a horse gaining on him. He has to move fast. The moment the cops catch up to him, they'll shoot first and ask questions later.

He reaches for the spigot again and forces it all the way open. The liquid starts flowing out onto the street with a deafening whoosh. The driver looks in his side-view mirror and spots a man with a baseball cap pedaling feverishly next to his truck. The driver swings the truck violently to his right. The American is knocked to the side and is about to crash down to the pavement when he's scooped up by the Australian on horseback!

The Australian shouts, "Looks like we've got ourselves a couple of live ones here, Yank. Now, if you don't mind, you get back on that little tanker and take care of business. There's another truck that I've got my eye on."

The Australian motions to his right. A Pingrati water tanker is coming up the access road.

Kidd stands behind the Australian as he maneuvers the horse to the side of the truck. The truck swerves again but the Australian anticipates it and slows the horse enough to get behind it. Kidd leaps from the horse onto the back of the tanker and scurries to the top. The Australian immediately cuts across a wooded area heading for the other truck.

Kidd works his way along the top of the tanker just as the tanker reaches the crest of the hill. Down in the valley on the other side, is a sea of bright yellow...SCHOOL BUSES! One hundred fifty-five of them. One for each country in the Olympics. More than five thousand kids.

Over on his right, he can see the Australian closing in on the other tanker. They both better move fast. The two roads will intersect in less than a minute and then it's straight downhill to the school kids.

Kidd finally reaches the cab of the tanker. Off to his right, he hears a shot. The Australian reaches over the dead driver's body but the driver's shoulders have slumped through the steering wheel, jamming it. He desperately tries to control the truck.

At the other truck, Kidd pulls out his gun and hangs over the driver's side. The driver thrusts open his door, smashing the window into the American's face. His sunglasses go flying off. The driver sees his piercing blue eyes and is terrified. He now knows his situation is hopeless...he's up against a legend...he's up against Kidd Black, the Black man with the Blue eyes.

The American aims and fires. The bullet strikes the driver's temple. The truck swerves, sending Kidd flying off it just as the two tankers collide at the top of the hill.

The explosion immediately kills the Australian. Kidd is thrown across the highway and down a grassy slope. As he loses consciousness, he whispers, "Dalakos!"

2

IN SAN FRANCISCO, sweat trickles down Devon Williams' cheek as his eyes are glued to the screen. The nuclear plant is going on line in five hours.

In Washington, the President knows he has to make a decision. The best-case scenario is nine thousand human shields dead...if the attack is perfect. The other choice is to do nothing and then have to deal with a nuclear weapons black market open to the highest bidder...and the President has a very good feeling who the highest bidder will be.

Fifteen American satellites are now in position. Keeping them in place is like juggling fifteen hot potatoes at once, possible but not easy.

The next step has never been done before. The software has to be able to line up fifteen more satellites so that all thirty will have a clear firing line. At the same time, their solar panels have to be kept at just the right angle to the sun for the power supply.

Four hours and thirty-nine minutes later, the thirty satellites are all in place. Each satellite is armed with the laser to end all lasers...the LAZER.

If the calculations are correct, if the software doesn't freeze up, if the hardware doesn't break down, if the President gives the order, Devon will finally know if the years of work have paid off.

At four hours and fifty-three minutes, still no word. Plenty of words from

CNN though. The Human Shields are in a frenzy counting down the last seven minutes.

At four hours and fifty-five minutes, the call comes through from the President: "Lazer it!"

Devon takes a deep breath, presses a button and waits for all hell to break loose. Thirty lazers strike the complex at the same time. One giant lazer by itself can't do the job without enormous "collateral damage" but thirty pinpoint lazers can do all the damage he needs.

Three minutes later, it's all over. The complex has literally collapsed in on itself, like a black hole. In fact, a black hole is all that's left. That and thousands of speechless Human Shields.

Devon rushes out of his office only then realizing that it's daylight. He's worked through the night...again. He shouts, "It worked! It worked! Monique, we did it!"

He flies downstairs past the framed Time Magazine cover with his steely-eyed face on it.

Devon Williams

Man of the Year/Man of Action

He knew hanging the cover on the wall was vain but after all, it was his first "Man of the Year." How was he supposed to know there would be three more?

He runs through the house shouting for his wife, Monique. He doesn't care if he wakes up their ten year old daughter, Sabrina Rose, actually he wants to wake her up and tell her the news, too.

Though it was all only a simulation, a computer game of sorts, it had finally worked. Monique's theory was correct. You could use small manageable lasers together to make the most powerful pinpoint weapon ever invented. Now, it was only a matter of time before they had a working prototype.

The only problem being, how to get the billions for thirty satellites. He sighs. If I have to, I'll just pay for it out of my own pocket.

But his wife and daughter are nowhere to be seen. Devon remembers that Monique had gone to a week-end conference in Washington and taken Sabrina Rose with her. But, they should be back by now.

Devon picks up his cell phone and sees there's a text message. He clicks on it and then just stares blankly at it. He looks at it from all angles as though it was something that had arrived from another planet.

Dear Devon,

Please don't take this news too hard. I truly admire you and thank you for all you've done. I'm sorry to tell you that I've fallen in love with the most incredible man I've ever met. Sabrina Rose and I are leaving. Don't try to follow, you won't find us. Good-bye and may God be with you.

Monique

He tries to call his wife back, gets her answering machine and leaves a message. "Call me."

Back in his private office, Devon knows there are a hundred things to do. There are logical ways to find someone. It's just a matter of finding the logic and connecting the dots. Like writing software code.

But before he does anything, he has to make one more call. As he picks up the phone, he takes one more look at the message.

Devon presses his speed-dial button #1. It picks up after one ring. He says, "Mr. President, this is Devon Williams."

The President quickly puts on the speaker-phone so Amanda Mason, his chief-of-staff, can listen in. Before the conversation is even over, they're both thinking, Why would any woman leave Devon Williams?

3

AMANDA MASON is in a hurry. She's never been late for a PACT meeting before and she wouldn't have been late for this one if it hadn't been for Devon's phone call. Devon wanted the President to get on it right away. The President promised Devon he would, but told Amanda to wait at least forty-eight hours. "Give Monique Williams a chance to come to her senses. No reason to bring in those cowboys over at PACT unless we have to."

So, Amanda thought, I've got forty-eight hours before they call out the bloodhounds. Amanda laughs to herself. I could tell that just the mention of Monique's name got the President breathing heavy...I wonder what it would be like to have that kind of effect on men.

As she heads into Virginia horse country, Amanda starts thinking back to when she had first met Devon. It was at West Point and Devon was her professor, even though he was a year younger than she. He was kind of goofy but he sure knew his way around a computer.

I always wanted to invite him over to my room to show him my computer but having a man over was strictly against all the rules. Not that it mattered. Once I introduced Monique to Devon, it was as though I had become invisible.

Amanda pulls her car into the underground garage at the "Silver Meadows Horse Farm." This is the unofficial headquarters of PACT, the President's Advisory Council on Terrorism.

PACT is more than just another government advisory board. PACT has a secret side. Its own budget, its own infrastructure and most important of all, its own agents...the elite, the best of the best.

She gets out of the car and takes a quick look in the rear view mirror. She runs a hand across her short hair and gets out. She had tried long hair and she had tried shoulder-length. You name it, she had tried it. But, once she realized that there was nothing that would make her the kind of woman men would go out of their way to meet, she had settled on short hair. Might as well be comfortable.

She knew what it was like to be in a room full of people and be invisible. She'd make a great bank robber. The tellers would describe her as a female Caucasian, average height with an average face. She liked to think that they'd at least notice that she kept in great shape, though she doubted they would.

But, she had smarts and ambition. And when you can do something for someone, they notice you. And, she certainly liked being noticed.

As she heads across the paddock into the Guest House, she can't help smiling. It's been almost twenty years and I'm still glad I turned Monique in when I had the chance.

Amanda's the last one into the meeting. She has the bad luck to come in just as Ike Muslow, the "retired" former head of the CIA and present head of PACT is speaking. He's just turned sixty and has the robust complexion of a man who has lived well all his life. With his tailored suits and rigid posture, you could immediately see he was a man who was used to getting his way. It almost seemed that the bald spot and the gray hair were added just for effect.

Ike looks down at her over his glasses and nods. Amanda feels like a schoolgirl who's late for class. Nothing to do though but smile weakly and take her seat. There's an open place by Caroline, the young woman who is PACT's computer specialist.

Before Amanda even has a chance to whisper hello, Ike clears his throat and motions to the present head of the CIA who looks at his notes and continues, "The economic ramifications of another peso devaluation will have a ripple effect throughout Latin America that could come back to us as a tidal wave."

While the presentation drones on, Caroline passes a note to Amanda:

Guess who's back on the market? For the answer, flip this over.

Amanda quickly turns over the note and reads, Devon Williams that's who. His wife left him! There's hope for us yet!

Amanda thinks how it didn't take long for the cat to get out of this bag. When it comes to siphoning information, Caroline is incredible. She probably knew Monique had left Devon before Devon did.

While Amanda allows herself the luxury of fantasizing where she'd go on her honeymoon with Devon, Caroline starts typing on her computer. She pulls up a file on Monique and whispers, "She was last seen at the conference, 'Computer Viruses as an Offensive Weapon.' It was right here in Washington yesterday."

Amanda leans over the computer screen and reads, The illustrious Monique Williams was the featured speaker.

Caroline sighs and continues, "She's drop-dead dazzling. If that's Devon's type, I don't have a chance."

Amanda thinks, What's she talking about? Caroline's not even thirty and turns heads wherever she goes. Sure, she wasn't just another pretty face, but it wasn't her face people remembered, it was those breasts. The kind of breasts women would fly to Brazil for, the kind of breasts women would take out a loan for. She told me that it was tough to be taken seriously when everyone just concentrated on your looks. I should have such problems. She even wore glasses though she didn't really need them.

Amanda lightly touches Caroline's arm. "I thought you were happily married."

Caroline types and mumbles, "Yeah, yeah."

She hits the enter key and says, "Check this out from the security camera. Monique's leaving with a guy."

"And it's definitely not Devon Williams."

"Let's just see if we have his photo in our database."

The two of them are now huddled over the computer waiting for an answer. Ike looks at them quizzically. The screen flashes "no match," and Amanda moans. "Damn. I sure wish I knew who that gorgeous guy was."

Ike once again clears his throat. Caroline and Amanda reluctantly give him their undivided attention. He then pulls out a file and addresses the Head of the Joint Chiefs of Staff, "I see here that the Saudis have launched another weather satellite. What's going on here?"

The head of the Joint Chiefs of Staff says, "We're building them for them. They're just that. Weather satellites."

Ike disdainfully asks, "Weather satellites? It's the god damn desert! It's hot during the day and cold at night. Why do you need thirty-three satellites to know that?"

Amanda jumps in, "It's the President's opinion that these satellites encourage inter-Arab cooperation under our auspices and as such should be viewed as a positive development."

Ike groans. "It's not the President's job to have opinions of his own."

Amanda glances at the Joint Chief before saying, "Ignoring that last remark, this is a huge contract for Microtech. The President's message is, and I quote, 'Don't fuck it up.'"

Ike pretends he didn't hear that remark and says, "That's all we have time for. So, next time..."

Caroline interrupts him. "But I haven't given my presentation yet."

Ike sighs and reluctantly announces, "Alright. Caroline Crimmins will give us a very brief update on her latest pet project."

Caroline clicks her mouse, the lights in the room dim and a picture of two young kids, a boy and a girl, come up on the screen.

Caroline smiles and says, "Here are my two kids, Jack and Sandra."

Ike quietly groans some more and looks at his watch.

Caroline continues, "I've been working on a system that takes into account bone structure, projected diet and other actuarial variables and put together an algorithm that extrapolates what that person will look like in twenty, thirty or even fifty years."

She looks at Ike. "It's a project I've been working on, on my own time."

She clicks and there's a picture of a middle-aged man and woman. "These are what my kids will look like in thirty years."

Ike's had enough. "Knowing your expertise with computers, there's no doubt in my mind that is exactly what your children will look like and while I see a tremendous market for that as a birthday novelty gift, I don't see any practical value for PACT."

Caroline patiently waits for him to finish and says, "Recently I had the idea to work backwards. Take a photo of an adult and match it with a photo from when they were younger. I've got a prototype and I'd like to show you how it works."

She clicks again and there's a photo of the Washington Redskins football team.

"For example, I can take this photo, match it with my international database of runaway kids and tell you if any of these men were missing children."

Amanda interrupts and jumps in. "What I want to know is who ran away with Devon Williams' wife."

A buzz fills the room. That certainly got everyone's attention.

Caroline hesitates and says, "Uh, I could try."

Up comes a photo and Caroline says, "This is Monique Williams leaving yesterday's weapons conference here in Washington with an unidentified man."

Ike quickly adds, "Which doesn't mean she ran off with him." Caroline mumbles, "Yeah, yeah…

I've done a search for a physiogenic match in all known databases and come up with nothing. So, let's see if I can match his photo today with any photos of children over the last thirty-five years."

She hits "search" and while the computer works, she explains, "There are any number of people who have photos on record as kids but nothing as an adult. There are also any number of people who go out of their way not to be photographed."

A beep sounds and up pops a newspaper photo of a boy of about ten sullenly standing between two policemen. It's easy to see that the cops aren't American. Beneath the photo is something written in Greek.

Ike and the rest of PACT lean forward now, their full attention on Caroline.

Caroline clicks again and triumphantly says, "Let me just get a translation of this and hopefully it will tell us the name of the man who Monique was last seen with."

Ike casually says, "No need for that. I speak Greek." He says it as though it was the most normal thing in the world.

With his eyes glued to the screen, Ike starts translating. "This is the orphan who was caught soaking live stray dogs and cats in gasoline and lighting them on fire. He is the same child accused of putting peanut butter in a classmate's lunch who was allergic to peanuts. The nine year old classmate died of anaphylactic shock but it could not be proven that Christopher Dalakos..."

For the first time in her life, Amanda watches Ike turn pale. He picks up the red phone next to him and tries to hide the panic in his voice as he says, "Get me Kidd Black!"

4

KIDD'S THOUGHTS can't help but drift skyward as his hang glider reaches altitude."Almost Heaven, West Virginia..." My father used to sing that song.

My mother used to make fun of him for being a John Denver fan. Well, Dad, here I am halfway to heaven in West Virginia.

Yeah, my father. Couldn't resist a joke, no matter what the situation.

I had a dream the night John Denver crashed his plane into the ocean. My father asked me, "What key does John Denver sing in?" Before I could even try to guess, he said, "Sea-flat."

I laughed a little and said to him, "A Baptist, a Jew and John Denver show up at the Pearly Gates. St. Peter says, 'I'm sorry, John Denver jokes are out.'"

K.Y.A."Know Your Audience". Rule number one for telling a joke...In my dream, my father laughed a lot when I told him that joke. Not because it was so funny but because his son came right back with a joke of his own. It was a laugh full of pride. The pride of a father who had raised his son right.

Sure, he was proud of all the awards and attention I had received and he was thrilled about the appointment to West Point but nothing made him happier than to sit around with his son and tell jokes.

For the first time in years, I woke up with a smile on my face. Yeah, like father like son.

Of course, Kidd didn't really look like his father, who was pasty white. To most people he looked like his mother. When your mother is black and your father is white, people see you as black. That's just the way it is. If it wasn't for the scars, a knife wound here, a burn there, you'd think he had just been dipped in fine milk chocolate.

Kidd's mother was a doctor. The only black pediatrician in the Roxbury section of Boston. His father taught high school history...the kind of teacher who inspired kids to one day become teachers.

From his mother, Kidd saw what raw determination could accomplish. From his father, he learned a sense of history. From both of them, he learned what was right and what was wrong...and that sometimes you had to fight for what was right.

What people remembered most about Kidd, more than his height, two inches over six feet, and more than the long piano player fingers—oh, how his mother wanted him to keep playing the piano—were his eyes. The surprise of a black man with blue eyes. A blue so deep, you could get lost in them.

An endless blue, like falling out of an airplane.

But now his eyes had a sadness to them. A sadness not from seeing too much killing but a softness from having spent eighteen years alone, from eighteen years of being a ghost.

Kidd Black heads the hang glider straight towards the ground. The wind whips across his face as he speeds downward, deathward. His veins popping out and his muscles straining, Kidd forces the glider against its will to take him back skyward.

Nothing can kill me. I'm already dead! When you sign up for PACT, you sign on as a dead man. No family, no friends, no one to put in danger, no one to slow you down.

Kidd smiles, a smile that's half wonder half pain, and thinks, Not only am I dead, but I've got a recording of my own funeral. Made it myself. Hid a microphone in the Chapel on the day I died...

Kidd's mind drifts back eighteen years to his "funeral" at West Point. Everyone was there...

Barry Feldman...chubby, slow but so full of life. My best friend right through high school. He was the first one to speak. He hated the idea of speaking in public but he wanted to say something.

Barry's voice shook when he said, "Top Cadet, Top of his class, Top of his game...The most amazing guy I ever met. Killed in a car accident. That's like Superman dying from slipping on a bar of soap in the shower..."

Devon Williams, West Point's youngest professor, the computer wizard, was up next. Devon could see the future and was showing the Army where the future was headed. The Army could also see where Devon was headed...Straight to the top.

Devon's voice was strong but full of pain. "I've only known Kidd for a year but we immediately became close...He always had something to say, something worth saying and something worth listening to."

Devon's voice lost its strength. He stopped for a moment to collect himself. Then he said, "If I had known he was going to be leaving us so soon, I would've found a way to record every moment we ever spent together..."

Next up was Amanda Mason, the new Top Cadet. She was direct and to the point. Always was and always will be. Back then, I suspected she didn't like me that much. Now I know my suspicions were correct. Plus, Amanda being Amanda, I expected her to talk more about herself than about me. I was right. She started off by saying, "I didn't know him well, but listening to everyone else today, I wish I had."

After her, the room became silent as my father walked unsteadily across the stage, his white skin probably even paler than usual. I can just imagine him grasping the lectern as he said in a barely audible voice, "My wife and I, we come from different backgrounds and as anyone can see, different colors. We are a family...we were a family...that loved to tell jokes. I asked my son to tell this joke at my funeral. I never thought I'd be telling it at his."

There was a sudden commotion. That had to be when Monique walked in. She always had an amazing effect on people. Maybe it was the long flowing auburn hair or the green eyes or the firm athletic body. Everyone saw something different...Everyone saw something they liked.

Of all the people who were asked to say something, she's the only one who refused...Only she and I would ever know why.

My father took a deep breath and started his joke. "Unable to attend the funeral after his father died, a son who lived far away called his brother and told him, 'Do something nice for Dad and send me the bill.'

Later, he got a bill for $200.00, which he paid. The next month, he got another bill for $200.00, which he also paid, figuring it was some incidental expense.

Bills for $200.00 kept arriving every month, and finally the man called his brother again to find out what was going on.

'Well,' said the other brother, 'you said to do something nice for Dad. So I rented him a tuxedo.'"

I imagine a few people smiled but it was certain that no one laughed.

My father's voice became quiet, almost inaudible as he said, "Today I want to remember Kidd Black for who he was and not who he could have been. Today, I'm going to smile, not cry, and I ask you all to do the same. And most of all, I want you to never forget my son, whose friends and foes alike called him, 'The Black Man with the Blue Eyes.'"

Kidd's beeper starts vibrating, snapping him back to reality, back to earth. He looks at it: Code One which means a helicopter is coming to pick him up to take him to the "farm."

Ike's in a hurry to see me. That's what they pay me for. It's not much, but nobody joins PACT for the money. If they did, then they'd really be nuts.

Kidd goes into his final maneuvers before landing and spots the helicopter on the ground. He thinks, Whoa, they're already here. This must be big!

Kidd lands and is told to leave his hang glider, someone will take care of it. When he gets into the chopper, the pilot takes one look at him and thinks, It's the legend himself, the Black Man with Blue Eyes. The best we've got.

From the time he's beeped to the time he gets to the "Farm," thirty-four minutes have passed. As soon as Kidd walks into the meeting, he can see that it hasn't been a particularly pleasant thirty-four minutes either.

Kidd has never seen Ike so agitated. Ike shouts, "Where the Hell have you been?" Before Kidd can answer, Ike gruffly tells him, "Sit down."

Kidd sits. Ike doesn't. He paces around the room for a few seconds and then starts talking. "Kidd, Monique Williams has run away with Christopher Dalakos."

Now it's Kidd's turn to be pissed off. "You brought me all the way here for something this ridiculous. Come on, Ike, have you guys at PACT been using yourselves for drug experiments or what?"

Ike ignores Kidd's question. "Caroline put us on the trail and now we have fingerprint confirmation. As if that wasn't bad enough, Devon Williams has been working on a very hush-hush project for us. It's a laser, which he prefers to call 'THE LAZER.' He said the 'z' gives it a certain finality. Monique Williams is the only person outside of PACT who is in on the whole picture."

Ike nods to the Head of the Joint Chiefs of Staff who says, "The only thing laser weapons today can do is burn from a great distance. They're not particularly effective. Devon's prototype implodes and explodes everything between two points. It simply sucks out the oxygen taking all life with it. According to his latest calculations, if he had enough satellites hovering over a target, he could incinerate Manhattan in a matter of hours. And he could do it without touching an inch of the Bronx."

Ike takes back over. "Monique knows just about everything there is to know about this weapon. It appears that she's gone with Dalakos on her own free will. I don't really care why or how this happened. I want you to find Dalakos and kill him. It should be easier now that he's traveling with a woman. Their last known whereabouts were here in Washington, yesterday."

Kidd sits there motionless, trying to suppress a thousand memories. *Monique coming to his room. I can still smell her perfume and it was eighteen years ago. Before I joined PACT. Before I was dead. Before she married Devon. The only woman he and I are ever going to love. One dose of her and you're hooked for life.*

Kidd is so lost in his memories of Monique that he almost forgets about Dalakos...almost.

He snaps back to reality when he hears Amanda's voice. "We're working under the assumption that Monique is a willing participant with Dalakos."

Kidd hasn't seen Monique in eighteen years. Still, he jumps right to her defense. "A willing participant? That's a pretty big assumption. In fact, it's just plain ridiculous!"

Amanda is too professional to show any surprise but she makes a mental note of Kidd's outburst. She continues, "As Ike said, this isn't the time to look into motivation. Which means, shoot first and ask questions later. There's too much riding on this. As for me, I'm going to deal with Devon Williams. You've got excess baggage with him. I'll handle Devon, you handle Monique and Dalakos. Got it?"

Kidd says, "Yes, ma'am. Yes, of course."

Kidd accentuates "ma'am," just to let Amanda know that he hates taking orders from her. He hates it that she knows his past, that he couldn't ever let sleeping ghosts lie as long as she was there to remind him of his previous life. Amanda glares back at him.

Ike is the first one to speak. "Amanda is right. It doesn't matter if Monique is a willing participant or not. The bottom line is that she's with Dalakos. This is just too big."

Kidd doesn't say another word and heads for the door.

Ike's voice gets tense. "One more thing, Kidd. We have reason to believe that there's a ten year old child traveling with her...her daughter, Sabrina Rose."

Kidd stops cold and faces Ike. Ike looks right into Kidd's blue eyes as he speaks. "She was last seen yesterday with her mother at the conference here in Washington. Do everything you can, everything possible so that nothing happens to her..." Ike's voice trails off and he looks away. They both understand the sentence he didn't complete. The sentence that starts with 'but' and ends with, "there are millions of innocent lives at stake here. Keep that in mind, too."

5

DEVON WILLIAMS leaves his mansion on Pacific Heights and heads for the airport. His private plane is waiting to take him to Washington.

He's not exactly sure what he's going to do when he gets there, but he can't stay here. At least in Washington he can keep an eye on everyone and everything. Telephones, faxes, and e-mails are great but they're no substitute for a good kick in the ass.

As he waits impatiently at the light at Divisadero Street, his passenger door flies open and a black man jumps in. Before Devon can say a word, the man orders, "Drive!" But Devon can't drive. He can't move. Devon doesn't see the blue eyes, he only sees the black skin.

Devon finally says, "I'm sorry, I don't have much cash on me. Do you take credit cards?"

The black man shouts, "I'm not here to rob you, now drive!" Devon takes off, not sure where to go. So, he speeds through the city, heading south towards the airport all the time cursing himself for leaving the house without a bodyguard.

"I need to ask you some questions and I know how difficult it is to get an appointment with you."

Devon relaxes a little. "Go ahead, shoot...Not literally of course."

"My organization might be the only ones who can save your daughter and wife. Do you have any idea where they are?"

Devon jams on the brakes. "If I knew where they were, do you think I'd call the President and ask him to find them? If I knew where they were, do you think I'd be on my way to Washington right now? If I knew..."

The black man says, "I guess that means no. Question number two. What does Monique know about the Lazer?"

Without a moment's hesitation, Devon says, "I don't know anything about a laser."

"I was hoping you would be a little more cooperative." Devon shouts, "Who the hell are you?"

The black man says, "Well, here goes. My name is Kidd Black."

BOOM! Devon rams into a truck...or a truck rams into Devon. Doesn't really matter. Like the old saying goes, "If the stone hits the window or the window hits the stone, it's going to be bad for the window."

Then comes that sickening sound of metal against metal, of flesh against glass...

6

OUT ON CHRISTOPHER Dalakos' boat, Monique Williams is lost in a fog. Lost in a dream…But she's worse than lost. She thinks she knows where she is…She thinks she knows the man she's with…

Dalakos stands over Monique, proud of his catch, thinking, Months of preparation. Months of sitting through those endless weapons conferences.

But, after every conference there was a cocktail. Little by little I gained her trust. After all, who could resist the charms of Christopher Dalakos?

But, just in case, he made sure there was a little help from his "pharmacist." Every time he saw her, he slipped some drugs into her drink.

All she knew was she was happy to see him whenever she saw him.

A voice, his voice, brings her closer to reality. "Here, drink this." He hands her another glass of orange juice. Monique's voice is hazy like she's in a daze. "I wonder why I'm drinking this, I don't even like orange juice!"

"Drink it."

She'll do whatever I tell her. If I told her to write to Devon Williams saying I was the greatest lover in the world, she would do it...

He smiles to himself when he thinks of her writing every word he had dictated, especially the sentence, "I'm sorry to tell you that I've fallen in love with the most extraordinary man I've ever met."

Dalakos stares at Monique and then says. "There is to be no discussion." Monique drinks the orange juice.

Unsteadily, Monique stands up. "I'm going to check on Sabrina Rose..."

Dalakos smiles to himself at the mention of Sabrina Rose's name. Anyone who knows Monique knows she would never run away from her husband without her daughter. So, it was imperative that the little kid come too.

The world had to think Monique ran away from her husband...

I need the time alone with her...without everybody and his uncle coming to try and claim the reward her husband would surely have offered if he thought she and their daughter had been kidnapped.

I waited for all the stars to be aligned in the right place. Weekend conference, her husband home working, a nearby port.... Everything was in place.

On what appeared to be the spur of the moment, I invited Monique and Sabrina Rose to come on my yacht. Sabrina Rose couldn't wait! Especially when Monique told her there was a swimming pool on it!

Now that I have Monique on the boat, I can use whatever drugs it takes to get the information out of her. And, if for some reason the drugs don't work, there are always other means. Another reason to have the kid along.

Monique continues, "She just loves that swimming pool!" Dalakos sighs. That's enough for now. I'll let her check in on the brat and then I'll get back to coaxing the information out of her.

Dalakos opens the cabin door and says, "Yes, she's a great kid. A great kid. You can be really proud."

7

SHOCK...YOUR body goes into shock. There's nothing you can do. But Kidd, even in a state of shock knows what to do. Stop the bleeding. Get out of the car. Get Devon out of the car. But first, stop the bleeding.

Kidd's right arm is spouting blood. A shard of glass has pierced his brachial artery. He takes his left hand and squeezes the artery shut. But, there's no way to keep it closed without removing his hand. He's got to get Devon out of the car. Devon's dazed, moaning, slumped over the steering wheel.

Cold. His right arm is getting cold. Sensation. He's losing all sensation it. It's going to have to be now or never and never is coming on fast.

Kidd shoves Devon off the steering wheel and rips off his seat belt. He lifts up the door handle with his foot and kicks open the door. He then kicks Devon out of the car. Kidd gets out and rushes over to get Devon away from the car. Already, the gas fumes are strong. Could be an explosion any second. Don't want to die the same way I died the first time. In a car accident.

Kidd pulls Devon away thinking, My friend, you've put on a few pounds since West Point.

With Devon out of harm's way, Kidd rushes over to check on the truck driver to see what he can do for him. Kidd thrusts open the door to the truck cab. He's going to have to let go of the artery to pull the guy out.

Just as Kidd is about to let go of the artery, he freezes. There's no color in the dead man's face. The blood has already settled in his abdomen. He's already cold. The man was dead before the accident...

It was no accident. Someone is trying to kill him or Devon or both of them.

8

MONIQUE IS LYING in a luxurious bed. The kind of bed that molds around your body. The kind of bed you never want to get out of.

She's cold. Very cold. Dalakos lies next to her with his arms wrapped tightly around her. She shivers slightly. She doesn't notice, but Dalakos is sweating from the heat.

She hears his voice, distant but insistent. "You were telling me about some lazer. What about the lazer?"

Monique is disoriented. "A lazer? The lazer? I wasn't talking about that, I was talking about 'him.'"

Dalakos is cool. He's the ocean. Eventually everything will flow to him. He tries again. "No, you were talking about the lazer. It must be important to you. You kept saying, 'the lazer.'" Dalakos takes her face in his hands and looks her in the eyes. He whispers, "The lazer."

Monique doesn't hear anything. She just sees the Blue Eyes.

"I met him when I was nineteen. He was eighteen. Devon's best friend. Devon's only friend. The three of us were always together. He was the most amazing man I ever met."

Dalakos pulls off the covers. Monique is wearing a blue skirt. Monique reaches for the covers. "I'm cold. So cold. Give me back the blanket."

"First tell me about the lazer."

Monique puts her arms around her breasts. "I was working in the computer center at West Point. I was a townie. I wanted out. Devon was going to be my ticket. But I couldn't resist. He was so cold, so strong, so...so....so unattainable. So, of course, I had to have him."

Dalakos sighs and gives her the blanket. She greedily wraps it around her.

Drugged and lost in her memories, she mutters, "I was wearing red. I had my back to him. I was bent over his desk. He knew I wanted him and I knew he wanted me. But, he would have to make the decision, make the move. There I was in his room. That in itself was against the rules. No women allowed in Cadet quarters. Part of the Code of Conduct. Enough to get him thrown out of West Point . But he wasn't focusing on the Code of Conduct. He was focusing on my ass. I was bent over for what seemed like an eternity, pretending to check some equations. Finally, hesitantly, he came up behind me. For the first and only time in my life, I felt him tremble."

9

DEVON WAS dazed but he could function. Kidd helped him walk and they move quickly away from the "accident." Kidd's not that afraid of an explosion, that was mostly Hollywood stuff but no sense in taking needless chances. He's more scared of the sirens coming his way. No time to deal with the police. And he didn't want it to get back to PACT that he had gone to see Devon.

Devon and Kidd cut across a park. Kidd heads for the first car he sees with Devon right behind. Kidd tells him, "Okay, Devon. You've got two good arms. Take a rock and smash in the rear passenger-side window."

"Who the hell are you and why should I do anything you want?" For what would turn out to be the first of many times, Kidd says, "If you want to see your daughter again, just do as I say."

Devon smashes the window.

"Now get in the car and get ready to take off."

Devon opens the car door. Kidd dives under the dashboard with blood spurting from his arm and hot wires the car within a matter of seconds.

Kidd moves over to the passenger seat, Devon gets into the driver's seat and they're off. Devon takes a look at Kidd's arm and says, "We've got to get you to a hospital."

A hospital. Too many questions. Too many papers to fill out. Too many cops. And, I've got to keep out of the long reach of PACT. Devon's right though. Got to get my arm fixed.

Kidd says, "Take me to 129 Fell Street off of Divisadero. There's a medical office building there. Fifth floor. Room five sixteen. Doctor Barry Feldman."

10

"I WAS HOOKED. I was his. There was a mirror by his desk. The whole time I was looking in his eyes. Those blue eyes."

Monique closes her eyes and breathes deeply. She's never forgotten the moment. She'll never forget the moment. Dalakos thinks, Nothing to do but wait. I'll never find out what I need until she's finished with her pointless story.

Monique continues. "And then all hell broke loose. Someone saw me go into his room. Someone who either hated me or hated him or hated us both. Or even someone who hated Devon. After all these years, I don't know who it was. It could've been anyone. But, there was a hearing. An open and shut case. But, they weren't going to hear anything from me. I quit my job. They couldn't make me testify."

Monique closes her eyes and starts to drift away. Dalakos thinks, That's the trouble with these drugs. You never know how much is too much and how little is too little.

He coaxes her back awake and pretends to listen with interest to her words.

"Devon never asked me what exactly had happened. But, he knew. And he knew his best friend was going to be thrown out of West Point. The only thing his best friend ever wanted to do was serve his country. To do what was right. To do good. And because I threw my ass in his face, he was going to lose it all.

The day of the hearing, Devon stood up and 'confessed.' 'Yes, Monique was in Kidd's room. But, the only other one there was me.' Devon handed in his resignation and left the room. A year later, I married Devon."

Now Monique starts crying. "I'll never forget Kidd Black. The black man with the blue eyes."

11

DEVON PULLS the car into the parking lot of the Medical Arts Building on Fell Street. Kidd knows the place by heart. The outside anyway. When Barry Feldman first moved to the Bay Area, Kidd had to fight off the desire to go see him. It's not easy being a dead man.

He'd hang around sometimes late at night. He wouldn't admit it to himself but he hoped that maybe Barry would run into him. Barry, his best friend when he was a kid. Barry, the only one he could talk to. Of course, they never talked much, but just knowing he could talk to someone if he wanted to was enough.

I was kind of a loner but Barry always searched me out at lunch time. I couldn't put my finger on it but there was something about Barry that I just… liked. I enjoyed watching Barry tell stories about things that had happened that day. Even stories that weren't at all interesting, Barry could make them exciting just by waving his arms and changing his voice. Barry, with his pear-shaped physique and uncombed hair, would be gobbling down his thick, fatty corned beef sandwiches while I would be slowly eating my fresh fruits, grains and yogurt, savoring every mouthful. Barry did most of the talking but would always try to get me to talk. I rarely spoke but when I did, I knew that he learned something new and appreciated it.

It was seven o'clock and Barry's office lights were still on. An early night for him. There might be better surgeons on this planet but there were none more dedicated than Dr. Barry Feldman.

Kidd and Devon get to the revolving doors. Locked. Devon pounds on the door and the security guard slowly makes his way over. Kidd squeezes the artery harder. The blood is down to a trickle but he's lost a lot.

Kidd keeps saying to himself, Compartmentalize. Compartmentalize. One of the tricks he learned when studying hand-to-hand combat with the Gracie Family in Brazil. Compartmentalize the pain. Don't let it seep into your consciousness. Compartmentalize the pain. You control the pain, the pain must never control you.

The security guard finally makes it to the door. Devon's thinking, What do you expect for eight fifty an hour and they have to pay for their own uniforms.

Kidd shakes his head when he sees that the guard is carrying a gun. There's nothing more dangerous than an amateur with a gun. The guard sees Kidd's bloody arm and still asks, "What can I do for you?"

Devon explodes, "We're here to see a doctor!" He pushes past the guard.

Kidd says, "Excuse my friend. He's not used to seeing blood. Do we need to sign in?"

The guard says, "Naw. Don't bother. Just try not to bleed on the carpet. If you do, I've got to clean it up."

Kidd smiles and says, "I'll do my best."

Devon's already at the elevator. It opens and they head for the fifth floor. On the way up, Kidd is thinking, What am I nervous about? I've almost been killed fifty times in the last eighteen years. I'm going to see my oldest friend and I'm worried about it?

Kidd laughs and shakes his head. Devon looks over and wonders what's going on in this man's head. The man who dares to call himself, Kidd Black.

FIFTH FLOOR: Kidd and Devon get off. Some blood trickles down to the carpet. Kidd sighs and says, "The guard's not going to like that."

Devon says, "I have a mind to buy this building just to fire him."

They quickly find 516. The light is on inside. Kidd says to Devon, "You better go in first. If I remember correctly, Barry doesn't like surprises. I don't want him to have a heart attack before he fixes my arm."

Devon shakes his head in wonderment. This guy is going to keep on insisting that he's Kidd Black. But, he might be right about one thing. He could know where my daughter and wife are. I don't know what his price is yet but when the time comes to pay up, I'll gladly pay. Every cent.

12

DALAKOS TURNS pale. Monique doesn't notice. She's too lost in her tears, too lost in her memories. He can't believe what he's just heard. It keeps rolling around in his head like an echo that just won't quit.

The Black Man with Blue Eyes. In Greek, he's known as O Mavros Anthropos Me Ble Matia. In Arabic, Rajoul Aswad Zu Ayoun Zarkaa. In any language, this spells trouble.

But, how could she know The Black Man with Blue Eyes? One thing for sure, The Black Man with Blue Eyes, the Legend himself, has not been dead for eighteen years. For eighteen years, he's been a pain in the ass for everyone in my chosen profession.

Oh yeah, there are those who say he doesn't exist. Never did. And there are those who say they killed him. Well, if they killed him, who was The Black Man with Blue Eyes who ruined my Olympics extravaganza?

I worked on it for four years. Four years of getting the nitroglycerin together. The trucks, the drivers. Turning the drugs into cash. Finding the perfect target. More than five thousand children. AT THE OLYMPICS! It would have been front page news for months!

Just the thought of that target getting away almost makes him sick. But, he's a man of self-control. He forces himself to relax and puts his arms around Monique. He tenderly cuddles her. She slowly stops crying.

Ten seconds later, he's had enough of foreplay. He literally rips off her dress and gets on top of her. He looks down into her eyes and shouts, "I am the man with the blue eyes. I am the man with the blue eyes!"

She tries to close her eyes and look away. Dalakos takes her head in his hands. "Look at me!"

Dalakos pumps faster, thinking, Too bad I'm having your husband killed. But, now that I have you, I don't need him alive. Just the same, he might have known something about this Kidd Black. Well, it's too late now.

The thought of Devon dead, killed on his orders, gets Dalakos pumping like a madman.

Monique looks into Dalakos' blue eyes and in her drugged state, sees only another man with blue eyes, she sees only Kidd Black. She wraps her arms around Dalakos and pulls him towards her.

But Dalakos no longer even notices that Monique is there. He's thinking, Kidd Black. If I killed Kidd Black the Legend, I'd become a Legend...Like the old Greek saying goes, "To become a legend, you have to slay a legend."

13

THE DOOR opens. Toni, Dr. Barry Feldman's thirty-something nurse, is there putting on her make-up. She looks up and sees Devon followed by Kidd. She's obviously getting ready to go out and is none too happy to see anyone this late. She makes an effort and asks, "Hi, what can I do for you?"

Devon answers, "My friend has been injured. He needs to see Doctor Feldman."

"I agree he needs to see a doctor. But it's not going to be Doctor Feldman. He just left. I'll call an ambulance."

Devon isn't used to hearing the word 'no'. "Please. Call Doctor Feldman and tell him that Devon Williams needs his help. It's an emergency."

A look of recognition comes over the nurse's face. She quickly picks up the phone. While it rings, she discretely checks herself in the mirror.

"Hello, Doctor. Devon Williams is here...THE Devon Williams. Here in your office...A friend of his is injured. He wants you to come help him."

She listens for a moment and then hangs up. She takes a deep breath before speaking. "Uh, Doctor Feldman says to take your friend to the hospital. He's already late for his basketball game."

Devon Williams looks at her incredulously. Kidd just smiles knowingly. The nurse continues. "Uh, you see he plays on this team and if they win tonight they go to the playoffs and..."

Kidd interrupts. "Would you mind calling him back and telling him that the name of Devon's friend is Kidd Black?"

14

IKE MUSLOW paces anxiously around the paddock. Chataqua, his favorite horse, wanders aimlessly outside the fence nervously watching his owner. Ike turns to the head of the FBI and asks, "Charley, what's the latest on Dalakos?"

Now it's Charley's turn to look nervous. "He left Washington, accompanied by a beautiful woman and a young girl and flew to Port Au Prince, Haiti, and boarded a cruise ship, The Paradiso, which set sail for Bermuda. And, and..."

Ike explodes. "And when the ship got to Bermuda, there was no Dalakos!"

Charles Baker mumbles, "Uh, that's exactly right! We found the ship though."

Ike shouts, "What's going on over there? How hard is it to find one world famous terrorist traveling with a woman and a child?"

Charles wants to say, "Apparently pretty damn hard," but instead just mumbles something about "the CIA screwed up too."

Ike pretends not to hear. He knew the FBI would blame it on the CIA and vice versa. They've been rivals from the day the CIA was formed. The only thing they ever seem to agree on is that they, not PACT, should be given the most important missions. The only thing they dislike more than having to work with each other is taking orders from PACT.

Ike shakes his head and thinks, Back when I was head of the CIA, I too hated the idea that orders came from PACT and worked its way down to the rest of us "mortals". Even though I was part of PACT as head of the CIA, I didn't like having to reach a consensus with the FBI and the Joint Chiefs and whoever else happened to be there that day.

Ike laughs to himself and thinks, But now that I'm head of PACT, I see how useful it is to have a centralized organization coordinating everything... not to mention that PACT has the best agents we've got!

Amanda Mason, the President's Chief of Staff, comes speeding up in her red Mustang Convertible. Ike walks over to meet her. Now Ike is muttering. But Charlie can just make out the name Kidd Black.

15

SABRINA ROSE is just waking up when Monique comes in. Monique looks at her as though she was seeing her for the first time. The prettiest girl she'd ever laid eyes on in her life. Monique bends over to kiss her. Sabrina says, "Ti kanis."

Monique asks, "Ti kanis?"

"Yes. That's Greek for, how are you?"

Monique smiles. "Luckily for you, you have my looks and your daddy's brains."

"Where is Daddy?"

Monique says, "Daddy? He's probably working at home. And that's probably where he'll be when we get there."

Sabrina doesn't smile. "How long are we going to stay on this boat? I'm ready to go home."

Monique says, "Don't tell me you're bored already. What about the pool?

I thought you loved the pool here."

"I do but I don't want to spend another night on this boat!" Monique laughs.

"Another night? What're you talking about? We've barely just gotten here!"

Sabrina Rose's first reaction is to say, "We've been on this boat for a day and a night already!" but she looks up at her mother and sees something strange. She can't put her finger on it, but her mother seems different. Instead, she asks, "Mommy, do you love me?"

Monique has a moment of clarity. She doesn't hesitate. She takes Sabrina Rose tightly in her arms. "Of course, I do. Why would you even ask such a question?"

Sabrina Rose hugs her mother tightly. "And I love you too. I really, really do. And if anything ever ever happened to you..."

But, Monique is already lost again in a drug-induced haze.

16

DR. BARRY FELDMAN jumps out of his blue four-door Volvo. No pretentious Porsches for him. He's wearing a crisp white sweat suit with matching white high-top sneakers. On the back of the sweats is written, MAGIC MEDICAL MEN.

He doesn't wait for the elevator. He runs up the stairs. At the first floor he's thinking, If I miss this game, I'm firing my nurse, suing Devon Williams for a billion dollars and punching out this idiot who says he's Kidd Black.

SECOND FLOOR: But, she did say he was a black man with blue eyes. What if he isn't dead?

THIRD FLOOR: Of course he's dead. I was there at his funeral. Everyone was at the funeral!

FOURTH FLOOR: If I miss this game, I'm firing my nurse, suing Devon Williams for a billion dollars and punching out this idiot who says he is Kidd Black!

Not even winded, Barry races up the last flight of stairs ready to beat up everyone in his office, including Toni, his nurse. Especially Toni. He throws open the door and freezes.

17

THE MOMENT Amanda Mason, the President's Chief of Staff, pulls into the farm, she knows Ike is worried. She knows Ike is worried because the damn horse looks worried.

He gets along a lot better with that horse than any human I've ever seen him with. But, being the head of PACT isn't a popularity contest. Still, having a few more friends around Washington wouldn't hurt when push comes to shove. And this Dalakos thing is definitely headed straight for shove.

She can see him walking Chataqua across the field coming towards her. He's talking to himself or talking to the horse, she can't really tell which but it doesn't matter. What she has to say isn't going to help his mood any either.

Amanda gets out of the car. Ike puts out his hand to shake hers but she doesn't put hers out. Ike Muslow, formerly of the CIA, formerly of the Marines and formerly of Yale, knows when bad news is coming. He gets right to the point. "All right. What's the problem?"

"Kidd Black didn't show up for his flight. Just never showed."

Ike laughs and turns to Chataqua. "You hear that? That's it. That's all? Kidd is rarely where one would expect him to be. It's part of his charm."

Amanda looks at the horse. The horse isn't fooled and neither is she. Ike is a very worried man and no, this didn't help

18

MONIQUE IS PLAYING chess with Sabrina Rose. Monique's already lost four games in a row including a very embarrassing "fool's mate." But, one rarely plays one's best chess in a drugged stupor. Sabrina Rose insists, "It's your move!" Monique laughs and says, "Oh, I was hoping you wouldn't notice."

Not that Monique likes playing chess. She learned it because Devon was passionate about it. But, already Sabrina Rose gives Devon a better match.

Monique sighs. She has to admit that he is a good father...and a billionaire. And these days those are two qualities that are hard to come by in a man.

Dimitra, Sabrina Rose's baby-sitter, walks into the bedroom. Dimitra apparently never sleeps. She's ready to watch Sabrina Rose anytime, anywhere. But never sleeping hasn't done anything to diminish Dimitra's dark

Mediterranean looks. She somehow always manages to look breathtakingly beautiful.

Dimitra glares at Monique, thinking, Christopher was mine until she came along. And he will be mine once again...once again when this bitch is gone. Which will be soon. But, not soon enough.

Monique senses that Dimitra hates her and for the life of her can't figure out why.

Dimitra says, "Ti kanis."

Sabrina Rose says, "Ti kanis," and Monique says, "Hi." Sabrina Rose tells her mother, "Dimitra doesn't speak a word of English."

Monique says, "Everyone speaks some English, whether they know it or not."

Dimitra points at Monique, motions towards the door and says, "Christopher. Go!"

Monique laughs and says, "See, honey, I told you she speaks English."

Before Sabrina Rose can answer, Monique says, "I'll be right back."

On her way out Monique points to the chess board and slowly says to Dimitra, "Play with her. But be careful, she's tricky."

19

BARRY FELDMAN squints hard. He's no longer the gangly chubby pear-shaped teenager he once was but he still needs glasses the size of telescopes. The man on the left he recognizes. That's a no-brainer. That's Devon Williams. The woman behind the desk is his nurse. He's sure of that.

It's the other one. Thirty-something. Light-skinned black man with the confident smile on his face. Barry Feldman takes a few steps closer. Blue eyes. Proves nothing. Contact lenses?

The guy's as solid as a rock. Nasty gash on his arm. Very nasty gash on his arm. Barry says, "Let me take a look at that. Follow me."

The four of them head into his treatment room. Now Barry's no longer worried about who this man is. He's no longer worried about missing his basketball game. There's an injured man in his office who needs his help.

20

GODDAMN IT!!! Another slice! I could blow up the world, literally blow it up with a wave of my hand, I can go on TV anytime I want, I can sleep with a whole lot of great looking women (as long as my wife doesn't catch me)...but I can't get that golf ball to do a damned thing!

The President of the United States of America, fifty-eight years old, looking forty-five and feeling like he's twenty, surveys the fifteenth hole, all four hundred twenty yards with a wicked dog leg. There's a lake dead ahead at a hundred yards but even my grandma could hit it over that.

He tees up the ball and takes one look around the spacious, empty golf course. Clearly the best part about being President is that you can go on the course anytime you want. Why they'd even put up lights if I told them to. Yes sir, it's a great day to be alive and a great day to be Number One.

The President is about to swing when he sees a golf cart coming his way. Amanda Mason is there along with a Secret Service Agent. The President sighs. If Amanda is coming out here, something's up and that something is not going to be good.

The President swings anyway. The ball heads straight for the lake and refusing to listen to the shouts of the "most powerful man on the planet," goes right in. A bad sign if there ever was one. Yes sir, a bad sign indeed.

Amanda gets out of the cart. She doesn't even bother with small talk. No, "Good morning Mister President" and no, "Bad luck about that shot, sir." No, she's got bad news and bad luck written all over her face.

"Mr. President, Devon Williams is missing. He was last seen headed for his private plane that was to take him to Washington. Never showed. His car was found a mile from his house. Blood stains everywhere. Only some of it his."

The President nods his head presidentially. "Get PACT on it and keep me informed."

Amanda is tempted to tell the President that she's already informed PACT but she didn't get this high up in the Government by saying whatever comes into her head. Instead she asks, "Is there anything else?"

"Next time don't hesitate to call me. That's what phones are for."

Amanda takes a deep breath and says, "Yes sir," and heads back to the golf cart.

The President forgets about the ball in the lake, takes another ball out of his pocket and tees it up. One of the advantages of being President. If you want to stretch the rules a little bit, no one is going to tell you not to

21

MONIQUE WAKES UP, sees Dalakos standing over her and thinks, What's Christopher doing here? Christopher....Christopher. I can't recall his last name. He had told me once but it was five syllables in Greek and we agreed that calling him Christopher would make my life a lot easier.

Monique sits up but feels dizzy and lies back down. She asks, "What am I doing in your bed?"

Dalakos says, "You weren't feeling well so you came to lie down."

He hands her a glass of orange juice. "Here, this will make you feel better."

She takes the orange juice and is about to say something when Dalakos cuts her off. "Sabrina Rose is fine. She's out by the pool."

Monique drinks the orange juice, lies back down and closes her eyes. Everything is so strange. I don't know if I'm dreaming or awake. I know that I made love to Kidd, I know that was a dream, a delicious dream I often have.

Dalakos sits on the bed next to her, strokes her hair and whispers, "I'm so happy that you're feeling better my love."

Monique thinks, My love? My love?

The last thing she thinks before passing out is, What a strange dream.

22

"YOU'VE LOST a lot of blood."

Kidd says, "You've always been the master of the obvious, Barry."

Barry Feldman reaches for Kidd's arm and tells him, "This is really going to hurt."

"Like I just said, thanks for telling me something I don't already know."

Barry smiles to himself and thinks, If I didn't know better, I'd think this really was Kidd. Smart-ass, confident, and not the least bit stressed. Either he's semi-comatose or his heart rate is off the charts. I've never seen a heart rate so low on someone who was still breathing.

Kidd had insisted on no anesthesia. He didn't want drugs that could slow him down. He had to stay alert.

Barry applies the sutures to the wound. Kidd doesn't even flinch. Barry thinks he's in a trance but Kidd is there alright, feeling everything. Something else he learned from the Gracie family, the greatest Ultimate Fighters on the planet. If you can't compartmentalize, feel the pain, every bit of it. Use the pain. The pain is yours. Take it with you wherever you go.

Barry says to his nurse, "Call SF General and tell them I'm going to admit this man who calls himself Mister Black."

Kidd says, "Don't bother. I've got to be going as soon as this is over...And thanks but it's time for me to get back on my head."

Barry flinches at the words, "back on my head."

Barry says, "No way. You've got a brachial artery laceration and you're in shock whether you admit to it or not. If you drop dead in the hallway, I'm not losing my license for that."

Devon has a solution, "We don't have time. If anything happens, I'll be personally responsible...I'll buy you your own hospital."

Barry looks over at Devon. "I have all the money I'm ever going to need and unlike some people, I know when I have enough."

Barry shouts over to his nurse, "Call SF General and tell them to expect..."

Barry looks disdainfully at the "impostor" with the blue eyes and continues. "Whom should I tell them to expect?"

Kidd shrugs and asks, "Kidd Black?"

Barry throws down a bandage and says, "Alright, enough of this. If you're really Kidd Black, who was the starting line-up on the Bradford Hills Bombers the day we played at Middle School?"

Kidd closes his eyes for a moment. "The Bradford Hills Bombers...Let me think..."

"Just what I thought. The Kidd Black I knew would never forget the starting line-up. It was the greatest day of his...no, my life."

"Let me see. Maybe it'll help my memory if I name the subs first...Let's see, there was Little Duane, who could only play on every third Saturday because he had to help at his father's store. And then..."

The memories come flashing through Barry Feldman's head. We had a football game against the Bloods. Now the Bloods were tough. It was tackle, no equipment. They were all black except for "White Chuck" who was really black anyway. They also had "Black Chuck" who was even better than "White Chuck."

We were known as the Jewish guys, though only a couple of us were Jewish. We musta played 'em 20 times and lost by an average of thirty to nothing.

Kidd continues, "It came down to one play. We were at their five yard line. I gathered everyone around said, 'I'm going to carry the ball in and you're going to move those guys out of the way for me to do it.'

We put our hands together and I said, 'Okay, break's over. Back on your heads.'"

"Back on your heads" sends Barry back in time. We all knew that joke so we all laughed. It broke the tension and we moved those guys out of the way in order for Kidd to smash into the end zone.

From that day on, Kidd was a legend. I tried to stay close to him even though he was always busy. Work, school, martial arts and a joke for every occasion. He only had time at lunch. He would take his time when he ate.

You could actually see him appreciating the taste of every bite. And every time he told a joke, I learned something. He never said things directly if a joke could get his point across. Seems like we spent a lot of time swapping jokes.

I remember telling him this one...

What country has the longest national motto?

The answer is Canada.

Their motto is: Don't blame us -we're not Americans.

Kidd didn't laugh. He didn't even say, "That's not funny."

He went right into a speech about America. Stuff that I never even thought about. He said, "Hey, I know America's not perfect but, do you know why America's the best country? Because if you've got a dream and you work hard, you can be whatever you want to be. Look at my parents."

I never told him a joke that made fun of America again.

But, with all his talk about loving his country, I didn't think his country had been so nice to him. He was always the outsider. The white kids considered him black and the black kids considered him white, white and rich, because his mother was a doctor.

He wanted to do something for his country and that was that. He was always pushing himself to get in better shape. He used to say, "If I'm not accepted at West Point, it won't be because I failed the physical!"

Somewhere in the back of his mind, Barry can hear Kidd saying, "That's the end of the story, back on our heads," but Barry has already stopped listening because the realization has come over him. It really is Kidd Black.

Doctor Barry Feldman, a man of science says, "I know there's a rational explanation for all this but for now, let me just believe it's a miracle."

Then Barry does something he's never done before in his life. He wraps his arms around Kidd and squeezes him as though he'd never let go. He whispers, "A miracle. A god damn miracle."

23

BARRY STITCHES Kidd's arm. "Nothing to it. What we in the business call a simple surgical technique. Of course, that's easy to say when it's someone else's skin."

Kidd doesn't say anything. He's too busy concentrating on how his arm feels. Barry puts in the last stitch and says, "Kidd Black. Kidd Black is back. Kidd Black is back in one piece."

Devon explodes. "This guy shows up after eighteen years, describes a football game to you, information that he could've learned about from anyone. From 'White Chuck,'

'Black Chuck' or any number of Chucks and you say, 'Okay, it's a god damn miracle.'"

Barry shakes his head and says, "Oh, woe unto those who are the Unbelievers."

Devon turns to Kidd. "Tell me this, where have you been for the last eighteen years?"

Barry says, "Can't you see? He's a secret agent. Like James Bond."

Devon says, "Like James Bond, huh? Is that true?"

Kidd knows the only way to convince Devon is to tell the truth, at least some of it anyway.

"My death was planned to protect my friends and family. I'm an agent for the US government, a very special agent. And, the only way to be in the club is to be 'dead.'"

Devon relaxes the tone of his voice and asks, "Okay, a definite possibility. Tell me, if you're such a special agent, does the President himself know about your existence?"

"Of course."

The moment he says it, Kidd realizes that he's fallen into a trap. Devon takes out his cell phone and says, "Well, that's easy enough to verify. I'll just put a call to him right now."

Like lightning, Kidd grabs the phone away from him. "You can't do that."

Devon looks at Barry and says, "Just as I thought. I'm out of here. You can keep the god damn phone."

Devon makes a move towards the door but Kidd grabs him and when Kidd grabs you, you're not going anywhere fast.

"Let go of me!"

"I can't let go of you, you idiot. I'm under orders to kill a man and if I have to kill your wife in the process, so be it and if I have to...

Kidd's voice trails off. He can't get himself to say, If I have to, I might have to kill your daughter too.

Devon's shoulders slump. He understands. He doesn't need Kidd to finish the sentence.

Kidd continues. "I'm under direct orders NOT to contact you. I came because I was, I am, your friend. I owe you, more than you can imagine. If I'm pulled off this case, the next guy in line won't care one way or another about your family. Now, I'm going to let you go, but I'm begging you, answer my questions before you do."

Barry says, "Come on, Devon, answer the guy. Kidd Black or not, looks to me like he's your best shot."

Devon hesitates and then says, "Okay, let's just say that you're Kidd Black. To tell the truth, I don't care who you are if you can help me find my family."

"Now that we've got that straight, what does Monique know about the lazer?"

"Lazer? I don't know what you're talking about."

Kidd says, "This isn't getting off to a very good start." Devon says, "I'd prefer that your friend here leaves the room, no offense, Doc."

Barry says, "No offense taken. I'll just..."

Kidd interrupts. "I'd prefer that he stays. If something happens to me or to you for that matter, I'd be happier if there's someone I trust who can carry on for us."

Kidd turns to Barry and says, "This lazer is a super secret weapon of some sort. That's all you need to know for now."

Devon says, "Well, now that he knows this much, he might as well stay."

Barry nods to Kidd and Kidd nods back. They understand. That's how it is with friends, no reason to say, "Thanks for the vote of confidence."

Devon continues, "Monique knows just about everything there is to know about it."

"Just about?"

"There are some things that you just have to feel. Monique's brilliant at the numbers. The numbers don't lie. But, like I just said, some things you just have to feel."

"So, why are you really going to Washington?" "I just told you..."

"If I'm going to help you, I'm going to need you to help me."

"Okay. I've found out some things. I've got some sources that you people don't. Personal contacts, favors called in, you name it. Anyway, Monique apparently ran off with some Greek playboy. Don't know his name yet but the head of Microtech Greece is checking into it for me. I don't care what her text message says, I'm going after her and I'm going to find her."

"What text?"

"This text." Devon pulls out his cell, looks at it like it's covered in Plague, clicks on it and hands it to Kidd. Kidd reads the text and says, "What makes you think she wrote this. It's a text message, anyone could've written it."

"Unfortunately, no. Monique and I have a security system for private messages like this. You need a code and it has a biometric check. And if you think she was kidnapped, don't. She has too much security. She could only get away like that if she wanted to. Plus, in case you haven't noticed, the key ingredient of a kidnapping is missing...the ransom demand."

Kidd looks at the note again. Good-bye and may God be with you. Monique. Kidd asks, "Since when does Monique have anything to do with God?"

"She doesn't. She used to get pissed off whenever I took Sabrina Rose to church."

Kidd hopes there's something there. He doesn't want to kill Monique but he will, if he has to.

Kidd says, "I just don't understand why you're so ready to think that Monique just took off like that. That you won't even consider that just maybe she was kidnapped!"

Somewhere deep in the back of Devon's mind is a demon. A demon that keeps whispering, She never got over Kidd. She will never completely love you and someone who can't completely love you is capable of anything!

Devon changes the subject. "Why are you so interested in what Monique knows about the Lazer, anyway?"

There's a knock at the examination room door and Barry says, "Come in."

Toni enters and says, "I'll just clean up these bandages before I leave, which means I'm leaving very, very soon."

Barry says, "Don't bother with those. I'll take care of them. I haven't forgotten that you have a date."

She smiles. "Thanks, Doctor. I and my date appreciate it." Kidd tells her, "I and my arm appreciate that you stuck around."

She looks disdainfully over at Devon. "I couldn't leave you all alone with this one. Every time the blood spurted, he looked like he was going to throw up...again."

Devon sheepishly says, "I was always better with computers than people."

Kidd says to the nurse as she heads for the door. "Uh, by the way, we'd appreciate it if you didn't mention to anyone that we came by."

She stops and sarcastically says, "Wait a second. I can't sell my story to The Star or The Enquirer? I can see the headline: 'Billionaire and Buddy Meet Beautiful Nurse.'"

Devon doesn't quite catch the sarcasm in her voice. He quickly says, "Name your price. Just don't tell anyone."

She smiles and says, "Hey, I was just kidding. Doctor-patient confidentiality extends to nurses, too. So, if you'll excuse me, bye Doctor. Bye Gentlemen who I've never seen before in my life."

Barry says, "Have a good time and..."

Before he can finish his sentence, she's out the door. The moment the door closes, Kidd says to Barry, "You should marry that girl. You could do a lot worse."

"Believe me, I have done a lot worse. And what about you? Do secret agents have time for a wife and kids?"

Kidd doesn't answer. He just flexes his wounded arm. His muscles ripple like sculptured steel. Barry says, "Careful Kidd. You got to give that arm some rest."

Kidd stops flexing. "Whatever you say."

Barry starts cleaning up, collecting all the bloody bandages. "Kidd, you know when I decided to become a doctor? At your 'funeral.' I wasn't satisfied with the medical treatment you had gotten."

Kidd shakes his head in disbelief. "You gave up a promising career in sports for me?"

"Yeah? You think I could've gone all the way to the pros?" Kidd can't stop from smiling. "Yeah. With your mouth, you would've made a great sportscaster."

A cell phone rings. Barry doesn't pick it up but says, "My basketball game! We've got to get going."

Devon asks, "We?"

Kidd says, "Actually, Barry...Devon and I have some unfinished business to take care of. I'll get in touch as soon as I can."

"I hope it's not another eighteen years." Kidd says, "Over my dead body." The three of them laugh, like old friends.

Devon says to Kidd, "Why are you so interested in what Monique knows about the Lazer, anyway?"

Kidd stops laughing. "This Greek playboy that your wife is with, either of her own free will or otherwise...His real name is Dalakos. Christopher Dalakos."

Silence. Barry and Devon are speechless. It's like their tongues were cut out. Neither can mutter a sound. Devon knows the implications of that and Barry can easily guess.

The office phone rings. And rings. Finally, Barry asks Kidd, "Would you hit the speaker button? I'm full of your blood."

Kidd hits the button. Barry says, "Hello."

A man's voice asks, "Is this Doctor Barry Feldman?" "You got him."

"This is Brad Walker with First Ambulance. The security guard said you were still in your office. We've got a woman with a fractured sternum. It happened right in front of the building. Can we bring her up? She's in rough shape."

Barry says, "Sure. I'll get ready," and then mumbles, "So much for basketball."

Kidd hangs up the phone. He then slowly and painfully flexes his injured arm. "I hope you did a good job. I'm going to be needing this arm...How many exits are there out of here?"

"Who cares. I've got a patient coming up."

Kidd grabs Devon and Barry by the arm. "Listen, both of you. That guy who called. If there's an injured woman downstairs, why did he take the time to tell us that the security guard said you were still here? And that security guard doesn't know anything...AND if he was in such a hurry, why the hell didn't he hang up the phone when you said, 'Sure. I'll get ready.' He waited for you to hang up."

Barry, not at all convinced says, "You seem to know the answers to everything. Tell me then, why is this guy coming up?"

"I'm not exactly sure..."

Now even more skeptical, Barry adds, "Uh-huh..."

"I'm not exactly sure if he's coming up to kill Devon...or me...or all three of us."

24

DALAKOS IS GETTING impatient. What I should do, what I would like to do, is take that little brat, that little Sabrina Rose and pull out a few of her teeth. Now, that would get her mother focused on the Lazer.

Dalakos smiles briefly at the thought but then a cloud returns over him.

I need to get Monique to cooperate. Getting the information might not be enough. I might need her around to help me get it working.

Monique finally starts to wake. Now's the time. While she's still dazed from the drug-induced sleep.

Dalakos crawls into bed with her and whispers in her ear, "What did you mean, 'It's in the computers?'"

Monique slurs her words. "The program, the equations, everything is in the computers...But why do you want to know about the Lazer?"

Dalakos sighs. That's the trouble with these drugs. You have to keep repeating the same things over and over. I could've used Rohypnol but it has the unfortunate side-effect of making the victim lose their memory...which makes it just fine for "date-rape," but not at all what I need.

Ah, it's a shame that I'm in such a hurry, that I have to use these drugs at all. It was just a matter of time before she was really mine, before she would've done anything I said. But, I'm definitely in a hurry. And the best way to speed things up is to convince her that I'm in love with her and that she's in love with me...And, of course, to keep her pumped with drugs.

Dalakos holds her tight and whispers, "I love you and you love me...and we both love Sabrina Rose. But, we're all going to need money to be together and I know someone who will give us money for the information."

Monique nods. Dalakos can see she believed him. She liked the part about the little brat, too. Even drugged, there's some part of her brain that is always thinking about her daughter. I'll have to file that away. It could come in handy. But now, I just want to shake Monique, slap her, make her scream...with pain, not pleasure.

But, he fights off the feeling and asks, "Did your husband trust you enough to give you the access codes?"

Monique laughs. "Of course he trusted me. Everyone trusts me."

She stops laughing and starts to cry. "Everyone who trusts me gets hurt. Devon, Kidd Black..."

Dalakos doesn't want to hear about anyone else, especially Kidd Black. Dalakos wheels over a computer to the bed.

Monique keeps talking. "But not Sabrina Rose. She trusts me and I'll never hurt her."

Dalakos takes her head and looks into her eyes. "This is very important. Listen carefully. I want you to use this computer and get me the information about the Lazer."

Monique pushes him away and starts laughing. "I can't do that."

"You have to do it. For me!"

"But there's a system. You can only access the computer if you're at the computer."

"But you said computers!"

"There's a network of three computers where Devon keeps his personal research files. One at each of our houses. Only he and I can access the information."

"You're the only ones?"

"It can only be accessed by retinal identification."

Retinal identification...It only works if the tissue is still living. Lucky girl.

Dalakos is breathing heavily. He's so close. "And where are your houses?"

"One in San Francisco, one in New York, and one in The Bahamas."

Dalakos relaxes. The Bahamas-right on our way home. How convenient. "So, I'll just send someone to the Bahamas to get it."

Dalakos picks up his phone.

Monique speaks as though she's talking to a child. "You can't just take the computer. There's a force field. To get past the force field with the computer, you have to get past another biometric ID system. Fingerprints and DNA. Mine or Devon's. No fingerprints. No computer."

Dalakos sighs. He calls the Captain and orders him to set a course for The Bahamas.

25

"DEVON, GO down the backstairs to the front desk. The guard will be dead."

Kidd reaches to his pant leg and hands Devon a small pistol. "I hope you remember how to use this."

Devon grabs the pistol and nods his head yes. Even the instructors at West Point were expected to know the rudiments of firing a weapon.

Kidd continues, "If the guard isn't dead and he isn't the same one you saw on the way in, shoot to kill. Call me on Barry's private line and keep me posted where they are from the monitors, then get your ass out of there. Now go."

Devon starts to say something but thinks better of it and heads out the office.

Kidd turns to Barry and stares at him. He doesn't look too scared. Good. I have to remember he's not the pudgy guy he was eighteen years ago. He's a surgeon now. And he's in shape. He can take the pressure...I hope. I've got enough to worry about without having to worry about him.

"Barry, you hide here and I'll go wait for them in your office. Try to find a weapon just in case. And don't try and be a hero. Bye."

Kidd walks quickly out of the office leaving Barry alone. Barry just stands there. Hide? Weapon?

The only weapons Barry can think of are scalpels. He opens one disposable scalpel and uses that to open fifty others. Now what? He sees the fire extinguisher hanging from the wall, rips it down and pulls out the hose. He then uses a scalpel to cut off the rubber tubing from all the IV bags.

He's soon standing in a large puddle. He ties the tubes together and ties them around the water release of the extinguisher. He stuffs the hose with scalpels and drags it into the recovery room while holding the rubber tubing. He uses another tube to tie the hose to an IV pole and aims it at the door. He goes into the operating room and peeks through the door, thinking, It's an old variation on a medical school prank, but this is all I've got.

Over the intercom, he hears Devon's voice. "Kidd, the phone lines are dead. I had to reach you this way. They're all on the fifth floor. I used the security system to lock all the doors. They can't leave there."

Kidd thinks, The fifth floor. Barry's as good as dead.

Barry thinks, Uh-oh. This is the fifth floor.

Then BOOM! The door blasts open and a well-disciplined pattern of bullets fill the room. Barry is in a state of shock. You never know how loud bullets can be until they're coming for you. Barry closes his eyes and pulls the tubing.

The four killers stare at the fire hose as it quickly comes to life. It rips free from the IV pole shooting water and scalpels everywhere. One killer gets a scalpel in the jugular and one gets stabbed in the leg. The other two just get wet as the giant snake writhes and squirms as though it has a mind of its own.

Barry locks the door and is looking for a place to hide in the operating room when he sees the tanks. Oxygen. Ether. Sodium pentothal. He opens them all and runs through to the scrub room.

A match. A match. I need a match. Toni! She smokes. In her desk. Funny, smoking will kill her but it may save my life. It will save my life!

Sight and sound suddenly become slow motion. The door to the Operating Room flies open. Shots are fired and then...the EXPLOSION!

26

IKE MUSLOW, the head of PACT, is not used to being kept waiting. But, Amanda had told him not to rush in. "We don't want to make the President too nervous, do we?"

She didn't have to say more. He knew exactly what she meant. PACT had all the means of the Government at their disposal and some means that the Government would just as soon not know about. It's what they called "Believable Deniability."

It's easier for the Government to lie if they don't know what the truth actually is. Still, when all was said and done, PACT answered to the President.

She's right. We don't want to make the President nervous. Who knows what he'll do if he panics? And for now, there's no reason to panic...For now.

Amanda comes into the waiting room and announces, "Let's go." She turns her back to him to lead him into the Oval Office.

Ike should be concentrating on the business at hand but his mind keeps slipping into images of Amanda wearing black riding boots out at his farm. He's thinking, Not a very original fantasy but right now it's the only one I've got.

Amanda turns around to let Ike in. His eyes quickly dart up to her face. Amanda notices that Ike is blushing. She doesn't know if she should be flattered or amused. She says loudly, "The President will see you now."

27

KIDD RUNS up the stairs and sees that the door to the fifth floor has been blown open. He hurries to the operating room and sees a pool of blood-tinged water. He sees another door that is partially blown off the hinges. Smoke is pouring out of the room. He counts two dead bodies as he rushes to the door with his gun drawn.

He yells, "Barry!" He hears a moan but can't see who it is. He quickly gets to his knees and puts his face to the floor to get as much oxygen as possible. This common-sense move saves his life. A round of automatic weapons fire bursts through the air where he was just standing.

A muffled voice calls out. "We've got your friend here. Throw your gun this way or he's dead."

A dull thud is heard as the man kicks Barry in the stomach. Barry grunts sharply and then gasps for air. The smoke is going to finish him off if the killers don't.

Kidd's mind is racing. Gas masks. These guys came prepared. Kidd rips off a piece of his shirt, dips it in the blood-soaked water around him and thrusts it to his face. He reaches over to the dead body of one of the killers and grabs his gas mask and automatic pistol.

Kidd shouts, "Here's my gun!"

Kidd slides the gun across the floor. He immediately thrusts the gas mask over his face and rolls aside. Just as he expected, a round of weapons fire hits the spot where he just was. But, he still can't see anything. It's only a matter of seconds before they kill Barry.

Kidd stands up and opens his arms wide and rushes in the direction of the gunfire. In the smoke, he feels a body and reaches for his face. A gas mask! One of the killers! Kidd's momentum carries them toward the window and they crash up against it.

A surge of rage and adrenaline rushes through Kidd. He doesn't feel the stitches in his arm tear as he picks up the killer and thrusts him through the window. He barely hears the man scream through his gas mask as he tumbles to the street below.

Kidd whirls around. Smoke billows out of the window. The room starts to clear. Kidd notices a man running out of the room. He doesn't follow. He rushes over to Barry and drags him out into the hallway where the air is clearer.

Kidd tilts Barry's head back and pinches his nostrils. He lowers his mouth over Barry's and starts to breathe into his lungs, not even thinking for a moment that he just might be trying to revive a dead man.

28

WHENEVER CHRISTOPHER Dalakos needed some killing done, he could always count on Karl. Karl certainly didn't look like a killer...if there is a look that killers have. He was an extremely fit middle aged Austrian with dark hair and rugged skin.

He had average looks, average height and a gift for languages with the associated accent down pat. He could fit into any setting depending on his wardrobe.

Yeah, when it was time to kill someone, Dalakos could always count on

Karl...that is, until now.

Dalakos is furious as he paces around his spacious cabin. A decoded message from Karl lies on the floor.

Devon Williams is alive! He has an army with him! Their numbers unknown. Send reinforcements!

Finally, the phone rings. Dalakos picks it up. It's Karl. Dalakos can hear the fear in the voice on the other end. Good. Maybe I'll get some answers.

Dalakos demands, "Tell me how many men there were!" "It's hard to say exactly. A lot."

Soothingly Dalakos says, "I know how difficult it is in battle to remember specific things. Just concentrate and describe to me the ones you actually saw."

Karl hesitates a moment and says, "Well, there was the security guard who we killed right away. And the nurse, who was in the wrong place at the wrong time, of course she's dead too. And then there was Devon Williams as you already know...and the Doctor. And the black man. Those are all the ones I had a clear look at. The other ones were too fast." He quickly adds, "And too many!"

Devon Williams is with Kidd Black! Maybe it's time to speed up the plan. Take the helicopter to a plane and head for the Bahamas. But their satellites are everywhere. They'll see me coming! No, don't panic, above all, don't panic. If I wait, MY satellites will be everywhere! Everywhere! I'll wait. I'm safe on this boat.

Dalakos stops listening to Karl's excuses and shouts, "The black man. Did you kill the black man?"

Karl is so full of fear that he's almost inaudible. "I think he got away."

Dalakos' voice sends a shiver down Karl's spine. "Stay where you are. You'll be hearing from me soon."

Dalakos hangs up the phone. This makes things a little more complicated. But in a project this big, one has to expect complications. Now I'm going to have to kill the biggest "complication" of all...

Back when I was a boy reading comics, I was the only kid I knew who was hoping someone would kill Superman, that smug typically American super-hero...

But before I kill Kidd Black, I'm going to have to find him...Unfortunately, one doesn't simply "find" Kidd Black. One sets the trap and waits for him to come...And a trap is only as good as its bait.

29

FLANNAGAN'S BAR on Geary Street...It's a typical Irish pub. Typical in that no one bothers anyone and no one asks any questions. And that's just what the three men sitting in the corner booth need right this moment.

The three of them didn't look too good on the way in. Kidd mentioned something about a rugby match and the bartender just nodded knowingly.

There was just enough time to wash the blood and the smoke off their faces. Just enough time to grab some clothes and head out of Barry's office before the cops showed up. Kidd insisted. This was not the time to have to explain anything to anyone. The only problem is that shock doesn't wash away so quickly.

Barry can't get it out of his mind that Toni is dead. She was so full of life. Just wanting to help. After all, nurses aren't in it for the money.

Barry looks at Kidd and hopes he tracks those people down and makes them suffer. Not a very noble thought from a doctor, but there you have it. And he has to admit, the idea of vengeance makes him feel better.

For the first time since the attack, Kidd manages a smile and says to Barry. "You know, eighteen years ago I never would've thought that you could've held up your end the way you did."

Devon doesn't give Barry the time to enjoy the compliment. He says to Kidd, "I hate to interrupt but I have a daughter to get back."

Kidd quickly adds, "And maybe a wife."

Devon glares at Kidd and says, "What do you mean 'maybe a wife?'"

Kidd takes a deep breath before he answers. He makes sure that Devon can hear him take the breath before he speaks. "Listen Devon, before writing off Monique, I'm going to need more proof than what we've got."

Devon glares at Kidd. "You can't believe it can you? You know why?"

Devon says slowly, painfully, as though each word is tearing him apart. "BECAUSE-YOU-STILL-LOVE-HER!"

Now it's Kidd's turn to glare at Devon. His famous blue eyes get colder than cold. His voice is even colder than his eyes. "First I'm going to find your wife and daughter, then I'm going to take care of Dalakos and then I'm going to find out what really happened with Monique...and then with great pleasure, I'm going to punch you so hard in that famous head of yours that no one will ever make the mistake of ever again calling you a genius."

Barry nods his head approvingly. Devon and Kidd just stare at each other.

Finally, Devon looks away. "I'm sorry. I'm really sorry."

Barry stands up and says, "Well, it looks like it's time for me to go. It's been a pleasure to meet you Mr. Williams. And Kidd, when you're done doing what I hope you're going to do, come back and see me."

Kidd stands up and puts a hand to Barry's shoulder. "I'm sorry, Barry, I really am.

I hate to tell you this, but you're not going anywhere."

30

SWEAT IS TRICKLING down Dalakos' face. He remembers now. He turned off the air conditioner half an hour ago to make her sweat. Now he's feeling confident. I've got her now. She's finished. It's all over but the crying.

He leans forward and studies the chessboard. Chess. It's just a question of marshaling forces on your enemy's weakest point. Find the weakest point and squeeze. Squeeze until they snap...and everybody has a weak point. It's just a question of time before it's found.

Sabrina Rose sits across from Dalakos pretending that she's looking at the board but she's studying Dalakos. Who is this guy? Why is he here? Why are we here? One thing I know, something tells me that he's the last person I should ask. Something tells me, he's up to no good. No good at all.

She watches the sweat trickle down his face. A smooth face. A face that doesn't look like it has a worry in the world. She remembers something her father had told her. "Chess is a lot like poker. You can learn a lot from the way someone breathes, from the way their hands are...But you won't learn anything from the face. Everyone has years of practice hiding what their face is giving away. Don't look there, look any place but."

Sabrina Rose glances at Dalakos' hands. The knuckles are white. He's excited, he's up to something, he thinks he's going to win. Go ahead. Go for my king...A trap is only as good as the bait you put in it.

Sabrina Rose almost smiles but stops herself. Already she knows not to let her face give her away.

Dalakos brings out his queen. It's about time the bitch did something besides looking pretty...boring the king.

Now Sabrina Rose can smile. She calls out the cavalry, her cavalier, her Knight in Shining Armor. Her knight forks Dalakos' King and Queen. The game is virtually over, for now his King or Queen must die. According to the rules, there is no choice. The King must move aside and let the Queen die. Normally, this is a rule that Dalakos finds both logical and convenient. You might even say it's his philosophy of life in a nutshell. But, not today.

Dalakos kicks the board across the room, scattering the two armies everywhere. He has to fight from kicking Sabrina Rose too. Without a word he marches out, slamming the door behind him.

31

BARRY IS no longer standing. He's slumped down in the booth. Kidd sits next to him and says, "I'm sorry. You can't go home. You can't go anywhere until this is over. It's too dangerous. For you, and for me. I can't be slowed down worrying about where you are and what's happening to you."

"Why would anyone want to kill me? I can see why they would want to kill you and maybe even Devon but why me?"

Devon's voice is soothing and encouraging. "Listen Barry, it's like Kidd said. So in order to stop us from being slowed down, you're coming with us. From now on it's the three of us. We're going to be just like Curly, Larry and Moe."

Kidd says, "I was thinking more along the lines of the Three Musketeers." Barry moans. "Did you know in the original story all three Musketeers died horrible deaths?" Kidd puts a fist to the table. "Here's a chance to rewrite history." Devon gets into the spirit. "Yeah, we'll do the Hollywood version."

The waitress brings over the check and Barry reaches for his credit card. Kidd pulls Barry's credit card out of his hand and bends it in half.

The waitress says to Barry, "Looks like your friend really wants to pick up the check. If I were you, I'd let him."

As soon as the waitress walks away, Kidd says, "No more credit cards. It's the easiest way there is to track somebody. From now on, it's cash. Nothing but cash."

Barry's not at all happy with the turn of events. "How are we going to eat? On our good looks?"

Devon answers, "Believe me, cash will be the least of our problems."

Kidd says, "Okay, then. By now, I'm sure that my organization knows I've come to see Devon. Just coming to see him at all is a good enough reason for them to pull me off the case. So, for now, we're going to have to do this ourselves."

Devon throws a hundred dollar bill on the table and gets up. Kidd says, "That's a hell of a tip. Even for a billionaire."

Devon smirks and says, "Don't worry. Like I said, there's plenty more where that came from."

Kidd picks up the hundred dollar bill and puts down twenty dollars. "You said cash was going to be the least of our problems. It's bad enough your face is on the cover of magazines. Dumb move for a genius."

32

ANOTHER ROTTEN rainy day. His golf game canceled, the President was already in a bad mood before he learned that Amanda and Ike were coming to see him. He says to himself, When those two get together, it's like having a jinx around. Never any good news. Never.

The President lines up the putt on the carpet and with a smooth swing, eases the ball into the cup. He smiles and says aloud, "Nerves of steel, that's what I got. Bad news coming and I'm cool as a cucumber in the dog days of summer."

There's a knock on the door and the President says, "Come in."

As the door opens, he takes one more quick putt that goes across the room and right into the cup. He triumphantly looks over at Amanda and Ike who don't congratulate him on a great shot. At that moment, he realizes that this is going to be really bad news.

Ike gets right to the point. "Mr. President, we have a problem."

The President says, "Oh, now it's WE is it? The only time I ever hear anything from PACT is when all of a sudden their problems become my problems."

Ike continues. "Uh, concerning the disappearance of Monique Williams..."

The President says, "I hope you've made some progress. Devon Williams is a personal friend of mine." He doesn't bother to add...And a very major contributor.

Amanda says, "You see, sir, we have reason to suspect that Monique Williams hasn't disappeared in the strictest sense of the word."

The President starts rubbing his temples. "Amanda, why can't you speak in straight sentences like a normal person?"

Amanda looks at Ike but he signals her to continue. "We, uh, have reason to believe that Monique Williams has run away, not been taken away."

"And whom might she have run away with?"

Silence. Amanda looks at Ike who says, "Christopher Dalakos."

The President is surprisingly calm. "Now, that's a great way to start off my day. So, Devon Williams' wife is keeping company with the world's most-feared terrorist. So, according to you, that 'Greek Playboy' Devon mentioned is really Dalakos. Is that right?"

Ike says, "Yes sir, that's correct."

Ike and Amanda see this is going much better than they had hoped.

The President asks, "And Kidd Black? What's the news from him?"

Amanda doesn't feel that this is the moment to talk aboutKidd but she has no choice. "Uh, he seems to have disappeared too. We haven't had a word from him or Devon."

The President of the United States does something he hasn't done since he lost the high school golf championships when he missed a "gimme." He takes his putter and smashes it on his desk sending papers and gifts from around the world flying across the room.

Amanda is taken by surprise. "Mr. President, don't!"

Her pleas have no effect whatsoever. He continues pounding the desk and shouting, "You don't know where Devon or Kidd are? You're PACT, God's gift to the world of cloak and dagger. You're supposed to know everything. Everything! Why don't you call Devon and ask him where the hell he is?"

Ike says, "We've tried every channel we have."

The President takes one more mighty whack at the table and throws the dented putter across the room. He picks up his portable phone." Devon called me today. So, I'll just call him back at the same number. Not very complicated, is it?"

Amanda and Ike make eye contact as if to say, President or no President, this guy is really wasting our time.

33

DEVON WILLIAMS comes strolling out of the Automatic Teller Machine in Palo Alto carrying a gym bag. No ordinary gym bag, but a gym bag full of crisp new hundred dollar bills. He walks over to the car that Kidd has "borrowed" and gets in.

Barry says, "I'm never going to trust an ATM machine again if it's this easy to break into them."

Devon smiles for what feels like the first time in days. "I'm the one who invented the programs for these machines. I know everything there is to know about them and then some."

Kidd is smiling too. "Plus, nobody's going to suspect a billionaire of being a bank robber."

Devon pretends to look hurt. "Robber? Let's call it a loan." Barry snorts and says, "Tell it to the judge."

Devon's phone starts ringing. Instinctively, he reaches for it. Barry's good mood moment quickly disappears. "You're not going to answer it, are you? They'll find us in a second, whoever 'they' are."

Kidd is quick to say, "Not everyone who would call is necessarily an enemy. I say you answer it."

Barry isn't convinced. "It'll be like shouting, 'Here we are. Come get us!'"

Kidd says, "For all we know, it could be Sabrina Rose." Devon presses a button and says, "Devon Williams."

34

THE PRESIDENT smugly looks over at Ike and says into the telephone, "Devon. This is the President. We had a meeting scheduled for today and I was wondering where the hell you were. It's not nice to stand up the most powerful man in the world."

Ike leans forward trying to catch some of the conversation. The President is really enjoying himself now. "Devon, I'll come right to the point. There's one of these spy-types here in my office who thinks your wife is with Christopher Dalakos, the terrorist...I'm sorry, of course you know who Christopher Dalakos is."

The President continues. "Anyway, as always, there are some complications. So, why don't you come to Washington and we can put you up to speed on the whole matter?"

The President's voice gets quiet. "I'll tell him. Good-bye." The President turns to Ike. "Mr. Williams' exact words were,

'Tell Ike Muslow and PACT to stay out of this. This is a personal matter.'"

35

THE LAST eighteen years hadn't been easy for Lawrence and Nadine Black. Life was tolerable except around Kidd's birthday. For a month before and a month afterwards, they wondered what their boy was up to. For them, he had remained a boy. Forever stuck at eighteen. They wondered if he had been killed on some secret mission or if he was happy or if he needed a helping hand or some advice.

Life was bearable except around Thanksgiving. All the other families getting together and the two of them sitting down to dinner for two. Nadine just didn't want to be around a lot of people then.

After Thanksgiving came the one-two punch of Christmas and New Year's. A time of joy and celebration for most people but just another lonely holiday for the Blacks...No, the last eighteen years hadn't been easy for Lawrence and Nadine.

Nadine remembers the time that Kidd told them that he was "going off to war" and he wasn't coming back. Yeah, he was going to have the privilege of dying for his country. Dying for your country is one thing, killing your parents is another.

He knew it wasn't a good way to start off his new life—disobeying a direct order, but he had to say good-bye to his parents before he went away. He had to know that they knew.

He had to let them know that in order to be a PACT agent, you had to "disappear." No trace. No way for someone to threaten one's loved ones, to murder one's loved ones, to blackmail, to compromise...PACT was a phantom army, an army made up of ghosts. And as everyone knows, it's very difficult to kill a ghost.

Lawrence remembers the "discussion" he and Nadine had had about naming their son. He wanted to call him Kidd right from the start. Every dad thinks his son is going to be special but Lawrence was sure. Because his mother was so special. A black woman from a poor neighborhood who wouldn't take "no" for an answer. A woman who wouldn't stop until the whole world called her "doctor."

Me? I just gave him a spermatozoa and a last name. I wanted the world to know he was my kid. I would've called him 'My kid' but I knew Nadine would never go for that. In fact, I knew she would never go for "Kidd."

Lawrence smiles to himself. Even after all these years he wouldn't tell

Nadine how he had played her like an old fiddle.

The baby was already born and we still didn't have a name. We were taking him home but we had to give him a name first. I said to her, "Let's call him Orchid." She said, "Orchid? Are you nuts?"

I said, "Orchids are the most valuable flowers in the world." I pulled out a book and began to read: hybrids are more adaptable than their parents, and will tolerate conditions which are to some degree either side of those best suited to their parents. "And, of course, our son is definitely a hybrid."

Nadine shouted, "Orchid? Orchid?" Why don't we just call him "Our Kid?"

I said, "Our Kid." That's not bad. I tell you what, let's just call him Kidd.

With that I filled in the name Kidd Black on the birth certificate, picked up my son and walked out of the hospital as fast as I could. I heard Nadine complaining but I knew she'd follow. And I knew she'd come around to liking the name. A special name for a special baby.

Once again Lawrence starts laughing to himself. His laughter is cut short by a knock at the door. A knock that they had been waiting for for almost eighteen years.

The man at the door said he had a message from their son.

36

AMANDA AND IKE walk out of the President's office. Ike is livid. He's not used to having anyone talk to him like that—President or not. Amanda isn't smiling either.

She says, "I think you should put another agent on the case. I don't trust Kidd Black."

Ike cuts in. "You don't trust Kidd Black? That's like the Pope saying he doesn't have faith in God. If you can't trust Kidd, you can't trust anybody."

Amanda smiles to herself and plays her ace. "Very poetic Ike but not very convincing. For the first time since I've known you, I know something you don't."

Ike smiles condescendingly and says, "What is this? I'll show you mine if you show me yours?"

Amanda thinks, Don't you wish. She says, "Kidd Black is in love with Monique Williams."

"Ridiculous. He doesn't even know her."

"He doesn't know her but he knew her. Eighteen years ago, at West Point.

Kidd and Monique. There was a scandal. Kidd should've been thrown out, but Devon Williams saved his skin."

Ike quickly says, "Preposterous," but his voice doesn't sound as convinced as before.

"Like I said, put another agent on the case. Kidd can't be trusted. He'd let the world blow up before he'd lay a finger on Monique Williams."

Ike's thinking, Put another agent on the case? There is no other agent like Kidd Black. He's the best we've got...I know. I was the one who recruited him.

Without a word, he turns and walks away from Amanda.

37

THREE MEN, each one carrying a gym bag, are out in the Pacific Heights area of San Francisco. They're heading up their fifth set of stairs carved into the hill. They don't call it Pacific Heights for nothing.

Devon catches his breath just enough to say, "This is getting a little ridiculous. Why didn't we take a cab?"

Barry, not the least bit winded, smirks. "All those years of sitting behind a computer are coming back to haunt you now, aren't they? A little exercise now and then is good for you."

Kidd keeps walking as he says, "Too many people are looking for us. And we can't keep on stealing cars. Sooner or later our luck will run out...We're not exactly the most forgettable group in the world, are we? Three guys carrying a fortune in hundred dollar bills. A world-famous billionaire, a black man with blue eyes, and a doctor who talks way too much."

Barry asks, "What's the difference between 'way too much' and 'too much?'"

Kidd ignores him and says, "So, Devon, how long is it going to take to get that computer out of your house?"

"Five minutes. Tops."

Barry says, "Sounds like a piece of cake."

Devon is full of confidence. "And then once we get the computer to a safe place, we go to my other two houses and destroy the two computers that are left."

Kidd asks, "Why can't we erase the other two computers from this one?"

"Impossible. That's the beauty of the back-up system I designed. It's a network of three but each computer can't access the other. There's no way to access them except to be there in person."

Kidd is clearly getting impatient. "While we're doing this, Dalakos could be on his way to the other computers. Tell me where they are, and I'll get someone to keep an eye on them."

"It's not that I don't trust you but I don't trust anyone when the life of my daughter is at stake."

Kidd asks, "Meaning?"

"Meaning, as long as one of the computers is intact, there's a reason to keep Monique and Sabrina Rose alive. So, once I have one computer in hand, you can go ahead and do all the destroying you like. But, not a second before."

Kidd surveys the area and asks, "How much further to your place?"

Devon looks out in the distance. His voice falters. "Over there, by those flashing red lights."

38

RIDING LIKE the wind. Ike has taken his horse, Chataqua, across the flat fields of the Farm. Actually, it's Chataqua taking Ike but Ike needs to feel the wind in his face. Chataqua knows when Ike needs the adrenaline rushing through him. Finally, Ike slows Chataqua down to a trot.

"There's something I'm missing here, Chataqua. What is Dalakos up to? He wants the software for the Lazer that's for sure and he's either found a way to make it operational or he's going to sell it back to us. Ah, if that were only the case. I'd happily pay a fortune for it."

Chataqua hears the car pull into the farm before Ike does. The horse turns his head in that direction. Ike races Chataqua back to the stable. It might be awhile before they get to ride like this again. By the time they reach the stable, Caroline, PACT computer whiz, is waiting for them by the stable.

Ike says, "Can't say I'm happy to see you. You only bring bad news."

"A typical case of blaming the messenger...I haven't slept in two days. We're picking up a high amount of chatter about Dalakos and something or someone called Archimedes."

Archimedes. The name sets Ike drifting back to a happier time. To studying the Classics. To living in a simpler world. A world that's been gone for more than 2,400 years. Or certainly since the 11th of September.

Caroline continues, "Our best guess is that Dalakos and Archimedes are one and the same. Why he would want to use some long-forgotten Greek scientist as an alias is beyond me. Those Greeks, always living in the past."

Ike sighs. Long forgotten Greek scientist indeed. He wasn't Greek and he certainly isn't long-forgotten.

No coffee, no small talk, no waiting for Chataqua to be unsaddled. Caroline opens up her briefcase right by the stable and sets out her papers. "Whatever it is, it's taking place soon. I've never seen this much static. It sounds like there's going to be some sort of pow-wow from Murder Incorporated from around the world and the host is Mr. Dalakos."

Caroline's papers are all out. All neatly stacked on the railing of the corral. It's as though she's about to say something that she doesn't want to say. "It seems it's no longer a question of if but of when."

But Ike is only half listening. He's gone back 2,400 years. Back to the Siege of Syracuse...

The soldiers in the besieged city knew that the end was near. Their own King had lost his mind. He was under the spell of that madman mathematician, Archimedes. For two months they had been making and polishing mirrors. No other preparations, just mirrors. And now, the Roman Armada was fast approaching Syracuse.

Every able bodied man was put in position, not with a weapon, but with a mirror. A mirror! Archimedes was making calculations up until the last moment and then gave his orders. The soldiers did as they were told as soldiers usually do. They followed his orders and waited to die. They angled their mirrors so that the sun's rays focused on the attacking wooden boats.

To the astonishment of everyone, everyone except Archimedes that is, the boats began to catch fire and burn.

Ike realizes that he's sweating. Caroline looks at him curiously as he wipes his brow. But Ike doesn't notice her. He's only thinking how Dalakos must know his history, too. He's going to harness the power of the sun and smite his enemies.

Ike closes his eyes and thinks, And it is we who are his enemies.

39

"WOULD YOU like a cup of coffee?"

Karl smiles at Nadine Black and says, "No thanks. I really can't stay long." His voice drops to what can only be described as a conspiratorial whisper. "In fact, I shouldn't be here at all."

Karl notices a picture of Kidd on the mantelpiece. It's him from what must be twenty years ago but it's definitely him.

No doubt about it. I've come to the right place. I don't know how Dalakos does it, but he's the best. It's a pleasure to work for such a genius.

Mr. Black fumbles with a cigarette. Nadine looks at him disapprovingly. He ignores her and asks Karl, "Mind if I smoke?"

Karl asks right back, "Mind if I join you?"

Lawrence hands him a cigarette and they both light up, taking deep drags. Nadine asks, "Are you in the same, uh, organization as our son?"

Karl smiles to himself. Me in PACT. That'll be the day. He says, "Yes. I am. Now, first of all, your son is fine. He wants to see you and I'm supposed to take you to him."

Lawrence can barely hold back his excitement. "Right now?" "As soon as you're ready."

Lawrence answers, "I'm ready. Let's go!"

Nadine says, "I'm not going anywhere until I put on some make-up and a proper dress."

"Oh, come on, Nadine. He's your son. He's not going to care if you're wearing lipstick or not."

"I haven't seen him in eighteen years. He can wait another five minutes."

Nadine walks upstairs without looking back.

Karl says, "I just want to tell you that at some point today I'm going to have to blindfold you both. I'm sure you understand why."

Lawrence takes a long drag from his cigarette and then says, "I understand."

Nadine comes down the stairs and stands behind the couch and faces Karl. Her voice is cold and steady. "I don't know who you are Mister, but we're not going anywhere with you."

Karl says, "Excuse me?"

Nadine says, "Maybe this'll help you to understand plainEnglish."

She reaches into her purse, pulls out a pistol and points it at Karl.

40

KIDD HANDS a pair of mini-binoculars to Devon and says, "It's nothing but charcoal now. Burned to a crisp."

Barry sighs and sounds exhausted. "I tell you what I think. I've been in the spy business for about five hours now. It was no accident and no coincidence. These people we're after, who by the way, seem to be after us too, always seem to be one step ahead of us."

Kidd says, "Someone definitely torched the place. The only question is, did they get the information they wanted or not?"

Devon quickly answers, "My guess is not. You can't just turn the computer on and access it. It has a retinal identification system. They couldn't do it without me watching, so to speak."

Barry says, "At least that's some good news."

Kidd asks, "Is there anyone else who can access the computer?"

Devon turns away from both of them. "No one. No one that is..." His voice is barely audible. "No one that is, except Monique."

Barry breaks the silence. "Why didn't they just pick up the computer and bring it to Monique?"

Devon patiently answers, "I'm sure they tried. But, move it out of the force field without the right fingerprints, mine or Monique's, and it self-destructs. I learned that from 'Mission Impossible.'"

Barry says, "Yeah, but in 'Mission Impossible,' self-destruct didn't mean burn the whole place down."

Devon smiles just a little bit sheepishly. "I, uh, gotta work on that."

Kidd says, matter-of-factly, "One down, two to go."

41

AMANDA GETS the news. As the gatekeeper to the President, she controls what and who has access to him.

For now, I'm going to keep this to myself. That's the trouble when you work outside of channels. You just can't count on the quality of the people you're working with. But we need that computer. If we destroy it, we'd lose years of work. With that lazer we'd be invincible. Invincible! But, on the other hand, if it gets into the wrong hands...

Amanda pours herself another glass of water. You ask a simple thing like steal me a computer and what happens? They nearly burn down Pacific Heights. If I want this done right, I'm going to have to do this myself. Maybe all that West Point training is going to pay off after all.

The President walks out of his office and into Amanda's. He says, "You think this fire at Devon Williams' had anything to do with Dalakos?"

Amanda says with a shrug, "PACT doesn't know anything about the fire."

"PACT doesn't know anything about a lot of things. Maybe it's time for a shake-up over there."

Amanda tries hard to hide her interest. "What are you going to do? Cut out their polo budget?"

"Whether you notice or not, Amanda, I am the President of the United States. With a wave of my hand I could put Ike out to pasture and...put anybody I wanted in that post. Someone I trusted. Someone who would have some answers."

Amanda breathes deeply, choosing her words carefully. "I'd think very carefully about taking on PACT. After all, as they say out at Ike's farm, you're only the President."

"ONLY the President? That condescending, arrogant bastard. Well, I might be ONLY the President, but I have a few surprises in store for Mr. Ike Muslow.

The President marches purposefully back into his office and slams the door. Amanda smiles and then smiles some more.

42

THE THINGS that run through one's head when a gun is pointed right at it. Karl knows he should be thinking about how to get the gun away from Nadine Black but all he can come up with is, what is everyone going to say when they hear he was shot by a sixty-five year old woman?

He's killed more men and women than he can remember. But now, he's frozen. Frozen with embarrassment.

Lawrence is the first one to speak. "Nadine, what the hell are you doing?"

Nadine doesn't take her eyes off of Karl as she speaks. "I remember the last time I saw our son. He said, 'Mama, look at the bright side. Drinking and smoking are out of the question...not to mention drugs.'"

Exasperated, Lawrence says, "What's your point?"

"He smokes. He's no secret agent. At least not for our side." Karl's thinking, That's pretty slim evidence. My guess is she's not convinced. Gotta pick my words carefully here.

Karl speaks in a clear confident voice. "Mrs. Black, I commend you on your deductive reasoning, but I'm afraid there's a hole in your logic."

Nadine waves the gun at him. "There's going to be a hole in your head in a minute if you don't start telling the truth."

Lawrence, more exasperated than ever, says, "For God's sake, Nadine, let the man speak."

Karl's thinking, Why didn't I wear a bulletproof vest? I'm getting over-confident or maybe I'm getting too old for this job.

Karl says, "It's true I smoke, I drink and I used to have a 'problem' with drugs. But that doesn't make me any less an agent than your son.

I wish we could call him and have him confirm who I am but that's impossible."

Nadine says, "Tell it to the police. They're on their way." Lawrence says, "You called the cops? Now we won't get to see Kidd."

Karl sighs and thinks, The police? It's always something.

Nadine says, "If this man says who he is, he'll be back on the street in ten minutes."

Karl keeps his voice cool and calm. "I have proof. I have a tattoo under my arm with my blood type. It proves who I am. Every PACT agent has one."

Luckily for Karl, PACT used to tattoo their agents that way. It saved the lives of a few because it sped up blood transfusions but it got a lot more killed because it didn't take long to identify who they were either.

Nadine hesitates. Karl continues. "All I ask is that you take a look at it."

Lawrence and Nadine both know that Kidd had been tattooed when he joined PACT. Lawrence says, "Let us see it."

Karl slowly takes off his jacket and holds it in one hand. He unbuttons his shirt and turns to show them his tattoo. As he turns, he reaches for the gun strapped to his back. He flings the coat at Nadine. While it's in the air, he grabs Lawrence, pulls him in front of him, and puts the gun to his head.

Using Lawrence as a shield, Karl stands there facing Nadine. Karl calmly says, "Now, I suggest you put that gun down. As you see, I've got a gun pointed right at your husband's head.

Nadine forces her voice to remain cool but the hand holding the gun starts to shake. "I've got a gun pointed right at your head mister. I suggest YOU put the gun down."

Karl laughs. "There's a much better chance that you'll kill your husband than me."

Nadine says, "That's a chance I'm willing to take.' Lawrence, his voice shaking, manages to ask, "You are?"

Karl looks Nadine right in the eyes as he says, "There's one thing you're forgetting."

Nadine doesn't even have time to ask, "What's that?" Karl fires and hits her in the hand holding the gun. The gun drops. He drags Lawrence with him and walks towards Nadine. She looks at him terrified. Reflexively, she takes her left hand and tries to stop the bleeding from her right hand.

Karl says, "The one thing you forgot is, you've spent your entire adult life saving people's lives. Before taking someone's life, I knew you'd freeze. Maybe for just a second, but I knew you'd choke."

Lawrence and Nadine are indeed frozen. Not a word, not a movement.

Karl throws Lawrence next to Nadine. Lawrence immediately puts pressure on his wife's hand to try and stem the bleeding.

Karl pulls out a pair of pliers from his back pocket. He looks at Nadine and then Lawrence and then back to Nadine. His voice is no longer calm. There's an excitement to it as he asks, "Now, who wants to go first?"

43

SABRINA ROSE might be smarter than most children but she's still a child and she sees the world in black and white. She knows Christopher Dalakos is evil and for some mysterious reason her mother can't see it. If they're going to get off of this boat, she's the one who's going to have to arrange it.

Sabrina looks out from their elegant prison, the top deck of a yacht. Actually, it's more like a small cruise ship than a yacht. They have their own pool and sun deck. It's Sabrina's only excuse to be out of her room.

Floating. I've spent so much time in this stupid pool, I feel like a fish. But, it's time to get out and do something.

We've got to be heading somewhere and my guess is once we get there it's not going to be good...Where's my daddy? He'd know what to do...But he's not here. It's up to me. It's up to me.

Sabrina Rose climbs out of the pool and walks up the stairs only to find a muscular man waiting for her at the top. She tries to walk past him. He motions to her that she can't. She tries to talk to him but he doesn't speak any English. So much for charming my way past him.

At the other end of "her" deck is a stairway up to the Captain's bridge. Behind that is where my mother goes. It must be his room. There's no escape that way.

She surveys the decks below. At the far end is a helicopter.

If I could hide in the helicopter I could fly out of here, call my daddy and rescue my mom. It's not a great plan but it's a plan and like daddy always said, "You gotta have a plan..."

Where is my daddy?

44

IKE SIGHS, feeling weary already and his day has just begun.

It's a sad day for PACT when I have to get my information from CNN. Now it's too late. Way too late. Too late to keep it out of the papers and too late to stop Kidd from hearing about the murders. Now I have to decide what to do about Kidd. When an agent takes his "contract" personally, he starts making mistakes...But when all is said and done, he's still the best I've got. I don't know how in the world Dalakos found out about Kidd's parents. And there was no doubt it was Dalakos. Blew up their whole house. Almost nothing left. All that the police found were...

Ike shudders and then finishes his thought...several teeth.

He sighs again when he sees Amanda's car come speeding up to the "farm." Why doesn't she use the god damn phone? Why? Because she and/or the President want a decision and she's not going until she gets it.

Amanda pulls right up next to Ike and doesn't even wait to get out of her car before saying, "This is getting out of control. It's time to bring in Kidd."

"One doesn't just 'bring in Kidd' unless he wants to be brought in."

"I think you overestimate the great Kidd Black. Just send a bunch of your PACT agents up to the funeral and bring him in."

Ike thinks, You're a clever one, Amanda. No doubt about it. I don't think Kidd would miss the funeral either. I just hope that Dalakos isn't half as clever as you.

Ike says, "Alright, I'll send someone up there just in case he shows."

"Good. And the President wants you to put someone else on the case."

Before Ike can say anything, Amanda adds, "And he says if you don't, you can bet he'll be all over your case."

45

TWILIGHT. SABRINA hears the light-blue helicopter before she see it. It blends in with the ocean and then at the last moment it pops up out of nowhere.

Just as long as the helicopter doesn't take off right away, my plan might just work. After all, there are only three ways off of this ship. The helicopter, a lifeboat and swimming. Though it's a long shot, the helicopter still seems like my best bet.

Sabrina Rose hadn't seen her mother all day. She knows that she's going to be coming by to see how her daughter is soon. So, now's the time. She's ready. As ready as she's ever going to be.

That's one of the great things about Sabrina Rose being a kid. She doesn't really know when to be afraid. Because if she did, she wouldn't be trying this, that's for sure.

The sun is going down. In the Caribbean, the sun hangs on the horizon, deciding what it's going to do and then once its mind is made up, quickly disappears out of sight. It's as though someone literally turned out the lights.

Sabrina Rose sees her mother leave the Captain's deck and head down the stairway toward Sabrina's cabin. Her mother looks somewhat dazed, almost drunk. She walks into the cabin and closes the door.

Come on, Mom. The cabin isn't that big. How long does it take to realize I'm not there? My plan isn't getting off to a very promising start. And this was supposed to be the easy part.

Finally, her mother comes out of the cabin, not yet worried, but showing the first sign of concern. Sabrina Rose ducks into the dumbwaiter that brings the meals up from the galley and hides herself behind a pile of tablecloths. Nothing to do but wait. Same as chess. Patience.

46

GOOD NEWS can wait. Bad news travels like lightning. They had a plan.

They all agreed, you had to have a plan. The computer in San Francisco was destroyed. That means there were two left. They would take one computer, disable the security and retinal identification system and install a homing device. They would then trade it for Monique and Sabrina Rose. Then, through the homing device, they would track down Dalakos and kill him before he could do any more harm. Unfortunately, Devon couldn't be in two places at the same time.

So, Barry, Kidd and Devon would go to New York to the first computer and Ike would go to the Bahamas to keep an eye on the second computer. Once Devon had taken care of the computer in New York, Ike would destroy the second computer. If there were any problems in New York, the second computer in the Bahamas would be a back-up. What wasn't an option was this: They couldn't destroy both computers.

As long as Dalakos thought there was a chance of getting the information, Monique and Sabrina Rose would stay alive. As long as Dalakos thought there was a chance of getting the information, they could trap him. And a trap was only as good as its bait.

They were heading towards New York. A private plane, hired in a private airport. The pilot was on his way to New York to pick up some clients on a corporate jet. He was happy to have the money (cash, of course) and would never tell his boss anyway.

Devon, Kidd and Barry are sprawled out trying to get some sleep. Kidd has insisted. Sleep can be just as effective a weapon as a gun. But Barry can't sleep. He's still wired from all the excitement. Being a surgeon had its own adrenaline, there were lives at stake on the operating table every day. But the difference here was that it's his life that is on the line. No, he won't be getting to sleep for awhile. The way he feels, in fact, he thinks he'll never get to sleep.

Barry sees that Kidd is awake and says, "So, a guy walks into a bar and notices everyone is sleeping..."

Kidd cuts him off before Barry can finish the joke. "Get some sleep. I'm not in the mood for jokes."

"Not in the mood? What're you talking about? You were always in the mood for jokes. Remember how you said it relaxed you? I can't believe it!"

"Barry, you're thinking of someone else. Someone you knew eighteen years ago. Sorry, but killing has a way of beating all the laughter out of you. Now, try and get some sleep."

Kidd closes his eyes and Barry stares at the ceiling, thinking, Not in the mood for jokes!

Barry changes the subject. "Remember when you told me you were going to go to West Point?"

Kidd doesn't open his eyes but says, "Sure. You said, 'Why the hell would you want to go there? Their football team stinks.'"

They both laugh. Barry says, "And I remember what else you said. 'It's one thing to want to do something for your country but it's another thing to have the means to do it. West Point is going to give me the means to do good.'"

Kidd opens his eyes. "I said that? How corny!"

Barry says, "I laughed at the time. But, you know what? I'm glad you did it because it's guys like you who are gonna protect guys like me, not to mention little kids and helpless old ladies from guys like Dalakos!"

"Now look who's sounding corny!" Barry says, "And another thing…"

Kidd closes his eyes as Barry talks. "Remember that story you told me? How when you were ten, you used to practice running up your bedroom wall and touching the ceiling and how one night there was a fly in your room. You told me you focused on it, then ran up the wall, leapt backwards and caught the fly in mid-air on your very first try. You then opened your window and let it free. "

Kidd doesn't say a word. Barry continues, "I've always wanted to ask you this...Did you really set the fly free?"

Barry looks over at Kidd and sees that he's sound asleep. Barry continues anyway, "Wouldn't hurt a fly. I sure as hell hope you've grown out of that idea!"

Barry spots a pile of papers. Typical for a corporate jet, they were all the latest business magazines, newsletters and newspapers. Each one claiming to give that inside edge that would make you rich. He glances at the front page of the Wall Street Journal. The small article on the front page catches his eye: "Prominent Physician and Husband Slain in Boston."

Nothing like news of a doctor getting murdered to get Barry Feldman to read further. He freezes when he reads that it's Kidd's parents. According to the article, Kidd's mother had called 911 saying there was an intruder in the house. According to neighbors, there was an enormous explosion. By the time the police got there, the house was burning out of control. The only way the police could identify the bodies was from Nadine and Lawrence Black's dental records. The only sign that they ever lived there, that they ever lived at all...was when the police found a few of their teeth in what was left of their house.

47

SABRINA ROSE tells herself she isn't going to peek out of the dumbwaiter until she hears what she wants to hear, which is a whole lot of searching going on. But there's only silence.

And it seems like it's lasting an eternity.

A little peek won't hurt. If there's no sound, it means they haven't started looking for me yet and if they haven't started looking for me yet, I can take a peek. But, if they haven't started looking for me yet, there won't be anything to see.

Sabrina Rose finally convinces herself to stay put and wait for her mother to form a search party.

She's got to round up a posse. I'm her daughter. No matter how strange my mom's been acting lately, she's still my mom and she'll come looking for me. That's one thing I can count on...though it seems like she's been gone a long time.

At last some footsteps are heard trudging up the stairs.

It's not like they're in a hurry to find me.

More footsteps come up the stairs. This time she can hear her mother calling. "Sabrina. Sabrina Rose, where are you?" Her mother's voice rises a little in pitch as she asks, "Where could she have gone?"

Two bodyguards stand near the dumbwaiter and mumble to each other in Greek. Sabrina Rose can't understand them but she imagines that they're thinking about the terrible fate that will befall them if she's not found. The thought makes her smile. Maybe they'll all kill each other off so mom and I can go back home to daddy.

What they're actually saying is that they hope the kid fell into the water so they won't have to baby-sit her any more.

Sabrina Rose can now hear Dalakos' voice. He screams out something and all of a sudden there's a loud commotion as everything on the boat is being turned inside out. Now's the time. A plan so bold it borders on ridiculous.

Sabrina Rose presses the button to send the dumbwaiter down to the deck below. It's just one more noise in all the commotion. By the time she gets one floor below, pandemonium has broken loose. Monique is now on the loudspeaker pleading for Sabrina Rose. A loud slap is heard as Dalakos takes out his frustrations on Dimitra, her nanny/bodyguard.

Sabrina Rose slowly opens the dumbwaiter a crack and takes a peek. Nothing. She opens it the rest of the way and climbs out. She doesn't hesitate. She rushes out onto the deck and jumps over the railing.

48

DEVON IS SILENT. Barry asks Kidd, "How do you know it wasn't a robbery gone bad or something like that? That's what the papers say!"

"I made a few phone calls." "And?"

Kidd sighs as though that should have been enough of an explanation. He continues. "They went in to kill right from the start. Your everyday thieves don't carry military grade explosives with them to rob a couple of old people. The total destruction of the house, almost impossible to find a trace of the bodies."

Kidd grimaces for a moment and then continues. "Just a couple of their teeth. It reminds me of that time in Germany. We had captured someone who we thought could lead us to Dalakos.

But, in capturing him, he lost a lot of blood so we took him to a hospital. Dalakos blew up the whole place in order to kill the man and one PACT agent.

A hundred people died. The destruction was so complete even their bones were melted.

No, my parents' death has got Dalakos' fingerprints all over it! That I'm sure of. That I know. What I don't know is how they found out who I was."

Barry feels he's in over his head. He asks, "Don't you think it's about time you told me who 'they' were?"

Barry has never seen Kidd look more intense as he says, "They are the bad guys. They are like the Hydra. One head springs up, you chop it off and another takes its place. Right now, the head that's springing up belongs to Christopher Dalakos. And regardless of what happens afterwards, my job is to cut off his head...after I go to the funeral, of course."

Devon says, "Your parents are dead. Going to the funeral isn't going to bring them back and it's not going to get us any closer to Dalakos. The best thing we can do is head for my computer in New York and safeguard the lazer information. Plus, everyone knows you're going to go to that funeral."

"It's true that Dalakos thinks I'm going to the funeral. PACT thinks I'm going to the funeral. Well, for once in my life I'm going to do the expected. And for me to do that, it'll be unexpected."

Barry says, "Life was a lot simpler when all we had to worry about was if we could round up enough guys for a baseball game."

Kidd says, "That's the idea. Every generation has to chop off a Hydra head so kids can keep playing baseball. And if you think that's too corny, all I can say is 'fuck you,' because it's true!"

Kidd heads for the pilot's cabin. On the way, he reaches into one of the gym bags and grabs a fistful of hundred dollar bills.

49

SABRINA ROSE gropes along the gunwale of the boat. All she can hear is the loud roar of the sea as the boat speeds towards its destination. She doesn't know enough to be afraid. Instead, she just concentrates on her next foothold, her next hand hold. She doesn't even know enough not to look down. So down she looks. She's fascinated with how fast the boat is really going. It never seems that fast from up on the deck where she was being held prisoner. But, she can't admire the sea all day. She has to work her way down to the helicopter.

Sabrina Rose starts to laugh. She remembers how when she wanted to quit ballet lessons her mother said, "You'll thank me one day that I wouldn't let you." And how when she wanted to quit gymnastic class, her father said, "My one great regret in life was that I couldn't do a backward roll."

So, before she starts off, Sabrina Rose thanks her mother and takes strength from the fact that if everything goes right, how proud her father will be of her...if everything goes right.

It's a lot further than it looked. Actually, it's not that far if you're walking but when you're groping with your hands, fighting the wind and the slippery gunwale, it can feel like an eternity.

Twice she hears guards scurry past her. But, she knows that this is the last place they'll think of looking. It's certainly the last place she would ever think of looking.

Finally, she gets to the back of the boat, about twenty feet from the helicopter. But her arms won't hold her much longer. With a burst of strength she didn't even know she had, she thrusts herself over the edge and back onto the deck of the boat. She loses her footing and goes sprawling out on the deck. Her body tells her to collapse, stay down, give up. But then she hears her mother's voice again over the loudspeaker frantically calling out her name. Sabrina Rose picks herself up and staggers towards the helicopter.

50

THEY DIDN'T make it in time for the service. A dead man can't just call up and say, "Wait for me!" But they made it in time for the actual burial.

Kidd tells Barry and Devon, "Go ahead. It's perfectly natural that you both come to my parent's funeral. I'll circle around and join you once I know it's safe."

Barry says, "I'd like to get the guys who did this on my operating table."

Devon says, "Come on, super-hero, let's go."

Devon heads for the large crowd of people already gathered around the grave site and Barry hurries to keep up with him. Kidd is wearing dark glasses, a hat and a black suit. He'd be very surprised if any of his relatives recognized him. It's been almost eighteen years.

But, it's not them he's worried about. He holds a large bouquet of flowers close to his face as he heads off through the wooded area that gives "Woodacre Cemetery" its name.

Right before he gets out of the woods, Kidd takes out a pair of binoculars and scans the crowd. It's like watching faded memories of his childhood except everyone he remembers has somehow aged. His cousins, uncles, neighbors are all there. There are a lot of people he doesn't even know.

Of course, funerals are for the living and it does make him feel good that so many people have come out on this beautiful sunny day to say their farewells to his parents.

He carefully checks out each unfamiliar face for a clue if they're working for Dalakos or not. He doesn't expect to find Dalakos himself. Not his style. One of the reasons that Dalakos has survived so long in a business with such a high turnover.

A voice whispers, "Hey, Kidd!"

Kidd is startled. A thousand thoughts rush through his head.

How did someone get so close? How does he know my name? If I don't do something quick, I'm going to die just like they planned and my parents will go unavenged!

Instinctively, in a flash, Kidd whirls around and drops to a crouch and then rolls behind a tree. By the time he stops rolling, his gun is out and ready to fire. The flowers fly off in the direction of the voice. The sunglasses are nowhere to be seen.

The voice laughs. "Very good. Very good. You must've had an excellent teacher."

Ike Muslow comes walking out from behind a tree and continues, "But I have to say it's not very impressive that you let an old man like me get so close without you knowing it."

Kidd doesn't move. "Ike, what a pleasant surprise. How nice of you to come to my parent's funeral. It's not out of guilt is it?"

"Guilt?"

"How did Dalakos know they were my parents? Or is it just coincidence that they died when I got involved in chasing him down?"

"It didn't come from our end, I assure you. The only people who know are PACT's inner council and the President."

"Sherlock Holmes said, 'Once you eliminate the impossible, your solution lies with the improbable, no matter how unlikely that is.'"

"Meaning?"

"Meaning you better check on your Inner Council and find out who sent the dogs after my parents."

Ike says, "Will do. Even though I think it's a waste of time."

"And while you're at it, check on the President."

"That I refuse to do...As for us, either you trust me or you don't. If you do, put down your gun."

Kidd remembers the first time Ike approached him. "We know a lot about you. We know that growing up you were neither accepted by white children nor black children. The beating you took from a bunch of older boys when you were ten and how you swore you'd never lose another fight again. How you worked and never stopped working so by the time you made it to West Point, you had the toughness and arrogance of a boy who never lost in whatever he did. But being the best isn't good enough for us.

We want someone who can think for himself but who will never forget where he comes from and why he's here. A man who believes in justice and equality and what the American way stands for. Are you that man?"

Ike knew a lot about me. But, he didn't know that I had slept with my best friend's girlfriend. I remember my own father talking to me about some political scandal, "He's an honorable man but I can tell you, when it comes to sex, all bets are off." As for me, all bets were off when it came to love.

I thought joining PACT would kill three birds with one stone. I could do something for my country. I could break away from Monique's spell and I wouldn't have to face my best friend Devon ever again.

Kidd looks at Ike and doesn't hesitate. If he can't trust Ike Muslow, the man who has been like a father to him since he effectively killed his own eighteen years ago, he doesn't want to live. Kidd throws down his gun.

Ike slumps down on a nearby tree stump. For the first time, Kidd can see how weary he is. Ike's spent his entire adult life putting out fires and the fact that the flames are once again licking at the door is almost more than he can take.

"Kidd, the President wants another agent on the case. He thinks you're taking this whole thing too personally..."

Kidd stares at Ike as he interrupts, "Dalakos killed my parents! You can bet it's personal!"

Ike doesn't avert his eyes as he says, "That's not what I'm talking about. The point is Kidd, the whole world's in danger and I don't give a damn about your feelings for Monique Robinson."

Kidd is startled that Ike knows about him and Monique but he does his best to remain unfazed. "You're not the best for nothing, Ike. But, I'm the best agent you've got. And I'm your best shot at getting Dalakos, so I think we should do things my way."

"Which is?"

"First we cut off Dalakos' arms and then we go for his throat."

In the background, the hearse can be seen as it slowly winds its way to the grave site. Ike takes a deep breath before speaking. Finally he says, "For the first time in my life, I'm going to disobey a direct order from my superior.

In this case, he just happens to be the President of the United States."

Ike manages a smile. "I was supposed to bring you in and take you off the case. I might still have to kick your ass for disobeying orders, but that'll have to wait until we take care of the likes of Christopher Dalakos. Now, what have you got?"

Kidd notices the hearse pulling up to the grave site and takes out his binoculars. Ike does the same. Kidd says, "I'm here with Devon Williams and Doctor Barry Feldman. Barry's an old friend who patched me up when Devon and I were hit. For better or worse, Barry's along for the ride."

"You were with Devon Williams? Amanda told you to stay away from him."

"I'm taking orders from two people in this world and Amanda's not one of them."

Kidd and Ike scan the crowd. Ike says, "If I'm thinking what you're thinking, Dalakos has to have someone here. Someone to finish you off while you're least expecting it. But whom?"

Kidd focuses on Devon as he scans the crowd. "Devon had three computers that contained the lazer algorithms and information. They were in each of his homes. The one in California has been destroyed which leaves one in New York and one is in the Bahamas. We'll take one computer, disable the security and retinal identification system and install a homing device. Then we trade it for Monique and Sabrina Rose...."

Ike interrupts. "...with me getting a message to Dalakos that we're ready to trade."

"It's that or look his number up in the yellow pages under terrorist..."

Ike ignores Kidd's remark and signals him to continue. "Then, using the homing device, we track down Dalakos and kill him before he can do any more harm. Unfortunately, Devon can't be in two places at the same time. So, we'll take care of the one in New York. You take care of the Bahamas."

Ike asks, "Where in the Bahamas?"

"It's on Paradise Island. Just ask where the Devon Williams' Estate is."

"I'll get on it right away."

Kidd grabs Ike by the wrists and pulls his face close to his. "Ike, under no circumstances is that computer to be touched. If something goes wrong in New York, it's going to be theonly thing keeping Monique and Sabrina Rose alive!"

Ike takes a deep breath. It sounds more like a sigh. Both men know that what Ike is going to say isn't going to be pleasant.

"That information is bigger than both of us, bigger than Devon Williams and unfortunately bigger than a woman and her child. It would be a tragedy if we lost it but a much bigger tragedy if it fell into the wrong hands."

Kidd tightens his grip on Ike's wrists. "I want you to promise me that you won't destroy that computer in the Bahamas! Put an army around that house, but don't touch that computer! DEVON CAN'T BE IN TWO PLACES AT THE SAME TIME! We need it as a backup in case there's a problem in New York. Only he can deactivate the security on it. He'll arrange for you to baby-sit the computer. Got it?"

"I promise."

"If you try to move it outside the force field, it blows up. BOOM! You understand? Fingerprints. Only Devon's or Monique's."

"I promise!"

Kidd pulls him even closer. "On the grave of my parents, I want you to swear!"

Silence. Eyeball to eyeball, neither one blinks. Finally, Ike whispers, "I swear."

Kidd nods his head and releases Ike. Kidd takes one more glance at the assembled mourners and says to himself, Coffee break's over, back on our heads.

Kidd picks up the flowers and they both head for the burial. Ike remembers Kidd's "funeral" eighteen years ago. Everything was the same and everything was different. The sun was shining -a Glorious day -and everyone was in black. Was it worth it? Tearing an idealistic nineteen year old away from his family? A family that would eventually be murdered because of what their child had become?

Ike clenches his fists and stands up straight. God damn right it was worth it. We're the Good Guys. It's people like us who are keeping the world safe from the likes of Christopher Dalakos. And that's something worth dying over.

After all the prayers have been said, the mourners file past the double-grave and throw in bunches of flowers. Kidd gets in line to do the same -to say a final farewell to his parents.

Kidd freezes. The grave digger. His hands. Manicured. Why would a grave digger have any manicure at all let alone an expensive one?

Kidd whispers to Ike, "Check out the grave digger. Is he carrying anything?"

Ike casually glances their way and says, "Can't tell. But that shovel looks bulky to me. Could be a weapon of some sort."

"Watch the hearse. Dalakos wouldn't send just one guy. Shoot first and ask questions later."

Kidd approaches the grave, keeping his head down. But not so far down that he can't see the hands of the grave digger. As he approaches, he notices Karl's hands tightly grip the shovel.

Kidd throws his flowers into Karl's face, momentarily stunning him. Like a cat, Kidd knocks the shovel out of Karl's hands. With a lethal combination of kicks and punches, Kidd sends him into the open grave.

The stunned mourners scream and run for cover. Barry and Devon rush around the grave to be by Kidd. Just then, the back door of the hearse comes flying open revealing a group of men with machine guns. Ike doesn't have a chance. But before he's going to die, he's going to take somebody with him. He ducks and rolls, firing into the hearse, hitting someone.

Kidd grabs the shovel, aims it at the hearse and squeezes the base of it. A rocket-propelled grenade heads right into the hearse, blowing it up. Kidd, Ike, Barry and Devon all stare at the shovel, very impressed. Ike yells, "Behind you!"

Karl, his face bloody, is halfway out of the grave. Kidd jumps on top of him and they plunge back into the grave. Body kicks are worthless here. It's too confined. They're stuck between the caskets and the soft earth.

Afterwards, Kidd barely remembers the thrashing, gouging and grunting as fists and faces collide.

All he remembers is when he finally had Karl turned around, his arms locked behind his back. Kidd had a flash of the first man he ever killed when he was twenty.

Then he started smashing Karl's head against the nearest casket. He didn't know if it was his mother's or his father's...And for the first time in his life, Kidd actually enjoyed killing someone

51

SABRINA ROSE had fallen asleep. When she wakes up, she isn't sure where she is. Then she remembers. She's snuggled behind the back seat of the helicopter. She decides to take a peek. She hopes against hope that maybe, just maybe, she has slept so soundly, the helicopter is already somewhere on land. She slowly pops her head up and is disappointed to see she is still on the ship.

I guess that was a lot to wish for...Still, I'm here and they haven't found me yet. Now, if only they'll send someone off on this helicopter before I have to pee. Now that's something they don't talk about much on television. Secret agents don't ever have to go to the bathroom. Well, sooner or later this one is going to have to.

Footsteps-coming closer. The helicopter door opens. Sabrina Rose is frightened and excited at the same time. Four men climb into the helicopter grunting and groaning. The helicopter is built for four, but just barely. The motor turns over and the noise is deafening.

Sabrina Rose takes the moment to stretch her muscles. It might be the last chance she gets for awhile. But keeping still is something she's good at. She was a champion player of "hide and seek."

One of the men in the rear seats chooses this moment to stretch his legs but there's nowhere to put them. The man adjusts the chair back to get a little more room. But, the chair won't move back. A master plan foiled because some guy's legs are a few inches too long.

They pull her roughly out of the helicopter, shouting as they do. More loud shouting. Dalakos comes running towards her, fire in his eyes. Luckily, Monique is right behind. But, Sabrina doesn't even notice Dalakos' screams. She barely notices Dalakos' slap across her face or her mother's protests. Sabrina Rose's mind is fixed on the sound of the helicopter taking off. She doesn't dare look at it until it's safely away. But she knows it's gone now. Maybe it'll help and maybe it won't. But it's something. And when you don't have anything, something starts to look like a lot.

Scrawled in her mother's lipstick, on the bottom of the helicopter is:

HELP!
MONIQUE + SABRINA ROSE WILLIAMS
THE ARGONAUT

PART TWO

1

"THERE ARE MORE than fifty-five thousand registered ocean-going boats on the high seas. Not to mention assorted unregistered pirate, gun-running and drug-smuggling craft.

Of course, there are airports but I doubt that he'd try that. It's not too difficult to watch an airport. On the other hand, an ocean is a little tougher. Especially when we don't know exactly what we're looking for."

The President rubs his temples and tries to concentrate. Ike has been briefing him for only fifteen minutes about the "situation" and it hasn't been pleasant.

Well, I am the President, after all. I'm going to have to make a decision about this sooner or later. Let's start with the essential."But if he gets his hands on this Lazer software, he still needs a satellite delivery system."

"That's right, Mr. President."

"And satellite delivery systems are very hard to come by, aren't they?"

Ike isn't encouraged by the hesitant tone of "aren't they" but he admits to himself that he's not too encouraged by the "situation" either.

Ike answers, "There are only a handful of known satellite launching facilities in the world. Some of them can be ruled out."

"Don't rule out anyone, God damn it!"

"Yes sir. I didn't mean 'ruled out' per se, I meant there are unlikely and likely candidates. The unlikely candidates with known satellite launching capabilities are Israel, China, India, Russia and the Europeans."

"And the United States."

Ike agrees, "And the United States."

"Unless, of course, there are rogue elements there who are working for Dalakos for a price...or for ideological reasons."

Ike replies, "We're keeping our ears wide open but there's nothing to indicate that that's happening."

"I'm more worried about the usual suspects." The President goes through the litany of bad guys starting with the Russian Mafia.

"They're making too much money as it is without tangling with us."

"Al-qaida?"

"They would if they could, but they don't have the means...yet"

"Iran?"

"They might if they could, but they don't have the means either."

"Pakistan?"

"They've been behaving ever since the head of their nuclear program confessed to selling the farm to anyone who could afford it."

The President hesitates before mentioning them. "The North Koreans?"

"They might have the means and they'd dream about doing it but I doubt it."

"Well, that makes me feel relieved. Would you like to elaborate?"

"I don't think Dalakos plans on using an established government. Our retaliation would be massive. Dalakos wouldn't care but the governments would."

"God damn right!"

"Dalakos has some other way in mind. Some other way to get hold of the necessary satellites."

"Such as?"

"Mr. President, I wish I knew. God, I wish I knew."

2

THE MEETING is in ten minutes and it takes her nine minutes to get there. She takes pride in not being late just as she takes pride in everything she does. One of the many reasons Lise Henry has been so good for Microtech just as Microtech has been good for her.

As she gets to the door, her computer beeps and a voice says, "Please read this e-mail." Surprised, she stops. Not only had she turned off that voice function on her computer but she had disconnected the sound card. Computers, unlike children, should be seen but never heard.

At the risk of being late for the meeting, she goes back to her computer and sure enough, there's an e-mail marked URGENT: ATTENTION LISE HENRY MICROTECH BAHAMAS

> MEMO: Dear Lise Henry, My wife, Monique, and my daughter Sabrina Rose are in your neighborhood for a well-needed vacation. Of course, they're traveling with their usual security contingent. But, as I'm sure you're aware from the newspapers, Monique will take any opportunity to escape them. If you hear any news about them of any kind, please contact me immediately.
>
> Sincerely, Devon Williams

Lise sighs. Being rich isn't all it's cracked up to be. In the Bahamas, there's a saying, "The trees can't grow to the sky." But Devon Williams' tree is up in the clouds and I imagine it's a very lonely place. Not to mention dangerous.

She snaps out of her daydream and heads for the door. If she runs, she can still make it to the meeting on time.

3

THE STOCKHOLM SYNDROME is a psychological state in which the victims of a kidnapping or persons detained against their free will develop a relationship with their captor(s). This solidarity can sometimes become a real complicity, with prisoners actually helping the captors to achieve their goals or to escape police.

Monique definitely has the Syndrome...But for her it's the worst possible kind. She's drugged and doesn't even realize that she's been kidnapped!

I wish he hadn't slapped Sabrina Rose..."That hurt me more than it hurt her." That's what he said. He said he was so upset that something had happened to her, that he couldn't help himself. He hit her because he cares so much for her and me. In fact, right now, he's making it up to her.

Three decks below, in the spacious galley, Dalakos is alone with Sabrina Rose. Dalakos couldn't be happier. Sabrina Rose couldn't be more apprehensive.

"So, little Sabrina Rose, I have a surprise for you."

"I'm not hungry, thank you. I should get back to my mother." "Your mother needs to rest. Let's give her some time to be alone. Some time for us to get to understand each other."

Warning sign: Sabrina Rose notices he didn't say, "Let's get to know each other but let's get to understand each other."

Dalakos continues, "But first your surprise." "I'm still not hungry."

"I said surprise, you little brat! I didn't say anything about food!!"

Dalakos picks her up with both hands and holds her above his head.

He then lowers her down so her face is inches away from his. "Now, if you don't want anyone else to get hurt, including your mother, behave yourself!"

"Let me down or I'll scream!" "Scream! Go ahead and scream!"

Sabrina Rose whimpers. "Please, let me down!"

"I said scream! SCREAM!"

Sabrina Rose starts to howl. A scream comes from the bottom or her soul. She screams for herself, for her mother, for her missing father.

Dalakos shakes her. "Louder!"

Sabrina Rose can't scream any louder but she tries. Finally, Dalakos has had enough. He gently sets her down.

"If you say one word to your mother, I'll kill you...while she watches. And then I'll kill her. Do you understand?"

Terrified, Sabrina Rose nods her head yes.

4

SAMSON HENRY is in a hurry to get out of his house. His mother-in-law is coming over to watch the kids and he hates to be around the woman. She's never happy. At least he's never seen her happy. But he's caught in a dilemma. He can't leave the kids alone and since she's coming to watch the kids, he can't do anything but wait for her.

Not that it matters if he's late for work. As long as the boats are cleaned before morning no one cares. But she cares. Every other word out of her mouth is, "How did my daughter end up marrying such a good-for-nothing?" He doesn't mind. He feels sorry for her.

Samson looks out the window of their modest bungalow and watches the sea. Peace and tranquility wash over him. He loves the Bahamas and he loves his wife. Of course, he adores his kids. And it doesn't matter to him, to his kids or his wife that she has a better job than he. But, oh, it matters to his mother-in-law. So, he goes back to watching the ocean. Sometimes he gets the feeling that the ocean is watching him too.

But then, his daydream is smashed like the waves against the shore. That woman is coming his way. The human cloud marches purposefully up the steps. She walks into the house without knocking, like she owns the place. She sees him and doesn't even bother to smile, doesn't even bother to say hello.

"I'm here, Samson. You can go and do whatever you do now."

"Hello to you, too."

"My daughter told me there's a man at Microtech who appreciates her very much. I wouldn't be surprised if she gets another promotion."

Samson isn't jealous. He's just glad that his wife might get another promotion. "Ah, she's a clever woman, my wife. After all, she was clever enough to marry me."

Samson smiles and kisses his mother-in-law goodbye only because he knows she hates being kissed by him just a little more than he hates kissing her.

5

DALAKOS IS LYING on his bed, headphones on, listening to his iPod. He closes his eyes just as he gets to the best part.

"But first your surprise." "I'm still not hungry."

"I said surprise, you little brat! I didn't say anything about food!!"

He smiles at his choice of words and thinks, That's good. That's very good.

He feels himself getting aroused as he once again hears Sabrina Rose's voice. It's the screaming that gets him going. He had tried sex with children before but never saw what all the excitement was about...but creating the screams, the fear, the pure fear, now there was something magical about that.

"Let me down or I'll scream!" "Scream! Go ahead and scream!"

Sabrina Rose whimpers. "Please, let me down!" "I said scream! SCREAM!"

Now very turned on, he picks up the phone and tells Dimitra, "Send up Monique. Immediately!"

Dimitra hangs up the phone and goes to do as she's told. She's seething with anger. But she's not angry with Dalakos. It's that woman she hates. Dimitra is certain that if she wasn't around, Christopher would be hers again.

6

THE PRIVATE JET heads up the Hudson River. The pilot announces, "Gentlemen, we're going to start our descent into New Paltz. Please fasten your seat belts."

Barry says to Kidd, 'Well, back on our heads."

Kidd nods in agreement. "Yeah, back on our heads."

Devon asks, "Hey, didn't your mothers ever tell you that it's not polite to tell private jokes in front of people?"

Barry says, "Private joke? Everybody knows that joke." Kidd adds, "Apparently, everybody but you."

Devon says, "Forget it."

Barry looks at Kidd, shrugs his shoulders in disbelief and says, "Okay, okay...A guy dies and arrives at the Pearly Gates where St. Peter tells him, 'Welcome to heaven. But, before you can enter, you have to decide between heaven and hell.'

St. Peter gives him a tour of heaven. 'People have to go to work, pay bills and taxes. It looks a lot like life on earth.'

Then St. Peter takes him to hell. In hell, guys are sitting around watching wild naked women dance and do unspeakable things. The guys are sitting around drinking cups of coffee. The only negative side is that they're all sitting on barrels of shit.

The guy says to St. Peter, 'I've made my decision. I'm choosing hell.'

St. Peter wishes him well and disappears.

The guy takes his place on a barrel of shit and once he gets used to the smell, is really enjoying himself.

Just then, the Devil walks into the room, blows a whistle and says, 'Alright, coffee break is over, back on your heads!'"

Devon doesn't laugh and says, "So, whenever you guys are facing a difficult situation, you say, 'back on our heads.'"

Kidd and Barry smile and say, "You got it."

Devon says, "For some odd reason, I expected more."

Barry says, "You know what you should do with all your money? You should buy yourself a sense of humor."

Kidd laughs. "Now that's funny."

Devon snorts and says, "You guys were made for each other." Barry stops laughing long enough to say, "Come on, Devon, life is too funny not to laugh."

7

PARADISE ISLAND, THE BAHAMAS...Paradise alright. If you're Devon Williams, I guess you settle for nothing less. At sunrise, Ike is checking out the mansion from a boat. The security he can spot is impressive and he's sure there's plenty more that he can't see. It looks like the only way in there is through the front door with a written invitation in hand.

Ike wonders, What does Dalakos think he's going to do? Just drive up with Monique and pick up the computer? If he does, we'll nab them both.

Maybe he doesn't know that Kidd is on the case. No, he must know by now after the funeral. Maybe he thinks that Kidd and Devon are dead. Maybe they are dead. Well, I gave my word that nothing is going to happen to that computer and nothing will...until I hear from Kidd.

Ike walks up to the gate of the estate and rings the bell. Maxwell Fynes, a well-dressed black man, comes out from the gatekeeper's house.

"Mr. Muslow, we've been expecting you. Welcome."

Ike takes a step through the gate. Maxwell stands in front of him. "Just one second, sir. You have to answer one question first. Mr. Williams' orders."

Ike smiles. "Of course, we don't want just anyone coming in, do we?"

"No, we certainly don't. So, please tell me, what is a furlong?"

Ike smiles again. "A furlong is a unit of length. 220 yards to be exact. The standard measurement of horse racing. The origin of the word is actually Arabic and..."

The gatekeeper relaxes. "As I said, welcome."

Ike also allows himself to relax...for a moment. Kidd must have told Devon about my love of horses. So, Kidd is still alive. Or was alive...I'm not going to worry too much about it and just take care of what I can take care of. And my job is to take care of that computer until Devon and Kidd arrive. And then? Well, I guess we'll think of something. We almost always do. Almost.

8

KIDD, DEVON AND BARRY walk out of the airport terminal and get in the only cab there. The cab driver looks like he's right out of central casting. Early 40s with a beer gut and the Yankees game on the radio. He mumbles, "Welcome to New Paltz. Where to?"

The moment Devon says, "Mohonk Mountain House," Kidd flinches.

The cab driver nods and says, "You got it."

The cab slowly winds its way up through the lush green of the Shwangunk Mountains towards the hotel. Kidd remembers running up that mountain, rushing to see Monique. Her aunt was a gardener there and Monique had a summer job baby-sitting the guests' kids by keeping them busy on the tennis courts.

Most of all, Kidd remembers that she had a two hour lunch break. Two hours that kept them both in shape.

I would run up the mountain, it seemed like nothing and then it seemed like everything. She stayed in shape, too. She never had time for lunch. We lived for our moments down at the old boathouse. It was built by Old Mr. Johnson back in the late 1800s but hadn't been used in decades. Back then, they say Mr. Johnson was quite the "swordsman" and was rumored to have put it to quite a bit of use himself.

The cab pulls up to the main gate. There's a sign:

No Private Cars Allowed Past This Point.

The gatekeeper says: May I help you?

Devon announces: "I'm David Wilkshire. I have a room here." Kidd smiles to himself. Every amateur chooses his own initials when thinking up a fake name.

The gatekeeper looks at a list and then says, "Welcome to Mohonk Mountain House, Mr. Wilkshire."

Devon steps out, hands a bill to the cab driver and says, "Thanks. We'll walk from here."

9

THE PRESIDENT is speechless. Amanda fills the space. "Against your direct orders, Kidd Black is with Devon Williams. They were last seen together at the funeral of Kidd's parents."

"Last seen? Which means that you don't know where they are now, doesn't it? We spend a trillion dollars a year for these gadgets that are supposed to be able to find anyone anytime. You know how much a trillion dollars is?"

Now it's Amanda's turn to not say a word.

The President continues, "Actually, I don't know how much a trillion is either. What's Ike have to say about all this?"

"Uh, that's the uh, part, I uh, was getting to."

The President winces. "I'm not going to like this, am I?" "No sir, you're not."

10

SAMSON HENRY has done an honest day's work for an honest day's pay. He wishes he could say the same for his crew. Mostly young kids, they just want to get the job done as quickly as possible and go out and spend their money to cool down with some hot women. Samson smiles at the thought. He used to be just like them but a wife and two kids teaches you a few things about responsibility.

Well, it being Friday night and all, he let the crew off early and checks the line before he heads home. Everything is fine until he gets to the helicopter. He gets down on his hands and knees and looks under it and sees some writing in lipstick.

He curses to himself. Probably some obscene graffiti. I've told these guys a thousand times that the bottom is just as important as the rest. But no, they just stick the hose under it and that's that.

Samson can read the last two lines clearly but the first line has been smudged by the water from the hose.

HEL
MONIQUE + SABRINA ROSE WILLIAMS
THE ARGONAUT

He crawls back out and comes back with an industrial strength sponge. He shakes his head and thinks, Who the hell would go to all that trouble just to impress a couple of tennis players, the Williams sisters, Monique and Sabrina Rose?

He scrapes off the graffiti and thinks, All this just to say "hello" to two girls who play tennis. Don't know who "The Argonaut" is. Probably the nickname of some boy or some teen slang that I'm too old to understand.

He laughs a hearty laugh and thinks back to that night when he climbed all the way up the water tower on Mayaguana Island. He rubs the sponge harder as he remembers her face when they came by on the ferry and she saw written in big blue letters:

Marry me Lise!—I LOVE YOU—Samson.

11

THE THREE OF THEM WALK UP the stairs of the Tower where a three floor suite right out of a medieval castle awaits them. To Kidd, nothing has changed. He half expects to see Monique appear at any moment.

Devon opens the door and it's just as Kidd remembered. Kidd had been up the stairs only one other time. Monique had gotten the key from housekeeping and they had done it right in Mr. Johnson's room. He had never been so excited or so scared in his life. Never, not even when..."

Devon interrupts Kidd's daydream and says, "Make yourself at home."

Barry asks, though he's sure the answer is yes. "You got cable?"

Devon says, "Sorry, I don't watch much TV."

Barry thinks about saying, How can I make myself at home without cable? but just says, "Oh."

Devon opens up a desk drawer and pulls out five tall stacks of hundred dollar bills.

Barry says, "I guess it's good to keep a little 'pocket money' around."

Devon opens up his gym bag and says, "One man's pocket money is another man's fortune, Barry. And after paying off those pilots, we're running low on the dough."

Barry says, "Yeah, looks like we're in desperate need of a transfusion."

Devon closes up the gym bag and says, "I'm going out to the boathouse to check on the computer."

Kidd says, "I'll go with you."

Devon picks up the gym bag and says, "No, it's okay. This is Mohonk. It's like Shangri-la. The outside world stops at the gate."

Kidd jumps up and says, "If this is Shangri-la..."

But Devon is already out the door. Kidd sighs and finishes his sentence anyway, "then why are you checking on the computer?"

Devon had his own reasons for going to the boathouse alone. This was a place for just him and Monique. She always wanted to make love there. How he loved it there. This is where he did his best work. This is where Sabrina Rose was conceived. He didn't want Kidd coming to the boathouse with him. This was his. The one place where Monique was really happy. The one place where he felt at peace with the world. But his world was no longer at peace. The world was no longer at peace. Devon thinks, Maybe Kidd is right. Maybe Monique was kidnapped. Maybe all this stuff about her still being in love with Kidd is nothing. He shakes his head, feeling embarrassed. After all, we've been married for a long time now. We've got a great daughter.

That demon named "Jealousy" rears its head up but Devon fights it off. She was only with Kidd that one time. Anyone can make a mistake...One time is a lot closer to zero than it is to two.

With that comforting thought in mind, Devon heads for the boathouse.

Barry looks out the window and watches as Devon walks past the basketball court completely oblivious to the game and the world around him.

Barry says to Kidd, "You never did tell me what you've been up to for the last eighteen years."

"You know what I've been up to." "Vaguely."

"My life's been like playing on a professional basketball team. You practice a lot and then hope it all comes together on game day. Except, in my league, only one team walks away alive."

Barry says, "Yeah, well even the pros have lives outside basketball."

"I had a girlfriend once. But, she decided she didn't want a long distance relationship. Meaning, she preferred to be with a guy who was a little more down to earth...one who was alive."

12

DALAKOS STANDS over Monique as she lays bent over across the table. Dalakos is wearing headphones. He's listening to his latest creation. Sabrina Rose's screams. Looped. It goes on forever. Every scream excites him. With every scream he thrusts into Monique. He's never been more turned on.

For Dalakos, Monique isn't there. It's a perfect match. Monique lays across the table and thinks of Kidd. She hasn't shouted his name in twenty years.

For twenty years, she tried to make love to Devon and not Kidd and sometimes she actually did. But Kidd always came back to her. Always. Always Kidd.

But, in her drugged state, she imagines she's with Kidd. For the first time in twenty years, she screams Kidd's name. Twenty years of pressure explodes as she shouts out his name.

Dalakos can't hear her. He's too lost in Sabrina Rose's screams. He opens his eyes and looks down on Monique. He slaps her ass and watches her react. He slaps her harder but, suddenly, a red light by his phone goes on and ruins the moment. There's an emergency somewhere and as much as he would like to continue, he stops. He's a professional and professionals have control.

He stops thrusting and throws off his headphones...Monique freezes. Dalakos grabs the phone and listens.

Dalakos then throws the phone against the wall and thinks, Contingency Plans. If PLAN A doesn't work go through the alphabet until one does. I didn't become the most feared man on the planet without backup plans. Well, they've thrown a double monkey wrench into my plans today, haven't they?

Ike Muslow has arrived at Devon Williams' estate. Kidd Black is with Devon in New York. PLAN A was to send Monique to get the computer while I entertain little Sabrina Rose. But, I don't think our good friend Ike Muslow will allow that.

PLAN B is looking better all the time. PLAN B: Bring on the Chameleon, my right hand man. The only man I really trust. In a previous lifetime, the Chameleon was a computer wizard. His only "mistake" was that he was living in London and ended up at the wrong place at definitely the wrong time.

There was an explosion in the underground and he was rounded up. An English interrogation went wrong and he ended up with a little too much bleach down his throat. He tracked me down and convinced me to let him sign up.

I was so impressed that he could find me, I gave him a try. He was as ruthless as he was a quick learner. Seems like there was no situation that the Chameleon couldn't fit in. Except socially, of course. Not with a voice like that.

Dalakos smiles to himself. If for some strange reason, the Chameleon can't take care of it, I've got to admit, things are more complicated than I imagined.

But, I'm not a legend for nothing. I've got Plan C up my sleeve. Plan C that I'm saving for the proverbial rainy day. And when it starts raining, it's going to pour! It's going to pour Plan C all over Mr. Kidd Black.

Dalakos is no longer smiling to himself, he's laughing out loud.

13

NADINE BLACK is now more confused than ever. Her shoulders slump as she sits back on the bed in their cramped cabin.

First that man comes to our house and tells us that he's bringing us to our son. I smelled a rat and I was right! Then he yanks out a couple of my teeth and then my husband's. Next thing I know, we're on this yacht going who knows where. We don't even know who's holding us here or why but I'm sure it has something to do with our son. Now, if what my husband says is true, what the hell does it all mean?

Lawrence interrupts her thoughts. "I'm 100 per cent sure it was Monique Williams."

"I think you've been hitting that whiskey a little too hard." "You're the one who said we've got to fight off any infection."

"That was before we got on this boat. One thing you've got to say for our 'hosts', that doctor takes good care of us."

"Which is besides the point. I saw Monique Williams on this boat! Just now! I walked towards the swimming pool before I was stopped. I only had time to look at the pool for a moment but I'm sure it was her."

Nadine sits up and takes Lawrence's hands. "Okay, let's say she is here."

"She's here alright! With a little girl. She's got a daughter right?"

Nadine and Lawrence, like most of the planet, had been following Devon's rise to the top. But, for them, Devon was mostly a sad reminder of their son, of what he might have become.

Nadine and Lawrence think the same thing. Devon and Kidd were great friends. They had met Monique once. Once before Kidd "went away." They had arrived early for a visit to West Point and found Kidd and Monique together. Alone and together, in public and in private at the same time, sitting on the library steps. But, there was something strange, as though Kidd was feeling embarrassed, almost guilty about it. The last time they saw Monique was at Kidd's "funeral".

But, that was almost twenty years ago. They had read about her having a baby girl with Devon.

Nadine is the first one to speak. "So, she's here with her daughter. Maybe, just maybe, Monique can give us a clue about where we are and why. What do you say we go talk to her?

"You took the words right out of my mouth. Let's go talk to her. How hard can that be?"

14

DEVON WALKS down the path through the woods until he comes to the lake. Just the smell of the pine trees is enough to make him miss his wife. His wife who ran away. Why didn't he see it coming? What could he have done about it? What would he have done about it? She must really hate him. It's one thing to leave your husband but it's another to take their daughter away. The more he thought about Sabrina Rose, the worse he felt.

He remembers something his mother had told him. "Any problem that money can take care of isn't much of a problem." And right now, all the money in the world couldn't make him happy.

Devon reaches the boathouse and walks up the three wooden steps to the front door. He puts his eye to the retinal identification system and then punches in a code. The door pops open.

This is his favorite place on earth. He breathes in and lets the sensuality of the place waft over him. This was a place that belonged just to him and Monique. Like Bogart would've said if he were in Devon's shoes, "No matter what happens, we'll always have Mohonk."

Devon slowly snaps out of his reverie and gets to work on the computer. He puts his eye up to the retinal identification system and embeds the homing chip in the computer.

He hears footsteps and then a knock on the door. Irritated, he gets up to open it. What's the matter with those guys? I told them to leave me here alone.

Devon turns the handle and as soon as he does, the door flies open.

15

I'VE DONE a lot of things in my day...Ike sighs. In my day...

He knows his day has passed. The proof is that he's here baby-sitting a computer. He laughs at the whole idea and once again wonders if he was right to come alone. But, over the years, he learned the hard way that the best way to keep a secret was to tell no one. But, he wants Dalakos to know he's here. So, he walked up to the front gate in broad daylight knowing, hoping, that Dalakos was keeping an eye on the place.

For the third time in an hour, he checks in with the men stationed around the house. Everything is quiet. In every "B" movie he's ever seen, that's always followed by "too quiet," but as far as Ike is concerned, "too quiet" is just fine with him.

There's a knock at the door. Ike tightens the grip on his gun and calmly says, "Yes?"

Maxwell, Devon Williams' gatekeeper, announces, "There's a woman here."

Ike thinks, Maybe it's Monique thinking she can just show up and waltz away with the computer.

"Who is she?" "Amanda Mason."

Ike immediately wishes it was Monique, or Dalakos. Anyone but Amanda.

"Is she here to see me, see Devon or 'just here?'"

"She's here to see you and she doesn't look like someone who is used to being kept waiting."

Ike doesn't want to let the computer out of his sight but Amanda would immediately become suspicious if he stayed in Devon's office.

Ike sighs again and heads for the front gate. As he's walking, he hopes beyond hope that it's not really Amanda and just an impostor.

As he approaches, he sees her telltale impatient look, arms folded, pacing. It's Amanda alright and she doesn't look happy.

16

"COME ON, NADINE. That's not like you to give up at the first hurdle."

"First hurdle? We're stuck in the back of the boat and Monique, if it is Monique, is at the front of the boat. Divided by a swimming pool which might as well be a moat! How are we going to get to the front?"

"It's called the bow."

"What's called the bow?"

"The front of the boat is called the bow. The back of the boat is the stern."

Nadine is beside herself. "You know, Lawrence, I have a mind to just throw you overboard."

Lawrence looks at her, smiles and nods his head. "Overboard. That's it! I'll climb along the outside of the boat and knock on her porthole."

"Lawrence, do I have to remind you that you're not twenty years old anymore. And, even when you were twenty, you couldn't even climb a tree! It's out of the question. Have you lost your mind?"

Lawrence stands up and wavers. He then falls back on the bed and with a huge effort gets back up again.

Nadine bolts up. "Lawrence, are you okay?"

Lawrence smiles and says, "Yeah, I'm just practicing losing my mind."

17

BORED, BARRY STARES out the window and watches some guys playing basketball. "You know, that Devon's a funny guy."

Kidd is lying on the bed. "Funny? The guy couldn't tell a joke if his life depended on it."

"Naw, funny like strange. Richest guy in the world and all that. It must be tough, that's all."

Kidd adds, "Especially when your wife and daughter have just disappeared."

"You know, I think it must be better to be just an ordinary guy like me or 'dead' like you." Barry shakes his head in disbelief. "Not only can't those guys out there shoot, but half of them are wearing running shoes. Great way to keep orthopedic surgeons in business. Try and move laterally on those and you'll rip an Achilles tendon."

"Barry, when this is over, you should get Devon to buy a basketball team and make you the team doctor."

"Yeah, right...Look at those guys. Two of them left the court to smoke cigarettes. There are two left, let's go challenge them, sneakers or no sneakers. Standing around here is driving me nuts."

Just then there's a collision on the court. One man shouts, "Owah," and the other "Ai!"

Kidd bolts up from bed. Before he "died," before he traveled the world, he thought everyone just said "ouch" when they were hurt but the Portuguese say "Ai!," and the Germans say "Owah!" It all comes rushing to him.

Guys playing basketball with running shoes...leaving the court to smoke cigarettes. Two foreigners...Something's wrong. Something's definitely wrong...They've come for Devon!

His voice urgent, Kidd says, "You wanna play some ball? Keep those guys busy! Go challenge them to a game and if they say no, persuade them with this."

Kidd throws Barry a gun and adds, "If they insist on not playing, use it!"

Barry looks at the gun and says, "That's one way to get picked."

Kidd is out the door and running down the stairs. He hears Barry running effortlessly behind him. Kidd calculates that by the time he gets past the guys on the court, if he gets past the guys on the court, Devon could be dead or kidnapped.

His only hope is to go back into time. Back twenty years. He stops by a door on the ground floor. He gets ready to kick it open, stops and tries the handle. It's locked. He then kicks it open and takes a step down to the basement and freezes for a split second as the musty familiar exciting smell of that time dazes him. He takes a breath and flies down the stairs. The basement is cluttered. Good sign. It looks like it hasn't been used for a long, long time.

18

BARRY SHUFFLES over to the basketball court. The two men listlessly playing basketball eye him warily. The ball comes rolling off the court in Barry's direction. He picks it up but doesn't throw it back.

Barry is all friendliness and innocence as he asks, "How about a little game of HORSE?"

The shorter of the two says, "HORSE? What's that?"

Barry enthusiastically says, "I take a shot and you try and match it. If you don't match it, you get a letter and if you spell H-O-R-S-E you lose."

The short one says, "No thanks. We'd prefer to play alone." He then puts out his arms to catch the ball but Barry isn't throwing it.

Barry pleads, "Come on guys, it'll be fun."

Barry then dribbles the ball on the court, takes a long shot and hits it. The ball making a sweet swishing sound as it glides through the net. Barry grabs the ball and throws it over to the taller of the two. He shouts, "Your go, big guy."

The tall one realizes that the only way to get rid of this nuisance is to play. So, he shoots and misses. Barry gets the rebound and throws it to the shorter man.

"Tough break, big guy. You've got an 'H.' Now you, little man."

Another shot, another miss...Barry thinks that he'd better miss a couple of shots or the game will be over much too soon.

19

IKE PUTS ON his best smile. "Amanda, what a pleasant surprise. Did Devon invite you down here, too?"

"I've always respected you, Ike. I've even looked the other way when I had to. I can't look the other way on this one."

"I'm not sure what you're..."

"Please Ike. Your behavior is unbecoming. You think you can round up this many ISSF agents without me finding out about it?"

Ike's smile quickly disappears. He says, "There are things in play that I can't tell you about. You'll just have to trust me and don't go on about how you've always respected me. I don't want your respect, I want your trust."

"Save the pretty speeches for your memoirs. The bottom line is, you're disobeying a direct order from the President himself."

"Like I said..."

"Ike, please give me a good reason why I shouldn't have the President remove you from PACT. Please."

Ike hesitates. Another sign that his day has passed. There's that old spy adage, "If you can't think of any other possible explanation, try the truth."

"Okay, Amanda. This computer is the only thing keeping Monique Williams and her daughter alive. If the computer is moved outside the force field without the proper fingerprint ID, it goes boom and so do the two of them."

"Ike, have you ever sent someone on a mission, knowing full well, they probably wouldn't come back?"

She doesn't wait for him to answer.

"You did it because there were bigger things at stake than one life. And there are bigger things at stake than the life of Monique and her daughter. I'm sorry, I can't take the chance that that computer will fall into Dalakos' hands. I'm going to make sure that never happens."

Ike doesn't hesitate now. He puts his gun against Amanda's head.

"I don't want to shoot you, Amanda, but if I have to, I will."

"Ike, you've got to be kidding."

She walks away from him and heads toward the estate. Ike puts the gun down, thinking, She knew I wouldn't pull that trigger. Not because it was her but because she was right.

A shot rings out. Amanda freezes, shocked that Ike took a shot at her. But Ike too is shocked. Soon, all hell breaks loose. A helicopter marked POLICE comes into view and hovers over the estate. Flashing lights pull up to the gate. It seems the entire Bahamas SWAT team has shown up unannounced and uninvited.

Ike's men around the house are surrounded. They don't know what to do. Outnumbered and faced with legitimate police, they hesitate to shoot without explicit orders from Ike himself.

And Ike isn't talking. He's cursing himself for leaving the computer alone. More than ever, he feels his time is long gone, long over and way past its due date.

20

THE SHIP'S DOCTOR is sweating. Dalakos' words couldn't have been clearer. Under no circumstances is anything to happen to the two old people. Dalakos didn't have to add anything more. The or else was understood.

Nadine speaks in her most professional voice. "I'm a physician and it's clear that my husband needs immediate medical attention! He's had Alzheimer's and schizophrenia for years now. You need to give him his Haldol."

Lawrence giggles, stands up, twirls a bit, sits down, starts crying and then smashes his head against the wall. The doctor swears under his breath and then asks. "Where the hell am I going to get Haldol?"

Nadine quickly answers, "If you don't have any Haldol, take us to your office. Let me see what you have. I should be able to make a homeopathic remedy that will at least keep him alive until we get to shore."

The doctor perks up at the words "keep him alive". Once the old geezer is off this boat, I could care less what happens to him. But, if she can keep him alive till then, she'll be keeping me alive, too!

The doctor sighs and thinks, Why didn't I listen to my father and go to law school?

21

Kidd works his way past what is probably twenty years of clutter. Old whiskey bottles, cigarette stubs and the occasional condom. A brief panorama of recent American history starting with the AIDS epidemic.

An old broom with a metal handle is stacked against the wall. Kidd picks it up. Another thing his mother told him, "One should never show up at a party empty-handed."

Across the room, the wall is full of animal head trophies. Kidd notices the stuffed head of the black bear. He remembers the first time he saw that head. He remembers it like it was yesterday when he said to Monique, "I wonder how fast that bear was going when he hit the wall."

Out of an old reflex from a long time ago, Kidd reaches into the bear's head and pulls on a lever. The wall creaks open and Kidd rushes through the passageway. He runs with the lightness of another era, rushing to a different kind of danger. Back then he was rushing to betray his friend, now he's rushing to save his friend's life. He wonders if that makes them even.

Kidd works his way through the narrow passageway. He has just enough light coming from behind him to see where he's going.

I'm getting too old for this or...I'm letting my emotions get the best of me. What would it have cost him to stop and be sure that Barry knew how to use the gun? A few seconds? But, a few seconds could be the difference between a dead Devon or a kidnapped Devon!

He makes his way along the damp floor to the boathouse. He can hear voices. Male voices. None of them are Devon's. He silently works his way to the wooden wall of the guest house. Twenty years ago, he had made a peephole in the wood. Even after making love to Monique, he couldn't get enough of her. After she thought he had left, he would circle back just to stare at her through the cut he had made in the wooden wall. He'd watch her make the bed, thrilled at every gesture, thrilled every time she'd bend over to adjust the sheets. The sheets where they had just been.

But the new owners, Devon and Monique, had painted over the walls. A real paint job here. Two coats and primer to boot. And insulation.

This house was made for winter use as well...But there were still slats in the wood. If he had the time, he could cut himself another peep hole. Did he have the time?

He takes out a Swiss Army knife from his pocket. Never leaves home without it. All the high-tech junk in the world can't match a good old Swiss Army Knife. He takes out the metal toothpick and cuts his way along the slats in the wood. As he cuts his way into the room, he hears a strange sound. It's a raspy rumble, kind of like sandpaper across stone. When he finally cuts his way through, he realizes it's someone's voice.

"Mr. Williams, we don't want to kill you and we have strict orders not to kill you but don't think about doing anything stupid like running away or fighting back. All we need is your eyes, and there are many other very unpleasant ways to keep you alive and keep your eyes intact."

Kidd takes it all in, thinking, That voice is so weird, it can't be real, but it apparently is. I heard another voice but now I hear only one. Voice number two could be waiting outside. It's like being blind. I'm blind and I don't like it. No, I don't like it one bit.

Kidd hears Devon say, "If you're in this for the money, I can pay you a lot more than your boss. In fact, there's a pile of cash in the desk drawer..."

Before he can finish the sentence, a loud slap is heard. Kidd hears that weird voice again. "I'm not in it for the money."

Devon groans. Kidd takes the opportunity to carve out a bigger slice of the wall.

Another slap. Another groan.

"Money! Money! For you, it's money! Money!"

Kidd can see now. Not the whole room but he gets his first view of the man known as The Chameleon. White, six feet tall, well-built, blue eyes, blonde hair. Looks like he could be a movie star but with a voice like that, he'd have to hope they bring back silent films.

Devon is in a chair, his hands cuffed behind his back. Kidd shakes his head distastefully, Beating a guy whose hands are tied behind his back. But, I can't do anything about it now...He said he's not going to kill Devon and I'll have to take him at his word.

The Chameleon opens the drawer and pulls out the cash. He throws it at Devon. Some of it sticks to the blood trickling down Devon's face and the rest floats to the floor.

"Blood money!" The Chameleon laughs at this and then slaps Devon again.

There's a sharp rapping on the door. The beating stops and The Chameleon says, "Okay."

Kidd hears the door open. The Chameleon rasps, "I'll take him to the boat."

Kidd thinks, A boat? Where the hell are they going in a boat? There's no way out from the lake! Just wilderness on the other side!

The Chameleon pulls Devon out of the chair and puts a coat over him to cover the handcuffs. He picks up the laptop and says, "Let's go slow. Nobody goes fast, we all go slow."

Devon's mind is racing. I need the computer intact now that the homing device is in place. But, if I tell them about the security function, they'll become suspicious. Looks like I have no choice.

He's about to speak when The Chameleon says, "Okay, put your fingers into the biometric identification slot."

Devon tries to look disappointed when he says, "It seems that you know everything."

The Chameleon spits out, "I work for someone who knows everything."

Devon puts his fingers into the slot and The Chameleon pushes him towards the door. He then says to the other man, "Pick up all the money. Put it in that backpack and hurry up!"

He then says to Devon, "Money CAN buy happiness. Guns, bombs, people."

Devon and The Chameleon move out of Kidd's line of sight. He hears the door close and another man quickly moves into view. White male, brown hair, younger, around twenty-five. He quickly picks up the money off the floor and starts stuffing it into a backpack. He looks back toward the door and then stuffs two large handfuls into his pockets.

Kidd laughs to himself, So for this one, money has some value. There's some hope for the world after all. But no more hope for him...I hope.

Time to go for broke. Kidd takes the broom handle and thrusts it through the wall. There will be just enough room to put his gun through the hole. Kidd will have to shoot blind. If the young man freezes, he dies. If he doesn't...When there's barely a PLAN A, there's certainly no PLAN B. The guy has to freeze.

22

MARTIN WILSON, the corpulent Chief of the Bahamas Police, stands by at a safe distance as one of his men approaches Ike. The Chief calls out, "Set your gun down and raise your hands. The slower the better."

Ike does as he's told. Amanda's arms are already raised. The sooner they get done with the formalities, the happier she'll be.

Amanda is the first to address the Chief. "I'm a representative of the United States Government and I demand to know what's going on here!"

“We’ve had reports of gunfire coming from the estate. And unlike your country, that’s highly illegal here.”

Amanda erupts. “That’s preposterous. I’m here as an invited guest of Devon Williams and this is Mr. Ike Muslow, my bodyguard. I insist that you let us go! My government and Mr. Williams will not look pleasantly upon this decision.”

“Bodyguard?”

The Chief turns to Ike. “May I see your permit for that gun, please?”

Ike calmly says, “If I may speak with you just a moment, sir. I’m sure all of this can be cleared up.”

The Chief and Ike move out of range of both Amanda and the policemen. Amanda is furious, the other policemen have seen this before.

Ike whispers, “As my colleague said...”

“Oh, now she’s your colleague? I thought you were her bodyguard.”

“My point is, I am a personal friend of Devon Williams and a personal representative of the President of the United States of America. Two men who have access to vast sums of money and incredible power. I guarantee you that it would be worth your while financially as well as politically to forget about this gun and leave these premises. Do we understand each other?”

Ike looks the Chief in the eye. He’s dealt with these type of corrupt officials countless times. When it comes time to pay up he will and he’ll pay well. The Chief knows it, too. But, the Chief also knows that if he doesn’t play along, it’s very unlikely that Ike will have him killed.

He might have him fired but he is planning on retiring anyway. On the other hand, he knows for certain, that if he backs out now, Dalakos will have him killed and probably his family too. In the Bahamas there’s an old expression, “When you sell your soul to the Devil, it’s forever.”

The Chief steps away and from Ike and announces, “Drugs have been sold here. Search the premises for evidence.”

Amanda shouts, “Drugs? Are you crazy?”

Ike can’t believe it. He didn’t go for the bait. What’s going on here?

Ike’s concern now is that they are going to try and move the computer out of the estate causing it, as Kidd so aptly said, “to go BOOM!”

He needn’t have worried about that because the Chief announces to his men, “The computers are to be guarded but not touched. Under no circumstances are any computers to be moved!”

The Chief might have just as well announced that he’s working for Dalakos. Amanda and Ike know it won’t be long before Monique shows up with

Dalakos and waltzes away with that computer.

Ike is not happy about the situation but not totally unhappy either. He's keeping his part of the deal in a roundabout way. Monique and Sabrina Rose can live a little longer until something can be done about Dalakos. Most kidnappers are caught when they come for the ransom and in this case the ransom is the computer. Now, they just have to find a way to get away from these police and stake out the computer. "Simple" as that.

But, Amanda doesn't see it that way. No, not at all. Her concern is the millions who would be at risk if Dalakos gets his hands on that computer. The life of a ten year old girl and her mother don't count for much when the stakes are this high. And certainly, the life of one Presidential Chief of Staff doesn't count for much either.

Having come to a decision, Amanda Mason, West Point Grad twenty years ago, a woman who takes pride in wearing the same size dress she wore at graduation, a woman who has stayed in shape her entire adult life, kicks off her heels and makes a dash for the main house of Devon Williams' Estate.

23

SILENCERS ARE by definition, silent. Screams by definition, are not. Barry and his "basketball buddies" hear the screams of a man who has been shot. The screams of a man who is dying.

Barry says, "Here try this shot."

He takes the ball and heaves it as hard as he can into the face of the tall guy. He's more than tall, he's a giant. The giant's nose is clearly broken and when the blood is done spurting it pours down his face but he's still standing!

Barry pulls out his gun and says, "This should get your attention," but the giant is literally seeing red. He doesn't see the gun through the blood, just the foggy outline of the man who broke his nose open.

Barry has spent his whole life saving lives. The Hippocratic oath and all that. "Whatever you do, don't do any harm." Well, one more principle out the window.

There's an old saying, "If you're going to attack a giant, be sure to kill him."

Barry points the gun, pulls the trigger and just like that, the giant is dead. Nothing like the movies, in real life there are body parts everywhere, lots of liquid. Kind of like surgery.

As for the little guy, he's off and running in the direction of the boathouse. Barry heads off after him, not realizing that he's emptied the gun into the Giant. He has no bullets left. If he had known that, it's not so sure that he would have taken off as fast as he did.

24

KIDD PULLS the lever to open the secret door to the boathouse. Twenty years of not being used, twenty years of paint jobs and insulation slowly give way. Kidd finally forces the door to slide open. He glances at the writhing body on the floor, instantly decides that he doesn't pose a threat and rushes out the door only to see The Chameleon rowing across the lake with Devon and the computer.

Lifeguard training. The first thing you do before jumping into a body of water is to strip down. Kidd kicks off his shoes, rips off his shirt and drops his pants. He hears Barry yell, "Kidd, look out!"

A classic case of being caught with your pants down. The little guy plows into Kidd knocking him over. Kidd can't kick and he can't move very well. He tries to roll away but the little guy is strangling him from behind. Kidd's options are limited. No kicking, his pants are hanging around his ankles. Kidd reaches behind him and grabs for anything he can but the wiry guy isn't letting go.

Barry shouts, "Stop or I'll shoot," but the little guy doesn't hear or doesn't care.

Barry fires and the gun clicks. Out of bullets.

Kidd starts to black out. Suddenly, he's rolling towards the lake. Barry has dived onto them and his weight is forcing them into the lake.

The little guy won't let go but Barry jumping on to them causes the little guy's grip to loosen momentarily. Kidd gets a breath as the three of them roll into the cold waters of Lake Mohonk.

25

AMANDA RUSHES across the manicured lawn of the Williams Estate. The surprised police are slow to react. The Chief shouts, "Stop her! Stop her!"

A policeman starts running towards Amanda but he has to get by Ike first. Ike, a former Yale football player himself, is well-versed in the fundamentals of tackling. As his coach had instructed him a long time ago, "Keep your eye on his jock strap, it doesn't move. Grab him at the waist, hold on and pull him down."

Like the Old Coach had also said, "It's going to hurt whether you tackle him or not, so you might as well hold on and bring him down." To Ike's surprise, he hasn't lost that much power since he last played football more than forty-five years ago and just like the Old Coach promised, the two of them go tumbling to the ground.

The policeman is more than surprised. An old man just doesn't behave like this. Another cop comes over and roughly pulls Ike off and points a gun at his head. The Chief yells, "Get the girl you idiot. Forget about him!"

Amanda is now in full stride. The closed front door of the house is fast approaching. If it's locked, she's dead. Simple as that.

Maxwell, the gatekeeper, watches from the house as the drama unfolds. He sees Amanda running towards the house and he has to make a decision. Should he open the door for her or not? She seemed to be a friend of Ike's and Ike is certainly a friend of Mr. Williams so it would make sense that she's a friend, too. One thing is for sure, she's no friend of that fat corrupt Police Chief and that's good enough for him.

A policeman is fast gaining on her, shouting for her to stop or he'll shoot. He's close enough to get a good shot, but his heart's not in it. He fires in the air, hoping that'll get her to stop. If anything, it just gets her to run faster.

She makes it to the door and like Moses and the Red Sea, it "miraculously" opens. She bursts into the house and Maxwell slams the door shut.

Breathlessly, she asks, "Where is Devon Williams' computer?" There is furious banging at the door and it startles Maxwell. Amanda pleads, "His computer? WHERE IS IT?"

Maxwell points to the winding stairway across the spacious marble floor. Before he can say a word, she rushes to it as bullets shoot off the lock to the front door. Maxwell ducks for cover as the door is forced open. Police rush in as Amanda runs up the stairs towards Devon's office.

26

NADINE QUICKLY surveys the doctor's office on Dalakos' boat. Without asking the doctor, she heads for the medicine chest and rummages through it. More or less, just what she expected.

Lawrence is now singing the same gibberish line over and over again.

"Her name was Annie, she had such a big fanny, that she couldn't even fit through the door."

Nadine thinks, That's right, honey, if anyone can overdo it, you can.

Lawrence stands up and tries to dance with the doctor. The doctor impatiently sets Lawrence back down.

Nadine asks the doctor in a tone that is more command than question, "Would you go to the lunch room and get me some salt?"

The doctor is more than happy to get away from Lawrence. He jumps up and says, "Of course."

The moment he's out the door, Lawrence perks up and says, "Okay, let's do it!"

27

WHEN YOU FIGHT underwater, not only can't you breathe but you can't see much either, especially if you've lost your glasses somewhere back on land as you rolled into the lake. Not that having his glasses would have helped much, the water's dark. Barry can't even make out the color of the skin of the man he's holding onto.

Fifty-fifty. He could grab a neck, break it and hope for the best but what if he's wrong? He can't stay underwater forever.

Kidd is going to have to do something or he is going to stay underwater forever. The pressure around his neck is getting to him. His only hope is to get his legs free but the water has tightened the pants around his knees. Too tight to kick them off.

He thrusts his legs apart and the material groans. He does a scissors kick and then spreads his legs apart again, too quick for the material to contract. Ten thousand miles of running, a hundred thousand sit-ups, enough leg lifts to build a pyramid, one more scissors kick and the pants split apart.

With his legs free, Kidd kicks back into "little guy's" groin. The shock causes his grip to loosen just enough for Kidd to rip his hands from around his neck. He has to make an instant decision, go in for the kill or go up for air. He decides to go in for the kill but "little guy" has had enough. He makes a break for air. Kidd follows him up and grabs him by the shoulders, thrusting himself up for air while keeping "little guy" down.

Kidd finds himself face to face with Barry. Kidd gasps for air, all the time holding "little guy" under water. Barry asks Kidd, "You need any help?"

Kidd shakes his head no and with one more effort, "little guy" is still. Kidd gasps, "When he floats to the surface, make sure he's dead."

Kidd disappears underwater and then twenty yards away surfaces like an alligator, with only his eyes out of the water. He's swimming towards Devon and The Chameleon. He doesn't waste a second. No time to catch his breath and no time for anything but chasing down that rowboat.

Devon sits in the rowboat, his hands handcuffed behind his back, coolly weighing his options. You don't become the richest man on the planet by not knowing all your options. And his options appear to be very limited.

Very limited indeed. Devon wonders why the guy rowing is looking so confident. There's no way out around this lake. It's protected virgin wilderness. The only way out is back through the Hotel. In the distance, Devon hears the first sound of what can only be a helicopter and his heart sinks to the bottom of Lake Mohonk.

Barry is startled as "little guy" floats to the surface. His face is contorted and bloated. Sure sign of drowning. Barry's first impulse is to reach for a pulse to see if he's dead.

His first impulse is to revive him.

But, Barry thinks about every sport he's ever played or watched. When you've got them down, finish them off. Don't give them any chances. The champions have the killer instinct. Go for the jugular, knock them out when they are down. And with those thoughts in mind, Barry comes up behind the body and thrusts it under water.

28

AMANDA THROWS OPEN the door to Devon's office and spots the computer. She locks the door behind her and then unscrews the cable connecting it to the screen. Footsteps come running up the stairs. She's got to get the computer outside the force field.

Pounding on the door. Bullets against the lock. No way out through the door that's for sure. The door is forced open. Amanda grabs the computer, runs to the balcony, spots the swimming pool below and jumps.

Amanda free falls towards the pool. She clutches the computer to her chest and hits the surprisingly cold water. She comes up for air, gets oriented and heads for the pool ladder. She wants to get out of there as fast as she can. Already, the pool is heating up…

Police come running towards her, guns drawn, shouting for her to put her hands up. She gladly obliges them and as she does, the computer explodes, sending water shooting up in the air, just like Old Faithful.

29

BARRY STAGGERS ONTO land and wants more than anything to just sit but he grabs a rowboat and heads out towards Kidd who is furiously swimming towards Devon and The Chameleon.

The Chameleon calmly stows his oars at the sound of the helicopter. Devon says, "If you're going to kill me, please, first tell me how my daughter and wife are."

The Chameleon rasps, "Your wife is fucking my boss day and night. Won't let him sleep. The poor guy is exhausted. As for your daughter, you don't even want to know."

Furious, Devon makes an effort to lunge at the man. The Chameleon laughs and easily pushes him back down. "Don't worry, if I wanted to kill you, I would have done it a long time ago."

The helicopter is getting closer. It can clearly be seen now. It has US COAST GUARD written on it. Devon mutters, These guys think of everything. No one will stop to wonder what the US Coast Guard is doing so far from the Coast, they'll just keep out of their way.

The smug look on The Chameleon's face disappears as he spots Kidd swimming relentlessly towards him. He pulls Devon up and puts a gun to his head.

"Sorry, I might have to kill you after all."

Kidd slows down when he sees The Chameleon with a gun to Devon's head. The man is clearly shouting something to Kidd but not so clear that he can make out what he's saying. When Kidd gets close enough to hear, he comes to a complete stop.

"That's far enough. Come any closer and I'll kill your friend."

Kidd shouts back, "You kill my friend and I guarantee that you will be dead before that helicopter comes for you and that computer."

"Ah, yes, the computer."

The helicopter is now at treetop level slowly and effortlessly working its way towards the rowboat. Kidd knows he could dive now and get to the rowboat without The Chameleon seeing him but if he goes underwater now, Devon is a dead man.

The closer the helicopter gets, the louder they have to yell. The Chameleon shouts which makes his voice almost indecipherable. "I'm giving you a choice, my friend. You can save this mere computer or you can save your friend."

With that, he shoves Devon overboard. Fully dressed, with his hands cuffed behind his back, he sinks like the proverbial stone.

Kidd knows it's no mere computer. His choice comes down to saving his friend or saving the world from massive terrorist attacks. But, when your house is on fire, the first thing you do is put out the fire and worry about who started it later. Kidd makes decision. He dives underwater and heads for Devon.

The helicopter is now hovering over the rowboat as a scaling ladder is lowered down to The Chameleon.

Barry rows frantically towards Kidd. He watches helplessly as the helicopter takes off with The Chameleon and the computer. Nothing to do but wait for Kidd and Devon to come up for air. Barry slumps over, exhausted.

30

LAWRENCE LEANS against Nadine just in case the doctor returns from going to get salt from the cafeteria sooner than expected. They work their way down the hallway.

Nadine whispers, "What makes you think we'll find her?" "This isn't the Queen Mary. We walk down the hallway and listen."

Nadine sighs, "You told me you had a plan. That's it?" "Uh, yeah. Now let's get moving before that quack comes back."

They slowly walk down the hallway willing some sounds, any sounds, to come out from behind closed doors. They hear deep snoring from one room and make a mental note to eliminate that one. They get to the end of the hallway without knowing for sure where Monique and Sabrina Rose might be.

Nadine whispers, "Time is running out. The doctor will be back any moment."

Lawrence whispers, "There are only two possibilities left.

You try that door and I'll try the other one. We don't have a lot of choice."

Lawrence heads for the far door. Nadine opens the door closest to her. Two of Dalakos' men are there, lying on their beds, wide awake!

One of them jumps up and asks, "What the hell are you doing here?"

Nadine nervously shouts, "It's my husband. He's disappeared! Please, get the doctor! Hurry!"

31

BARRY SLOWLY ROWS the three of them back to shore. A group of people have gathered. Nothing like gun shots in Paradise to bring out the crowds.

The crowd can only marvel at the sight of the three men, one of them handcuffed, all of them the worse for wear, as they arrive at the dock. The three of them stagger forward and without saying a word to the crowd, walk into the boathouse and close the door.

Devon freezes once he sees the passageway. He looks at Kidd and then quickly looks away. A cloud comes over Devon. Not anger but gloom. The gloom that fills a heart when shining memories have been irreparably destroyed. Memories of the good times with Monique. Memories of the good times with Kidd. Even the memories of battles won have been torn apart by seeing that passageway.

As the expression goes, "You don't have to be Einstein to figure this one out." And Devon is about as close to Einstein as you get these days.

Devon thinks, The only way that Kidd could have known about that passage is if he had been here before. And that before was when he and Monique were together. Monique was always happy here. She was happy here because she felt close to Kidd. How often had she made love to me and thought of Kidd? How often had she made love to Kidd? As Barry would say, "Life is too funny not to laugh." Yeah, life is funny all right, a real cruel joke and it sure looks like the joke's on me.

32

AMANDA LEFT THE Bahamas Police Station almost as soon as she got there. She is, after all, the Chief of Staff for the President of the United States. The Chief of Police wasn't sorry to see her go. Ike on the other hand, was another story. He was a private citizen as far as the world was concerned. He couldn't just say he was head of PACT, could he? The reality was, Amanda wasn't in much of a hurry for Ike to be on the loose. For the time being, she was more than happy to know where he was, even if that meant jail. She boarded a special jet for Washington and was at the White House in under two hours.

The President was in a mostly great mood. The world had been saved, thanks to Amanda, but he had to do something about Ike. Letting one's personal feelings interfere with one's performance just couldn't be tolerated.

The President says, "Amanda, I've read the reports from the agents in the Bahamas. This bit about Ike's behavior. I want you to change the locks on the doors to PACT, so to speak. I want Ike's clearance taken away. He did a great job there but it's time to put him out to pasture. Bring in some new blood. Someone I can count on."

Amanda's heart is beating a hundred miles an hour. He's talking about me. He's got to be talking about me.

"Amanda, I want you to take over PACT."

She thinks, I feel like a schoolgirl who just got invited to the Senior Cadet Ball by the Number One of the Class. But, Devon never asked me. Well, this will have to do.

"You can count on me, Mr. President. I'm going to be hands-on all the time. You won't be getting any unpleasant surprises on my watch. That's a promise."

The President tells her, "Good, now come up with a reason why you're resigning as my Chief of Staff. Writing a book, having a baby, you'll think of something. Just let me know what it is before you announce it to the press."

33

KIDD, DEVON AND BARRY come into the boathouse. They all need sleep and they all know they won't be getting any for awhile. First of all, there's a dead body lying across the floor.

Kidd examines the body for anything that will give them a clue as to where they can find Dalakos, the computer or both and comes up with nothing.

Barry puts a mock-serious tone to his voice. "I feel as a licensed physician that I can safely say that this man has been shot at close range from what appears to be a secret passageway."

Devon, his voice full of irony, looks at Kidd and says, "Gee, it was lucky you stumbled upon that secret passage."

Barry, not in on the situation, says, "Yeah, without it, you were a goner, Devon. Dead as a doornail with a cherry on top."

Kidd, desperate to change the subject, says, "We've got to get out of here before the police come."

Devon says, "There's a crowd of people out there. If we want to be invisible, we have to go back out the way you came in…"

Devon lets his voice trail off. Kidd looks at the intense way that Devon is staring at him. He never imagined in a million years that he'd be walking through that passageway with Devon...but he's right. It's the only way out.

Barry looks at the two of them glaring at each other. He has no idea why and for the moment, he could care less. He says, "So, what are we waiting for?"

The three of them step into the passageway.

34

LAWRENCE TURNS the door knob, forces his way into the room and startles Sabrina Rose. He spots Monique on the bed and sees that she's sound asleep. Lawrence motions for Sabrina Rose to be quiet.

Lawrence whispers the first thing that comes into his head. "I'm a friend of your father's. I've got to talk to your mother."

Sabrina Rose perks up at the news and says, "Okay, let's wake her up."

Lawrence sits down next to Monique on the bed and lightly shakes her. She moans and then opens her eyes. Somewhere deep in her memory, she recognizes the face.

"I'm Kidd Black's father."

Monique is now sure she's dreaming. She smiles wistfully and says, "Hi. It's been awhile."

Lawrence looks at Sabrina Rose who shakes her mother. "Mom, wake up. This man is here to save us." She turns to Lawrence and asks, "You are here to save us aren't you?"

Monique, slurring her words, asks, "Save us from what, honey?"

35

IKE PACES AROUND his cell. He's been in worse jails, that's for sure. There are no rats, no other prisoners, just a camera watching him 24/7.

He's a little surprised that he hasn't been released already. If he stays any longer, his surprise is going to be raised to the level of real concern.

In the spy business, you use what you have at hand. Hi-tech, low-tech, you gotta go with the cards you're dealt. When he was young, Ike would use his charm and his good looks to get what he wanted. If need be, he could also sell coals to Newcastle and snow to Eskimos. But now that's rarely an option so he has to use what he's got and what he's got is a lot of money and old age. He knows he can't outbid Dalakos so he has to go with Old Age.

Ike waits for his dinner meal to be delivered. Like most things in the spy business, it's best done at night. When he hears the footsteps coming, he gets his mouth frothing and throws some water on his face.

He gasps and as the door opens he clutches his heart just to be sure the guard knows what's going on. He doesn't speak. The guard looks at him with a mix of fear and irritation because the guard has to make a decision and guards aren't comfortable making decisions, they're just comfortable guarding.

The guard takes a halting step towards Ike. Now, Ike is ready for the Grande Finale. He falls to the floor and pisses in his pants. The guard doesn't come any closer. He goes quickly out of the cell looking for help.

First step is a success. Next step a hospital. This jail is too small to have its own medical staff and they won't take a chance on his dying here. No, if they wanted to kill him, they would have done it already. He isn't sure what his next step will be, he just knows that by staying here he isn't going anywhere fast.

36

THE DOCTOR on Dalakos' ship tells the two crewmen to go back to their cabins. "Nothing to worry about. I'll take care of it."

The last thing he wants is to set off a general alarm that will notify Dalakos. The two men happily head back to their cabin.

The doctor asks Nadine, "Now, where do you think he went?" "He said he had to go to the toilet. When he didn't come back, I panicked and went looking for him everywhere! You don't think he jumped overboard do you?"

Just at the thought, the doctor turns pale.

Below deck, Lawrence too is turning pale. He thought finding Monique would be the hard part. But, the more he tries to talk to her, the more he realizes that she's barely coherent.

He asks again, "What are you doing here? Why are you here?" Before Monique can even try and answer, Sabrina Rose asks a question of her own. "Why are you here?"

Lawrence sighs and says, "I'm not sure. But something tells me that if my wife and I are here, the fact that we're still alive can only mean one thing. The reason we're still alive must mean that our son, Kidd Black, is still alive!"

Monique doesn't move. But for a brief moment, a fog seems to clear from her face. Something more powerful than Dalakos' drugs has hit her. Something more powerful than all the darkness she's felt since Kidd "died". It's not enough to snap her out of her daze but still, it's that first ray of light that could one day become a bright new dawn. In the distance, somewhere in her subconscious, Monique sees a glimmer of something she hasn't felt in what seems like a long time—hope.

Lawrence turns to Sabrina Rose "My wife's here with me on this boat. She's a doctor. I'm going to try and have my wife take a look at her."

One thing about kids, they're not afraid to ask direct questions. "Is my mother going to die?"

Lawrence takes her in his arms. "No, no, of course not. It's just that sometimes people need a second medical opinion. Maybe the boat's doctor doesn't know things that my wife does."

"When is she coming to take a look at my mother?"

"Uh, soon. In the meantime, I have to go get her. Take care of your mom till we get back."

37

EVERYTHING IS GOING according to plan. To the new plan, that is. Devon explains, "The homing chip in the computer gives off a signal to a satellite. The satellite gives the signal to us. It's as simple as that. It's accurate up to 15 feet. Not bad, designed it myself."

They are in a helicopter following the computer which is in another helicopter flying east. Of course, if they could have just phoned in, life would have been a hell of a lot easier. But, if they did, the police and Amanda would know where they were and the computer would never lead them to Dalakos.

Amanda would destroy it.

Kidd is hesitant to call in PACT without talking to Ike. Kidd tries again but Ike isn't answering. This makes Kidd nervous. Ike always answers. Always.

38

MOST SPY WORK is rather humdrum. Sure, there's a place for the Kidd Blacks of the world, but usually information is gotten at cocktail parties for either cash or ideology. I remember blackmailing a few unwilling people with compromising photos but most of the info I got was from people with their hands out.

So, here I am in the ambulance heading to a hospital. There's a young Emergency Medical Technician and a not so young cop to keep an eye on me.

No other guards. I guess I'm not considered dangerous enough. Another indignity of growing old.

Ike studies both men. No sense in talking to the EMT, he's not the one with the gun. Ike doesn't need to be reminded that he's supposed to have had a heart attack. He's hooked up to an EKG machine and has an intravenous tube stuck in his arm. With an exaggerated effort, he sits up and in a weak voice, says, "So, as a cop here in the Bahamas, how much do you make in a month? Two thousand dollars? Three?"

The cop snickers and says, "I should be so lucky."

"I'll give you BOTH ten thousand dollars cash if you let me out of here. How does that sound?"

The cop answers, "It sounds great but how do we know you'll pay? I would bet that if you were good for the money, you would have been out of jail a long time ago."

"They seem to think I'm important enough to keep around." The EMT joins in. "That's the problem. If they think you're important enough, they're going to miss you and it'll be our asses on the line."

Ike mulls it over. "You got a point there. In that case, how much would it cost me to make a call on one of your cell phones?"

The EMT reaches for his cell phone but the cop says, "No can do. They'd trace the call and that's all she wrote for us."

Ike sighs, lies back down and thinks, Looks like I'm going to have to do this the old-fashioned way.

The ambulance slows down at an intersection. Ike leaps up from the cot and as he does, the tubes and leads rip out of his body. He bull rushes the cop.

His shoulder slams into the cop's chest and they bang into the back doors. The doors fly open and the cop half-flies out of the ambulance.

Ike makes a split-second decision. With one hand, he grabs the cop's belt and with the other holds onto the ambulance door for dear life. The ambulance begins to pick up speed.

Ike shouts to the EMT, "Give us a hand!"

The EMT is frozen. Ike screams, "I can't hold on to him forever!"

The Emergency Medical Technician springs to life. He grabs onto the cop and he and Ike pull him back in. The EMT and the cop roll back into the ambulance.

The cop reaches for his gun. Ike has to think quick. He could head butt the cop, break his nose, probably before he can get his gun out.

Probably.

Ike doesn't want to push his luck. He jumps out of the ambulance, hits the road and rolls as delicately as possible...which isn't very delicate at all.

39

DALAKOS IS IN a good mood...

So much work to be done. Invitations to be sent out. Menus prepared. Seating. Ah, the seating. Always the problem. Who hates who, who likes who, well, nobody really likes anyone, so who hates who the least and so on and so on.

And the date. It has to be the right date. It would be a pity if someone missed it because of a previous commitment. But, who would miss this?

This is the World Cup, the World Series, and the Super Bowl all in one. No, I could say it was tomorrow and everyone would come.

Dalakos is in a good mood. A very good mood. He got word that the computer is as good as his. It could have been better, of course. He could have had Devon Williams as his personal guest, but he has the next best thing in Monique. In one way, she's a lot better than having Devon around.

As far as that little brat, I was getting tired of that tape of her screaming. I'll have to make a new one. Yes, a new one with a lot more screaming and a lot more crying.

No doubt about it. Dalakos is in a very good mood, a very very good mood indeed.

40

DEVON'S EYES ARE GLUED to the computer screen as the helicopter heads east across Massachusetts. Kidd sits across from Barry and says, "You might not realize it, but you're in shock. In shock from killing those guys."

Barry nods his head in agreement.

"Yeah, don't worry, I realize it." Devon's eyes never leave the computer as he says to the pilot, "Take us down into New Bedford."

Barry says, "New Bedford, Mass. It's not the end of the world but you can see it from there."

Barry laughs at his own joke and Devon mumbles, "Being in shock hasn't made his jokes any funnier."

Barry pretends he doesn't hear him and asks, "But, why New Bedford?"

Devon says, "It makes a certain amount of sense."

Kidd adds, "New Bedford, the largest Portuguese Community in the U.S."

Devon says, "Just a hop skip and a jump to Lisbon from there. We know for sure, based on Kidd's analysis of the way one person said 'ouch,' that at least one of the gang is, was, Portuguese."

Kidd interrupts, "Fishermen. Greeks, Portuguese, they all have a long tradition of sailing. Dalakos feels safest at sea, always has. He hates to be on land. The only thing he hates more is to be in American Territorial Waters. Either way, I figure we're going to need a boat at some point. All quite elementary my dear Barry."

Barry says, "Too bad we can't just phone the FBI and pick them up. That's their job, right?"

Devon adds, "Yeah, and watch them blow up that computer before your eyes; it would be like watching them kill my daughter."

Kidd can't help but notice that he said his daughter and not his family. That secret passageway looks like it destroyed more than their friendship. But, that will have to wait. For now, there's nothing to do but try and get some sleep but he knows sleep will be slow in coming. Kidd can't stop wondering, Where the hell is Ike?

41

AMANDA WALKS INTO the room with the President beside her. No longer walking in before him, no more walking in after him. Everyone in the room stands. They stand for her as well as for him. Yes, it's going to be just how she imagined it.

The President says, "As you know, Ike Muslow has resigned from PACT. The new head is Amanda Mason. And as you know, I have some Affairs of State to take care of. I hope the country will still function without Amanda around to make sure I'm where I'm supposed to be when I'm supposed to be there. To finish off, I want to say I have the utmost confidence in her and well, you know the drill."

On that note, the President leaves the room. Everyone continues standing waiting for Amanda to sit down. Yes, indeed. She likes this already. Amanda lets the moment linger and then sits down. When everyone sits, she says, "Ike Muslow was a great man but the President has his reasons for dismissing him. No time for second guessing and no time for sentimentality."

Amanda smiles to herself. The President said he resigned. I just wanted to make sure they know he was fired!

Amanda turns to Caroline Crimmins, PACT computer expert, and says, "Caroline, anything on Dalakos? Anything at all?"

Caroline, pleased to be the first one addressed, says, "Nothing. Zippo. Nada. Either he's the most disciplined discreet terrorist we've ever tracked, or he's dead, Amanda."

Amanda says to the computer expert. "I would prefer that from now on, you address me as Ms. Mason."

There is a cold look of recognition on Caroline's face that things will never be the same between them. Amanda says to herself, I'll tell her afterwards that when we see each other socially, of course, she can call me Amanda. And of course, we won't be seeing each other socially any more so I don't have to worry about it.

42

THE SHIP'S DOCTOR felt like he was going to throw up and he'd never been seasick in his life...but just the thought that Lawrence might have jumped overboard was making him sick.

He hadn't been searching long but every minute felt like an hour. It didn't help his mood that Nadine was so slow. And, he had to search discretely. He certainly wasn't going to say a word to Dalakos until he had scoured every inch of the boat.

And then, he heard the greatest sound he'd ever heard in his life. An out of tune male voice could be heard singing from Nadine and Lawrence's cabin…

"Her name was Annie she had such a big fanny
She couldn't even fit through the door
She ate so fast no matter what the food
Eating was like running a race

Hot fudge sundaes blueberry muffins
She just kept stuffing her face"

Though their cabin was the first place they had looked, the doctor rushes over to it, convinced that had to be Lawrence "singing". He throws open the cabin door and sure enough, there's Lawrence dancing to his own music. The doctor shouts to Nadine, "Here he is! Thank God!"

Nadine reaches the cabin door and before she can say anything, the doctor says, "Keep an eye on him. I'm getting someone to watch him every second. We don't want him disappearing again now, do we?"

The doctor pushes Nadine into the cabin and slams the door shut. Nadine moves close to Lawrence and whispers, "I kept him distracted as long as I could. How did it go?"

Lawrence moves even closer to her and whispers, "You have a house call to make!"

43

FOR MOST PEOPLE, when the phone rings in the middle of the night, it's never good news. Good news can wait until morning. But Kidd isn't most people. He shoots up from bed, takes a deep breath to clear his head and in an instant is wide awake. The only person who has this number is Ike. So, it has to be Ike or someone who has Ike.

"Yes?"

Ike knows from experience that every second is valuable. No pleasantries, right to the point.

"Kidd, the computer has been destroyed."

Kidd listens. This isn't the time, if that time ever comes, to say, "I counted on you not to let that happen. You gave me your word."

Instead, he just listens.

Ike continues, "Amanda came blasting in. She got hold of it and blew it up. I tried to stop her."

Ike then says something to Kidd, he's never heard him say. "I'm sorry. Really sorry. Now, where are you?"

"We're still on the case."

Kidd couldn't have been clearer. He can't trust Ike with everything. It's better that he doesn't know. Just in case Amanda comes "blasting in".

Ike says, "You don't have to worry about Amanda. I'm no longer with

PACT I've been put out to pasture."

"For what?"

"For trying to keep my word."

Now it's Kidd's turn to say he's sorry.

44

FOR TWO DAYS NOW, they've been in New Bedford. They would take shifts watching the location of the computer. It was in a small apartment complex right on the harbor. This gave them perfect access to any of the hundreds of fishing boats moored there. Kidd and Company were ready to move the moment the computer moved. But, for the moment, the computer wasn't moving. For the moment.

Barry's first impression of New Bedford was off the mark. Not a bad place really. Lots of beaches, lots of boats. Lots of widow's walks on top of every old house where years ago womenfolk would watch for boats to see if their menfolk were coming back from the sea. Barry knew that if they lost this computer, there would be a lot of widows and a lot of orphans for that matter. He tried not to think about it. He much preferred surgery. Things were a lot clearer.

Barry had wanted to keep a twenty-four hour watch on The Chameleon but Kidd was against it, saying, "They know what we look like already."

Barry had countered, "Didn't they teach you in spy school how to follow somebody?"

Kidd had said, "Yeah, they also told us not to do it unless it was an absolute necessity. And right now, it's nowhere near an absolutely necessity."

Kidd was out running. The moment he got off his shift, he was out. Sitting in front of a computer for three hours drove him nuts. For Devon, it was the opposite. They had to drag him away from the computer. But, they had agreed, not more than three hours. After that, you got tired. And tired people made mistakes. The constant pulsating signal from the homing device became hypnotic after awhile.

But, pulling Devon off of the computer just sent him over to another one. Constantly checking his e-mail, constantly surfing the internet. Surfing for Dalakos. Reading every conspiracy theory about him and there was a lot to read. He didn't know what he might find but he had to keep busy. Just clicking away, hoping for a miracle.

Then, like a bomb exploding, the signal stopped. It reminded Barry of surgery, when the heart stopped beating. But, in surgery, he always knew what to do, what to try. Now, he just stares at the computer screen. Is there a problem with it? Is the power off? Should he hit it to make it work? A thousand ideas run through his head, a sure sign of panic.

Barry grabs his phone and presses the speed dial for Kidd. Kidd picks it up and continues running. He's in such good shape that you can't even hear he's running, his breathing is so constant.

Barry spits it out. "The signal stopped. There's no homing signal!"

Now, Barry can hear Kidd's breathing. Now, he too is worried. Kidd says, "Call Devon. I'll be there as fast as I can. And, whatever you do, don't touch that computer!"

45

SAMSON HENRY lies back waiting for his wife to come to bed. The kids are asleep, the breeze is blowing in from the sea and he doesn't have a care in the world. Lise doesn't get undressed in front of her husband. She wants to keep some mystery in their relationship, and with two kids it hasn't always been easy.

When she finally does come in the bedroom, she's looking finer than fine. Samson can't wait any longer. He grabs her and pulls her to the bed. He rolls her over and goes right for her neck. Her favorite spot.

She closes her eyes and floats away. Samson whispers a couple of "you look so goods" and then he whispers, "You, you're my baby doll. My baby girl."

Suddenly, Lise jumps up leaving Samson to wonder what it is he said.

"Where do you think you're going?

He grabs her to pull her back to bed but she's too quick. She says, "I've got to get my phone."

"Your phone? What're you talking about?"

She tells him, "Devon Williams' wife and their daughter are in the Bahamas and there's something strange going on and I promised to be on call 24/7 for him."

"Well, whatever their problem is, I hope it can wait a few hours. I've got big plans for you."

"A few hours? You haven't had plans that big since we were seventeen."

"You hurry up and get that phone and we'll see about that. Seventeen my ass!"

Lise comes back into the room and puts the phone by the bed. "You know, I bet being that rich isn't all it's made out to be."

Samson says, "Oh, I think I could handle it."

"You think you could handle worrying every day that someone was going to kidnap your kids? You think you could handle worrying every day that someone was going to kidnap one of us?"

"If word gets out about what you do with that tongue of yours, I'm going to have to start worrying about kidnappers real quick."

Lise ignores him and says, "You know, I met Monique Williams once. There was something about her, something fragile, something unhappy."

Her voice drifts off and then she says, "Well, it's not for me to solve the world's problems. I got more important things to do right now."

She gets into bed and slides next to her husband. He's got a funny look on his face.

He looks right at her and asks, "This Monique Williams, her daughter isn't by any chance named, Sabrina Rose, is it?"

46

IKE WALKS OUT of the Farmhouse and heads for the paddock.

The communications equipment is gone along with the computers. There is no sign whatsoever that this used to be PACT headquarters. It didn't take them long. How very efficient that Amanda is. I just hope she's as efficient when it comes to tracking down Dalakos.

Ike stands there waiting for the horses to come up to him but they don't move. Ike wonders, Have I become that invisible? I'm a living ghost! Well, I'm not the kind of guy who lies down to die. If the mountain won't come to me than I'm going to the mountain.

Ike calls out to the horses but only Chataqua comes over. He saddles up his old friend and heads out across the fields riding nowhere fast.

47

THE TWO OF THEM have been hovering over the computer waiting for Devon's diagnosis for what feels like an eternity. Barry knows the look on his face. The same look Barry has when he has to announce that a patient didn't make it. The only sound out of Devon has been the occasional sigh.

Devon finally speaks. "There's nothing wrong with the computer. For whatever reason, the homing device isn't sending a signal or the satellite isn't picking it up."

Kidd asks, "Battery?"

Devon shakes his head. "Can't be."

Kidd suggests, "Could they have found the device and deactivated it?"

"If they did, then they're bigger geniuses than yours truly and we're not going to beat them ever."

Kidd tries again. "Could they have just taken out the hard disk and left the homing device behind?"

"No, the homing device is implanted in the hard disk."

Kidd gives it another shot. "What if they're going out to sea and put it in a waterproof something or other? Would that block the signal?"

Devon massages his temples. "Could be. Could be. Could be." Barry says the unsayable. He knows the reaction he's going to get but says it anyway. "Maybe we should've destroyed the computer when we had the chance."

Kidd doesn't say a word. Devon surprises them both when he says, "Maybe we should've. But we didn't. And because we didn't, my daughter is still alive."

Barry adds, "And your wife, too."

Devon glares at Kidd. "My wife is already dead." Barry is confused. "What are you talking about?"

Devon calmly says, "She's dead. And I know who killed her."

Devon and Kidd stare at each other. Devon turns to the computer. "Now, if you two would stop bothering me for awhile, I need to check if this satellite is still working."

Barry's thinking, I wish I knew what the fuck was going on around here.

48

DALAKOS STANDS AT the bow of the Argonaut as the icy winds of the North Atlantic whip across his face.

Yesterday was as close to New Bedford as I ever want to get. The Chameleon had arrived with the computer and it's now safe and sound in my cabin, protected by a state of the art waterproof casing. Even if the ship goes down, that computer will still be safe! Even in this horrible cold, it's enough to warm my heart!

When the morning arrives, he will be able to make out land. He'll be able to see the French flag flapping in the breeze. He doesn't like the land, never has. But, at least it's not American or Canadian

On the port side he'll be able to make out Nova Scotia. But, he's heading to St. Pierre and Miquelon, French territory. Twelve miles off the coast of Canada, but French territory nevertheless.

Not that the French wouldn't do everything in their power to get their hands on me, it's just that they don't have the means that the Americans do. The Americans and their sidekicks, the Canadians, have an unpleasant habit of stopping all boats in their territorial waters for "routine checks."

Plus, he knows the Prefect of Police there. Takes good care of him. There will be no mention at all of the Argonaut docking. Dalakos is pleased with himself. Years of preparation for this. Another fundamental belief of his: There's no such thing as an overnight sensation. And as far as luck goes, he never heard of it. Luck is, after all, what happens when opportunity meets preparation.

Dalakos smiles. Content...Patience. That's the key. Tomorrow morning, I'll bring in the boat to the docks.

I'll send one of the crew ashore to meet up with the Chameleon who's gone on ahead to arrange provisions.

And, I'll send another crew member to keep an eye on the first crewman. One thing I've learned, never underestimate the Americans...especially with the likes of Kidd Black on their side.

49

DOWN AND OUT. The end of the line. Rock bottom. It's like a wake. Devon, Kidd and Barry look at the computer willing the homing device signal back to life.

They're out of ideas. They'd rushed over to where The Chameleon should have been. The trail was cold. Nothing. A couple of empty pizza boxes and the sports section of the Boston Globe. It looked a lot like the hotel room where Kidd and the guys had been holed up for the last two days.

It seemed that they had no choice but to call in PACT. That would mean Amanda's gang coming in guns blazing. Goodbye Sabrina Rose and goodbye

Monique. It was time to admit that they were licked.

PACT could be in twenty places at the same time. They could cover the airports, the highways and the sea lanes.

Kidd gets on the phone and dials Amanda. She picks up on the first ring.

"Hello."

"Amanda, Kidd here."

Amanda is delighted to hear from Kidd. She presses a button on her desk which connects her to the President.

"Are you all right?" "Yes."

"Then, where the hell have you been?"

"I've been indisposed, but now I'm back. I spoke with Ike and…"

Amanda cuts Kidd off.

"Ike is no longer with PACT. I don't want you having any contact with him."

"Since when are you giving orders?" "Since I became head of PACT!"

Kidd is surprised but doesn't miss a beat. "Okay, you're the boss."

"Now, what do you have on Dalakos?"

"That's why I'm calling you. Dalakos has…"

From across the room, Devon is frantically waving his arms signaling Kidd to get off the phone.

Kidd doesn't waste a second. "Amanda, I gotta go." He turns off the phone.

Devon tries to remain calm but his breathing gives him away. "I just got an e-mail from one of my employees. We might be back in the game!"

Barry and Kidd rush to Devon's computer and look at the e-mail.

Dear Mr. Williams,

My husband, Samson, was washing down a helicopter that had just come from a ship and saw a note written in a child's handwriting, "If you're ever on the Argonaut, look up Monique and Sabrina Rose." I thought this might refer to your wife and daughter. I'm not sure if this is important, but I thought that is for you to decide. If you have any questions concerning this, please feel free to contact me day or night by e-mail or at my personal phone, 334-7889-75-72.

Sincerely,
Lise Henry,
Director of Personnel, Microtech Bahamas

Kidd smacks his hands together. "Bingo! The Argonaut, it must be Dalakos' ship."

Barry can't stand still. He moves around the room as he says, "We ARE back in business. This woman deserves a raise."

Devon says, "A raise? I think with the bonus I'm going to send her, she's going to retire!"

Barry stops moving. "Now, how hard is it to find a ship? With all the billions we spend on that kind of stuff, it should be a snap."

Kidd says, "It would be, if we could call in PACT, but we're back to avoiding them at all costs."

Barry starts circling again. "Devon, can't you just hack PACT computer/satellite system and find out where the hell this Argonaut is? You designed the thing system, didn't you?"

Devon's voice is full of confidence. He feels like he's back in control again. "I made sure there was no way for me to do that. If I fell into the wrong hands, I didn't want to be able to get into the system. Simple as that."

50

THE PRESIDENT is on the line with Amanda and he's not in a good mood.

"What do you mean you can't just call him back?"

"His phone is untraceable if he doesn't want to be traced."

"He works for us, doesn't he? I thought you were going to change things around PACT. Crack the whip and all? Well, get cracking, damn it!"

The line goes dead. That's twice in the last five minutes that someone has hung up on her. She doesn't like that one bit.

I can't fire the President but Kidd, that could be another matter. What the hell was he doing, hanging up on his new boss! That's complete disrespect. He would never have treated Ike like that.

51

IKE STANDS IN THE rain with an umbrella and a dog. The umbrella he already owned, the dog he had to borrow. He much prefers horses but the idea here was to be inconspicuous. Right out of a spy movie. Ike knew a lot about the people who worked for PACT. Some of it was for moments like this, some of it because it was interesting and he had to admit, titillating, to know about the private lives of people one knows. But, Caroline's life was as humdrum as they come. Husband, two kids, a mortgage and a dog.

Caroline comes out of her house, dog on a leash, right on time. He supposes punctuality was to be expected from a computer expert. Ike walks past her house. He knew that this was the route she would take. It's much less suspicious to have someone follow you than you to follow them.

He slows down his pace, not surprising for an old man out walking his dog. Caroline passes him on the sidewalk. Ike puts his umbrella above hers and sets himself under hers.

"Caroline, keep walking, I have to talk to you."

Caroline is momentarily startled. "Ike?" But, she manages to keep walking.

"I'm sorry to show up unannounced but under the circumstances, I couldn't very well call."

"No, I suppose not. You are persona non grata. Amanda only refers to you in the past."

"Caroline, I can't go into it, I have to ask you for a favor. I need some information and I need it right now and I'm afraid, you're the only person who can get it for me. The reason is…."

Caroline cuts him off. "Ike, I don't really care what the reason is. Chances are, you wouldn't tell me the truth anyway, would you? All that I care about is that you need help. Tell me what you want and if I can do it, I will."

"I really appreciate this. I really do."

Caroline didn't expect a thank you but she got it. She feels she's made the right decision.

"There's a ship. Somewhere in the Atlantic. Probably Greek registry. The Argonaut."

52

SABRINA ROSE rummages through the garbage in the kitchen. She comes across some moldy infested meat and quickly pulls her hand away. Finally, she sees what she's looking for. She grimaces, holds her nose and reaches deep into the garbage can and pulls out a cork. She takes the cork and forces it into an empty wine bottle. Empty except for the note she put in: *HELP!!!! My name is Sabrina Rose Williams and I'm prisoner with my mother and Mr. and Mrs. Black on a ship the Argonaut. My father is Devon Williams! HELP!"*

She then takes a candle, lights it and turns it upside down to let the wax drip over the bottle to further seal it up. She blows out the candle and satisfied with her work, takes one last look around the room. She heads for the door and freezes. Footsteps are coming her way. She desperately looks for a place to hide. There's nowhere. Nowhere except the disgusting garbage can.

The footsteps are getting closer. Sabrina Rose rushes across the room and hesitates at the garbage can. It was bad enough putting her hand in there but her whole body? She can't do it!

She unscrews the light bulb over the garbage can. She then tries to push it away from the wall to hide behind it but it's too heavy. The footsteps get closer. Sabrina Rose puts the bottle in the garbage and then jumps into it. Please God. No rats and no spiders!

The door opens and the lights come on but the garbage can is in shadow. Sabrina Rose tries to listen but can only hear her own heart beating wildly. She's as good as dead if she's found in the garbage, not even mentioning her message in a bottle. Finally, she calms down enough to hear some rummaging around.

Maybe it's just someone coming in for a late night snack. The rummaging stops and there is only silence. Sabrina Rose can't take the suspense. She pops her head out of the garbage just enough to see the back of a woman. It's Dimitra! She has two glasses of orange juice in front of her and is measuring something from a syringe. She takes the syringe and puts the contents into one of the orange juice glasses.

Sabrina Rose ducks back down into the garbage can. She no longer notices the disgusting things around her. She's thinking about the syringe, the orange juice. They're drugging her mother! Of course, her mother would never act like this if she weren't drugged! The lights go off and the door closes. Sabrina Rose knows she has to get back to her room before Dimitra does!

53

THE HELICOPTER SKIMS low across the North Atlantic. They can just make out the white caps of the choppy waves whenever the moonlight cuts through the clouds.

Barry wonders, Don't know what good I'll be doing here. But, it sure beats sticking around St. Pierre watching Devon watching the computer. Anyway, somebody has to stay in the helicopter just in case the pilot changes his mind...but with the money Devon is paying him, I'm pretty sure he'll keep his part of the deal.

When Devon gives the signal, the helicopter is to rise to three hundred feet, drop off Kidd and then plunge back down to just above the waves. It has to be quick enough so that Dalakos' radar will think it's a glitch of some sort on their screen.

Barry gets a signal on his earphone. "Kidd, I just got the word from Devon. Back on our heads."

Kidd puts his hand on Barry's shoulder and says, "Yeah, back on our heads."

The helicopter door opens and Kidd slides out onto the pylons and holds on with one arm. Barry passes out the hang glider to him.

The pilot says, "Let's do it." The helicopter rises.

Kidd can make out the lights of the Argonaut in the distance.

So far, Ike's information has been right on the money. All that's left is to board the ship, save Monique and Sabrina Rose and of course, at the same time, kill Dalakos and rid the earth of the deadliest of terrorists.

54

AMANDA DRIVES THROUGH the empty streets of suburban Virginia. It's late but she's heading to the office. Like she told the President, she's going to run a tight ship...unlike Ike.

I need to know who Ike has been in contact with besides Kidd. I need to keep an eye on everyone! But whom can I trust?

The answer to that comes quickly enough.

No one. Something I learned the hard way, by experience. The last person I ever trusted...the last person I ever loved, was Devon Williams. And what did he do? Barely acknowledged my existence is what he did...and ran off with Monique the first chance he had.

But, Amanda knows she's going to have to trust someone. She can't check out everyone and everything herself. She needs eyes and ears. She'll have to trust Caroline. Caroline is a magician. She really is capable of being in sixteen places at the same time.

Amanda pulls into the National Security Administration complex at Langley. To the guards she's just another woman with a top security clearance. But this is her Kingdom and here she's Queen. No wonder she spends as much time here as possible.

Amanda smiles a satisfied smile and walks towards a gray nondescript structure set off from all the other offices there. Very few people know what it is or what goes on in there. Even the members of PACT call it, "The Shop."

55

SABRINA ROSE knows there are two stairways on the boat but even if she runs to the far stairway and rushes down the other one, she'll never get back to her cabin before Dimitra. She could run into Dimitra and knock over the tray with the orange juice but then she'd have to explain what she was doing out of her cabin.

She looks frantically around the cafeteria, nothing. Then she looks up at the ceiling. A smoke detector! Sabrina Rose takes a match, lights a newspaper and throws it into the garbage. Smoke billows up. She rushes out the door just as the smoke detector starts screaming.

She dashes for the far stairway as the boat comes alive. Without missing a step, she heaves her 'message in a bottle' overboard, saying a silent prayer as she does.

Dimitra can't get down the other stairs as the crew members rush up towards the sound of the smoke detector. Sabrina Rose dashes into her cabin. Her mother is sound asleep. Sabrina Rose thinks, She's not asleep. She's drugged!

Sabrina Rose quickly washes off the grime from the garbage can and throws on some clean clothes. She then kisses her mother on the cheek but her mother doesn't move. Sabrina Rose asks herself, How do you convince someone on drugs that they're on drugs? They won't believe you because they're on drugs!

She pushes her mother, nothing. She shakes her, she barely moves. Well, at least she's alive.

She reaches over and takes the flower vase and hesitates for a moment. Then, she throws the cold water on her mother's face. At last. Monique's eyes open wide and the blankness begins to clear. She wakes up to the sound of the smoke detector screeching across the boat.

Monique says in a quiet voice, "What's going on?"

"There was a fire but I think it's under control."

"That's good. How are you, sweetie?" Without waiting for an answer, Monique slowly closes her eyes.

"Mom, you gotta stay awake. We have to get out of here." But Monique is already fading away.

Sabrina Rose puts her face close to her mother's and starts to cry.

"Mom, I need you. I need you. Mom, please." Sabrina Rose can't stop crying.

"Mom, this man is a bad man." She hesitates about telling her how he threatened her. If he finds out, he really will kill her. Instead, she says, "I don't like him."

Monique's eyes seem to clear as she says, "My baby. My baby. Don't cry. I'm here."

There's something about her mother's voice that gives her hope. For the first time, she feels her mother is back! She thinks, Something that Mr. Black said is bringing her back! Now's the time to tell her that *that man* is drugging her and that he threatened to kill me!

Just then, there's a knock at the door.

Sabrina Rose knows that it's Dimitra because if it was Dalakos he would just barge in. Dimitra doesn't wait for the door to be opened though, she just slips in carrying a tray of food and two glasses of orange juice.

Sabrina Rose knows the drill by now. Dimitra stands over them until they've drunk their orange juice and then leaves. She remembers the one time she reached for the "wrong" one, Dimitra quickly stopped her.

Sabrina Rose waits until Dimitra hands a glass to her mom. Then, she fills her mouth with as much saliva and mucous as she can, thinking, Now this is going to be fun!

She then "sneezes" right into Dimitra's face. Dimitra recoils and goes to wipe her eyes. At that moment, Sabrina Rose grabs the glass of orange juice out of her mom's hands and guzzles it down. She then sets the glass on the table just as Dimitra has finished wiping her face.

Sabrina Rose looks innocently at Dimitra and says, "I'm so sorry."

Dimitra sees the empty glass on the table, glares at Sabrina Rose and storms out of the room.

56

NADINE opens the cabin door. Just as the ship's doctor had promised, there's a guard sitting there. Luckily, the guard couldn't look more bored. Probably signed on for some serious raping and pillaging and here he is, guarding two old raisins old enough to be his grandparents.

Nadine tries to walk past him. "Where do you think you're going?"

Nadine sighs and says, "The doctor said you were here to watch my husband not me!"

"You sure about that?"

"You want me to call the doctor and wake him up? I don't think he'll be very happy about that, do you? Now if you'll excuse me, I'm going to the upper deck to take some air."

Right on cue, Lawrence comes out the door, full of energy. "Hello, Guardy, what do you say we go for a swim?"

At that, Lawrence heads for the railing. The guard grabs him. "Oh no you don't!"

Lawrence starts laughing maniacally. "Unhand me you brute!"

The guard grabs Lawrence and escorts him back towards the cabin. Nadine takes the opportunity to walk away towards the upper deck. The guard watches her walk away and thinks, The further that old bag keeps away from me, the happier I'll be.

He coaxes Lawrence back into the berth and says, "I bet you're happy to see her go too, aren't you Old Timer?"

57

KIDD HANGS FROM the helicopter pylons by his feet. He needs his arms to steady the hang glider as the helicopter rises. When it reaches three hundred feet, it hovers. That's Kidd's signal. He secures himself to the hang glider in mid air. He drops from the pylons and heads straight for the water. No reason to panic, he's done this a hundred times before. But, there's no reason to be overconfident either. He would've preferred to go up to four hundred feet but then the helicopter would've needed too much time to get below radar. So, he keeps his eyes fixed on the Argonaut even though he's heading straight for the ocean. No sense in staring down, he'd know soon enough if he hit the water.

In seconds, he's got updraft and is looping his way across the ocean. The wind rips across his ears. The hardest part is yet to come. He has to control the glider in order to land on a moving ship. And a glider, by definition, means that there's no gas pedal to get you where you want to be.

He glides across the water, making his descent. To land the hang glider, you have to stall it. As he approaches, he pushes the control bar as far out as he can. This tips the glider nose up, slows the glider down and eventually stalls it so you can land upright on your feet.

He picks his spot, just behind the lifeboat on the stern. But Kidd can see that his landing area is small and his landing has to be absolutely perfect. If this were gymnastics, a landing rated 10 might not do it.

And then he sees it. A flickering light. A cigarette! Some joker is sneaking a cigarette behind the lifeboat!

He's at the point of no return. Well, cigarette or no cigarette, I've got to land this thing somewhere.

Like a hawk, he swoops down and aims the glider at the Smoker's chest. In an instant, the point goes through the center of the Smoker's heart and pins him against the wall.

Kidd pulls the hang glider out of the wall and throws it overboard with the Smoker still attached to it.

58

AMANDA WALKS THROUGH the corridors of the Shop, PACT HQ. No one acknowledges her presence. Only the inner ring of PACT is supposed to know that she's the new boss. But, she feels that people are looking at her differently, like they know she's Ike's replacement. Further proof that even at PACT, secrets are hard to keep.

Amanda is surprised to see a light on in Caroline's office. She knocks once on the door and walks in. Caroline is sitting in front of her computer but has a startled look on her face. Startled because someone walked into her office at this time of night or startled because it's Amanda?

Amanda acts as though she didn't notice a thing as she says, "Hi. Glad to see someone burning the midnight oil around here. The bad guys never sleep so why should we?"

Caroline says, "I couldn't sleep either so I came in...to do some work. I suppose it could've waited but what the hell, I could use the overtime pay."

Caroline laughs and Amanda pretends to. She knows that Caroline has two kids, a husband and a dog. She's a brilliant efficient worker but when work is over, she's home with her family. Only an emergency would bring her out here at night.

Caroline asks, "Amanda, what do you say we go for a cup of coffee?"

Caroline stands up expecting Amanda to head for the door but instead Amanda walks towards Caroline's computer.

"Sure, but first I'd love to see what you're working on. Part of my hands-on management. I'm not going be like Ike and not know what the hell's going on around me until it's much too late."

Amanda sees the nervousness in Caroline's eye even though her voice remains calm.

Caroline lightly says, "Oh, it's just the recent satellite photos of the shipping lanes along the East Coast."

Amanda looks at the screen, smiles warmly and asks, "Really? Tell me all about it."

59

KIDD WALKS OUT from behind the lifeboat as if he owned the place. Someone looking his way would think he was part of the crew. No better way to draw attention than to sneak around like a burglar.

Now, to find a couple of needles in a not so big haystack. I imagine that they're somewhere up near the bridge. Best berths and all.

Kidd heads towards the bow and spots the bored guard, gun by his side, in front of a cabin. But, on the other hand, they could be right here. I doubt there's anyone else under guard here.

My priority is Monique and Sabrina Rose. I'm going to find them, put them in the lifeboat and have the helicopter pick them up. Then, I'll take care of Dalakos. Take care of Dalakos. How I'm going to love that!

Kidd walks right towards the guard who wonders, Why haven't I seen this guy before. After all, the crew isn't that big.

The guard reaches for his gun. Kidd rushes into him, pushes open the door to the berth, and the two of them tumble in.

Kidd shouts, "I've come to help. I'm a friend!"

Kidd fully expected to see Sabrina Rose and Monique. When he sees it's his father, he freezes. Just long enough for the guard to grab Kidd.

The guard pins Kidd against the door of the berth and bangs his head against it. The guard takes him and throws his head against the door again. A few more times and Kidd will lose consciousness.

With a strength he didn't know he still had, if he ever had it, Lawrence jumps on the guard from behind, wraps his arms around his neck and begins to pull with all his might.

Not enough to kill him, not even enough to knock him out but certainly enough to distract him. Enough of a distraction for Kidd to get free. In a matter of moments, the guard is knocked out on the floor.

Kidd looks at his dad and rushes into his arms. Kidd, barely recognizing his own voice, a voice on the verge of tears, says, "I can't believe it. I just can't believe it."

His dad whispers, "Wait until I tell your mother."

Kidd pulls back and looks at him hopefully. His dad says, "Yeah, she's here on the boat too."

Before Kidd can say another word, the guard moans and stirs a bit. Kidd reaches down and lifts him up. His dad asks, "What are we going to do with him?"

"We? You've already done enough. I'll take it from here."

At that, Kidd opens the door and pops his head out. Seeing no one is around, he drags out the guard and throws him overboard.

60

NADINE SOFTLY knocks on Sabrina Rose and Monique's cabin door. Nothing. She slowly opens it and enters. Monique is lightly snoring and Sabrina Rose is dead to the world. Nadine is about to wake up Monique when she notices that Sabrina Rose is barely breathing, in fact, she's worried that she might literally be dead to the world. Nadine has no way of knowing it now, but that dose of the drug-laced orange juice that Sabrina Rose drank was calculated for a grown woman, not a ten year old girl.

Nadine decides to not wake up Monique. Lawrence had told her to expect her to be incoherent. She can't lose any valuable time trying to explain what's going on. She picks up Sabrina Rose and heads out the door.

She quickly climbs up to the doctor's berth and bangs on the door. The doctor, half-asleep, opens it. He spots Nadine and jumps awake. He nervously asks, "Is your husband okay? Where is he?"

"My husband's fine." Nadine holds up Sabrina Rose. "But this girl isn't. Now, take me to your office. "

61

KIDD WALKS down the hallway where his father said he would find Monique, Sabrina Rose and his mother. He opens the door and there in the dimly lit room lies Monique, asleep on the bed. There's no sign of Sabrina Rose or his mother.

Kidd takes another look at Monique who looks as though she doesn't have a care in the world. He's gone through this moment a thousand times. Kidd heads for the bed and gently touches her arm. She stirs in her sleep.

Kidd kneels next to the bed and touches her a little more forcefully. He whispers her name, "Monique, you have to wake up."

Monique opens her eyes. "Monique, it's me, Kidd."

For once, because she hadn't had her "orange juice," Monique isn't in a drug-induced haze. Her mind is racing. She sees that it's not Dalakos in her room. It's a man with blue eyes, a light-skinned black man. What's this man doing in my room?

"Monique, it is me. I've come to take you and Sabrina Rose away."

Monique looks around the room. Where is Sabrina Rose?

Kidd doesn't know if Monique is going to cry or kiss him. Either way, he's ready to take her in his arms. A moment he's dreamed about for eighteen years. Kidd reaches for her.

Monique bolts up from the bed and rushes for the door. Completely taken by surprise, she makes it to the door before Kidd can react. Monique rushes into the hallway and screams. The men in the next room wake up for a moment, dismiss her screams as Dalakos having fun, laugh and go back to bed.

Kidd hurries after her. She makes it to the deck and shouts, "Christopher! Christopher! Help!" Monique's now completely hysterical.

Kidd grabs her from behind and puts a hand over her mouth.

He pleads, "Monique, it's me, Kidd Black. I'm not dead. Kidd Black. I'm not dead. Kidd Black. I'm not dead."

But, Monique doesn't believe him. She only knows that a man had broken into her room. A man who had reached for her.

A man who knew her daughter's name. Kidd had made the mistake of thinking she would do what he hoped she would do without thinking of every possibility.

From up by the bridge a voice says, "Kidd Black? On my boat, to see me, I imagine. What an honor."

Monique looks up and is relieved to see Dalakos. But, at the same time, she's confused. Christopher had called this man, Kidd Black! And that man in her cabin, the man she thought was just a dream, had said he was Kidd Black's father!

Kidd shouts, "Where's the little girl? Where's my mother?"

Dalakos says, "I don't think you're in a position to be asking questions, Mr. Black."

Kidd agrees with Dalakos but doesn't think this is the time to tell him that. Instead, he tries to bluff his way out of a bad hand.

"If you don't show me the girl and my mother, I'm going to kill Monique. And I don't think you'd like that, would you?"

"You're not fooling anyone."

"Try me."

Monique is thinking, This man will kill me. And where is my daughter? And why was he talking about his mother? The man is crazy!

Dalakos says something in Greek and Dimitra comes into view with Sabrina Rose held firmly next to her. The doctor comes out holding Nadine, her mouth gagged. Dalakos picks up Sabrina Rose and holds her close to him.

"Here's the kid. Here's your mother...

And now what?" Kidd and Monique can hear Sabrina Rose whimpering.

Kidd shouts, "Give me them both and you can keep Monique."

Dalakos says, "Okay, let's make a deal. You decide. Who do you want more? The girl or your mother. You decide! If you want the girl, go get her."

Dalakos picks up Sabrina Rose and holds her over his head. Dimitra stands behind Dalakos with a satisfied grin on her face. Sabrina Rose whimpers. Dalakos heaves her overboard. Her tortured screams resonate across the boat

Kidd lets go of Monique's mouth and she too screams. An ancient primeval scream. The scream of a mother who watches helplessly as her child dies.

Kidd runs to the edge of the boat, spots Sabrina Rose and without a moment's hesitation dives into the cold water after her. He comes up for air and can hear the motors as the boat moves away from him. Above the roar he can hear Monique screaming.

Kidd sees where Sabrina Rose is and swims towards her as she sinks. He grabs her just in time and pulls her towards him but it's not her at all. It's a life-size doll. Dalakos had thrown a doll overboard! A doll with a sound system. A sound system that plays a child's screams!

Shocked, Kidd contacts Barry to come get him. Painfully, he tells him that he's alone in the water. No Sabrina Rose, no Monique and certainly no Dalakos. He'll explain later about his parents. Nothing to do now but wait for Barry to come fish him out. He watches as the Argonaut heads across the horizon and out of sight.

Kidd waits in the cold water. Not moving but speeding his heart rate up to help fight off the cold. The heart is the only muscle in the body that works without the brain telling it what to do but Kidd has learned to control his heart rate.

He doesn't feel the cold, though he knows it's there. He's burning up inside.

Burning with humiliation.

Kidd hears the sound of a jet. He can't see it but he hears it fly over and head in the direction of the Argonaut. Then, he sees a flash of light and hears a massive explosion, followed by another flash of light and an even bigger explosion.

Kidd lies in the water and thinks about his parents. He buried them once already and now he's buried them again. This time for good. All because he wasn't up to the job!

A wave washes over his face, bringing him back to life. To life...The last place on this Godforsaken Earth he wants to be. Because now he has to face the question he doesn't want to ask. How the hell is he going to tell Devon that Monique and Sabrina Rose are dead?

PART THREE

1

AMANDA IS DOING her best to conceal her joy but she's not doing a very good job of it.

"Mr. President, I wanted to be the one to tell you personally that we got Christopher Dalakos. He's dead."

The President doesn't say anything right away. It's too unexpected. Dalakos dead is like the Berlin Wall coming down. Something bad that you thought would always be there.

Amanda fills in the space. "PACT came up with the location of his boat and gave the news to the Air Force and they took care of the rest."

Finally, the President smiles and says, "You've been head of PACT for less than a week. Amanda, you deserve a medal. A medal given in a private ceremony, of course, but a medal nevertheless."

Amanda quickly adds, "We'll give all the credit to the Air Force."

Amanda and the President both know that there is no sense in giving credit to PACT because the secret side of PACT "doesn't exist" but she also knows that it makes her look humble to suggest giving the Air Force credit.

The President swallows and then asks, suspecting he knows the answer already, "And Monique Williams and her daughter?"

Amanda puts on her serious look. "The boat was totally destroyed. We have every reason to believe that they were both on it at the time."

The President sighs. A sigh that is part sadness and part resignation. He says, "Better the two of them dead than having that Lazer in the hands of the likes of Dalakos."

"That's been our thinking from the beginning, Sir."

"I'll have to call Devon Williams. I don't know what the hell I'm going to say. Have you recovered any of the bodies yet?"

Amanda announces, "We're sending a boat to do that as we speak."

The President sits back in his chair and says, "Now, as soon as you have the photos of his body, get it out to the world."

"It's great to have some good news around here for once." The President says, "Good news? This is great news!"

2

BARRY AND KIDD sit silently in the helicopter as it skims across the water heading to where the Argonaut used to be.

Kidd hasn't said much since they picked him up. Barry is content to wait for him so say something. But Kidd keeps replaying the movie of his time on the Argonaut. What could he have done differently? Where did he go wrong?

Kidd closes his eyes and sighs. A sigh that is awfully close to crying. He knows where he went wrong.

Finally Kidd says, "Remember when your Mom told us that all dogs go to Heaven, that goes for kids too, right?"

Barry's not sure what to say. Kidd has always been like a super hero to him and it's not easy to see your hero beaten like this. This is completely new territory for him. Barry would love to speak in a language he knows Kidd will understand. But, no jokes come to mind. So, he mumbles a weak, "Yeah, that goes for kids, too."

The helicopter stops moving and hovers. The pilot says, "We're here."

Kidd's voice is distant and resigned. "Bring it down as close as you can and give me all the light you've got."

3

AMANDA SITS IN HER office thinking, Another perk of being head cf PACT. People come to see me. I don't have to go anywhere. And if I tell them to be here first thing in the morning, they come and they don't complain. At least, not to my face, anyway.

A young male voice announces, "General West is here." "Send him in."

The General walks in and as he shakes her hand he says, "Heard about your show in the Bahamas at Devon Williams' Estate. Of course, we expect nothing less from a graduate of the Academy."

Amanda doesn't like his tone of voice. A little too condescending for her taste. In a very business-like tone, she says, "Concerning the Argonaut. You've never heard of it. Nothing is to be written. No report whatsoever. As far as we're concerned, this case is shut."

General West is in too good a mood to notice the tone of her voice. "And the pilot shall be commended for a job well done with no specifics on his record. I imagine you'll want him there for the medal ceremony."

Amanda quickly answers, "Yes, of course," and thinks, The President just loves rubbing elbows with heroes.

4

KIDD AND BARRY peer down into the water. They're not sure what they're looking for but they keep looking, hoping that maybe, just maybe, somehow, that someone, Monique, Sabrina Rose, his parents, made it out alive. It's too much to even hope that all four could have survived.

Finally, Barry breaks the silence. "Come on, Kidd, let's get back to Devon. He could use the company. There's nothing here. I mean, nothing."

"I'm not ready to go back yet. Give me another minute." Barry shrugs and peers down into the sea. It's definitely better than looking at the pained look on Kidd's face.

When Kidd finally speaks, Barry barely recognizes his voice. It's a voice full of pain. "I just wish there was something to bring back. Something to bury. Something for a funeral. You know what I mean?"

Barry sees that there's nothing down there. A few pieces of boat, some articles of clothing and that's it. The Air Force knows how to do its job, that's for sure.

Barry quietly says, "Sometimes the sea is the best cemetery there is. Let's go."

Kidd doesn't say anything. A thousand times over the last eighteen years, he dreamt of coming to see Monique again. A thousand times, she would break into tears and rush into his arms. A thousand times they made love like they invented it. In an instant, he was eighteen again.

That look. She looked at me and saw nothing, nothing but fear. There was no recognition in her eyes, no love, no lust. No nothing. She had screamed for protection. She had screamed out for help from the world's worst terrorist. Help against me!

Kidd has the look on his face of a man who sees the world turning upside down and is having trouble just holding on. He tries not to think about his parents or Sabrina Rose but he knows that that pain can't be just wished away.

Barry looks at him and just sees a man who's beaten. He quietly says, "There's nothing for us down there."

Kidd slowly takes out his cell phone and says to himself, I've had it. I'm over the hill. I let my emotions get the best of me and because of that, four innocent people are dead.

Kidd whispers, "I'm done. I'm out." He takes the phone and heaves it into the ocean. He watches as it quickly sinks.

Barry shouts to the pilot, "Take us back in, would you?"

The pilot grunts an okay and the helicopter immediately heads for St. Pierre. Kidd just keeps on staring at the ocean—seeing nothing.

5

CAROLINE WALKS SLOWLY down the hall towards Amanda's office. She's been in the doghouse since that incident about Ike and the Argonaut. Caroline had claimed ignorance, that she didn't know Ike was off limits to all ISSF personnel. After that, Amanda had formally ordered her not to have any contact whatsoever with Ike. Caroline still can't believe that Amanda is bossing her around and even worse, ordering her not to have any contact with Ike.

She reaches Amanda's office and knocks gingerly. She was hoping to avoid any more delicate situations since her last delicate situation with Amanda but this can't wait.

Caroline hears, "Come in," and slowly opens the door. Amanda forces a smile. Amanda knows now that she can't trust Caroline and if she can't trust her, she can't trust anyone. She'd like to fire her but she prefers having her around where she can keep an eye on her. That famous quote of President Lyndon Johnson is stuck in her head. He was referring to J. Edgar Hoover, the head of the FBI. "I'd rather have him inside my tent pissing out than outside pissing in."

Caroline asks, "You got a minute?"

Amanda is wondering, Do I have a minute to talk, woman to woman, if so, no I don't have time for that kind of bullshit. If I have a minute for something important, then, yes I do. I guess the only way to know is to say yes.

Amanda puts a friendly touch to her voice. "Sure, what's up?" Caroline sits down and opens a folder. Amanda is thinking, Well, at least it has to do with business.

Caroline takes a short breath and starts. "I was finishing up the paperwork on the Argonaut 'incident.' As I'm sure you know, I make an encoded report on every ISSF action."

A warning light goes on in Amanda's head. She thinks, Where is this going? I don't know anything about these encoded reports!

Amanda feigns disinterest. "And?"

"And something doesn't add up. I took a look at the thermal target response and...."

Amanda interrupts her. "I'm sorry Caroline, but you know, I'm new to this job. What are you talking about?"

"The TTR is the infra-red satellite feed that confirms if the target was destroyed, partially destroyed or missed."

Relieved, Amanda can only smile. "You telling me that the Argonaut wasn't destroyed? We sent a ship to take a look. There were no survivors and the boat is firewood. I've seen the photos!"

Caroline isn't one to give up so quickly. "No, I'm not saying that at all. I'm saying the Argonaut exploded before the pilot even fired. I contacted General West who said there must be a technical problem with the satellite."

"I'm sure that's it."

Caroline thinks, I've gone this far, I can't stop now."I've checked and rechecked the satellite and the TTR system. It's all in order. I asked General West to let me talk to the pilot but he said the pilot was unavailable."

"What difference does it make? The Argonaut sunk. Dalakos is dead. That's what's important."

Caroline won't let go. "Amanda, you know, above all, I'm a mathematician and when something doesn't add up, it bugs the hell out of me. I want you to get me access to that pilot."

"Request denied. Now, if you don't mind, the President is coming over to pin a medal on yours truly and I've arranged for you to get one too."

Caroline laughs, "Me? Why me?"

"Well, if you hadn't found the Argonaut, we never could have blown it up, could we?"

"I was just doing Ike a favor. I had no idea what it was about. I found the Argonaut because Kidd and Ike got me the information. It was easy from there."

"I certainly can't give Ike a medal, he's no longer welcome around here. And as for Kidd, nobody seems to know where the hell he is. So, in the interest of your career and in the interest of making PACT look good with the President, I strongly suggest you be at the ceremony, all smiles and all dressed up."

Caroline tries to put some enthusiasm in her voice and says, "Yes, of course," but her mind is already a million miles away.

6

BARRY COMES INTO the room to find Devon at one end and Kidd at the other. It's impossible for them to be further apart.

Devon shouts, "Listen, Kidd, it's not your fault. You hear me? It's not your fault!"

Kidd shouts back, "Yeah? Then whose fault is it?"

Barry senses that this is getting out of control and going nowhere. He doesn't need a map to know what they're talking about. He too shouts. "It's Dalakos' fault! Enough! Let's leave it at that!"

Silence. Each guy can only hear his own heart beating and his own loud breathing.

Finally Devon says in a voice so quiet they have to lean forward to hear, "Okay. Like the good doctor said, 'Let's leave it at that.'"

Kidd and Barry nod their heads in agreement. After all, what's the sense of looking for blame? It would take them through a minefield of betrayal. Not only Monique's but Kidd's too. And they all knew that assigning blame wasn't going to bring back the ones who were completely innocent in the whole thing, Sabrina Rose and Kidd's parents.

Barry says, "Devon, I've made arrangements for a funeral if it's okay with you."

Devon's voice gets even quieter. "A funeral? It hadn't even crossed my mind."

Barry's voice drops a few decibels, "I thought we'd go out to sea, to the spot, and say a few prayers. I've arranged for a boat. There are some clergy available on this island if you want."

Devon is firm. "No, no clergy. I'd rather just the three of us go out there. At sunset. Sabrina Rose and Monique loved to watch the sunset."

Barry looks over at Kidd as if to say, "And for your parents?"

Kidd mutters, "No, no clergy is fine with me too."

7

MEDAL CEREMONIES AT PACT were usually low budget affairs with a low profile crowd. A table of drinks and potato chips. But, you could tell the President would be coming. Not only was it catered, even tablecloths had been set up in the briefing room. It was about as VIP as it could be. The "board of directors" of PACT was there. The rest of the room was filled with PACT staff members.

Amanda mingles. She's trying not to look too happy. She's been head of PACT for less than a week and already this!

Caroline walks into the room and heads turn. The men look at her with appreciation and the women who know her can only be surprised. She's wearing a white dress, black stockings and black heels. And, just enough cleavage to make it difficult for any man there to look her in the eyes. She thinks to herself, Thank God, it looks like I still got what it takes. I'll know soon enough.

Amanda comes up to her and says, "Don't you look great. This is a side of the 'nose to the grindstone computer techie' I've never seen. Never."

Caroline smiles graciously and says, "You did say we wanted to make PACT look good. Just trying to do my share. And, don't forget, the President will be here."

Amanda laughs and says, "Don't worry, I haven't forgotten." Amanda looks around the room for someone more important to talk to and spots someone. She speaks as though Caroline isn't even there. "Enjoy yourself. I'll see you soon."

Without waiting for Caroline to reply, Amanda makes a beeline for the Chairman of the Joint Chiefs of Staff. Caroline is left there standing alone. She heads for the bar. A drink will calm her nerves. She feels rusty and out of practice, that's for sure. She orders a beer. As she waits for it, she notices a man, early thirties, with his back to the bar. There's a small plate of untouched food next to him.

Caroline says, "I can always spot who the Secret Service Agents are. They're the ones who don't try to stuff themselves with free food."

The man barely acknowledges her presence with a polite smile and continues to look around the room. She points to his drink and says, "And they're the ones who don't drink." She didn't add, And they try and choose the ones with a nondescript face. The kind that blend well into a crowd. The kind that are easy to forget.

The man asks, "Excuse me, ma'am?"

Caroline smiles and adds, "And they're the ones who always say ma'am."

The man finally looks at her and says, "Looks like you're on to me. I'm Agent Dalton Roberts. Just call me, Dalton."

Caroline puts out her hand. "I'm Caroline..." Before she can finish her name, Dalton says it for her. "Crimmins."

"Should I be flattered or spooked?"

"Just because you're getting a medal doesn't mean we don't check up on you."

Caroline smiles coquettishly and asks, "So, how do I check out?"

The bartender discretely sets her beer down next to her. "You check out just fine. Husband, two kids, a dog, no strange cults, political affiliations and no affairs."

Caroline shakes her head sadly and says, "Sounds like Caroline Crimmins leads a very dull life."

"Just how we like it." He stiffens slightly and his eyes scan the room.

Caroline says, "Looks like it's show time."

As if on cue, the door opens and all heads turn in that direction. Everyone applauds as the President enters the room. He's accompanied by a young man in uniform. The guy has pilot written all over him. Cool, calm and straight as an arrow. Caroline spots a woman next to him. Judging by the matching rings, she'd say that this woman had to be the pilot's wife.

Caroline's heart drops. Not only is the pilot great looking, so is his wife. She thinks, Sure hope the old adage is true: "Behind Every Beautiful Woman, There's a Man Who's Tired of Having Sex with Her."

The President makes a beeline for Amanda and gives her a big hug in front of everyone. Amanda is beginning to think that this could be the best day of her life. Amanda takes the President by the arm and leads him over to Caroline. "Mr. President, thank you for coming. I'd like to introduce you to Caroline Crimmins, the woman you'll be pinning a medal on today."

The President likes what he sees and says, "It will truly be an honor."

He shakes hands with Caroline who says, "It's already an honor for me, Sir."

The President puts his arm around the pilot. "This is Derrick Jameson, our other hero. Derrick this is Amanda Mason and Caroline Crimmins."

Amanda shakes hands with him and says, "Great job, Captain. Great job."

Derrick's voice is deep and confident. "Thank you ma'am." Caroline puts out her hand and Derrick takes it. Caroline says, "Truly a pleasure to meet you, the real hero."

Derrick beams and says, "And thank you, too, ma'am." Caroline smiles at him and very, very slowly lets go of his hand. Somewhere in the background, she hears the President introducing her to Derrick's wife.

8

LE CHAT NOIRE, a thirty-five foot fishing boat, chugs its way towards the funeral. The Captain has French written all over him. A Gauloises cigarette dangling from his mouth, a long Gallic nose and sipping red wine. Everything was as one would expect but instead of a beret, he was wearing a Boston Red Sox cap.

Barry, Devon and Kidd are seated at the bow around a small wooden table, an empty bottle of wine next to them and a recently opened bottle on the table. The sun is just beginning to set, causing a cold wind to come across the Atlantic.

Barry had gotten the coordinates from the helicopter pilot and given them to the boat Captain. He was half hoping that there wouldn't be any sign of what was left of the Argonaut. But, no such luck. The Captain yells out, "Over there. That must be the spot."

He turns the boat towards the port side and in a matter of minutes they're next to some floating pieces of wood that must have come from the Argonaut. The three of them stand and Kidd asks the Captain to cut the motor. They stand there in silence until finally Devon speaks.

"This was Sabrina Rose's favorite joke. 'Why can't a steam engine sit down?' He pauses for a moment and almost smiles. "Because it has a tender behind." He lowers his head and slowly shakes it from side to side. And then he starts to quietly cry.

9

CAROLINE WAITS IN her office. It was like she was back in high school again. Feeling very naughty, very excited and very nervous. What if he didn't come? She had pulled out every trick in the book to get him. Crossing her legs, touching him when she talked to him, looking him in the eyes, looking away so he could glimpse her cleavage, listening to him as though his words should be written in stone, the whole nine yards. Then, she put her cards on the table.

"Okay. I need to see you alone. Right now. My office is on the first floor, 216. Take the stairs. Don't bother knocking. You won't be disappointed."

Without looking back, she walked out of the room, headed for her office and waited…

She hears footsteps. They stop in front of her door. She leans back on the desk and waits, thinking, This is going to be very embarrassing if it's not him.

The door opens and Derrick comes in. Caroline whispers, "Lock the door!"

Derrick quietly closes the door and locks it. He comes up to her and they kiss and grind and kiss some more. Caroline thinks, One very big downside of being married. You don't have moments like this. My first kiss with my husband was a long, long time ago.

Thinking of her husband, Caroline remembers why she's there. She breaks away from Derrick, gets behind him and pushes him towards the desk. He's content to see where this is going. Caroline starts working her way down his back with both her hands on his ass. Now, down on her knees she whispers, "Close your eyes."

Derrick closes his eyes and Caroline whispers, "That's a good boy."

She reaches for the handcuffs that are attached to her desk. She takes the free cuff and snaps it shut around Derrick's ankle. His deep voice has just gotten a lot deeper. "Now, this could be good."

Caroline takes a step away from him and coldly announces, "Okay, tell me what happened with the Argonaut. And don't give me any bullshit or you'll have to explain to your wife what the hell you're doing here!"

10

THE BOAT CAPTAIN was the first to hear it. He had respectfully cut the motor and kept his distance. He wondered what a helicopter was doing out here literally in the middle of nowhere. A few seconds later they all heard it coming closer. The moment was broken. For all practical purposes, the funeral was over.

The three of them are furious. Barry says, "What the hell is this all about!"

Through teary eyes, Devon looks up to see that the helicopter is coming straight for them. Kidd instinctively reaches for his gun knowing full well that if the helicopter is interested in killing them, there's not much he can do.

The helicopter hovers over them and a ladder is lowered out of it. The three of them go from anger to wonder. A helmeted man in a suit slowly works his way out of the helicopter and down to the boat. In order to reach the boat, he has to jump the last ten feet but he won't do it. He signals for the pilot to ease him down and he does. He stands there in the middle of Kidd, Devon and Barry, straightens his suit and takes off his helmet.

Kidd says, "Well, I'll be damned. If it ain't Ike Muslow himself."

Kidd puts out his hand and warmly shakes Ike's. Kidd turns to Barry and Devon and says, "This is Ike Muslow. He used to be my boss."

The three of them nod to each other. Kidd continues, "Hopefully he's going to tell us what the hell he's doing here."

Ike is indignant, "Why don't you answer your goddamn phone? That's what it's there for you know. To be answered. If you answered the goddamn phone I wouldn't have to risk my life to talk to you."

Kidd's smile disappears as he says, "I threw it away. I'm getting out. I'm done. I'm cooked."

Ike takes out a phone and hands it to Kidd. "Consider yourself uncooked. I need to talk to the three of you."

Ike turns to the Captain and says, "S'il vous plait, monsieur. Ammener nous au port, le plutôt possible."

The Captain snaps to attention. "Oui, monsieur. A vos ordres."

The motor starts up and Ike sits down. He looks at the wine and a disappointed look comes across his face, "Not the best but as my father, Colonel Muslow, used to say, 'Any port in a storm.'"

Ike sits down with the glass of wine and starts drinking. He looks over at the guys. "Gentlemen, I suggest you join me. We have a puzzle to solve."

Barry, Devon and Kidd sit down next to Ike. He pours them all a glass of wine and says, "This puzzle, there are some pieces missing and I'm hoping we can find them."

Devon says, "I'm sure this can wait. I'm really not in the mood for fun and games, Mr. Muslow."

Ike says, "There's nothing else to do until we reach St. Pierre. Please humor an old man."

Devon doesn't say anything so Ike takes that for an okay. Ike looks at the three of them and announces, "The Air Force jet didn't blow up the Argonaut."

A collective "what?" is heard from Kidd, Barry and Devon. Ike adds, "I thought that would get your attention. The Argonaut exploded just as the pilot pulled the trigger."

Devon jumps up. "Impossible! What makes you so sure about all this?"

Ike says, "I have it on the best authority." Devon insists, "Which means?"

Kidd joins in. "Which means he's sure."

Kidd turns to Ike. "Go on, we're listening."

Ike asks Kidd, "Now, where were you when the Argonaut blew up?"

A pained look comes over Kidd's face. "I was in the water waiting for

Barry to come fish me out."

Ike leans forward to ask Kidd the key question. "What did you see and hear while you were waiting in the water?"

"The Argonaut had just made it over the horizon when I heard a jet. Then I heard an explosion and saw a flash of light. And then…"

Kidd stops, carefully trying to figure out the significance of what he's about to say. "And then I heard another explosion and another flash of light. I assumed it was the fuel tanks going up."

"And what did you do once Barry fished you out?"

Barry answers for him, "We went looking for survivors." Ike says, "Just as I imagined. And what did you find?" Kidd is quick to answer. "We didn't find any survivors.

None."

Ike says, "I didn't ask if you found any survivors, I asked 'what did you find?'"

Barry, not sure where this is going, answers, "We found a blown up boat, some clothes, fuel, a floating bed…"

Kidd adds, "Yeah, that's about it."

Ike takes a long drink of wine and continues, "Are you familiar with Sherlock Holmes?"

Devon's had enough, "Oh, Jesus. Could you get to the fucking point already?"

Ike looks annoyed but his voice is calm as he continues. "In 'The Hound of the Baskervilles,' Holmes found the culprit because the dogs didn't bark. Here we have a similar situation. From your description, you didn't find any body parts in the water did you?"

Barry thinks for a second before answering, "Now that you mention it, no."

Ike says, "I have every reason to believe that once Dalakos realized that PACT knew his whereabouts, he immediately evacuated the Argonaut. And, as usual, he was right to do it."

Kidd asks, "Evacuated how? Why didn't we see the lifeboats?" Ike says, "There were no lifeboats. The Argonaut carried two minisubs. They took off underwater."

Devon's voice is a combination of hope and disbelief. "You mean to tell me that you think my wife and daughter and Kidd's parents are alive?"

Ike quickly answers. "That I don't know. But, I do know that at the moment the Argonaut blew up they were in the mini-subs probably headed back to St. Pierre."

Devon is almost speaking to himself. "Mini-subs. Yes, mini-subs. Sure, why not? That's why we lost the homing signal!"

Barry is excited. "And when the subs resurface, we'll get our signal back!"

Kidd says, "And that explains how the computer got to Dalakos' boat without us catching the signal. He probably sent a mini-sub to come pick it up!"

They fill Ike in on the homing signal just as the fishing boat noticeably slows. They can see the island of St. Pierre in the distance.

Devon lifts his glass and shouts, "We're back in the hunt!" The others immediately lift their glasses. Kidd lifts his so high he loses half of the wine in it. He shouts, "We're back in the hunt!"

The four of them shout, "We're back in the hunt!"

11

SABRINA ROSE surveys the situation from her cramped seat. He seems to be in a good mood for a man who had to abandon ship like the rat he is.

She looks to her left and sees Dimitra looking right back at her. At least on that ship, I didn't have to put up with her staring daggers through me. She wouldn't be unhappy to see me dead, that's for sure. Guess I could say the same about her, too.

Sabrina Rose smiles sweetly at Dimitra. No way I'm going to show her that I'm afraid. Her smile wipes away when she looks at her mother. Monique is passed out on the seat next to Dalakos. She had fainted when she thought Sabrina Rose had been thrown overboard and then fainted again when she saw she was alive.

But, Monique isn't passed out. Her eyes are closed but her mind is working overtime. That man. That man who said he was Kidd Black. Could it be?

Could it really be him? I guess it really doesn't matter now. He went overboard to save Sabrina Rose. Christopher had told me that his throwing the doll overboard was a ruse to save her from that man. But, "that man" was someone who without a moment's hesitation gave his life to save, so he thought, my daughter!

And that man who said he was Kidd's father—If he really was Kidd's father then that must mean that was Kidd! But, how could that have been Kidd's father on the boat? I had met him before. Years ago. It makes sense that that's what he looks like now…unless I was dreaming. Well, I'm not dreaming now, that I know!

Monique moans painfully. Dalakos puts a hand on her thigh and says, "Are you okay, my darling?"

Monique flinches. Just the thought of him touching her disgusts her. Those screams, those screams that cost the man who said he was Kidd Black his life, those were really my daughter's screams. How could I have been so stupid, so blind?

At least I have the answer to that question. Sabrina Rose told me about the "orange juice".

She's tempted to slap Dalakos when she thinks of the way she was drugged but instead takes all her energy and forces herself to open her eyes. She smiles sleepily at Dalakos and says, "I'm okay. I'm with you. That's all that counts."

Dalakos nods his head, not the least bit surprised, thinking, Once a woman has loved Christopher Dalakos, she's hooked. There's no escape, ever. I think the medical term is Dalakositis.

He laughs to himself. Dalakositis. That's very funny.

Dalakos takes his hand off of Monique's thigh and instinctively puts it on the computer. He didn't like the idea of taking it out of its waterproof casing, but there's only so much room on a mini-sub.

Monique knows they're not going to be in this mini-sub forever. And when they get out, she's going to find a way for her and Sabrina Rose to escape. And if the only way to escape is to kill Dalakos and that witch, Dimitra...she asks herself if she could do it.

Monique thinks long and hard and realizes that she could. Yes, she certainly, definitely could. With that comforting thought going through her head, she falls asleep.

12

IN THE OTHER mini-sub, Nadine and Lawrence haven't had a chance to speak to each other. The boat was evacuated in an instant. They were thrown into a mini-submarine and ordered not to speak. And just to make sure they don't, there's a burly crewman sitting between them.

Nadine and Lawrence are lost in their own thoughts with a lot to digest. And they're both thinking the same thing. Their son is alive…if somehow he survived that jump into the cold ocean. But, someone wouldn't just jump into the middle of the ocean without some kind of backup plan, would they?

They comfort themselves by coming to the same conclusion...Impossible that he didn't have some kind of plan when he jumped into the ocean!"

When you're a parent, you try and imagine what your children will look like when they're adults.

Kidd disappeared when he was nineteen. Now almost twenty years later, they see him again. It's like one day they were imagining what he would look like, what he was up to and poof! He was there in front of them.

They're beginning to believe anything is possible. And, they're also beginning to believe that their son can survive anything. Now, if they can just do the same, one day they'll be all back together.

13

DEVON IS ENERGIZED. He's convinced that Monique and Sabrina Rose are still alive. He was surprised to realize how decimated he was to think that Monique was dead. This time he's going to get them back. To lose them a second time would be unthinkable. And, if they're alive, Kidd's parents are alive too.

Kidd is pumped up. It's not very often that life gives you a second chance. He knows it's not life that's giving him this chance, but Ike. He's never been more impressed with him than he is now.

Barry originally felt he was just along for the ride. But, now, he's ready to do anything and everything to save Monique, Sabrina Rose and Kidd's parents...and to stop Dalakos.

Ike is worried. He knows at some point he's going to have to convince Amanda to put the full force of PACT on their side. If not, all this work could be for nothing.

Devon is back at his computer and the other three men are looking over his shoulder. Devon's heart sinks. "There's no signal from the homing device."

Barry looks at Ike and tries to hide the disappointment in his voice. "Which means that your theory might be just that, a theory."

Kidd doesn't sound worried. "Or, it might mean that the subs are laying low, waiting for the right moment. Or waiting for a boat or a plane to come get them."

Ike sounds confident. "If what I said is correct, there should have been some signal from the homing device after you lost contact with it."

Barry's excited. "Right. When they brought the computer from the Argonaut onto the mini-sub, the signal should have come back."

Devon clicks away and then shouts, "Bingo! The signal WAS back...for eighteen minutes."

Kidd peers down at the screen and says, "When I was lying in the water waiting for Barry to come fish me out."

Ike adds, "Eighteen minutes. Long enough to get off the Argonaut and onto a mini-sub."

Devon looks embarrassed. "When I was handling communications for you. I never even thought of watching for a signal from the computer. What an idiot!"

Barry laughs and says, "That's the first time I've ever heard anyone call Devon Williams an idiot."

Devon smiles and says, "Well, let's hope it's the last." Barry asks, "So, now what?"

Kidd, Devon and Ike all speak at the same time. Barry says, "Hey, glad you've all got ideas, but how about one at a time?"

Ike goes first. "We get ready to leave on a moment's notice. The moment being when we get that signal back. Devon, you order us a private plane and have it waiting at the airport. Barry, rent, buy or steal the fastest ocean-going boat around here."

Kidd is quick to add, "And we split up. Devon stays here at command central. There are only so many places on these islands for a plane to land or for a boat to dock."

Barry says, "And if they rendezvous with a sea plane or a boat already at sea?"

Kidd's thrilled to be back in the hunt. "Then it's PLAN B. We high-tail it to the airport and get our asses after them."

Ike says, "I'll get in touch with Caroline Crimmins at PACT. She'll be our eyes and ears on any and all traffic coming into these islands. We can count on her."

Like a college football team before the big game, the four of them put their hands together, and shout their own particular version of "Let's Go!"

Three of them are laughing. Ike is thinking about that phone call to Amanda.

14

A PREFECT IS THE French equivalent of Sheriff and Mayor all rolled into one. Being the Prefect of St. Pierre and Miquelon wasn't the first choice of anyone. But, Jacques Dinet was a man who knew how to roll with the punches.

When he learned he was going to be posted there, he decided to make the best of it. He became known as a man who knew how to get things done. And the way things got done was to make sure the wheels had a lot of grease and if some of that grease went his way, well, that's just the way things worked out.

He was a well-respected man in the community. He was able to keep services running smoothly here even after the cod fishing quotas put nearly everyone on unemployment. He didn't really consider himself corrupt. A corrupt Prefect accepts a lot more than he could ever need.

But, that all changed when the "Foreigner" came to the islands. He didn't know his name and didn't really want to know it. He referred to himself as Mr. D., but to Jacques Dinet he would always be the "Foreigner."

The Prefect didn't see anything wrong in doing some favors for the "Foreigner." The island had a long tradition of smuggling. Joe Kennedy himself had used St. Pierre as a floating booze warehouse in the '20s.

Kennedy made his fortune as a bootlegger and when they got around to legalizing alcohol he became a very respectable man. The "Foreigner" is probably moving some drugs. And they're going to make that legal some day and then the gravy train will come to a sudden halt. No, he decided, the time to cash in was now. The "Foreigner" was really a Godsend.

So, when the "Foreigner" wanted a zoning waiver to build an underground berth for his submarines over on Miquelon Island, he arranged it. It was supposed to be for an underwater tourist park which he'll believe when he sees the first tourist. When the "Foreigner" wanted his comings and goings off the record, he arranged it. And now, he apparently has another request.

When his secretary announces his visitor, he straightens his tie and glances in the mirror. He nods to himself as if saying, You're doing the right thing. You're doing the right thing.

He opens the door and is surprised that the "Foreigner" isn't there. But, he's certainly not disappointed. There's a twenty-something young woman, holding a black briefcase and dressed for success in black heels, he always notices the heels, and an understated black dress with discreet white pearls. But all the understatement in the world can't hide the fact that she's got nice tits. Very nice tits indeed.

Before he can say a word, she says in impeccable but accented English, "I'm terribly sorry but my boss can't make it. He asked me to come in his place, if you don't mind."

The Prefect maintains an even tone to his voice and says, "No, of course not. Please come in."

He holds the door open for her and as she walks into his office he smells her perfume and glances at her ass. No, he's not disappointed at all that the "Foreigner" couldn't make it.

Dimitra sits down and Jacques offers her a drink. She smiles and accepts. He pours her a glass of wine. She smiles again and says, "I like the way the French do business."

Jacques feigns a serious look and says, "Ah, yes, business. How can I be of service?"

"My boss has a special request. A very special request." Jacques smiles. A "special request" will mean a special amount of money and the "Foreigner" is nothing but generous.

He says, "I'm all ears."

Dimitra opens her briefcase, pulls out a folder and says. "As I'm sure you know there is an Air France flight from here to Paris twice a week."

"Yes, every Tuesday and Friday." Jacques is thinking, This is going to be a piece of cake. First class is probably sold out and he wants a few tickets.

Dimitra continues, "And, of course, there is always one plane at the airport as a back-up in case of any unexpected events."

Jacques, a little surprised that she is aware of that, says a little bit hesitantly, "That's right."

Dimitra looks him in the eyes and says, "He'd like you to arrange for sixteen passengers to fly to Paris tonight at three o'clock in the morning."

Jacques nearly spits out his wine. He stalls for time. "I, I, I don't know how I could do that. I'd have to arrange for a crew. I'd have to notify Paris and there'd be a lot of questions. A lot of questions."

Dimitra patiently waits for him to stop babbling and says, "Will this help you change your mind?"

She opens the briefcase and it's packed with one hundred dollar bills. "All used. The serial numbers aren't consecutive."

Jacques grimaces and says, "My superiors in Paris would frown upon me sending a plane with sixteen people there without a good reason. I'd love to change my mind but I don't see how I could spend the money in prison."

Dimitra was tempted to say, "You can't spend the money when you're dead either," but Dalakos had said that he was only to be threatened physically as a last resort. And, even then, it wasn't sure that threatening him would work. After all, he didn't know that the Foreigner was in real life, Christopher Dalakos, world famous terrorist.

Dimitra was really hoping the money would be enough to persuade him. Dimitra puts down the briefcase but doesn't close it. She uncrosses her legs and then crosses them again. "You drive a hard bargain and I'm glad you do. My client has authorized me to offer you a special incentive."

"And what's that?"

Dimitra looks him in the eyes and says, "Me."

Jacques makes an immediate decision. He stands up, walks to the door and locks it. He undoes his tie and says to himself, Sixteen people on a three AM flight to Paris? I'll think of something.

15

DEVON IS GLUED to his computer and Kidd and Ike are huddled over a map of the islands. Kidd says, "It's not so easy. Look at this. The airport is on the island of Miquelon and the harbor is on St. Pierre."

Ike shakes his head. "We don't have a lot of choice. We'll have to split up. Two of us at the airport and the others cover the harbor."

Kidd says, "It'll take half an hour with a break to get from one to the other. That's half an hour to hold them from leaving. Not easy."

Ike is agitated. "But, even at full strength we're only four!"

Kidd asks, "Is there any way to get the French authorities in on this?"

Devon's still glued to the computer but says, "I wouldn't risk it. We don't know these people and for all we know, they're friends of Dalakos."

Ike calms down. "I have to agree with Devon. We stick with the plan. We split up and the moment we get the signal from the homing device, we get all our firepower together. That's the only way I see it."

Kidd says, "The only thing we have going for us is that they don't know about the homing device."

Devon says, "What are you talking about 'the only thing we have going for us?' We've got Kidd Black!"

Kidd smiles wearily and Ike pats him on the back. Kidd says to himself, They think I'm Superman. How to God I wish I was.

Barry comes in with an excited look on his face and announces, "Good news. I found the fastest ocean-going boat on the island. Everyone I asked said that was the one to get hold of."

Devon doesn't look up from the computer but mumbles, "Good." Ike and Kidd, still huddled over the map, don't say anything. Barry says in a louder voice, "The bad news is that it's been rented. The crew has to be ready to ship out at three o'clock this morning! It's booked for two weeks."

That gets everyone's attention. Kidd and Ike turn their chairs toward Barry. Even Devon looks up from his computer.

Ike says, "Now, that's some interesting news."

Barry smirks. "Interesting? This is our big break! Let's take over the boat, hold the crew and wait for Dalakos to show up. Easy as pie."

Kidd says, "Since when have you turned into James Bond? There are a lot more of them than there are of us."

Barry says, "You got a better idea?"

Kidd says, "Yeah, first we try to buy our way onto the boat and if that doesn't work we'll go the James Bond routine."

Barry nods his head and says, "Sounds like you've got a better idea."

16

THERE'S NEVER A SOUND in the harbor on St. Pierre at two o'clock in the morning. Never that is, unless there's money to be made. Kidd, Barry and Ike watch from a distance as the ocean-going vessel, La Nouvelle Espoire, bustles with activity. There is a crew of six. Six sailors, bodies forged by the sea, tough, no-nonsense men who know what it means to work for a living.

Ike moves around the corner and talks into a microphone hidden in his jacket. "Can you hear me?"

Kidd answers, "All clear and good luck."

Ike comes out of the darkness and walks purposefully along the dock towards the boat.

Kidd says to Barry, "If Ike can't close the deal, I don't want to fight these guys. I don't really have the stomach for it. Anything could happen, like us losing or us winning which means these innocent guys get hurt. Sorry, Mr. Bond, you'll have to save your fighting for another day. If we can't have the boat, we'll wait for Dalakos right here and intercept them before they get on."

Barry asks, "And if they don't come walking across the dock? If they come by submarine?

Kidd quickly replies. "Then we have no choice."

The crew sees Ike coming and looks at him, not suspiciously and not threateningly but curiously. When they see that he's walking directly towards them, all work stops.

The man who appears to be the Captain comes forward so that Ike can't get all the way to the boat. Back in the darkness, Barry and Kidd listen in from the signal sent by Ike's hidden microphone. Just in case they're needed at a moment's notice.

Ike says, "Good evening, do you speak English?"

The Captain says, "I speak English. It's a little late to be out for a walk, non?"

"Actually, I'm in desperate need of a boat. I saw you and your crew and I've come to see if it's available."

"I'm sorry, it's already rented.

Ike feigns a surprised look. "I don't think you understood me. I don't want to rent your boat, I want to buy it."

The man looks surprised, really surprised. "I'm sorry but I'm not used to strangers coming by at two o'clock in the morning to buy my boat."

"I'll pay in cash. Right now. Name your price."

The Captain calls to the crew and shouts in French, "Hey guys, this old man wants to buy my boat. Right now. In cash."

The crew comes over and gathers around. Ike starts again, "Like I said, just name your price."

The Captain says to the crew, "What a day. A woman comes by and rents the boat for five thousand Euros a day and now this! But she was certainly better looking and she had the cash on hand!"

Ike patiently waits for an answer.

The Captain says to the crew, "How much should I ask for?" One yells out, "Five hundred thousand!" The crew is now having a great time. They know the boat is worth about eighty thousand dollars, if you could find a buyer that is, and around here boats just aren't selling.

Another one yells out, "A million!" The men are now rolling with laughter and the consensus is that a million is the price.

The Captain says, "A million and the boat is yours, mon ami." Ike asks, "Would that be dollars or Euros?"

The Captain says, "I am not a greedy man. Dollars will be fine."

At that, the men howl with even more laughter.

Ike puts out his hand and takes the Captain's. He says, "A million it is."

The Captain says, "Now, when you show up with the cash, the boat is yours. In the meantime, I have a ship to prepare."

At that moment, Kidd and Barry come out of the darkness and walk along the dock. Kidd is carrying a suitcase with him.

The crew turns to face them.

Ike says, "Gentlemen, I suggest that we get on board my ship. I'd prefer to count the money in private."

17

IT'S SOMETHING RIGHT out of a bad dream. Sabrina Rose is roughly awakened to see a woman she doesn't know standing over her. The woman is saying something in a foreign language that she doesn't understand. Sabrina Rose calls out to her mother but there's no answer. She looks around her room and her mother is nowhere in sight.

And, worst of all, it's not a dream. When her eyes clear, she sees that the woman is none other than Dimitra and her "room" is the mini-sub.

As she feared, her mother is nowhere in sight. Dimitra is motioning for her to get up.

Sabrina Rose says, "I have to go to the bathroom."

She can see that Dimitra doesn't understand. Sabrina Rose mimics going to the toilet. Dimitra motions for her to get up. Sabrina Rose gets up and says, "One way or the other, I have to go to the bathroom."

Sabrina Rose follows Dimitra up the stairs to a dock. It's still night. Dimitra pushes her towards a portable toilet and Sabrina Rose goes in.

She's so happy to pee she hardly notices the pungent odor inside. When she comes out, Dimitra motions for her to follow. Sabrina Rose follows and when they get to the road she sees an ambulance. Sabrina Rose gets in and her living nightmare gets a lot worse. Her mother is lying motionless in the back of the ambulance with intravenous tubes coming out of her everywhere.

Sabrina Rose screams and Dimitra slaps her. For the first time in her life, Sabrina Rose hears Dimitra speak English as she growls, "Shut the fuck up!"

18

THE CREW STANDS over the Captain with wide-eyed amazement as he counts out the money. Ike sits across from him at the table. Kidd and Barry stand behind Ike. Everything is very relaxed, everyone is in a good mood. The Captain has promised to share his good-fortune with his long-time crew.

The Captain finally stops counting and says, "It's all there. One million dollars." And then just to hear himself say it again he repeats, "One million dollars."

The Captain says to Ike, "You'll have all the necessary papers first thing in the morning."

Ike, Barry and Kidd all are sure that they won't be on the island first thing in the morning but this certainly isn't the time to mention that.

Ike says, "That will be fine. Now, what can you tell me about this woman who rented your boat?"

The Captain says, "A woman one doesn't easily forget. Around twenty-five, black hair, black eyes..."

One of the crew members adds, "And world-class tits!" The rest of the crew nod in worshipful agreement.

Ike says, "And you have no way to reach her."

The Captain says, "How I wish I could. Now that I'm a rich man, I'd love to show her around my beautiful island, if you know what I mean."

The crew once again laughs.

Ike glances at his watch and thinks, It's two in the morning. Dalakos and his entourage should be arriving in the next hour. He stands and says, "It's been a pleasure doing business with you."

The Captain stands, shakes hands with Ike and smiles. "The pleasure is all ours. All ours."

He then looks at the money, then at his crew, then once again at the money and whispers, "All ours."

The Captain takes the money in one hand and with the other shakes hands with Barry and Kidd. The crew shakes hands with all of them too. Finally, they all leave the boat.

The moment they're off the boat, Kidd calls Devon. Kidd asks, "Any signal at all?"

When Devon tells him, negative, Kidd says, "I sure the hell hope they show up. Otherwise we just spent a million of your dollars for nothing."

19

DALAKOS COMES OUT from his underwater bunker carrying the computer. Next to him are two tough-looking men dressed in ambulance driver uniforms. One of the men gets in the driver's seat and the other gets in the back next to Monique. Dalakos gets in next to Dimitra and Sabrina Rose.

He says to Sabrina Rose, "Your mother is fine, don't worry. But, if you make any kind of scene at the airport, she won't be fine any longer. And the moment she isn't fine, you can be sure that it won't be good news for you either. Do we understand each other?"

Sabrina Rose nods her head yes. Dalakos quietly says, "I can't hear you."

Sabrina Rose finds him the most frightening when he speaks quietly. She answers, "Yes, I understand."

Dalakos smiles and says, "That's good." He then signals to the driver to get going.

20

DEVON STARES AT HIS screen willing the program to come to life. Finally, finally, the long-awaited beep sounds. He thanks God that he has the signal and he prays to God that his wife and daughter are alive.

He pinpoints the signal coming from over on the island of St. Miquelon. He immediately calls Kidd.

"We've got a signal! It's on St. Miquelon and it's heading your way."

Kidd shouts over to Ike and Barry, "Good news! Devon has a signal and they're headed our way." He then says to Devon, "I'll put on the speaker, stay on the line."

Devon says, "They're coming along the coastal road towards the bridge." His voice suddenly changes from excitement to what can only be described as panic. "They're going past the bridge. They're not taking the bridge!"

Barry shouts into the speaker, "Maybe they're taking another bridge."

Devon shouts back, "There's only one bridge. Only one fucking bridge! They've got to be heading for the airport! They're heading for the airport!"

Kidd says, "It'll take us at least an hour to get there!" Devon says, "I can be there in fifteen minutes. Get there as fast as you can!"

Devon grabs the laptop and is out the door. He rushes down the stairs to the street and jumps into his car. He starts it up, glances once more at his screen, sees that they're still heading for the airport and takes off through the deserted streets of St. Pierre.

Devon runs the only red light he sees and is across the city in five minutes. He hits the coastal road where he sees a sign that says the bridge is only five kilometers away. He'll be at the bridge in three minutes. Two and a half minutes later, Devon is forced to jam on the brakes.

The drawbridge is up! A sign reads:

Horaires d'ouverture 6h-22h. En cas d'urgence sonnez ici.

Devon translates with his high school French. The bridge is closed until six in the morning. In case of emergency ring here.

Devon thinks, Who the hell closes a bridge at night? He starts leaning on the buzzer like there's no tomorrow and knows that if he doesn't get across that bridge soon, he just might be right.

21

THE AMBULANCE PULLS up to the small airport. As Dimitra had arranged, the plane is waiting and is ready to take off. Sabrina Rose gets out and sees the entire crew of the Argonaut. Some of them she recognizes and some she doesn't. One of the ones she doesn't recognize is The Chameleon. And they're certainly not there to say goodbye. They're coming on the plane with them.

And standing with them is Mr. Black, the old man who came to their cabin on the boat. Next to him is the black woman who carried her to the doctor's office. She said she was a doctor too. Well, it's gotta be good news that they're coming. They're on our side. I'm sure of that!

Lawrence and Nadine make eye contact with Sabrina Rose and smile at her. Sabrina Rose smiles back but there's no chance of talking to them. The crew of the Argonaut is between her and them.

Monique is wheeled out and a uniformed French policeman comes out and asks, "Can I be of some assistance?"

Dalakos says, "Yes, could you help her through security?" The policeman says, "Yes, of course." He motions to the man next to Monique to follow him.

Dalakos looks at Dimitra and nods his head in approval. Dimitra is proud that she had thought of everything. She had insisted that they go through security before boarding the plane in order to erase any doubts from the Prefect's mind about their flight. Of course, the Prefect was thinking mostly about seeing her out of her dress, but later, she didn't want him to have any regrets. As far as her part of the deal, she was sure he had no regrets. She smiles to herself at the thought. Older men are just so appreciative.

22

FINALLY A LIGHT comes on in the bridge master's house. What seemed like an eternity was in reality only five minutes. Only. When every second counts, five minutes is a lot. In what seems like another eternity, the door opens and a sleepy middle-aged woman dressed in a nightgown comes to the door. "Oui?"

"The bridge, the bridge. I have to cross the bridge!" Without saying a word, she turns to the stairs and shouts something in French that he doesn't catch. A moment later, a paunchy middle-aged man, even sleepier than his wife, comes slowly ambling down the stairs.

Devon shouts to him, "The bridge! Please, I have to cross the bridge!"

The man groggily asks, "Why?"

Devon hesitates for a split second. He never imagined that he'd have to say why. Finally, he screams at the bridge master, "My wife! My wife is having a baby!"

The woman's eyes light up and the man smiles at him and says. "Of course. Of course. I'll get the bridge down immediately."

23

SABRINA ROSE follows listlessly behind Dalakos as they pass through security. She wonders what would happen if she started screaming out that they've drugged her mother and kidnapped them. But, it's clear to her that everyone except for the old couple is here with Dalakos and even if they weren't most of them wouldn't understand what she said anyway.

She smiles weakly. She knows once she gets on that plane nothing good can happen to her or her mother.

As she goes through the metal detector, the security technician, a rather plump middle-aged woman who seems very happy to be of service, says, "Don't worry. You'll be in Paris in no time and then your mother will have the best medical care in the world."

Sabrina Rose begins to cough and holds her stomach. "A toilet. I feel sick. I need a toilet."

Dimitra suddenly becomes very talkative. She firmly says, "There's a toilet on the plane."

Sabrina Rose coughs even more and grabs her stomach. She looks plaintively at the friendly-looking technician and says, "Please, a toilet! A toilet! It's an emergency."

Before Dimitra can say anything, Nadine comes out of nowhere and takes Sabrina Rose gently by the hand and announces, "I'll take her to the toilet. Don't leave without us!"

Nadine rushes her to the toilet.

24

DEVON STANDS WITH the bridge master next to the mechanism that lowers the drawbridge. He loudly asks, "What are we waiting for?"

The bridge master says, "I remember when we had our first child. I was a nervous wreck. Just like you."

Devon makes a huge effort not to throttle the man and tries again, "What are we waiting for?"

"For the signal from my wife. She's letting all maritime traffic in the area know that the bridge is coming down."

Devon looks around and says, "There's nothing in sight!" "Don't worry, she'll be done in a minute." As if on cue, she comes out to them and says, "It's all clear."

The bridge master immediately presses the button to set the mechanism in motion.

The woman smiles at Devon and says, "Is this your first child?"

Devon, exasperated says, "Uh, no. We already have a daughter. We're hoping for a son."

He turns to the bridge master and asks, "Can't you make it go any faster? I'll pay you for any damage! Cash!"

The harbor master laughs. "All the money in the world can't make this go faster. It will be down when it is down."

Devon asks, "How long will it take?" "Twenty-two minutes. Not a moment less."

Devon tries to remain calm. He gets on the phone to Kidd. "I'm stuck here waiting for the drawbridge! I won't be there for half an hour!"

Kidd says, "We're on our way!"

Devon asks incredulously, "On your way? You'll be too late! Too late!"

Kidd says, "We're coming by boat. We should get to the airport about the same time you do."

Devon says, "Don't come by the bridge. They're lowering it as we speak! Keep me posted. I have to make another call."

Devon gets off the phone and runs back to ask the bridge master, "What's the number for the police?"

"Seventeen."

Devon says thanks and steps outside. He dials seventeen and waits more than two minutes for someone to answer. When they do, he says, "My name is Devon Williams and I'm calling to tell you that there's a bomb on that plane getting ready to leave!"

"What plane are you talking about?"

Devon tries again, "There's a plane leaving St. Miquelon airport very soon. There's a bomb on it. You have to stop that plane from taking off!"

The voice audibly sighs and says, "You must be drunk," and the line goes dead.

25

SABRINA ROSE walks into the stall and locks the door. She figures as long as she's there, she might as well pee. As she's peeing, she's trying to figure out a way to not get on that plane.

She hears Nadine's voice. "We've got to keep you off that plane. Once we come out of here, pretend you're very ill. I'll explain to them that I'm a doctor and we'll rush you to the hospital. Can you do that?"

Sabrina Rose answers, "What about my mother? I can't just leave her here."

"One thing at a time. I don't want to leave my husband here but it won't do us any good to all get on that plane! Are you with me on this?"

Before Sabrina Rose can answer, the bathroom door flies open. She hears a commotion and then a muffled voice or voices, she can't tell.

The she smells a very particular odor similar to the hydrogen peroxide her mother used to put on her cuts in what seems like a previous lifetime.

Sabrina Rose nervously asks, "Are you still there?"

No answer.

She sees a pair of black high heel shoes before she hears a voice. But, she knows that it's Dimitra who whispers in a very threatening tone, "You see this?"

A cloth is thrown over the stall. It has the same particular odor she had just smelled.

Dimitra continues, "If I have to, I'm going to knock you out with this, too. Then you're really going to be sick. So, it's your choice. I'll count to ten and then I'm kicking this door in and taking you out!"

Sabrina Rose doesn't even wait for her to reach one. She flushes the toilet and says, "I'll be right there."

26

WITH IKE AT THE HELM, Barry and Kidd have nothing much to do. Kidd says, "The airport is at the far side of St. Miquelon.

We have to go the long way around. Devon's getting them to lower the drawbridge."

Barry says, "And when we get to the airport? What then?" Kidd says, "You and I get on that runway and find a way to stop that plane."

Barry says, "And what if everyone at the airport is in on it?"

Ike's voice gets loud. "This is not Microtech we're dealing with. They're not a world-wide corporation. Dalakos and his thugs are just that, a bunch of thugs! A small band of little thugs!"

Barry mumbles, "Yeah, sure," but he doesn't believe it and sees no advantage in arguing about it.

Kidd says, "First we stop that plane and then we can worry about convincing them who we are and who Dalakos is."

27

DEVON WATCHES AS the bridge is nearly lowered. He's very tempted to drive his car up one side and come down the other. He's seen it a million times in films. But, he's not so out of control as to actually do it. It would save him a couple of minutes but could cost him any chance of getting to that airport if he misses.

He gets in his car and revs the motor. The bridge master's wife says, "This is so exciting! What are you going to name the baby?"

Devon says, "If it's a girl, Monique. If it's a boy, Kidd." The woman looks distastefully at Devon and says, "Kidd? What kind of name is Kidd?"

Devon answers, "Good question."

A bell sounds and before their conversation can go any further, he's racing across the bridge. He follows the sign towards the airport and speeds off down the road.

28

LIKE A ZOMBIE, Sabrina Rose walks up the stairs towards the plane. She feels like she's being made to walk the plank on a pirate ship. The stewardess welcomes her and Sabrina Rose doesn't even bother to try and smile back.

As she enters the plane, the stewardess makes eye contact with Dimitra as if to say, "That poor girl."

Dimitra says, "We have every reason to hope that her mother will be okay."

The stewardess smiles and says, "There's certainly no shortage of seats. Sit wherever you like."

Sabrina Rose says, "I'll sit back by my mother." The stewardess says, "Yes, of course."

Sabrina Rose walks past Dalakos and his crew, through first class and into business class where her mother lies, still knocked out. She can see the black woman and Mr. Black through the curtain in economy class. The black woman looks like she's asleep.

Sabrina Rose plunks herself down on the aisle seat and takes her mother's hand. Dimitra is taking no chances. She takes the seat behind Sabrina Rose, smiling at her sweetly as she walks past.

29

THERE'S NOTHING KIDD hates more than attacking without proper intelligence. All they know about the airport is what they remember when they landed there. It's on a peninsula on the western side of the island. No one remembers if there was a fence, electronic or otherwise.

He doesn't even know how deep the water is where they're going to arrive. He imagines though, or likes to think, that there's not much in the way of guards considering that it must be an unscheduled flight in the middle of the night.

Ike slows the boat down and they can clearly see a passenger jet on the tarmac.

Ike announces, "Okay, guys. Here's where it gets interesting. I'm taking us in as far as we can go. Once we're grounded, you're off. Brace yourself and good luck."

They nod back at Ike as he heads the boat right for shore. Kidd and Barry lie face down on the deck of the boat and wait. There's an excruciating screech as the bow smashes into the rocky shore and comes to a crashing halt.

Kidd and Barry climb off the side of the boat and let themselves slowly down into the sea. They find their footing along the rocks and work their way to shore. They immediately come to a high fence topped with barbed wire. Kidd studies it to see if its electric, sees that it isn't and takes out his wire cutters.

Barry says, "Don't bother." He points to a hole in the fence big enough for the two of them to crawl through.

Kidd says, "I guess you can't blame 'em. Who would ever attack the St. Miquelon airport?"

They climb through and get oriented. They're about a half a mile from the plane. It's a straight line. A sprint.

30

THE AIR FRANCE copilot goes through the routine of getting the plane ready for takeoff. He and the pilot weren't that surprised that they got the call to go to Paris on a moment's notice. After all, they've been around long enough to have flown Ministers' mistresses to different parties around the world and once even had a case of champagne as their only passenger. What did surprise them was the time. Three o'clock in the morning. But, when they heard it was for a medical emergency, they were more than happy to do it.

The copilot gets on the microphone and goes through the safety procedures. He hands it over to the pilot who welcomes everyone aboard. They get clearance from the control tower, taxi down the runway and then prepare to turn into the wind.

The control tower announces, "Hold on a second. It seems that we have two men running towards you on the runway. Now, I've seen everything. Keep your motors idling. I'm sending the cops out to take care of it."

The plane comes to an abrupt halt. The pilot announces, "I'm sorry everyone. We have a slight delay due to, uh, two guys running down the runway towards us."

Both pilots chuckle.

Dalakos gets up, goes to the business class section and motions to Dimitra. She comes forward to the first class section and sits next to Dalakos. He doesn't need to say anything to her. She heard the pilot's announcement. They look out the window and see the flashing lights of a police car speeding down the runway.

Kidd and Barry also see the police car's lights. They don't slow down but keep running toward the plane. The police car blocks their way.

One policeman gets out of the car while the other one stays inside. The one outside shouts to them in French and gestures to them not to move. With his gun pointed at them, he's very persuasive.

Kidd and Barry raise their hands and Barry shouts, "We don't speak French! No parlez-vous français!"

The cop says, "Ne bougez pas!"

Kidd says to Barry, "The guy doesn't speak English! No way to convince him to stop that plane. Guess it's PLAN B."

Barry whispers, "No one said anything about a PLAN B!"

Kidd pretends he's drunk. He staggers and everyone knows what drunks do. Apparently, they cheer! He starts chanting and acting out their high school fight cheer.

"Lean to the left, lean to the right, stand up sit down, fight fight fight!"

As everyone who ever went to William Nottingham High School knows, when you shout "fight fight fight!" you punch the air each time you shout "fight."

Barry joins in and the cops watch with a bemused expression as Kidd and Barry cheer. The cop in the car tells the control tower that there are two drunk men on the runway and that they'll get them off as fast as they can.

The control tower notifies the plane that as soon as the drunks are off the runway, they're cleared for take-off. The pilot then notifies the passengers of the situation. The copilot's laughter can be heard as the pilot signs off.

Out on the runway, the cops move closer to Barry and Kidd to get them off the runway. When they're close enough, Kidd makes his move. Barry watches in amazement as Kidd goes into action. Both cops are incapacitated in a matter of moments.

Kidd and Barry jump into the police car and head for the plane. At that moment, Devon drives right up to the terminal entrance, jumps out of his car and races inside. The two policemen who were supposed to be there are out cold on the tarmac so Devon can run right past the surprised security woman without anyone stopping him.

Devon bursts out on to the tarmac and grabs a tire iron from a baggage truck. He's going to get to that plane and smash the tires before it can take off.

Sabrina Rose looks out the window and sees a man wildly waving a tire iron running towards them. As the man gets closer, Sabrina Rose sees that it's her father! Her father is coming to rescue her. She's thrilled but she's not in the least bit surprised. She always knew deep down inside that he'd find a way to save them!

But, Dalakos sees him coming, too. He nods to Dimitra who reaches under her skirt and pulls out two plastic guns from between her legs. She hands one to Dalakos who then knocks on the cabin door.

The moment the door opens, Dalakos points his gun at the pilot and calmly says, "I'm sorry gentlemen, but it's a matter of life and death that my wife reaches Paris tonight. If she dies, so do I and if I die, so do you. These men out there are trying to kill my wife. I suggest you get this plane moving or one of my men, a trained pilot, will do it over your dead bodies."

The pilot says, "You're a very persuasive man." Dalakos says, "Notify the tower that it's getting too dangerous on the ground. We're taking off! And please be aware that my assistant," he points to Dimitra, who smiles and salutes with her gun, "speaks perfect French."

The pilot tells the tower that it's getting too weird down there and he's taking off.

The tower tells him that he's not cleared. The pilot doesn't respond. Devon's within fifty yards of the plane when the engines come to life. He sprints faster but the plane moves away from him.

Head-on, the police car speeds toward the plane. Dalakos calmly says, "Looks like a classic game of chicken. Gentlemen, I assure you that they'll blink first. Please, continue."

The pilot says, "I can't. I can't"

Dalakos says, "It seems that I'll have to kill you first and then we'll see if your copilot is willing. If not, I promise you, that I'll kill him too."

The pilot and copilot exchange a helpless glance and then put the engines into take-off speed.

Barry and Kidd can hear the engines roar over the sound of their siren. Barry shouts, "You got a PLAN C?"

Kidd guns the motor and the police car speeds towards the plane. Barry braces himself and says, "Not exactly what I had in mind."

The pilots see that the police car is still heading their way. Dalakos puts a pistol to the pilot's head and says, "We're at the point of no return. Even if we wanted to stop now, it's too late."

The pilots tighten their grips on the steering wheel. They know that Dalakos is right.

Kidd too realizes the same thing. He jerks the wheel to the left and the police car swerves away from the plane. The plane hurdles past them and is soon off the ground.

Devon comes running over to Kidd and Barry. "God damn it, we were this close!"

Barry says, "Now we know where they are. We'll get the French to arrest them when they get to Paris and that'll be that."

In the background, sirens can be heard coming in their direction. Kidd takes out his phone. "I got to fill Ike in on what's going on."

The sirens get louder. Ike picks up on the first ring. "Monique, Sabrina Rose and my parents are on that Air France flight with Dalakos. They're headed for Paris. The three of us are on the runway about to be arrested. Get someone to meet that plane! And then, get us out of jail."

Ike says, "Kidd, I was about to call you for help. It appears that the entire French navy is coming my way."

Police cars have now crossed onto the runway and are speeding towards them.

Kidd says, "Okay, how long before they get to you?"

But Ike doesn't answer. Instead, a voice in French says, "Oui, âllo?"

Kidd turns off his phone and asks Devon, "You got any I.D. that says you're Devon Williams?"

Devon instinctively reaches for his pockets and says, "Yeah, sure."

Kidd says, "That's the first good news I've heard all night. Now, if I were you, I suggest you let go of that tire iron."

The police cars surround them and the cops, guns drawn, rush out.

31

NOW THAT THE PLANE IS safely airborne, Dalakos takes a seat in the cockpit and calmly says, "Don't worry, we're not suicide maniacs. We have no intention of crashing this plane into anything and no intention of killing you. If we wanted you dead, it would have been done a long time ago."

The pilot says, "To tell you the truth, the only thing that will make me feel better is landing in Paris."

Dalakos says, "I'm very sorry to disappoint you but we have make a slight detour. I assure you though, that after that, you're free to fly anywhere you like. Without us, naturally."

The copilot says, "Naturally."

Dalakos says, "Please set a course for the Azores. Specifically, the airport on the island of Corvo Flores."

The pilot says, "I'll get on it."

Dalakos signals Dimitra who comes over towards him. He switches to Greek and says, "We'll be landing in an hour. Make sure she's ready to travel."

Without a word, Dimitra reaches up into the overhead bin and takes out a leather bag.

Back in business class, Sabrina Rose has been tightly holding her mother's hand. She leans over and whispers in her ear, "I saw Daddy. I saw Daddy."

Monique squeezes Sabrina Rose's hand. Sabrina Rose says in a louder voice, "I love you, mom." Monique squeezes her hand even harder.

Dimitra walks back into business class and Sabrina Rose squeezes her mother's hand even tighter. The stewardess sits up, afraid of the unexpected.

Dimitra sees the stewardess and curses to herself. Doesn't she have anything to do? I hate having to be nice to that little brat when someone else is around. I don't want to cause any more tension than there is. Tension causes people to crack and people who crack have been known to do very stupid things.

Dimitra forces herself to smile sweetly at the stewardess and says, "I'm sorry to bother you, but the men in first class would like something to drink."

The stewardess slowly gets up and says, "Sure, okay." She walks away thinking, As far as hijacking goes, it could be a lot worse. Plus, they don't seem like the kind of people who will fly this plane into a building, but you never know.

As soon as the stewardess leaves, Dimitra puts her face next to Sabrina Rose's and whispers, "Take your hand away. I have to give your mother a shot."

Dimitra knows she could put the shot into Monique's other arm, but she quite enjoys terrorizing the kid.

Sabrina Rose pleads, "No! You're going to kill her. No!" Dimitra says, "Listen, this shot is to wake her up. We need her alive. As for you, we definitely don't need you alive.

You understand? Take your hand away or I'll cut it off. And you know I'm not kidding."

Sabrina Rose takes her hand away but very slowly. She looks Dimitra in the eye in an effort to show her that she's not afraid of her.

And she no longer is. She knows that her father is on the case. Sooner or later he'll be back and then these people will be very, very sorry. That's one thing she's sure of.

Dimitra takes out some alcohol, rubs it on Monique's arm and puts the needle to her. "She'll be waking up soon. Don't shock her. Just smile when you see her. Got it?"

Sabrina Rose spits out, "Yeah, I got it."

32

THE PILOT TAKES OFF his headphones and says to Dalakos, "There is no airport at Corvo Flores!"

Dalakos calmly answers, "Yes there is. It's just not opened yet. The Grand Opening is next week. We're doing them a favor, trying it out for them ahead of time. It'll be daylight soon. Nothing to worry about."

The pilot shrugs to the copilot and says, "Let's bring it in."

He looks back at Dalakos and says, "You've got everything thought out, haven't you?"

Dalakos says, "Everything? No, not everything. But, I've given a lot of thought to this."

Dalakos shouts out behind him, "Please come up here
'Captain.'"

The Chameleon comes forward without saying a word.

Dalakos gets up and says to the Chameleon, "Captain, take my seat."

The Chameleon takes Dalakos' seat and Dalakos says to the pilot, "I want you to turn off your transponder. And, please, do as you're asked. This man is a trained pilot."

The copilot looks at the pilot who nods. The copilot presses a few buttons with the Chameleon carefully watching him. The Chameleon nods to Dalakos who then goes and takes a seat in first class.

As he sits down, Dalakos says to himself, The Chameleon knows as much about flying planes as I do. But, as long as the pilot and copilot don't know that, they'll do as they're told.

Dalakos sits back in the plush first class seat very satisfied with himself. Now, I've thought of everything.

33

KIDD LOOKS OVER at Devon and Barry. They're bruised but still f unctioning.

The sound of opening doors can be heard. Then footsteps and then some mumbling in French. Then another door opens and a man wearing an expensive suit motions for the guard to open their cell door.

He says, "Please, Mr. Williams, you and your friends, come with me."

Devon stands up and brushes off his clothes. He looks at Barry and Kidd and says, "I guess it pays to be famous."

34

SABRINA ROSE keeps saying the same thing over and over. "I saw Daddy! I saw Daddy! He was running towards the plane with a big stick!"

Monique is now conscious. The shot has done its job. She's still groggy but feeling more awake by the moment.

Monique says, "That's great. That's great," but she doesn't believe for a second that by some miracle her husband appeared out of nowhere "running towards the plane with a big stick."

But, she has bigger things to worry about than the overactive imagination of her daughter. Everything seems like a haze to her. And there's that image of the man who said he was Kidd Black. Was it a dream?

Sabrina Rose sees that her mother is fading away again. She shakes her and says, "If you look behind the curtain, you'll see that man, Mr. Black, who came to our cabin and his wife. They're on our side! The woman tried to help me escape!"

Monique stands up and pretends to lose her balance. She knocks against the curtain separating business from economy forcing it open. She peers back into economy class where she spots Lawrence and Nadine. Nadine looks to be asleep.

Seeing them gives her hope. That has to be Kidd's parents. And, if that's Kidd's parents, it would make perfect sense that that was Kidd. And then why not Devon coming to their rescue too!

Monique feels herself regaining control when the stewardess comes towards them and tells them to get ready to land. Monique asks, "Land where?"

The stewardess says, "I'm sorry. For the first time in my career, I just don't know."

The stewardess makes sure that they've fastened their seat belts and then she takes a seat herself.

Up in the cockpit, the Chameleon watches carefully as the pilot and copilot begin their descent. The landing is a piece of cake. The runway was clear, no wind and the sun was already up. They come to a stop and Dalakos says, "Well done, gentlemen."

Dalakos opens the cabin door and takes a deep breath. "Ah, it's a beautiful day to be alive, don't you think?"

The pilot hesitantly says, "Yes, it is."

For them, this is the most tense moment. If they're going to be killed, it will be soon.

From across the runway, Dalakos spots two of his men pushing a stairwell towards the plane. He shouts to his crew in Greek and they all prepare to exit the plane.

He then walks back to Monique and Sabrina Rose, smiles and says, "Ah, looks like you're feeling much better. Dimitra had to give you something to keep you calm. Your heart rate was way up."

He comes over to her and gives her a warm hug. Monique hugs him tightly but over his shoulder she looks at Sabrina Rose and rolls her eyes. Sabrina Rose would love to laugh but doesn't dare.

Dalakos breaks off the embrace and says, "Let's go. As quickly as possible. I'll explain later."

He ushers them out of their seats towards the open cabin door. The stairwell has reached the plane and Dalakos' crew has gotten off. Dimitra helps Monique down the stairs. The fresh air feels great. Sabrina Rose is next.

Dalakos turns to the pilot and copilot and says, "Gentlemen, I need you to turn over your portable phones."

The pilot and copilot each eye Dalakos warily, reach into their flight bags and hand over their cell phones.

Dalakos thanks them and then says, "Now, if you would just step into first class and make yourselves comfortable."

The pilot and copilot go out into first class and sit down. They are comforted by one fact: Why would he ask them for their cell phones if he was going to kill them?

Dalakos nods to the Chameleon, who proceeds to destroy the radio in the cockpit.

Dalakos thinks, He might not know anything about flying a plane, but he's great at smashing things up.

When the Chameleon is finished, he rasps, "Anything else, Mr. Dalakos?"

Dalakos says, "No, I'll meet you outside."

The Chameleon leaves and the pilots and stewardess look terrified. They now understand that they've been hijacked by Christopher Dalakos. They're as good as dead.

Dalakos turns to the pilots and the stewardess and says, "One of my men will be stationed outside so please don't think about leaving the plane. I'm sure someone from the Portuguese administration will notice your plane on their runway sooner or later. Now, thank you and goodbye."

The pilots and stewardess, fully expecting to be killed look relieved and surprised.

Dalakos adds, "Despite my reputation, I'm not a cold-blooded killer. I'm a business man with political ideas and killing you will neither make me money or further my cause."

With that, he leaves and walks down the stairwell all the time thinking, I want them to tell the world about the genius of Christopher Dalakos and it doesn't hurt once in awhile to do a little public relations.

35

KIDD, DEVON AND BARRY walk into a spacious office and find Ike sitting with a well-dressed man who looks like he's about to be sick.

Ike says, "Gentlemen, this is Jacques Dinet, the Prefect of these islands. Luckily, I used to work with someone who knows someone in the French government who was finally able to convince Mr. Dinet that we are the 'Good Guys' and that the men on that airplane are the 'Bad Guys.' You see, Mr. Dinet was until now, a well-paid employee of one Christopher Dalakos."

Jacques protests and says, "I, I had no idea who he was."

Ike snorts. "You just thought he was your friendly local drug dealer. But, that's not our concern right now. The bottom line is, you're going to do everything in your power to help us."

Jacques stands up. It's clear that he's been sweating and he can't stop moving his hands when he speaks. He says, "As what I'm sure will be one of my final acts as Prefect here, I'm going to order that plane to be met in Paris and everyone on board held in custody. The plane should be arriving in two hours. If there's anything else I can do, just name it."

Kidd explodes, "You actually think that plane will arrive in Paris? What kind of an idiot are you? Have you been tracking it? Send your Air Force to intercept it! Send our Air Force! Just send somebody!"

Mr. Dinet says, "Yes, of course," and picks up the phone. When he hangs up, he says, "Done."

Kidd is clearly worked up. He asks Ike, "Why didn't you tell him this?"

Ike replies, "It took me all this time just to convince this moron to get you guys out of jail! You think that I think there's a snowball's chance in Hell that plane's going to Paris?"

Devon says, "I need my computer back. Right now!" Mr. Dinet says, "Yes, right away."

Another phone call and the computer is immediately brought into the office. Devon grabs it and gets to work.

The phone rings and Jacques answers. He hangs up and in a very weak voice says, "There's no sign of the plane. It was last seen on radar in the middle of the Atlantic three hours ago. We've sent an AWAC team to scour the area."

Devon shouts to him, "Get the hell out of here! We've got work to do."

Jacques Dinet walks quickly out of the room.

Barry says, "What an asshole! I can't believe it!"

Clearly tense, Devon turns on the computer. "Well, they're certainly not dead. Or at least the homing device isn't dead. They left Libya an hour ago and are heading east across Sudan!"

Ike shouts, "They must be headed for Mogadishu!"

Kidd says, "Sudan! That plane didn't have enough fuel to get to Libya let alone Sudan!"

Barry asks, "Maybe they refueled."

Kidd says, "Doesn't make sense They'd have to find a place to land, refuel, take off again. You don't just land a jet that size without anyone noticing."

Devon looks at the log of the homing device. "They landed for ten minutes at an island called Corvo Flores. It's part of the Azores."

Ike says, "You can't refuel a plane in ten minutes." Barry jumps in. "But you can switch planes."

Devon is subdued. He says, "Once they land, they're eventually going to transfer that software to a supercomputer. And then, no more homing signal."

Kidd says, "Ike, one of us has to call Amanda." Ike sighs and says, "I'll do it."

Ike picks up the phone on the Prefect's desk and asks, "Is there a speaker function on this thing?"

Clearly jumpy, he presses some buttons but to no avail. Devon reaches over, pushes a button and the dial tone is heard.

Ike dials the number from memory and they all hear the call go through.

Barry says, "You think she'll answer?"

Kidd says, "She'll answer this number, believe me."

Right on cue, Amanda picks up, with a note of concern in her voice. She knows that if someone is calling on this number, it's an emergency. A real emergency.

"Yes?"

"Amanda, Ike here. I'm with Kidd and Devon."

Her voice immediately softens. "Tell Devon I'm sorry about his family."

Devon grits his teeth and doesn't say anything. He knows she gave the orders to kill Dalakos knowing full well that meant the death of Monique and Sabrina Rose.

Ike says, "I'll tell him. But first..."

Before he can say another word, she says, "And where the hell are you?"

"We're on the island of St. Pierre." "Where on earth is that?"

Ike says, "It's French territory. Off of Nova Scotia." "What the hell are you doing there?"

"Listen, what we're doing here isn't why I'm calling. Christopher Dalakos is on a plane that just crossed Libya into Sudan."

"Christopher Dalakos is dead."

Ike persists, "He's got Devon's computer. We've got a homing device on it, but we might lose contact."

Devon says, "The plane is dropping altitude."

Ike says, "It looks like the plane is going to land in Mogadishu. We need your help to get the three of us in there."

Amanda says, "Listen Ike. I just came back from getting a medal from the President of the United States for my role in killing Dalakos. Now you're asking me to go tell him that I'm sending the three of you to track him down?"

Ike tries again. "Don't tell the President anything. We just want logistics and papers to get into Mogadishu! Is that so much to ask?"

Amanda tries a different track. She softens her voice and asks, "Why don't the three of you come to see me in Washington and we'll talk about it?"

Ike says, "Yeah, sure. Goodbye."

He hangs up and Kidd says, "At least we tried. We had to try."

Devon says, "The plane didn't land in Mogadishu. It's heading across the Red Sea."

Kidd, Barry and Ike rush to the computer and stand over Devon's shoulder.

36

AMANDA IS PISSED OFF...Ike will make up any story to make me look ridiculous. He'll do anything to get his job back. I can't believe he wants me to think that Dalakos is alive. Yeah, right, I'm going to say that to the President!

There's a knock on her door. She regains her composure and says, "Come in."

In walks Caroline, dressed in low heels and an ankle-length beige skirt. She says, "Hi, you wanted to see me?"

Amanda asks her to sit down and then says, "Gee, you look nice."

"Thanks. I'm going to a PTA meeting tonight. You don't think it's too austere?"

Amanda lies and says, "No, as always your taste is just right."

Caroline smiles appreciatively. "Thanks."

Amanda says, "PTA, work, kids and a husband. I don't know how you do it."

"And a dog."

They both laugh.

Amanda says, "I think you'll like what I'm going to tell you. In honor of your good work, not to mention your medal, I'm giving you two weeks off, paid of course."

Caroline asks, "Really? That's great. You're a million times better boss than Ike ever was."

"I'll remember you said that the next time I ask you to work all night."

"Okay, then. I'll finish up today and be back in two weeks." Amanda smiles. "Don't bother. You can take off right now.

I've arranged for someone to cover for you."

Caroline gets up and says, "Okay, then. For once, I'll pick up the kids at school."

Amanda smiles as Caroline leaves. She crosses one more thing off of her mental checklist. Ike's going to contact her to go behind my back. I don't know what he's up to or who he's chasing but it sure has nothing to do with Dalakos. The best way to put a stop to that is to get Caroline out of here as soon as possible.

When Caroline gets back to her office, there's a muscular young man sitting at her desk. She says, "Excuse me, but what are you doing here?"

The man says, "I'm taking over for you for the next two weeks. I'm Rod Clarkson."

"I'm Caroline Crimmins."

Rod says, "You don't have to introduce yourself. Everyone knows who you are."

Caroline is flattered. "Oh. I guess I'll be going."

Her phone rings. Caroline reaches to answer it but Rod is quicker.

He says, "Hello."

There's a long pause and Caroline notices some hesitation in Rod's voice but he finally says, "One moment, who's calling?"

Caroline reaches for the phone and asks, "Who is it?"

Rod says, "He wouldn't say." He raises his eyebrows and with a twinkle in his eyes says, "Very mysterious."

Caroline picks up the phone and says, "Caroline Crimmins." "Hi, it's Ike."

"Hi. What's going on?"

Ike says, "I need another favor. A big one. And I'm sorry but you have to keep Amanda out of this loop."

Caroline sits down in the chair facing Rod and says, "Listen, honey. It's nothing that can't wait until I get home. We'll talk about it then. I'm on my way now...Love you, bye."

Caroline hangs up the phone and shakes her head as she says to Rod, "Husbands."

Rod laughs along with her and Caroline says, "I'll be going. If you need any info, just give me a call."

"Will do."

Caroline gets up and as she does, she bangs her knee against the desk. She falls back down into the chair, groaning with pain.

Rod immediately jumps up and asks, "You all right?"

Caroline blinks her eyes and says, "I'm a little dazed. That really hurt. Could you get me something cold from the machine? It's at the end of the hall."

Rod says, "Yeah, sure. I'll be right back."

The moment Rod leaves Caroline reaches into her purse and pulls out her key chain. It's got a one gigabyte hard disk on it. She never thought she'd ever use it but it was a present from her husband so she always had it with her. She puts it into the USB port of the computer and sits down at her desk. With a couple of clicks, she begins downloading all her access passes to PACT system. Data banks, satellite imaging, electronic eavesdropping, the works.

She stares at the screen willing it to go faster but it'll take another two minutes to finish the download. She hears footsteps coming. She has to delay Rod from going back to the screen and at the same time, stop him from seeing the key chain sticking out of the USB port.

She rushes back to the other side of the computer and puts her back up against it to cover the USB port. Rod walks in carrying a can of coke.

She stands there "in pain." Rod says, "You doing any better? Should I call for help?"

Caroline says, "I think I'll be okay." She pulls her skirt to just above her knee and asks, "How does it look?"

Rod fights the temptation to say "It looks pretty good," and says, "It's not black and blue or anything."

Caroline starts slowly massaging her leg thinking, I've got his attention now, but what am I going to do for another minute and a half?

She reaches out a hand and says, "Thanks for the coke."

He hands it to her and says, "Sure, no problem," and heads for the seat by the computer.

She quickly asks him, "Could you reach in my bag and pull out some hand lotion?"

He stops and reaches for her bag. "Sure."

She's thinking, This'll kill thirty seconds. No man can find anything right away in a woman's bag.

But, he immediately comes up with the lotion. She thinks, Gee, I hope he's not gay.

He hands it to her but she says, "Would you just rub a little bit on my thigh?"

He says, "Uh, it's hand lotion."

Caroline grimaces and says, "Thighs, hands, It's all skin. I think it'll help."

Rod shrugs and pours some into his hand and gets down on his knees to put it on. Caroline's thinking, If it wasn't for the stress, this secret agent business could be alright.

Rod rubs in the hand lotion, wondering what the hell this is all about. As much as he'd like to, he doesn't dare reach his hand up any higher on her thigh. After all, she's head of all information technology for PACT. No, if anything's going to happen, she'll have to make the first move. Or did she already make the first move? Is she going to think he's a wimp if he doesn't do anything? He finds himself rubbing harder and faster as the questions swirl around his head.

Caroline reaches behind her and slips the key chain out of the USB. She knows now that it's fish or cut bait. She sighs.

The key chain reminds her that she's married. Plus, having sex with someone besides her husband and in addition someone who works for her is just plain stupid and she likes to think of herself as anything but. And, to top it all off, she's got a job to do. But, all in all, it's been a pretty good week.

She's glad to know she can still seduce a man if the need arises.

She breathily says, "Thanks. You'll never know how much that helped me."

She stands up and straightens out her skirt. Rod is still on his knees wondering how stupid that must look.

Caroline reaches for her bag and puts the hand lotion in it. She looks down into Rod's eyes and says, "I gotta go. Take good care of the place for me."

Caroline walks out into the hall clutching her key chain and gets back down to business. I should've known Amanda giving me two weeks off had something to do with Ike. I'll find out what it's all about soon enough. And if he needs me, I just might be able to help.

37

IKE HANGS UP THE PHONE..."She can't talk right now. I'll try her at home in forty-five minutes."

Devon says, "The plane's landed. At Yanbo." Ike sounds surprised. "Yanbo?"

Kidd asks Ike, "You know it?"

"Yes. It's the closest port in Saudi Arabia to Medina." Barry asks, "Medina? Never heard of it."

Kidd says, "Medina is the home of Mohammed's Mosque. Every Muslim must visit it once in their lives if they can."

Barry says, "I thought that was Mecca."

Kidd says, "Mecca and Medina. They're both important places." Ike asks Devon, "Are there any supercomputers in Saudi Arabia?"

Devon answers, "Off the top of my head, I can think of only one. It belongs to, uh, Microtech."

Ike's voice takes on an accusatory tone. "And it has something to do with that contract for weather satellites, doesn't it?"

Kidd asks, "What contract?"

Devon looks away and starts typing on the computer.

Ike says, "Thirty-three weather satellites, that's what. Thirty-three god damned laser equipped weather satellites. Microtech did the software for them!"

They all look at Devon and Barry asks, "Can you do a lot of damage with these lasers?"

Devon looks like he's going to be ill. He says in a near whisper, "If you get them coordinated so the effect is one big laser, you can do a lot of damage. A lot."

Barry sighs. "You don't have to be Devon Williams to figure out that we've got a big problem on our hands."

Devon says, "The supercomputer is located between Mecca and Medina.

In the middle of nowhere. I'm not kidding. It's in the middle of the desert. There's only one road. Security reasons."

Ike says, "Well, at least we won't need Amanda to get us into Saudi Arabia. I know Prince Abu Fariq, the Royal Governor of the Province of Medina."

Barry asks, "Is he a friend of yours?" "He is, except when he isn't."

PART FOUR

1

THE FED-EX PILOT knew something was up when he heard that he was going to have a flight engineer onboard as well as his usual copilot. Then they came and took out all the cargo from the plane. He had heard about something like this from another pilot, some kind of hush hush VIP trip.

When they loaded the bay with hay, he knew this routine flight to Paris was going to be nothing but routine. The clincher was when they brought in the oats. By now, he knew he would be flying a horse to Paris and sure enough, ten minutes before they were scheduled to take off, a woman dressed in white marched a majestic black thoroughbred onto the plane.

The copilot said she was a vet. They both agreed that it had to be a hell of a valuable horse to travel with its own vet. They both agreed that the vet was kind of cute to boot. Unfortunately, they were under strict orders to talk to no one unless they talked to them first. That could make getting a date with her in Paris a little bit difficult.

The final word came through. They were to avoid all turbulence, even if they had to fly out of their way. This ride was supposed to be as smooth as humanly possible.

2

ON ANOTHER PLANE, things weren't as comfortable. They had landed and didn't know where they were. No one was telling them either. No sense in asking, they'd probably just lie anyway. One thing, though, with the air conditioning off, it sure was hot. And it was about to get a lot hotter.

Dimitra comes into the rear cabin and throws some clothes at Monique and Sabrina Rose.

"Put these on and hurry up about it. We're leaving in ten minutes." She then marches out back towards the front of the plane.

Monique unfolds the clothing and just stares at it. At first she isn't sure what it is and then realizes it's one of those full-length coverings for women. She had seen these on documentaries about the Middle East and Central Asia. She even once saw a woman in New York wearing one. She unfolds the other one and it's the same thing, only smaller. Clearly for Sabrina Rose.

Monique tries to make the best of it and says, "Gee, talk about fashion victims."

"We're going to boil to death in these," whispers Sabrina. "I don't think we have a lot of choice."

With that, Monique unzips her skirt and lets it fall to the floor. She pulls off her shirt and holds up the covering and grimaces before pulling it on over her head. Immediately, she's formless. Her once magnificent body is just a memory.

"Come on, Sabrina Rose, you're next."

Sabrina Rose strips down to her underwear. She too grimaces before pulling the covering over herself and says, "I'm never going to complain about clothes again. Never."

Monique says, "At least something good is coming out of this...adventure."

Sabrina Rose reaches into the bag and pulls out two heavy pieces of cloth clearly meant for their heads. "Things just got a lot worse."

Dimitra comes storming back into the cabin and says, "Come on. Get those on. We don't have much time."

She walks over to Sabrina Rose and grabs the larger piece of cloth from her. She then pulls Monique by the hair causing her to gasp. Sabrina Rose shouts, "Hey, don't!"

Monique says to her, "It's okay. It's okay."

Dimitra thrusts the cloth over Monique's head. There are only two tiny slits for her eyes. Dimitra says, "Be happy I'm letting you see anything at all, you little slut."

She then turns to Sabrina Rose and says, "Put it on. We're going."

Sabrina Rose quickly complies. She and her mother follow slowly behind Dimitra. Even going slowly they knock into the seats.

Dimitra gets to the cabin door and thrusts it open. The desert heat comes ripping through the plane. She takes a step down the stairs and says, "Ah, fresh air."

Monique inches her way to the stairs as the heat burns through her. She can only hear her own heavy breathing as she steps out into the blinding sun. She turns back to Sabrina Rose and tries to speak. Her voice sounds like it's coming from inside a cave. "Take it slow. One step at a time. You can do it."

Sabrina Rose nods her head but realizes that no one can see her nodding through this thing. She says in a weak voice, "One step at a time."

Monique makes it down the steps and is already dripping with sweat. She turns and waits for Sabrina Rose who slowly works her way towards her When she gets down the stairs, the two of them turn to face Dimitra but she's nowhere to be found. To make matters worse, the hot tarmac burns through their shoes. Monique thinks, All they need is a big sign, "Welcome to Hell."

From across the tarmac, a jeep comes towards them. Squinting into the sun and squinting through the coverings, they see it's Dimitra being driven by a man in traditional Arab costume complete with headdress.

The jeep pulls up and Monique takes a step towards it. Dimitra pushes her away and laughs as she says, "Follow us. On foot."

The jeep slowly crosses the tarmac and Monique and Sabrina Rose trudge behind. The jeep pulls ahead and stops at another plane. This one is much smaller and it's propeller driven.

They watch as Lawrence Black, painfully pushing a bed on wheels across the hot tarmac, arrives at the propeller plane. They can just make out a body on the bed. They imagine it's Nadine.

Monique and Sabrina Rose sigh. The sigh reverberates through their coverings and comes back to them as a hopeless echo.

3

THE FRIDAY AIR FRANCE flight from St. Miquelon to Paris has been cancelled. There aren't any planes. One is stuck on a runway in the Azores and the other one has already left, carrying Ike, Kidd, Devon and Barry to Paris. Devon, Ike and Barry have made themselves comfortable in first class.

Devon looks right at home here. With a computer on in front of him and a satellite cell phone to one ear, he looks as though he's spent his whole life in first class...which he almost has.

He says, "Listen Dick. I'm coming into Yanbo late tonight. I want to take a look at that satellite control center."

Devon listens a moment and then says, "Yeah, I know it's a pain in the ass to get in there on short notice but I'm sure you'll think of something. You always do."

Devon looks over at Ike and nods. "Notify the press. It can't hurt to shine a little light on all the good work we're doing there in Saudi. You know, play up the part about how many lives will be saved with reliable weather forecasts and all that."

He hangs up the phone and says, "It's all set on my end." Barry says, "You sure it's a good idea to have the press meet us? Shouldn't we just sneak quietly in there?"

Devon says, "No way. Dalakos will know we're there, press corps or not.

This way he'll have something to think about. And, it'll make it a lot easier to get an audience with the Prince."

Barry looks skeptical but adds, "Okay, you're the genius." Devon smiles and says, "That's right. And another thing. Since you're coming as my doctor, from now on, your name is Barry Riley."

Barry looks askance and says, "What's the matter, Feldman too Jewish for you?"

Devon says, "Not too Jewish for me but way too Jewish for the Saudis. They frown upon anyone with a name like yours coming into their country. So, don't be so paranoid."

Barry's voice raises. "Paranoid? Paranoia only exists if the danger is imaginary."

"Okay, you're not paranoid but if you want to come, you change your name. Simple as that!"

Barry shrugs and says, "I hope this story will be about the life of Riley and not his death."

Ike's phone rings. He listens for a moment, says okay and hangs up.

Ike announces, "All set on my end. Chataqua is going to meet us in Paris. Prince Abu Fariq has always dreamed of buying that horse and now he's going to get the chance. So, we all have a way into Saudi. Devon and Barry will meet up with Brewer and Kidd and I go in with Chataqua."

Kidd asks, his voice full of irony, "What am I going in as, your trainer?"

Ike says, "Exactly. Now I bet you're glad PACT training included horse riding. I'm sure you remember how to do it."

Kidd says in a relaxed tone of voice, "Like riding a bicycle."

But, Kidd is feeling anything but relaxed. In fact, he's looking downright ill.

Barry looks up from his Sports Illustrated, and asks him, "Are you alright? You look pale and for a guy with your complexion to look pale, that's saying something."

Kidd says, "I'm okay. Just a little airsick."

Barry says, "Drink lots of water and don't touch anything with caffeine in it." Feeling he's done his duty as a doctor he goes back to the magazine.

Kidd closes his eyes. He's sick alright but nothing to with being on a plane. Just the thought of getting back on a horse makes him want to throw up. It's been eighteen years since he rode a horse. He beat back the fear once, he hopes he can do it again.

4

MONIQUE AND SABRINA ROSE finally make it across the boiling tarmac and climb up the stairs into the small plane. Dimitra marches in behind them. Waiting inside is Dalakos.

He stands as they walk in and says, "Ah, my Monique and little Sabrina Rose. Sorry for those awful coverings, but it's best if no one knows you're here. You see, there are all sorts of terrorists around who would be more than happy to kill you both because you're infidels. As a matter of fact, they'd be happy to kill me too."

Monique and Sabrina Rose pull off their veils and take their first easy breath since putting them on. Monique asks, "And where is here?"

Dalakos smiles. "Welcome to the Kingdom of Saudi Arabia."

Just the mention of the place causes Monique's heart to sink. For her, Saudi Arabia is a place where women are invisible. And if you're invisible, it becomes very easy for you to disappear.

Monique spots Lawrence and Nadine sitting in the last row of the plane. Nadine is also wearing the same covering that they were forced to wear.

Dalakos speaks directly to Lawrence and Nadine. "It's a small world indeed. It seems Monique knew your son a long time ago. Well, when you see your son again, please be sure to tell him this. Monique much prefers me! Kidd Black is no match for me!"

Monique takes a deep breath. Just as I had hoped, but now I'm sure! It is Kidd's parents! Kidd is alive! Kidd is alive!

Lawrence musters up his voice and asks Dalakos, "And who are you? Why are you keeping us here?"

Dalakos smiles as he quietly says, "Did I say when you see your son again? I meant if...if you play by my rules. Rule number one: Don't speak to me unless I speak to you first!"

The propellers on the plane come to life and the plane is soon airborne.

Dalakos says to Monique, "Ah, where are my manners? You must be thirsty...Dimitra."

At his signal, Dimitra reaches into a cooler and pours out two glasses of orange juice. She hands one to Monique and one to Sabrina Rose.

Sabrina Rose has already warned her mother about the drugged orange juice but with Dimitra standing over them, they have no choice but to drink.

As soon as they're done, Monique says, "Excuse me a moment." She struggles to get up but makes her way to the toilet. Once inside the cramped space, she has a tough time to get on her knees. Nothing is easy when you're wearing a full body covering. Once on her knees, Monique thrusts a finger down her throat, trying to throw up the orange juice.

Nothing. She tries again with two fingers and this time pukes her guts out...and with her guts the poison, too.

5

IKE PACES NERVOUSLY around a private lounge at Bourget Airport, Paris' little-known third airport. It's usually used just for private planes and VIPs as well as the annual Paris Air Show.

Barry asks Kidd, "Ike sure is nervous. What's up?"

Kidd says, "It's Chataqua. Ike hates the idea of flying him around the world. That horse is like a son to him."

Barry shakes his head. "And he's going to sell his son to that Saudi Prince?"

Kidd says, "Yeah, something like that."

Devon comes into the lounge followed by two young men carrying large cartons. He thanks them and they leave. He announces, "This should be everything we need."

He rips open a box and says, "Five portable phones equipped with GPS." He passes them out to everyone. "And as they say here, the pièce de résistance."

He reaches into another box and with a flourish pulls out two large swords, complete with delicate inlays.

Devon continues, "It's too risky to try and bring weapons into the Kingdom. So, these are ostensibly presents for His Royal Majesty, the Prince. They might just come in handy. Collectors items, if there ever were. From the personal collection of one of the Louies. The sixteenth, I think."

Barry asks, "Does that mean Dalakos and Company don't have guns?"

Kidd says, "I wish. But, swords are way better than nothing." Ike watches out the window as a plane taxis towards the gate.

He sees the FedEx logo on it and says, "At last."

He heads for the door but before leaving, says to Kidd, "Come on. When Chataqua gets off, take him for a ride. There's a grassy area near the Air Show grounds."

Kidd makes an effort to keep his voice even but doesn't succeed. "Me? Why me?"

Ike says, "Because you're his trainer? Remember?"

Ike shakes his head in disbelief and walks out of the lounge.

6

MONIQUE AND SABRINA ROSE stare out the window from the propeller plane. Desert. Nothing but desert and a lot more nothing than desert. Every mile depresses them more. Then, in the distance, like a mirage, an oasis of green. Dark green. A lush green. It reminds Monique of upstate New York, of Mohonk Mountain House. Of Kidd, of Devon, of another life.

Dalakos says, "We'll be landing soon. Put on your veils." Monique and Sabrina Rose put on their veils and immediately enter into a world of darkness. It's like stepping into a time machine back to the Middle Ages.

Monique looks back and sees Nadine putting on her veil too. Once the plane has landed, Dalakos signals for Nadine and Lawrence to be taken off the plane. As they walk by Monique and Sabrina Rose, Nadine speaks through her veil. "If they wanted to kill us, they would've done it a long time ago. Remember that!"

Monique wonders about what Nadine said. If they wanted to kill us...Is 'us' the two of them...or is 'us' all of us, including Sabrina Rose?

Dalakos screams, "Get them out! Get them out!"

Nadine and Lawrence are roughly removed from the plane and forced into a waiting car.

Dalakos returns to his usual calm self. He smiles and says to Monique and Sabrina Rose, "Shall we go? Our chariot awaits us."

Sabrina Rose and Monique are whisked off into a waiting van with tinted windows.

Ten minutes later the van stops and they go into a white bungalow. In the distance, through their slatted veils, they can see other bungalows, but theirs is clearly set apart from the rest.

They go into the bungalow and it's air conditioned! But, still in their coverings, they're sweating.

Dalakos comes in with a burly man who carries their suitcases and sets them down. Dalakos announces, "Why don't you take a shower and relax? I'll come back for you in half an hour. We'll be taking a trip together. We have work to do. Sabrina Rose, you stay here. Dimitra will entertain you."

Monique points to her covering and asks, "And this? Do I still have to wear this thing?"

Dalakos says, "Don't worry. You'll get used to it."

7

THE MICROTECH PLANE waits on the tarmac with its engines going. Devon, Barry and Ike stand by the walkway that leads to the plane.

Devon says, "When we get to Yanbo, we'll head for the SCC, the Satellite Control Center. When you get to the Palace, give us a call."

Ike says, "Count on it."

Barry asks, "Where the hell is Kidd?"

If Ike's concerned, he's not showing it. "Don't worry. Chataqua will bring him back."

They all shake hands and Ike walks down to the tarmac. The Microtech plane taxis down the runway. Ike walks up the stairwell to another waiting jet to get a better view and sees Kidd walking Chataqua towards him. Or is it Chataqua walking Kidd? Either way, they're going mighty slow.

When Kidd finally makes it to the plane, Ike says, "You were supposed to ride the horse, not walk him. Some trainer you're going to be."

Kidd says, "Don't worry about me. Let's get going."

The two of them set Chataqua on a baggage elevator and accompany him into the plane.

8

ONCE AGAIN, MONIQUE can do nothing but stare out at the world through two slits in her veil. They've left the lush oasis and are driving on a road that has clearly been carved out of the desert. It's completely straight. There's nothing but asphalt entirely surrounded by sand.

They've only traveled ten minutes and twice they've been stopped at what is either a toll or a checkpoint. It's hard for her to tell what it is exactly. They all speak in a language she doesn't understand. She does understand that the satellite center is very well protected. The soldiers are literally armed to the teeth and there are tanks at every stop.

Dalakos sits in the back seat next to her. After the second stop, he says to her, "When we get to the satellite control center, you will get access to the laptop with the retinal ID and then you will transfer the software to the mainframe supercomputer we have there."

Monique can't help but notice that he is no longer asking her but telling her what to do.

He continues, "Then once everything is ready, we will have a little celebration, you and I."

Dalakos puts a hand on her knee and says, "You know there's something sexy about this outfit you're wearing. Later, when we fuck, wear it."

When Monique hears this she thinks, Just what I was afraid of but didn't want to even think about. He's been raping me while I've been drugged.

And I've got to find a way to keep off his drugs. Which means, next time he rapes me, and it definitely sounds like there's going to be a next time, I'm not going to be drugged at all.

Monique really feels like she is his slave now. And, with Dimitra guarding Sabrina Rose, for all practical purposes, she is.

9

THE ROYAL TREATMENT. When Ike and Kidd arrived at the Prince Abu Faruq Airport, they were met by a limousine and an air-conditioned horse trailer. Ike rode in the limousine and Kidd and Chataqua rode in the horse trailer.

"Royal Treatment" or not, their bags were completely searched when they arrived. The police didn't bat an eye when Ike explained that the swords were a gift for the Prince. He would present them to him at the banquet that was to be held in his honor the next evening. For at least twenty-four hours, they had weapons, even if they were from the 18th century.

In the short drive to the Palace, they couldn't help but notice the amount of military activity. They weren't sure if it was to protect the Prince, the SCC or both. They were impressed with how green everything was. But, this was truly an oasis. On the flight in, it was complete desert until they arrived at the airport.

The Palace itself is something out of "Arabian Nights." Ike is reminded of a poem by that great Arabian poet, Omar El-Ski.

He tries to recite it and stops. A wave of exasperation briefly washes over him. I used to know the whole damn thing by heart. Another sign of old age.

As they drive through the gates to the Palace, Ike is pleased to see that the Prince himself is waiting to greet them. Ike thinks, Waiting to greet Chataqua is more like it but in Arab culture it's a great honor.

The Prince is tall, tanned and in full Arab gear. He looks like something out of Lawrence of Arabia.

The limousine stops in front of the Palace stairway. A soldier from the honor guard rushes to open the door. The Prince walks down the stairway as Ike steps out of the car.

The Prince embraces Ike and says, "Welcome to my Palace."

Ike says, "Thank you." Before he can get in another word, the Prince smiles broadly and says, "I never thought I'd see the day when you would part with that fabulous horse of yours. I promise I'll take great care of him."

Ike says, "You are the only person I would ever sell him to. Believe me."

The Prince says, "Oh, I believe you, I do."

Ike notices the Prince's eyes glance toward the horse trailer. Ike picks up the cue and asks, "Your Highness, would it be too soon to reintroduce you to Chataqua?"

The Prince says, "No, now would be more than fine."

Ike and the Prince walk to the horse trailer and prepare to open the door. They open the door and find Kidd rubbing Chataqua's ears. They look like they're best of friends.

Ike points to Kidd and says, "This is Mr. Washington, Chataqua's trainer."

The Prince nods in Kidd's direction but doesn't see him. He's staring at the majestic Chataqua. With his eyes riveted on the horse, the Prince says to Kidd, "Ah, you must be a fine trainer indeed. And now, the two of you must come inside for some refreshment."

The Prince motions to two men who gently guide Chataqua out of the trailer. He says, "Come, come. My men will take care of the horse."

Kidd says, "Yes, your Highness."

The Prince puts his arm around Ike and guides him up the stairs to the Palace. As Ike had told him to, Kidd follows two steps behind.

When the Prince and Ike arrive to the front door of the Palace, the Prince walks in but Ike hesitates. The Prince stops and asks, "Yes?"

Ike says, "Excuse me, but I don't see any sandals. I..." The Prince looks chagrined as he says, "Widowmakers. Men don't take their shoes off indoors because of the Widowmakers." He laughs and says, "Ah, the women, that's another story." Ike asks, "Widowmakers?"

The Prince says, "This was a small oasis and then we built the satellite control center. With that came people. With the people we needed water. So, we built a desalination plant and the desert bloomed. And with it bloomed this poisonous scorpion, leiurus quinquestriatus, otherwise known as the Widowmaker. This is their mating season. Paralysis starts in thirty seconds and they can kill you in five minutes. Even quicker if you don't remain calm."

Ike says, "Remain calm indeed. It's like Lord Byron's 'White Elephant Club.' To be a member, you had to sit in a corner and not think of white elephants."

The Prince adds, "Easier said than done." He then continues, "In the mosques, where we have to take our shoes off, it's an enormous problem. I tried to get a fatwa to keep our shoes on, but it was not possible. Sometimes, I think, the clerics are only interested in fatwas that kill, not those that save lives."

Kidd thinks, Yeah, you son of a bitch. You say that, and at the same time, you let the likes of Christopher Dalakos have free run of your province.

10

BARRY SINKS INTO the plush couch of Devon's personal plane as it taxis to the gate of Yanbo Airport. They're definitely not sneaking into Saudi Arabia. From the window he can see Microtech1and the blue and gold Microtech logo on the fuselage of the plane.

Barry thinks, I definitely don't want to get off of this plane. Especially when getting off means danger. This whole plan seems a little vague to me. The only part that is clear is that there are people here who clearly want to kill us.

Devon doesn't even notice the plane coming to a stop. His eyes glued to his computer, he talks to Barry without looking up. "We've lost the homing signal. Right at the SCC. Could be there's some kind of interference from all the electrical equipment."

Barry grunts an acknowledgment but thinks, This guy is a real optimist. There are a million other possibilities why the signal was lost and he picks the one where everything is okay. Kidd told me that optimists don't last long in the spy business.

The plane comes to a complete stop and Devon finally shuts down his laptop. He looks out the window and says, "There's Dick Brewer. The one with the baseball hat."

Barry, definitely not an optimist, says, "He sticks out like a sore thumb. Looks like an easy target to me."

Devon says, "Not here. There's never been a whiff of trouble since we set up shop here. Now I know why. The Prince has made a deal with the devil and devil is spelled with a capital "D" like in Dalakos. Believe me, Dalakos wouldn't rock the boat by killing us."

Barry says, "Maybe not you, but who's gonna care about anyone killing me?"

"Relax. Everyone here is a guest of the Prince. Dalakos isn't in a position to upset his host."

Barry adds, "Not until now, anyway. See how Dalakos feels if he gets his hands on that Lazer."

"Let's just make sure that doesn't happen so we don't have to worry about it."

They step out into the oppressive Saudi heat. This doesn't do anything to alleviate Barry's sense of foreboding, that's for sure.

Devon warmly shakes hands with Dick Brewer and introduces Barry. Barry likes him right away. He's got that easy-going confidence that makes other Americans feel right at home. Plus he soon finds out that Dick uses some of the same jokes that Barry uses. A sure sign for Barry that Dick has good taste.

Dick Brewer warmly smiles as he says, "Welcome to Yanbo, Dr. Riley. It's not the end of the world but you can see it from here. First, we check into your hotel, then we meet the press and then we take a flight to the Prince's airport. From there, we drive out to the SCC.

Now, that, that's the end of the world. Of course, the Prince would like to meet you. He's arranged a little dinner tomorrow night. Remember, 'little' to him might not be little to us."

"So, you're from Texas," Barry says.

Dick Brewer says, "Texas born and bred."

"Then you know the joke about the guy from Texas," Barry says.

Dick says, "You make it sound like there's only one joke about a guy from Texas."

"Don't we have a press conference to get to?" Devon asks hopefully.

Dick Brewer picks up the hint from his boss and says to Barry, "I'm sure it was a great joke but we've got to get going."

Barry says, "One of my best."

Dick says to Devon, "Okay, here's the set-up for the press conference. I introduce you. You make a short speech saying how happy you are to be here and how this satellite program, will bring more reliable weather forecasting saving lives and money. You take some questions…"

Barry says, "And then we go to lunch."

Dick ignores Barry and says to Devon, "It's show time."

The press conference goes smoothly. Barry thinks, Devon acts like he's done this a hundred times before which he probably has.

They are just about to wrap things up when a reporter asks Devon why he is traveling with a personal physician. Is he ill?

A buzz goes through the crowd. A personal physician?

Devon glances at Dick Brewer. A glance that asks, How the hell did they find out about that?

Dick Brewer swallows. Damn reporters. Must've gotten a tip from immigration. And what's this going to do to the stock price? I've got a hell of a lot of shares in this company.

Dick Brewer says, "Dr. Riley will, uh, be more than happy to explain his presence to you."

He looks over at Barry who is sitting with the press. All eyes turn towards him. He stands up and says, "I'm a doctor, but certainly not Devon's personal doctor. I'm along for the ride because I'm one of the few people on the planet Devon's capable of beating in golf."

Everyone laughs. Barry's got an audience now. He's just getting warmed up.

He continues, "Speaking of golf..."

Barry ignores Devon clearing his throat and says, "Stevie Wonder and Tiger Woods are in a bar when Stevie mentions that he plays golf.

'You play golf?' asks Tiger.

Stevie says, 'Yes, I've been playing for years.'

'But I thought you were blind; how can you play golf if you're blind?' Tiger asks.

'I get my caddie to stand in the middle of the fairway and he calls to me. I listen for the sound of his voice and play the ball towards him,' explains Stevie.

'But how do you putt?' Tiger wondered.

'Well,' says Stevie, 'I get my caddie to lean down in front of the hole and call to me with his head on the ground and I just play the ball to the sound of his voice.'

Tiger says, 'What's your handicap?'

'I don't have a handicap,' Stevie assures Tiger.

Tiger is incredulous and says to Stevie, 'We must play a game sometime.'

Wonder replies, 'Well, people don't take me seriously so I only play for money, and I never play for less than $100,000 a hole.'

Tiger thinks it over and says, 'OK, I'm up for that. When would you like to play?'

'I don't care—any night next week is OK with me.'"

The press corps loves it. They laugh and shout for more. Barry is on a roll. He says, "So, three golfers walk into a bar..."

Dick Brewer, laughing loudly, quickly walks over to Barry, puts an arm tightly around him and announces, "And now, may I suggest that we all go to lunch."

11

SABRINA ROSE isn't going anywhere. She's checked out the bungalow she's in and there's no way out. The windows are barred and there are guards by the front and back doors. To make matters worse, someone comes by randomly to check in on her. No, there's nothing to do but watch TV and wait for her mother to come back. The good news is that there's a remote control. The bad news is that the TV only gets one station. And, of course, it's in Arabic.

Then, a press conference comes on. A group of journalists wearing Arab dress are waiting to interview someone. Another man in Arab dress comes to the microphone and says something in Arabic but she thought she heard her father's name. Sure enough, her father walks to the microphone and begins to speak. The voice-over translation drowns out most of what he says but she distinctly hears the words Saudi Arabia and Yanbo.

My dad is in Saudi Arabia! He's close by and he's coming to save me and mom!

Sabrina Rose hears a car pull up and sees that it's Dimitra. She quickly turns off the TV. No sense in letting Dimitra know that she knows her father's not far. When she hears the door open, Sabrina Rose tries to look as miserable as possible. Dimitra enters and is more than happy to see Sabrina Rose sitting there looking bored to death.

12

IN A DIFFERENT PART of the housing complex, Nadine and Lawrence are on the sofa, watching TV. While Lawrence stares blankly at the screen, Nadine is deep in thought. In a voice just loud enough for her husband to hear, she says, "I'm shooting blanks. I'm coming up with nothing."

Lawrence barely hears her. His voice is lifeless as he says, "There's no way out. No way out."

Nadine leans over to him, wraps her arms around him and gently pulls his face close to hers. "All my life people have told me that there was no way out. No way out of that rat infested slum I was born into in Roxbury, no way out of not becoming who I was capable of becoming! I tell you, and you'd better listen to me, there's always a way out! Always!"

Lawrence hugs into her. "Well, if there is a way out, you'll find it!"

Nadine smiles and her voice is strong. "There is a way out and *we'll* find it"

Lawrence, now full of life, says, "You're goddamn right!" The Arabic from the TV drones on in the background...until they hear the name, Devon Williams. They both look at the TV and see Devon on screen. Behind him a banner is raised: *Yanbo Welcomes Devon Williams!*

Lawrence turns to Nadine. "Things are looking up already." "Yeah, if Devon's here, our son can't be far behind." Nadine pulls Lawrence even closer. "I've come up with a plan."

"Lay it on me."

"The plan is that we stay alive until we're rescued." Lawrence shakes his head and smiles. "A little weak on the details but you can count me in!"

13

DEVON, BARRY AND BREWER head down the highway to the SCC. Devon and Barry have really warmed to Dick Brewer. Helpful and funny. Something for each of them. Barry thinks Dick has a great sense of humor because he always laughs at his jokes. Devon likes him because he really knows everything that is going on at the SCC.

As they approach the SCC, Brewer's phone rings. He flips on the speaker and they hear a man with an American accent, "Dick, we've got a problem. The place has been evacuated."

Brewer's perpetual smile immediately disappears. "How's that, Cody?"

"That's all I know. Some local spotted a scorpion and the whole place went nuts. No one will work until the place has been checked out from top to bottom."

Devon says, "How long's that gonna take?" "A couple of hours minimum."

Brewer says to Cody, "I've got Devon Williams here."

Cody says, "Hi, Mr. Williams. Welcome. Sorry you're coming on such a lousy day."

Brewer says to Devon, "You want to look around anyway?" Devon says, "No sense in that. We'll come back later." Brewer says, "Later it is."

Brewer gets Cody on the case, turns around and heads back to their hotel.

14

MONIQUE STARES OUT the window of the SUV as it heads for the Satellite Control Center and thinks, I'll never get used to this thing, this heap of clothing.

The view doesn't help her mood either. Sand, sand and more sand. Then, in the distance, like a mirage, is the SCC. A two-story square functional building surrounded by antennas that are taller than the building itself. It has a surreal feeling to it. Plunked down in the middle of the desert, it looks like a set from a B movie about aliens.

She sits in the backseat by herself. Dalakos sits in front next to the Chameleon who drives. She wasn't introduced but remembers the Chameleon from the hijacked plane. Dalakos and the Chameleon barely say a word and no one speaks to her during the whole trip.

When they arrive at the SCC, the Chameleon produces a pass and they drive down into the underground parking garage. From there they take a service elevator and using a key, go down to a lower level even though there is nothing indicating a lower level on the elevator.

They arrive in a spacious office that holds only a small laptop. Dalakos notices Monique's surprise and says, "The supercomputer isn't here. We just access it through here with the laptop."

Dalakos moves close to her and dramatically announces, "Monique, now comes the big moment. I'd like you to access the laptop through the retinal ID and then transfer its software to the supercomputer."

He motions towards the Chameleon and says, "He's a computer expert. He will give you any help you might need."

Monique says, "I can't work with this veil on."

Dalakos glances towards the Chameleon who looks blankly at Monique. Dalakos walks closely to Monique and whispers, "I'm terribly sorry but you can't take off that veil until I tell you. It's for your own safety. Now, please, get to work."

Monique tells herself, For my own safety? More like the safety of Sabrina Rose. How did I get myself into this? Stuck in the middle of the desert with a man I don't know but thought I knew, a man who drugged me and kidnapped my daughter and me, a man I now can't say no to and to top it off...a mute weirdo who gives me the creeps has been added to the stew.

Monique connects the cables to the two computers. She turns on the laptop and puts an eye to the retinal ID. To her surprise, the retinal ID system has been disabled.

Strange, very strange. One of the main reasons I was needed was for my retina and now I see anyone could have accessed the computer.

She accesses the computer and then looks at the Chameleon out of the corner of her eye. He doesn't seem to have noticed anything out of the ordinary.

One hour later, the software has been transferred to the supercomputer. Dalakos and the Chameleon are very satisfied. Monique asks Dalakos, "Could I take this laptop back for Sabrina Rose? There's a chess program on it. It'll give her something to do while I'm here."

Dalakos looks at The Chameleon who sees no reason not to let her take the computer. Dalakos says, "Anything for little Sabrina Rose." He turns to the Chameleon and says, "I'd like you to leave us now."

The Chameleon immediately leaves the room. Dalakos stares into Monique's eyes and says, "You've done a good job so far, now for your reward. Get on your knees."

Without hesitation she gets on her knees. She doesn't want him to have the slightest inkling that anything has changed. He stands over her and unzips his pants. "Now, you can take off your veil."

15

CAROLINE WAS DOZING on the bed by the computers at Microtech headquarters. The most powerful computers in the world are at her disposal. All other work has been halted on them. This was the number one priority.

She hasn't seen her kids since she stopped by the house to pick up a few things. They and everything else in her life are on hold. She's armed with PACT passwords and Devon's computer arsenal. The phone rings.

There is only one person who would call her. She picks up the phone and says, "Ready to roll."

Devon says, "Caroline, we were on our way to the SCC when they shut it down because of a scorpion attack."

"You're kidding."

Devon doesn't even bother responding to that and continues. "Our tour's postponed until tonight. In the meantime, take a virtual look around and see what you can find."

"I'm on it."

Devon adds, "Check everything you can. Not only the SCC but everything concerning the Prince."

"I had already planned on it."

"Call me once you've done it. Even if you don't find anything."

"Will do."

Devon hangs up and paces around his hotel suite. I could use a drink. And, the one thing you can be sure you won't be able to get here is a drink. What a place. Invisible women and no alcohol.

Devon opens up the minibar again and looks through it hoping to find something he didn't find the last time he looked. I've got billions of dollars and I can't get a drink. The stress gets to you after awhile. All adrenaline, all the time, wears you out.

There's an old expression, be careful what you wish for because at that moment there's a knock at the door. Devon goes to the door and looks through the peephole. He sees a dark haired woman wearing a full body covering. Her eyes are visible and what eyes they are. Dark and inviting, the kind of eyes that make time stop.

Devon would be the first to admit that at this point, anything to release the stress he's under would be greatly appreciated. But he knows better than to even dream of a Saudi woman. He's heard all the stories of adulterers beheaded and he doesn't plan on being one of them.

Devon opens the door and asks, "Yes?"

The woman says, "I have a message from the Prince. May I come in?"

Devon hesitates for a moment. He glances down the hallway, sees no one and says, "Of course, come in."

The woman enters the room and Devon glances one more time down the hallway before closing the door. The woman takes off her head scarf. Her long flowing black hair comes tumbling down. Those magnificent eyes reveal all their promise. Devon is already lost in them.

The woman knows her spell is cast...Of course, it's working, working like a charm. The woman is none other than Dimitra.

She says, "These god damn coverings. Like walking around in a portable prison. Unbearable. Really unbearable."

Devon enjoys the sight and asks, "Can I get you something to drink?"

Dimitra answers, "A whiskey would be fine, thank you."

Devon laughs. "A whiskey? You can't get a whiskey here. You just can't."

Now it's Dimitra's turn to laugh. "I don't know the meaning of the word can't."

She slowly unbuttons her covering and strapped to her thigh is a flask.

The covering drops to the floor as she unhooks the flask. She's wearing a simple black dress underneath her body covering but still it causes a tinge of longing to come over Devon.

Devon reaches for two glasses on the mini-bar and says, "So, you said you had a message from the Prince?"

Dimitra looks perplexed. She says, "Did I say message? I meant to say that I have a gift from the Prince."

Devon looks around for the gift. Dimitra continues, "For the man who has everything."

Devon doesn't move. He doesn't say a word. He thinks, She's beautiful. I'm married. I was married. Monique ran off with another man.

Okay, maybe she didn't run off with him but she definitely ran off with Kidd, who was my best friend. Who used to be my best friend at the time.

And given the chance, why wouldn't she run off with him again? Obviously, I have other things to think about than this beautiful woman.

Devon says in a very unconvincing voice, "I'm married." Dimitra moves towards Devon. She stops inches from him. Her breath, her perfume, her beauty. He doesn't move. She won't make the first move. They stand there, eye to eye. Finally, Devon blinks.

He says, "I know enough about Arab culture not to refuse a gift from my host."

With that, he pulls Dimitra towards him who then pushes him back onto the bed and straddles him. She says, "I adore married men. They know how to make love."

They roll around the bed. Clothes are thrown away, in any direction as long as they're off. Devon finds himself behind Dimitra who is on all fours as they both face the mirror. She thrusts back at him as she reaches between her legs to caress him. She shouts, "Does your wife do this?"

Devon whispers, "No."

Dimitra shouts, "I CAN'T HEAR YOU!" Devon shouts, "NO! She doesn't!"

Dimitra opens the flask, reaches behind her and pours some over her body. She orders him to lick it off. As he does, she shouts, "Does your wife do this?" and Devon can only shout back, "No!"

During every position, using every trick in her book, she shouts to their reflections in the mirror, "Does your wife do this?" and Devon shouts back, "No! Never!"

16

DALAKOS IS GETTING dressed while Monique lies on the floor, filled with revulsion. But still, she's gone this far, she's not going to let on that she can't stand to be touched by him.

Dalakos says to Monique, "Now that the software is on the supercomputer I need one last thing. I need proof that it works."

Monique hesitates before asking, "What kind of proof?" Dalakos is excited. "I want you to send a Lazer beam down to earth. Simple as that."

Monique can't believe it. "You want me to send a Lazer beam to earth? You could kill someone. It's too dangerous. It's never been tested outside of a laboratory."

"I know it's never been tested. This will be a test. Just hit a target in the middle of the desert. No one will get hurt.

No one."

Monique says, "What's the rush? I could work out a computer simulation and have the results in a couple of weeks. I could simulate the thirty-three weather satellites already in place."

Dalakos patiently explains. He uses the tone of voice a teacher would use to a slow student. "I have some people who will invest in the project if you can prove the theory works. If they invest, we'll be rich. It might not matter now but you're a woman who is used to luxury. I'm just a poor heir to a small shipping fortune. You'll have your own money and you won't be in HIS shadow any longer. You'll get the respect and recognition you deserve. You're the genius, not your husband!

Even the dwarf who stands on the shoulders of a giant can see further than the giant. He's been standing on your shoulders too long!"

Monique doesn't believe him for a second but pretends to. She thinks, I don't see how this demonstration can do any harm. But, these investors he's talking about. Whoever they are, they can't be up to any good. For the moment, I don't have any choice, they've got Sabrina Rose. I can't refuse. I'll do the demonstration and then I'll stall as much as I can until I find a way out of here. After all, they can't do anything without me. I'll just make sure no one gets hurt.

She tries to put some enthusiasm into her voice. "When do you want the demonstration?"

Dalakos says, "Tomorrow night."

Monique doesn't flinch. Once again she says what she knows he wants to hear. "For you, anything."

She gets up and starts getting dressed. She'll never get used to this covering and she's still frustrated that it takes so long to put it on. It's like she's putting handcuffs on herself.

As she's adjusting the layer that goes over the layer she's already wearing, there's a discreet knock at the door. Dalakos opens it and the Chameleon hands him an envelope. Without saying a word, Dalakos closes the door. He pulls a DVD out of the envelope and inserts it into a DVD player. He walks over to Monique and says, "Come. Let's sit down. I have an educational DVD I want you to see."

Dalakos firmly guides her to the couch and they sit. He picks up a remote control and the DVD begins. It's Devon in what looks like a hotel room. The camera appears to have been placed behind a mirror in the middle of the room.

Monique, her voice quivering, asks, "What is this? What's this about?"

Dalakos puts up a hand and says, "Like I said, it's educational. You're about to learn something about your husband."

Monique turns back to the DVD to see Devon opening the door and having a conversation. A woman in a full body covering enters the room. A conversation about a drink follows and the woman removes her veil. Monique is horrified to see that the woman is Dimitra.

She feels like she's entering into some kind of nightmare. She's watching her husband have sex with the woman she hates. The woman who would gladly kill her and her daughter if given the signal from the man sitting next to her. As though this wasn't bad enough, soon her husband is screaming wildly that his wife, her, Monique, isn't half the woman Dimitra is.

Monique starts to cry. Dalakos puts an arm around her and brings her to his chest. Her tears become a flood as Monique explodes in grief.

17

NADINE STANDS by the front door of the bungalow. She looks at Lawrence who nods. Nadine opens the door and is immediately confronted by a guard. Nadine screams, "My husband is having an Alzheimer's fit!"

Behind her, Lawrence mumbles incoherently, walks unsteadily and bangs his head against the wall.

Nadine continues, "Please, get us to a doctor!"

The guard shouts something to someone behind him as Lawrence continues to knock into things. Nadine shouts, "Hurry!"

Another guard comes over. He's older and appears to be someone in authority. He surveys the situation. Lawrence goes into his full act, mumbling louder and smashing whatever he can.

Nadine, her voice shaking, says, "It's his Alzheimer's. Please, take us to a hospital."

The guard says, "Alzheimer's? It's not fatal. Take two aspirins and call us in the morning!" He and the other guard laugh and slam the door in her face.

The moment the door shuts, Nadine signals for Lawrence to stop moving around. Exhausted and depressed, Lawrence collapses on the sofa. Nadine flops down next to him and sighs long and loud. She then says, "Well, look at the bright side. At least you didn't smash the TV."

18

CAROLINE SITS BEFORE the world's most powerful computer and stretches her fingers. Just like a concert pianist before the big show. This is the moment she feels she's practiced for all her life. The good people of the world need her talent and she's not going to let them down. She has to find that needle in a haystack of billions upon billions of pieces of information.

She logs into PACT data banks and brings up the telephone logs of the Satellite Control System. Nothing out of the ordinary which means that there's nothing.

She taps into the Echelon project, the CIA's ears over Europe, and does a search through all the cell phone conversations. Keywords from one hundred languages and twice as many dialects. Nothing.

She checks the water usage since the center was built. She adds the number of people who have entered the center and compares it to the number of people who work there. The water usage is a little higher than might be expected but there's not enough there to keep her on that track. Too many variables. Parties, extra showers, nothing there to point to anything that could help Devon.

Then she starts casting a wider net. There's a big Convention Center by the Prince's airport.

Why in the world anyone would want to go to a convention there is beyond me. Those Princes just don't know what to do with their money...

There was a very recent order for Iranian Top Grade Caviar with a surcharge paid for immediate delivery. And, a large order for alcohol, Irish whiskey, and lots of it. And, on top of that, an entire wing of the hotel has been booked.

She makes a mental note: Tell Devon there's a big party going on at the Convention Center, probably international guests. Not sure what it means, but maybe he'll want to check it out.

Caroline gets up from the computer and walks around the room. Think. She's got to think. All she can hear is the whirring of the fans that keep the computer system from overheating. The fans. The fans.

Electricity. Caroline hurries back to the computer and checks the electricity grid for the SCC. As expected, it uses a lot of electricity. Especially, the supercomputer. Then she notices that the supercomputer is being used twenty-four hours a day, seven days a week. Strange indeed.

Every supercomputer has to shut down for maintenance and to cool down. Not this one.

She gets deeper into the electricity grid. The supercomputer isn't being used twenty-four hours a day. There's something else using the same amount of power. Could it be that there's another supercomputer there? Probably not. But what if there's some kind of bypass. If so, it must be some kind of Wi-Fi setup.

19

MONIQUE ONCE AGAIN sits in the back, wearing her full body covering. Dalakos sits in front as the Chameleon drives. Dalakos looks back at Monique who hasn't said a word since they got in the car.

Dalakos smiles to himself, That DVD did its job. She's speechless. Even if he begged her, she wouldn't go back with that man. Ah, a woman scorned is a beautiful thing to see.

Monique is surprised but she's not in shock. With everything she has on her plate, she can't afford to be paralyzed by the DVD.

She thinks, What was that expression. Something about the kettle calling the pot black?

I should talk. For twenty years, I couldn't forget the man I'd had an affair with, a man who was my husband's best friend...And, I've never seen Devon so turned on. And whose fault is that? I haven't always been one hundred per cent there when we made love, have I?

She laughs derisively to herself. Not one hundred per cent? How many times have I just thought of Kidd when Devon and I made love?

And I'm supposed to be shocked by a DVD of Devon with a beautiful woman? I am hurt though, hurt to see a mirror of how I acted.

Dalakos drops her off and says, "I'll send over your dress for tonight. You will be the prize of the evening."

Monique forces herself to look sincere and whispers, "I love you."

She turns and walks up the sidewalk to the bungalow. She makes a mental list of all that's going on. Demonstrate the Lazer to a group of so-called investors tonight; at least she doesn't have to wear this body covering. Check out the laptop to see why the retinal ID was disabled and most of all, see how Sabrina Rose is holding up.

There's an armed guard there, who opens the front door for her. Monique says, "Thank you," and then wishes she hadn't. What the hell am I doing saying thank you to this asshole? As Monique walks into the bungalow, she can hear the SUV drive away.

The moment she walks into the door, Sabrina Rose comes rushing into her arms, almost knocking her over. Sabrina Rose whispers in her ear, "I've got a secret. A good secret!"

Before Monique says anything, she spots Dimitra sitting across the room on the couch. Dimitra says, "Now you know how it feels, don't you?"

Dimitra smiles a cold smile and looks right at Sabrina Rose and says, "Your mother is a slut. Do you know what a slut is?"

Before Sabrina Rose can answer, Monique sets her down and walks straight over to Dimitra. She shouts, "Get out of my house!" and then with a force she didn't know she had, she slaps Dimitra across her face.

Dimitra's face turns red, red from the force of the slap and red with anger. She stands up and faces Monique. Sabrina Rose watches speechless.

Monique doesn't back down. She shouts, "Get out of my house!" Dimitra says, "You'll be taken care of later and you can count on it that I'll be doing the taking care of. Here's a down payment."

Dimitra spits in Monique's face and marches out of the bungalow slamming the door behind her.

Monique stands there, proud of herself but also surprised. I stood up to Dimitra. Probably a stupid thing to do but for the moment, they need me as much as I need them.

Sabrina Rose walks over to her mother and gently wipes Dimitra's saliva from her face. Sabrina looks at her mother with pride and respect.

She says to her, "I saw Daddy on TV. He's here!"

20

DALAKOS SENT OUT the invitations the moment Monique told him she could get the Lazer to work. A demonstration that would change the world. He had told everyone on his list to be ready to leave on a moment's notice. Now, the moment's notice had come. It would be tonight at midnight. Plenty of time for everyone to fly into the Prince's airport.

So much to do. Food to be prepared. Women to be found for those who didn't bring their own. It was important to have the women around. The men will be so much more civilized.

The rooms at the hotel had already been reserved. If more rooms are needed, guests would be asked to leave. If they refuse, I'll have them killed. Simple as that.

The target had to be prepared. Within sight of the hotel terrace but not too close in case Monique's aim is a little off. She assured me that wouldn't be the case but just as insurance, I'll make sure Sabrina Rose is close by. That'll encourage Monique to not make any mistakes.

And, the dress has to be sent to Monique for a fitting. Dalakos smiles. I think this will impress my peers more than the Lazer. I, Christopher Dalakos, with Devon Williams' wife.

21

DEVON SITS BACK on the bed in his hotel suite. I don't regret that at all. That's the test. Afterwards, if you regret it or not. And I don't. I really don't.

Who am I kidding? I sound like a guy trying to convince himself that just because she did something horrible to me at Mohonk all those years ago, it's okay for me to do the same. How many times have I told Sabrina Rose that two wrongs don't make a right...I'm not like that. That's not me.

Until I see Monique face to face and have her tell me it's over, I'm still married.

Devon shakes his head and laughs at the way he told Dimitra, "I'm married."

Got to get back to business. If I don't hear from Caroline, Barry and I will have to head back to the SCC and snoop around some more.

Don't know what good it'll do but it's better than sitting around here with our thumbs up our ass.

Devon turns on his computer just in case Caroline has sent an e-mail. Just in case there's a problem with the cell phone connection.

There's no e-mail but there is a signal from the homing device! He pinpoints the location. It's a bungalow in the worker's village. Bungalow number 7. Lucky seven. Why would the computer turn up there? Why?

Devon racks his brain. The man who has solved what many said were unsolvable problems, tries to will the solution. Rule number one. Eliminate the impossible. Whatever's left, no matter how improbable is the solution.

But, he keeps drawing blanks. He needs more data. Someone is going to have to check out this bungalow. He has to decide to go there with Barry or see if Ike and Kidd can do it.

The phone rings and with it his decision is made for him.

It's Caroline. There appears to be some kind of bypass at the SCC, something that needs to be checked out. Probably a powerful Wi-Fi setup.

And, there's a party going on tonight at the Convention Center. Devon thanks Caroline and asks her to be ready for anything.

He hangs up and thinks, I can't be at three places at the same time. Barry and I have to get back out to the SCC and Kidd and Ike will check out the party. On their way, they can check out bungalow 7 to see what the hell is going on with that homing device.

Devon phones Ike and gets his answering machine. He can't believe it! He tries again and this time leaves a message. "Call me."

22

THE PRINCE PUTS out his hand and he and Ike shake. The Prince says, "It's a deal. Now how would you like that three million dollars?"

Ike says, "A check will be fine."

The Prince is in a very good mood, He laughs and says, "A check? You are an honest man, my friend. Most of the people I deal with prefer cash or nothing at all. Now, what do you say we retire to the terrace to make a toast and watch the majestic desert sunset?"

Kidd thinks, The sunset? We've got to get out of here. We're not doing anyone any good by hanging around. Come on Ike, get the ball rolling.

Ike says to the Prince, "Your Highness, would you find it in your heart to permit me to take Chataqua out for one last ride?"

The Prince puts his hand on Ike's shoulder and says, "No, of course not. I understand. I'll have one of my men accompany you."

Ike says, "If you have a horse worthy of Chataqua, I would prefer to ride with my trainer."

The Prince says, "A horse worthy of Chataqua has not yet been born but I will have Scheherazade, my personal mare, saddled up. Who knows, perhaps one day she and Chataqua will breed."

Ike says, "Thank you, Your Highness, you are truly a Prince among Princes."

The Prince says, "But, you can't go out like that."

The Prince claps his hands a young man appears. The Prince says something in Arabic and then turns to Ike and Kidd. "These men will give you proper clothing. The desert is not as warm and inviting as you might think."

It's not long before Ike and Kidd are slowly riding west across the desert in the direction of the airport. They are dressed in traditional Bedouin outfits to protect them from the desert cold and sand. Once over the horizon from the Palace, Ike checks his phone machine and calls Devon. He's brought up to date on everything, including the caviar.

Ike hangs up and says to Kidd, "There's something planned for tonight at the hotel. But, our first stop is bungalow number seven in the village. Now, let's see what that horse of yours can do."

Like a timeless photo from a land without time, they speed across the desert. Their robes flowing in the wind, their swords glistening by their sides. Chataqua, thrilled to finally be let loose, leads the way.

Scheherazade, more than happy to follow the stallion, is right behind.

23

MONIQUE STUDIES THE laptop computer. Why in the world would the retinal ID be turned off? It was my insurance policy. Does someone want me dead? Did Dimitra disable it? I doubt it. It's very tough to disable it and not destroy the computer. Then maybe Devon disabled it. Would he want me dead? I could understand that but that would also put Sabrina Rose in danger and that he would never do.

Monique runs a series of tests and doesn't find anything out of the ordinary.

She goes into the bowels of the laptop and looks at the programming code for the Lazer software. She works her way backwards through the code, a variation of reverse engineering. It leads her to a chip buried within the chip of the computer.

A chip with a regular pulse, a pulse being sent out to nowhere. A signal being sent out to everywhere, to space. A homing device. Devon had put it in the computer. That's how he knows where we are! HE DISABLED THE RETINAL ID HOPING I WOULD FIND THE HOMING DEVICE!

Then it hits her. Her husband trusts her. He led her to the homing device confident that she wouldn't tell Dalakos, that she wouldn't set a trap for him.

This is proof that somewhere deep inside, he never really believed that I ran away on my own free will.

She almost breaks down in tears but quickly realizes that crying is a luxury she can't afford.

She calls to Sabrina Rose, "Bring me my bag and yours too. And turn off that TV."

"But maybe Daddy will be on again. Maybe he'll have a secret message for us!"

"Yeah, okay. Sorry. I'm not always thinking clearly."

Sabrina Rose gets up off the couch and brings the two bags to Monique. She gives her mom a hug and says, "Don't worry, Mom, Daddy and I are thinking clearly."

Monique gives her daughter a quick hug and begins rifling through the bags until she finds a metal nail file. She then unscrews the laptop casing. She studies the insides of the computer carefully and then goes through Sabrina Rose's bag. She pulls out a costume jewelry necklace and sets it beside the computer.

Sabrina Rose asks, "What are you doing?"

Monique doesn't look up but says, "I'm making you a new necklace. A necklace you can never take off."

Monique takes Sabrina Rose's face and pulls it close to hers. "Promise me you'll never take it off."

Sabrina Rose says, "Even when I take a shower." "Never except when you take a shower."

"What if I don't like it."

Monique glares at Sabrina Rose who says, "I promise." Monique then carefully takes out the homing chip from the computer and places it on a napkin. Next she takes out the lithium battery from the computer and reconnects it to the chip. She fastens that to the necklace and puts it around Sabrina Rose's neck. Sometimes the best place to hide something is in clear view.

Sabrina Rose looks in the mirror and says, "Style isn't what you do best, Mom."

Monique says, "Looks pretty good to me. And, it doesn't matter, you promised you wouldn't take it off. It's a good luck charm."

Monique stops admiring her work the moment she hears a car pull into the driveway. She hurries to the window and sees Dimitra, the Chameleon and a man she's never seen before coming towards the door.

The stranger is carrying a dress and has a measuring tape around his neck. Monique says, "I have to go to a party tonight. My dress is here. So, no discussion. I have to go. I have no choice."

The door opens and Dimitra marches in with the two men behind her. As usual, the Chameleon doesn't say anything. Dimitra announces, "In the bedroom. You have to be fitted for your dress for tonight."

Monique sighs and follows her three "guests" into the bedroom. Sabrina Rose follows behind her mom. When Monique walks into the bedroom, Dimitra bars the way to Sabrina Rose.

Dimitra says, "You, you wait out here. You don't want to come in."

Sabrina Rose stands at the door.

Dimitra says, "Go watch the television."

At that, she slams the door on Sabrina Rose's face. Monique freezes at the ominous tone in Dimitra's voice. Dimitra points to the tailor and says, "This man will take your measurements. Get undressed."

Monique looks at the Chameleon and asks, "What are you doing here?"

Dimitra answers for him. "Him? He's just here to watch."

The Chameleon speaks. It's the first time Monique has heard his voice. It's cold and metallic, almost artificial. More than ever, this guy gives her the creeps. He says, "Yes. I like to watch."

The Chameleon makes himself comfortable on the bed and Dimitra hovers behind Monique. Monique lifts up her T-shirt. Dimitra says to the Chameleon, "I told you she had nice tits."

The tailor moves towards her with his measuring tape. He says, "You'll have to take off that bra if I'm going to get a correct measurement."

Monique knows he's lying but she won't give him the satisfaction of saying so. It'll just make their little show more interesting for them.

Monique thinks, Let them look at my tits all they want. But, they better not touch me...

24

FREEDOM...Ike and Kidd ride towards the lights of the airport. From there, they'll go straight to the workers' village. Devon will call them if there's any change in the location of the homing device. It could be a dead end but they have to follow up on it.

Chataqua leads the way and rushes up a sand dune.

Scheherazade follows and slips in the sand. She and Kidd lose their balance for a moment but the horse quickly regains it.

But, that moment was enough to send Kidd back to his childhood. To his first time riding a horse, not a walking pony, but a real horse. He was six years old.

The old horse got spooked, who knows why. Doesn't really matter. Nobody knew that it could still ride so fast. Kidd lost his balance and was almost completely out of the saddle, a saddle that was too big for him anyway.

One hand clutched the bridle, his face inches from the stony ground. Out of control. Literally holding on for dear life. Using his stomach muscles he willed his free hand back to the saddle. He forced himself back on to the horse and then held on for dear life. Eventually, the horse got tired and slowed down. Kidd learned three things that day.

ONE: He would have to take care of himself. The adults, the people who put him on that horse, couldn't be trusted.

TWO: He was capable of taking care of himself and...

THREE: He vowed he would never get on a horse the rest of his life.

Though the desert night is cold, Kidd starts to sweat. He grabs the horse's neck to steady himself. The horse senses his fear and slows down. Ike and Chataqua pull away. Ike has to stop at the next hill and wait.

When Kidd finally shows up, Ike doesn't say anything. He's peering at the runway through a pair of computerized glasses. They look like ordinary glasses but are actually binoculars with night vision.

Finally, he says, "Put on your glasses and take a look at this."

Kidd puts on the glasses and everything takes on a greenish tinge. The cloud covered sky is now clear. He zooms in on the airport and watches as a private jet lands. The jet taxis to the terminal. There are already five private jets parked there.

Waiting on the tarmac is none other than Christopher Dalakos. Kidd asks, "Do you see what I see?"

Ike says, "Yeah. I see him. Now who on that plane is so important that Mr. Dalakos is coming to greet him himself?"

They watch as the passengers disembark. Two beautiful women are the first ones off. Elegantly but conservatively dressed, it's impossible to hide their bountiful curves. Next come the bodyguards. Muscular young men whose eyes are everywhere.

After a moment, one of them signals the plane. A white man, not a day under seventy, walks slowly down the stairwell and kisses Dalakos on each cheek. The two of them smile, like old friends.

Kidd says, "You know that guy?"

Ike's voice is cold. "Yeah, I know him. He was the head of the IRA. Back when that meant something. I was sure he was dead. Really sure. Twenty years ago, I killed him myself."

Kidd says, "Yeah? Looks to me like you missed."

Ike says, "Looks that way, doesn't it...The spy business isn't always an exact science."

What he didn't add was, I killed someone. I wonder who it was.

As though reading Ike's mind, Kidd says, "Don't worry. When we kill Dalakos, we'll be sure, believe me."

Ike adds, "Amen."

Kidd and Ike watch as plane after plane comes into the airport. Terrorist after terrorist gets off and is personally greeted by Dalakos. Ike snaps away with his zoom-equipped portable phone and says, "North Koreans, Basques, Chechens, Iranians...This is a page right out of the 'Who's Who of Danger.'"

Kidd says, "More like the 'Assholes of assholes.'"

Then Ike adds, "Strange bedfellows for a group of guys who hate each other."

Kidd stares down at the airport, formulating a plan in his mind. "We've got to do something about those planes."

Ike says, "What do you suggest? Two guys armed with swords ride down there and slash their tires? Maybe while we're at it we can write some graffiti, BAD TERRORISTS GO HOME!"

"I was thinking more along the lines of taking over one plane and rolling it into the others."

Ike rolls his eyes. "You've been watching too many James Bond films." He pulls out his phone. "We're going to need the cavalry on this one."

"I think you've forgotten that you're no longer head of PACT."

"Thanks for reminding me."

Ike then presses a button on his phone and Caroline immediately picks up.

"Caroline, it's crunch time. I'm uploading some photos to you. It's Dalakos and his friends. They're having a party. We're at Prince Faqir's Airport in Yanbo Province, in Saudi. Get the GPS location from my phone. Take everything you sent us with what I'm sending you and get it to Amanda. You've got to convince her to level this place."

Ike listens for a moment and says, "Give us as much warning as you can but don't wait for us to get out of range. There's too much at stake."

Ike hangs up and says, "Come on, let's get to that bungalow." Kidd adds, "And then let's see where all that caviar and whiskey has ended up. My guess is that there's a founder's meeting of Murder Incorporated Tonight."

Ike stops and says, "There's one more plane taxiing. Let's check it out."

They crawl back to their observation point. Dalakos is waiting on the tarmac to greet the plane. A breeze comes across the desert as the clouds move away to reveal the full moon. Dalakos seems to look right in their direction. He quickly walks to his car and drives away without waiting for the plane.

Kidd notices Ike's bald head is reflecting the moonlight. Kidd says, "Let's get out of here. I think we've been spotted."

The two of them slither away from the hill. They reach their waiting horses and mount up. They see a cloud of sand moving their way.

They take out their binoculars and see it's a machine-gun mounted jeep speeding towards them. Kidd and Ike signal their horses and speed away across the desert.

25

SABRINA ROSE sits in the back of the SUV with Dimitra next to her. The man with the funny voice is sitting next to Mom. She's wearing a beautiful dress, made by some French designer. She doesn't look too happy, which I can understand. I don't look too happy myself. But, at least she doesn't have to wear this body covering. Me, I'm stuck in it, veiled from head to toe. Thank God the car is air-conditioned.

The ride to the Convention Center Hotel takes only a couple of minutes. They turn a corner and it looks like the Limousine Dealers Convention. Limo after limo, broken up only by the occasional military vehicle. Whose military, it's difficult to tell.

Their SUV is spotted and after a cursory check, is whisked into the underground parking garage. From there, the four of them get into an elevator.

As soon as the door closes, Monique feels the Chameleon pressing against her from behind. Like a predator stalking his prey. Monique feels uncomfortable for more than the obvious reasons. If the Chameleon dares to take such liberties with "Christopher's woman" then he must feel that I'm "fair game" and that Christopher has indicated that the Chameleon can have me later.

Finally, the elevator reaches the top floor. The elevator opens onto a rooftop terrace with a panoramic view of the desert. Sabrina Rose peers out from her veil and says, "Look at that!"

She points to what looks like a giant American flag painted in black across the desert. In fact it's not paint, but something cheaper, oil.

Monique knows what it is. It's her target. She had seen it at the SCC, from the photos taken from the weather satellites. Just like in a cruise missile, the Lazer will match the photo from the satellite with the image on the ground. When there's a match, everything is blown to all hell! She just didn't appreciate how big it was. The "flag" is at least as big as a football field.

Once again, Monique wonders if she should go through with this. And once again, she weighs the pros and cons. She thinks, I've got to stay alive long enough for me or Devon to save us. He's not far away, I know he's not far away.

She takes one look at Sabrina Rose and says to herself, My God, I hope this Lazer works!

The Chameleon takes Monique by the arm and says, "Come on, it's time to go."

Dimitra grabs Sabrina Rose by the arm and says, "Come on, it's time to stay."

Before Sabrina Rose can protest, Monique forces a smile and says, "Don't worry, honey, I won't be long."

The Chameleon ogles Monique and says, "Yeah, but I might be." He laughs as he leads Monique away. A raspy laugh that sounded like it could become convulsions at any moment.

26

CAROLINE KNOWS THE easy part is over. I've gotten all the photos together with all the info for Devon and Ike. Now, to get them to Amanda in time. Which means, first I have to find her. I could check her secretary's computer, her computer, her credit card records to see her shopping habits. If I had time, there are a million things I could find out about her. But, since I don't have time, I'll try the obvious first. I'll try her computer.

It's child's play for Caroline to go through Amanda's computer. After all, she's the webmaster in charge of all PACT computers and she took all the passwords and entry codes with her when she left.

She looks at Amanda's agenda page: "KC" for tonight. What the hell is KC? Or who the hell is KC? On the same day's entry is: X location unknown. XX out of the way.

While she ponders that, she notices on the other pages, Xs next to entries every day. Sometimes one X sometimes two. She follows the entry backward through time and notices that the Xs go back for years.

It must mean something but I don't have the time to look into it. I've already wasted ten minutes. Then, like a light bulb going on in her head, she picks up the phone. I'll do it the old-fashioned way. I'll call her.

Amanda picks up on the first ring with a neutral, "Yes?" "Amanda, Caroline."

Amanda makes an effort to sound as though she's happy to hear from her. "So, how is vacation treating you?"

Caroline gets right to the point. "I need to talk to you. It's a matter of life and death."

Amanda says, "That sounds dramatic. I'm all ears."

"I need to see you in person. It's too big to go out over the phone."

Amanda says, "Alright. I'm leaving the office in twenty minutes. Be here before then or forget it."

Amanda hangs up before Caroline can get in another word.

Caroline calculates the distance to the office. She presses a button on the land line phone. "How fast can you get me to Langley, Virginia?"

27

KIDD AND IKE race to a hilltop and abruptly stop. They look behind them and see that the jeep is still heading their way.

Ike says, "We've got to do something about that jeep. The men we can take care of later."

Ike attaches his binoculars with night vision and surveys the desert in every direction. "I'm looking for an area that has no vegetation. Nothing."

Kidd watches as the jeep comes closer. Close enough for him to see that there's a driver and a uniformed man riding shotgun. But, in this case, shotgun is a 50 caliber machine gun. He knows it's a 50 caliber from the sound it makes as they begin firing at them.

Kidd thinks, They're still too far away to be accurate but they could get lucky.

Kidd says, "Well, here's to hoping you find it soon."

Ike doesn't say anything. Kidd thinks, Uniforms. Looks like the local police are doing Dalakos' bidding.

Finally, Ike puts the reins to Chataqua and says, "Follow me."

28

CAROLINE TELLS THE PILOT to put it down in the parking lot. The pilot shakes his head. "I was told to do whatever you wanted, but there's nowhere down there to put this baby."

Caroline says, "Sure there is. Get me as close to that pick-up as you can. I'll take it from there."

The pilot says, "If I get out of this alive, I'm asking Mr. Williams for a raise."

He lowers the helicopter to ten feet above the pick-up. A flinch here and they're goners.

Caroline thanks the pilot and slithers out the door and onto the helicopter pylons. She hangs down from the pylon and shouts up for him to go lower. Either he doesn't hear over the noise of the helicopter or pretends he doesn't. She lets herself fall, bends her knees to take the shock and lands on the bed of the pick-up.

She jumps to the ground, waves to the pilot and runs towards the front door of "the Shop." She runs past a uniformed chauffeur standing by a limousine right at the front door. Just as she heads in, Amanda comes out of an elevator. Black dress, white pearls, high heels, make-up.

It's Caroline's turn to be dumbstruck with how good she looks. Before she can compliment her, Amanda icily says, "Just in the nick of time."

Caroline pleads, "I really need to talk to you."

Amanda makes a point of looking at her watch and says, "I really don't have a lot of time."

A pained look comes over Caroline's face and Amanda says, "You can ride with me if you like."

Caroline hesitates. This limo wasn't exactly the place she had in mind.

Amanda says, "I'm going. Do what you want."

Amanda motions to the driver who immediately opens the door. Amanda gets in and before he can close the door, Caroline gets in too. The limousine takes off and Amanda says, "You look like you could use a drink."

Caroline says, "Thanks, I'm fine," and reaches forward to bring up the panel that separates them from the chauffeur.

Amanda says, "Okay, you've got until we get to the Kennedy Center to convince me what's so important. Tonight, I'm sitting with the President in his box and I have no intention of being late."

Caroline begins by saying, "Christopher Dalakos is..." Amanda reacts immediately. "Christopher Dalakos WAS! He's past tense, old news, he's dead."

Caroline takes out her coup de grace, the photos of Dalakos greeting all the terrorists at the airport and hands them to Amanda. "This is proof that Christopher Dalakos is alive. Tonight he's gathered everyone from our most wanted list in the same place!"

Amanda hands the photos back. "It could be that you're right. But, it could also be that the photos are doctored. You know what can be done with digital photos. How do I know when these were taken?"

Caroline says, "These photos are real. Kidd and Ike sent them to me! I talked to them by phone."

Amanda now knows where this is all coming from. Another conspiracy to get her to look ridiculous in the eyes of the President so Ike can get his job back!

Amanda tries to remain calm. "And, if I believe you that these photos are real, what do you want me to do about it in such a rush?"

"I want you to order Prince Faqir's airport leveled and I want you to send in a Rapid Deployment Team to eliminate those terrorists."

The limousine comes to a stop at the Kennedy Center. There are beautiful well-dressed people everywhere. Limos line the curb. It's Washington's big night out.

Amanda says, "You want me to bomb Saudi Arabia? That's what you came here to ask me? You want me to bomb Saudi Arabia?"

Caroline pleads, "Yes! Right now! Immediately!"

The chauffeur opens Amanda's door. As she gets out, she says to Caroline, "That vacation of yours. Make it permanent."

Amanda walks towards the entrance to the Kennedy Center without looking back. Caroline, standing there in sneakers, jeans and a blue work shirt couldn't possibly look more out of place.

The chauffeur asks, "Can I drop you somewhere?" Caroline says, "Uh, yeah. You could. Thanks."

She lets herself into the back of the limo and asks the chauffeur, "Could you take me around to the back entrance?"

The chauffeur, a little surprised, answers, "Sure, okay." They pull out past the long line of limousines, head towards the back of the Center but can't get any further. There's a concrete barricade manned by uniformed police. Caroline says,

"Thanks, this'll do fine."

She steps out of the limo, walks over to the first policeman she sees and says, "I need to talk to Agent Dalton Roberts. My name is Caroline Crimmins. It's a matter of life and death."

The policeman looks at her to see if there's anything dangerous or crazy about her and then says, "Please wait here a moment please."

He calls over to another cop and says, "Stay with her. I'll be right back."

29

KIDD AND IKE race over a hill with the jeep closing in. As they come flying over it, they split in two directions. The sand is softer here but the horses navigate it and head towards the next sand dune.

The jeep comes flying over and lands flat in a sand hollow. Stuck. Ike and Kidd hear the jeep engine straining to get loose. They turn their horses and take a deep breath. Ike had found a spot with no vegetation. No roots. No water. Only sand.

Kidd says, "Let's leave 'em. We don't need them dead." "Just like I taught you. Rule number I forget which one...

The less you fight the less chance you have of something going wrong and getting yourself killed. So, only fight when it's absolutely necessary."

Kidd says, "Which means, 'Let's get the hell out of Dodge.'" They take off across the desert but quickly rein in the horses. They can just barely make out the sound of a helicopter coming their way.

30

FIFTEEN LONG MINUTES later, Agent Dalton Roberts comes briskly walking over to Caroline. He signals for the cops to leave him alone and then gets right to the point. "Okay, what's this about a matter of life and death?"

"I need to talk to the President. It's concerning an imminent terrorist attack."

Dalton says, "Whoa. Come on, Caroline. We have channels for that. Procedures. Talk to your boss, not the President."

Caroline would've preferred not to say it but can't see a way around it. "I did talk to my boss and she didn't believe me. In fact, she fired me."

Her honesty has a positive effect. She can see Dalton's demeanor change.

Dalton softly says, "Sorry about you getting fired but I can't help you."

"Dalton, I just got a medal from the President himself. There is something big going on and it's going to happen soon. The only one who can do something about it fast is the President himself. I just need five minutes. Look, I'm not going to embarrass anyone and I'm not going to kill the President. I'm unarmed. I'll prove it."

Caroline unbuttons the top button of her shirt. Then the second. The other cops notice and their eyes are glued in their direction. As she reaches for the crucial third button, Dalton says, "Okay, okay. Let's talk inside."

As Caroline follows Dalton past the disappointed cops, she says, "Sorry fellas, maybe next time."

They get inside and stop by a service stairway. Dalton says, "Okay, Caroline. I've made an executive decision. I'm going to get you five minutes with the President. I hope whatever you've got in that dossier is convincing."

Caroline sighs with relief and says, "You won't regret this, I promise."

"Regret? I just don't want to lose my job."

Dalton talks into a phone. "I'm coming up the stairs with a woman. Have Sanchez meet us there. I'm bringing a message to Number One."

Dalton's hesitation is gone. He starts walking up the stairs and says to Caroline, "Come on, there's no turning back now."

Caroline marches up behind him. When they get to the top, Agent Sanchez is waiting for them.

Dalton says, "This is Caroline Crimmins. Stay with her until I come back with the President."

Dalton walks past two more agents and disappears into the Presidential

Box of the Kennedy Center. Caroline doesn't say a word to Sanchez. I think I'll quit while I'm ahead.

Dalton steps into the Presidential Box and immediately spots the President. Looking at the back of his head reminds him of the view John Wilkes Booth must have had before he shot President Lincoln at a theater not too far from this one.

This President is listening to some cowboy-hatted country singer twanging away. Lincoln was watching a comedy, "American Cousin."

Sitting next to him is Amanda Mason, PACT head and Caroline's boss, make that former boss. The gossip around town is that the two of them are having an affair.

One thing about being in the Secret Service, you really do know what goes on behind closed doors at the White House. The fact is that the President and the Mrs. sleep in separate rooms and nothing has happened between him and Ms. Mason. Nothing yet, anyway.

Dalton walks down the aisle to where the President can see him. The last thing on earth he would do is come up from behind the President. When he's sure the President has seen him, he takes a step past Amanda and whispers in the President's ear. "Sorry sir but I have to ask you to come with me for a moment. There's a situation that just can't wait."

The President asks no questions. He excuses himself to Amanda and follows Dalton. They step out into the brightly lit hallway.

Standing there is Caroline and Agent Sanchez. Two other agents hover nearby.

Caroline says, "Sorry to bring you away from the show, sir." The President says, "To tell the truth, I hate country music. But it makes me look like a man of the people, which I assure you I am, but that's another story."

Caroline says, "I'm Caroline Crimmins. You gave me a medal..."

The President cuts her off. "I know who you are. What's this all about?"

Caroline gives it her best shot. Photos, data, wiretaps, the whole nine yards. Then she tops it off with her request that the airport be leveled.

The President wavers. "Very persuasive. Amanda Mason is here. Let me get her opinion on this."

Caroline hurriedly says, "She didn't believe me. Do you?" The President says, "I need more confirmation than what you've shown me before I go and bomb Saudi Arabia of all places."

At that moment, Amanda comes out from the Presidential Box. "What the hell are you doing here? You ARE crazy."

Caroline pleads, "Please, Mr. President. If you don't believe me, talk to Kidd Black."

Caroline pulls out her portable phone and presses one button. Amanda walks towards her and reaches for the phone. "Give me that!"

31

CHATAQUA AND SCHEHEREZADE are having the time of their lives. An endless playground is before them. Running full speed to their heart's content. They loop back to where the jeep is stuck. The rolling sand dunes cover them. But, the fun and games are over now.

They get up a full head of steam and come stampeding towards the hill. A jumping horse has to have complete confidence in its rider. Chataqua would take Ike anywhere and is about to prove it. Luckily for Kidd, Scheherazade would follow Chataqua anywhere.

The helicopter is coming closer. Close enough to start firing. The bullets bury into the sand with a soft pop.

When Ike and Kidd come to the crest of the hill, they unsheathe their swords and signal their horses. They literally come flying over the hill. The two men in the jeep are frozen with fear. Out of nowhere, two men on horseback are charging at them. Not really at them, but over them. As they go by, they slash them with their swords across their necks. The two men don't even make a sound as they die. Their faces are now just frozen silent screams.

Kidd and Ike dismount. Ike has the two horses lie down in the sand. As Kidd zigzags back towards the jeep on foot, his phone starts buzzing. The helicopter chooses Kidd as the first target and fires as he jumps into the jeep.

Kidd swings the machine gun towards the helicopter and pumps everything he's got into the helicopter. The 50 caliber bullets tear through the fuselage. The exploding helicopter lights up the desert like a supernova. Noise, fire and then silence.

32

CAROLINE TAKES A STEP back and begs the phone to answer. Amanda moves closer.

Caroline says, "You'd do anything to stop Monique Williams from being saved. You hate her because you still love Devon Williams!"

Amanda keeps walking towards her but a little slower. "You're crazy."

"I saw it in your computer. You're obsessed with her. You kept pushing the idea that she had been kidnapped! That she had to be killed!"

Amanda reaches for the phone. "Give me that." NO!

Amanda screams, "NOBODY SAYS NO TO ME!" The President says, "Amanda, stop." Amanda shouts back at him, "Shut up!"

Amanda lunges for the phone. Caroline slaps Amanda right across the face sending her to the floor. The Secret Service Agents take out their guns but Dalton waves them off.

At last, Kidd answers the phone. Caroline says a prayer of thanks and then says, "Kidd, the President wants to talk to you."

33

LAWRENCE AND NADINE are watching TV. Lawrence stands up and yawns. "I've never watched this much TV in my life...and a station in Arabic to boot!

"It's our only connection to the outside world. Maybe, just maybe, Devon or Kidd can get a message to us and Monique and her daughter."

Lawrence is tempted to say, "If Kidd is still alive", but he doesn't see the point.

The door to the bungalow flies open. Nobody knocks at this hotel. Two guards come in. They grab Lawrence and signal Nadine to get up. Nadine slowly stands.

Lawrence, his voice shaky, says, "This can't be good."

One guard then pulls out two dark hoods from a sack. Nadine takes a deep breath and looks right at her husband. "My only regret is that we won't have a chance to say goodbye to our son."

Lawrence, his voice shaking, says, "Amen."

The guard goes to put the hood over Lawrence's head. Lawrence, surprising even himself with the strength of his voice, shouts, "Wait!"

The guard hesitates. Lawrence steps over to Nadine. Lawrence says, "Kiss me like it's the last time."

Nadine forces a smile and says, "Kiss me like it's the first time!"

They kiss passionately. Nothing like staring into the eyes of death to make you appreciate the wonders of life.

34

DILEMMA.. Kidd and Ike ride across the desert until they come to the outskirts of the workers village. They stop.

Kidd says, "I can't imagine anything more conspicuous than two Bedouins, one black and one bald, riding horses down the street. If that doesn't get the local police on the case, nothing will."

"We don't have a choice. It's the quickest way. We'll just say we're going to a costume party."

"No. I've got a better idea."

Kidd jumps off his horse and rips off his Bedouin outfit.

Kidd says, "I'll run there. It'll be just as quick and look a lot less suspicious."

Ike says, "You running around at night barefoot in your underwear isn't suspicious? But, I know that tone of voice of yours. No sense in arguing about it."

Kidd takes off jogging through the village. As soon as he gets out of sight, Ike's phone rings. It's Devon. The homing device has headed for the hotel. Ike says, "Kidd has taken off to check out bungalow 7. We'll get to that hotel as soon as he gets back."

Ike hangs up and curses himself for not thinking of having Kidd take his phone with him.

Kidd jogs his way through the village. It's set up like a typical American city complete with a mall, supermarket, and movie complexes. Each bungalow has a low white picket fence around it. They've obviously done everything to make the workers feel right at home.

Kidd follows Caroline's directions to a secluded area set off from the rest of the bungalows. He jogs by number 7. There's a man sitting idly by the front door. Well-built, white, around thirty, wearing a jacket. Judging by the way he touched his jacket when Kidd ran by, probably armed.

Kidd thinks, This is what I get paid for.

Kidd turns around and heads back towards bungalow 7. He stops right in front of it and watches as the guard tenses but doesn't react. After all, it's just some black guy, barefoot, in a T-shirt and his underpants.

Kidd proceeds to piss through the picket fence onto the sidewalk that leads to the bungalow.

Kidd thinks, Talk about low-tech. But, this has to get the guy going. One of the most primordial instincts is protection of territory. Here I am pissing on his territory. There is no more ancient insult.

The guard isn't thinking that deeply. He sees a crazy guy pissing through the fence. He shouts over to Kidd in a language he doesn't know but from the tone of his voice it's probably the equivalent of, "What the hell do you think you're doing?"

Kidd shouts back, "Fuck you!" Kidd remembers that the three most widely known English words in the world are Coke, okay and fuck.

The guard gets up and moves towards Kidd. Kidd thinks, This is more like it.

The guard pulls out his gun and curses in only slightly accented English, "Fuck you is it? Well, fuck this!"

The guard gets close enough. Kidd puts one hand on the fence, leaps up and kicks him in the face. Stunned but not down, the guard is knocked a step back. Kidd jumps over the fence and the rest is just a formality. Kidd takes the unconscious guard's gun, puts his penis back in his shorts and goes into the bungalow.

Kidd rushes through every room hoping to find Sabrina Rose or Monique. No one. He finds some clothes. Clothes that would fit a young girl and some that would fit a woman.

Kidd finds Devon's laptop. He studies it carefully. He can see from the scratch marks on the screws that they've been turned.

He takes a closer look at the gun. It's an Italian Beretta. He empties the gun of its eight bullets and throws it in the toilet. The last thing he needs is to be seen running through the village with a gun in his hand.

He leaves by the front door, checks to see that the guard is still out and jogs back to Ike.

35

DALAKOS SURVEYS THE roof top terrace from the security booth. The stage is a rectangle at one end of the terrace up against a wall. He doesn't like the idea of anyone coming up behind him. One can never be too sure. That old saying about there being honor among thieves or in this case terrorists never rang true for him.

The rest of his guests will be seated at circular tables. A truly international cast. One would think it was one of those do-gooder organizations. What a headache setting up the seating. Some tables, no alcohol, some no pork, some even no women. But they all have a thirst for power, a hunger for destruction.

Dalakos spots some movement on another screen. It's Monique and the Chameleon entering another dressing room.

He smiles and thinks, Monique looks truly magnificent. Fit for a King. What a coup. The stuff legends are made of. Devon Williams' wife, here, ready to do anything for Christopher Dalakos. Even so far as to deliver the ultimate weapon to him!

Maybe keeping her around wouldn't be such a bad idea, after all. Of course, I'd have to do something about that little brat.

He checks a screen that shows Dimitra and Sabrina Rose in a bare, well-lit room. Dimitra sits with her back to the door and Sabrina Rose sits across from her at an empty table facing her. It makes him smile to see how much they hate each other.

Dalakos checks himself in the mirror before going to meet them. Powerful, fit, the expensive white suit shows off his tan. He likes what he sees. He goes outside for one last check to make sure everything is ready for the big show before making his Grand Entrance.

Monique sits in the dressing room with the Chameleon. She sits at one end of the well-lit room and he at the other. He turns on the makeup lights that go the length of the mirrors making the room almost blindingly bright.

He says, "Cross your legs." His voice is even stranger than usual. To his usual rasp is added a breathy urgency.

In another circumstance, in a different life, Monique would have just laughed at him. Now, she stalls for time. She says, "I'm sorry? What did you say?"

The Chameleon is happy to repeat his request. It clearly turns him on. His breathing gets heavier, he rasps, "Cross your legs."

Monique hesitates. What would Christopher say if I told him this man, his underling, was coming on to her? Would he care? Would this man take the chance of incurring Christopher's wrath if he wasn't sure that it was okay? Probably not.

Monique looks him straight in the eye and crosses her legs. Nylon against nylon, silk against silk. The Chameleon puts his hand to his crotch. "Now uncross them."

Monique slowly uncrosses them and pulls her dress down below her knees. She wonders how long this is going to go on and when Christopher is going to arrive. She realizes the irony of hoping that Christopher will rescue her.

She can't dwell on her predicament too long because she hears, "Now, walk. Walk for me."

Monique thinks, If he unzips his pants, I'm making a break for it.

Monique walks across the room for him. She tries to walk as prudishly as possible but for the Chameleon it's now clear that whatever she does it's going to be great for him. He's slowly rubbing himself through his pants. He's got that far away look of a man who is about to climax.

She thinks, Normally you can tell if a man is going to come from his breathing but with him it's hard to tell what sounds from him are normal or not.

Monique hears footsteps. The door opens and in walks Dalakos. The Chameleon quickly pulls his hands away from his pants. Monique thinks, So, it looks like this ogre was acting on his own initiative. I suppose that's a good thing.

Monique is almost happy to see Dalakos and says, "I'm ready. Shall we go?"

Dalakos says, "You have never looked more beautiful.." He then looks at The Chameleon as he asks, "eh, my friend?"

The Chameleon looks bored and says, "I hadn't noticed but now that you say so, yes, she does look...better than usual."

Dalakos says, "Come, let's go."

Dalakos takes Monique by the hand and they walk across the hall towards the double doors that open onto the roof top terrace. The Chameleon is right behind. Dalakos pulls a veil out of his pocket and pulls her to him.

"Before I put this on you..." He stops and kisses her passionately. She has no choice but to kiss him back. He roughly pulls away and says, "Put this on. Don't say a word until I tell you."

He puts the veil over her face. They walk up the stairs to the terrace. All eyes turn towards them as they head for the stage. Monique peers out through her veil and sees a well-dressed crowd with beautiful elegant women. She feels relieved. She didn't know what to expect but didn't expect everyone to look so normal. They reach the stage. Dalakos signals Monique to stand next to him. She does.

Dalakos motions for the room to be silent.

"My friends. Welcome. Welcome to a historic evening. I'm sure once you see tonight's demonstration, you will be more than happy to invest. But, an investment is only as good as the team behind it."

Dalakos moves behind Monique and continues, "And the head of the team behind our project, is none other than Monique Williams, the wife of Devon Williams."

He rips off the veil from Monique and the assembled terrorists gasp in disbelief. Dalakos says, "Monique Williams will now give you a brief explanation of what you are about to see. Monique."

Monique stands. She's given dozens of demonstrations before and tries to convince herself that this is just like any other.

Her voice confident, she says, "Thank you, Christopher. Tonight we're going to show you the latest in laser technology. But, not lasers as you know them but the future of lasers and the future of lasers begins tonight. The beauty of these lasers is that they are inexhaustible. They're solar powered and because the lasers are in space, there is no limit to their power. As long as there is a sun, they will work.

Like anything, these lasers can be used for good or for evil. They can drill for oil or they can blow up oil wells, they can..."

Dalakos interrupts her and says, "I think it's time for the demonstration."

The assembled terrorists laugh. Monique says, "Yes, of course."

Dalakos says, "There are thirty-three weather satellites hovering above us. Thanks to the software developed by Monique, all the satellites will send a laser beam to the same spot at the same time. There has never been a system more pinpoint, more accurate. My guests, if you'll turn your attention over the terrace railing, you'll see what looks like a large American flag in the desert."

Dalakos turns to Monique and says, "Let the show begin!"

36

KIDD AND IKE RIDE across the desert. The full moon lights their way. The time for talking is over. They're riding like the wind, but faster.

Ike thinks, Devon said the homing device is in the hotel on the west wing on the top floor. That's the sixth floor.

Kidd thinks, Everything points to Monique and Sabrina Rose being in that hotel. With a little luck, we can kill a few birds with one stone. Get to the hotel, get them out and get away before the Air Force levels the place

37

ONCE AGAIN, Devon, Barry and Dick Brewer head down the desert road to the Satellite Control Center. Dick says, "It's just going to be the three of us at the SCC."

Devon asks, "Where is everyone?"

"Nobody'll go in until the Scorpion Men show up. That's what they call the bug killers around here. And they're not showing up until tomorrow. The only ones there are some pretty jumpy guards...if they're still there."

Devon says, "Alright then. As long as we can take a look at that supercomputer."

Brewer says, "Will do. Now, nothing for us to do but enjoy the ride."

They ride in silence across the desert road. Nothing for miles but sand, moonlit sand. The novelty has worn off and the monotony depresses Barry and Devon.

Brewer says, "Look, the first thing we'll do when we get there is crunch a few scorpions. You boys aren't afraid of a couple of spiders are you?"

Devon and Barry look at their feet. Not to avoid eye contact with Brewer but to make sure their shoes don't have any holes in them.

Brewer continues, "And the second thing we'll do is take a little tour of the SCC to check out that supercomputer and the third thing is have a little Texas barbecue. I doubt the cowards who ran away bothered to take all that fine prime rib with them. Flown in fresh from Texas."

Barry smiles politely and rechecks his shoes. Devon pretends to laugh but something is bothering him. When Brewer put out his finger to signify "first," he used his thumb. Then when he signified "second," he used his thumb and index finger. "Third," his thumb, index and middle fingers. Americans use the index finger for the number one.

Brewer said he was Texas born and bred. Would he have picked that up here? He doubts it. People always count in their mother tongue and he imagined something like this would be the same. Devon personally brought Dick into Microtech almost twenty years ago. His impressive credentials were thoroughly checked and he had turned out to be a brilliant and loyal employee.

Still something was nagging him. And if something wasn't quite right, someone is hiding something.

Devon picks up his phone and writes a text message to Caroline. "Check out Dick Brewer. IMMEDIATELY!"

38

DALAKOS AND MONIQUE walk to a table set up by the stage. He lifts off a cover and unveils the control system. He says, "Let Monique Williams be the one to turn on this historic switch!"

Monique checks the coordinates to be sure everything is in place. It should be a piece of cake, the target isn't moving and hasn't moved.

Monique clicks on the icon. Nothing happens. There is a murmur from the crowd but Monique isn't worried. She had explained to Christopher that the satellites were in orbit 22,500 miles above the earth. It took time for the lazer to get into perfect position. Anything less than perfect and they'd miss the target completely.

After two minutes the murmur has turned into a dull roar. Shouts of, "What is this bullshit?" in many languages fill the air. And then, out of nowhere, a beam appears from nowhere and from everywhere at the same time. It cuts its way perfectly along the outline of the "flag."

Smoke, fire. When the smoke clears, the "flag" has completely disappeared. A sixty foot crater has been dug into the sand without anything around it touched.

The room is on its feet. A man holds up his glass and says, "A toast. To the Chief of Chiefs!" Another man shouts, "To the Prince of Princes." Still another voice says, "To the King of Kings, to Christopher Dalakos!"

The room begins a rhythmic chant, "Da-La-Kos! Da-La-Kos! Da-La-Kos!"

Monique is frozen in shock. Dalakos? Christopher Dalakos? The terrorist? That's the only Dalakos there is! Oh my God! What have I done? If I had known it was Dalakos, I would've blown up this terrace with me and everyone on it!

She sighs a sigh of hopelessness and thinks of Sabrina Rose.

Or would I have?

Dalakos tries to shout above the crowd but they can't be stopped. Glory is his! Respect is his! Now for the final touch, the coup de grace!

He calmly begins to speak, knowing they will quiet down to hear him. "My friends, targets must be chosen. So, let the bidding begin. You have received envelopes. Make your bid, choose your target and once the money is confirmed, let the party begin!"

39

THE HORSES SAW IT FIRST...They stopped and looked off to the west across the desert. Kidd and Ike followed the horses' gaze and saw the light come down from the sky. Awestruck, they watched as the beam cut its way across the target.

Ike looks dazed. "My God! That can only be one thing!" "Let's not jump to conclusions. Maybe it's a hoax of some sort. A trick."

Ike's voice is quiet, almost a whisper. "That was no trick. That's the lazer. It works."

Kidd adds, "It works and Dalakos has it."

They take off towards the hotel in the distance, both of them thinking, Looks like it's on to PLAN C.

40

THE FIRST INDICATION that something was up was the radio turning to static.

Barry says, "Holy shit. Look at that!"

Brewer and Devon turn to see the beam come out of the sky. As soon as it starts to cut its way across the target, Devon knows that only the Lazer can do that. He feels a surge of emotion knowing that his years of work have finally paid off. But, at what price?

Barry says, "Is that what I think it is?"

Devon says, "Yes, but unfortunately, you can't even begin to think what it really is!"

Devon shouts to Brewer, "Step on it! We've got to get to the SCC!"

As Brewer hits the gas, a very tiny current of air causes some grains of sand to swirl across the desert. When the Lazer hit the ground, it burned a hole into the target, displacing the air and causing a depression.

The Lazer cut through the sand counterclockwise...counterclockwise, just like a hurricane.

41

DALAKOS STANDS BEFORE the room holding an envelope in his hand. It has all the markings of the Academy Awards but one could say that the stakes are a lot higher. He holds the envelope up and the room quickly becomes quiet. "I have here the highest bid which is for 1.4 billion dollars!"

A gasp comes from the crowd.

Dalakos says, "Yes, 1.4 billion dollars! And with the highest bid comes the honor of choosing the first target..."

He opens up the envelope and smiles. "Washington, D.C., USA." The room erupts into wild applause.

Dalakos has to shout over the ecstatic crowd to be heard. "We'll start at the White House and then burn our way across the city from there!"

Monique is in shock. I've put the lazer into the hands of Christopher Dalakos! I've got to find a way for me and Sabrina Rose to get out of here!

Luckily, without me, they can't use the lazer. Without me, they can't destroy Washington!

She desperately looks around the terrace for a way out and quickly realizes that for the moment, there is no way out...for the moment.

She forces herself to smile as Christopher continues to speak. "The money will be confirmed in two hours and then the heart of the United States will beat no more!"

Just when it sounded like the crowd couldn't get any noisier it roars even louder. A wild chant is heard from the back of the room and it soon becomes a wave of sound that crashes across Dalakos and Monique. "Two hours! Two hours!"

Dalakos turns to the Chameleon, "Put the satellites into position. Then wait for my orders."

Monique feels sick. They don't need me anymore. They watched me work and now they can do it themselves. They don't need to be perfect to hit the target! The target is all of Washington! I'm expendable. Sabrina Rose is expendable!

Dalakos turns to Monique and says, "My friend will take you to Dimitra and your daughter. I'll see you back at the bungalow."

Dalakos kisses her passionately in front of the admiring crowd. She decides to deny him this one little pleasure. She pulls away from him and slaps him across the face. The terrace immediately goes silent.

Dalakos is frozen in place. Monique has only a moment. She shouts, "You'll never get away with this! Devon Williams will see to it!"

At the mention of her husband's name, the crowd begins to laugh. If that's the only thing they have to worry about, it's not much of a threat. Dalakos takes the opportunity to grab her by the wrist. He pushes her towards the Chameleon and says, "Take her to Dimitra! You have more important things to do!"

The Chameleon pulls her by the hand and forces her towards the door. Before they're out, she shouts, "Kidd Black will see you roast in hell!"

The laughter stops. She had said the magic words. "Kidd Black."

Everyone speaks at once.

Everyone looks worried, everyone except Dalakos.

He holds up his hands and everyone eventually quiets down.

He grabs Monique with one arm, forces her to face the crowd, and speaks. "Kidd Black? You think I should be afraid of Kidd Black? There is no reason to fear Kidd Black! I can assure you that he wouldn't dare show his face here. He knows if he does..."

Dalakos waves his arms and a man and a woman, wearing black hoods are thrust on the stage next to him and Monique. Dalakos continues, "He knows if he does...Dalakos rips off the black hoods revealing Lawrence and Nadine—his parents will die a most horrible death!"

The crowd once again chants, DA -LA -KOS! DA -LA -KOS! Dalakos basks in their chanting. He pulls Monique close to him and quietly says, "Such a waste that you will see Dimitra before I have a chance to enjoy you one more time. When she's finished with you, there will be nothing left to enjoy."

Dalakos tries to silence the crowd to no avail. He shouts above the chanting, "Say goodbye to Monique everyone!"

The assembled multitude find this deliciously funny. They break out in laughter and shout, "Goodbye Monique!"

Lawrence and Nadine aren't laughing, they're terrified. So terrified they forget they're afraid.

Nadine whispers, "He's going to kill Monique, God bless her soul. If we can't stop that, there's a chance the little girl's still alive. We've got to find her!"

Lawrence surveys the terrace and whispers back, "And in order to find her, we've got to find a way out of here!"

Nadine thinks, We've already tried Alzheimer's. It worked once, the other time it was a complete flop. Gotta go with a sure thing, something everyone understands. Terrorists by definition don't get subtlety.

The moment Monique is escorted from the room, Nadine shouts, "My husband's heart! Oh my God!"

Right on cue, Lawrence grabs his heart.

Nadine takes a deep breath, swallows her pride and gets on her knees. She crawls towards Dalakos. "Please! My husband has a heart condition. His medicine is at our bungalow. Please, we have to get there immediately, please!"

Dalakos looks down at Nadine and announces in a voice loud enough for everyone to hear, "We don't want your husband dying... just yet!"

Everyone laughs!

Dalakos orders a burly guard to take them back to their bungalow.

42

CAROLINE HURRIES DOWN the hall at PACT accompanied by Secret Service Agent Dalton. She thrusts open the door to her office. The young man who took her job looks up at her, just like he's seeing a ghost. Caroline says, "Get the hell out of my office."

He sputters a few words. Dalton says, "You heard her, now get out."

The man hurries out and Caroline sits down in front of her computer. It's just like coming home. She gets into her photo ID program and runs a reverse ID search for Brewer's photo. It's like going back into time. She goes through Brewer's career at Microtech in rewind down to his first day there, him proudly smiling as he poses for his first ID photo.

Then it's off to Texas A&M Graduate School. Him and his PhD., in the newspaper for winning yet another science prize and then back in time to the University of Texas, where he was "The Boy Wonder."

She looks at his resume and goes searching for a photo of him at Sam Austin High School. Nothing. She checks every High School in Texas. Nothing.

She has the Power Of God. She shuts down all non-essential computer power at PACT and revs it up. She does a worldwide search for Brewer's facial features. Five minutes later, Bingo!

She looks at the results and runs the search again, thinking, It's worth another five minutes to double-check this.

43

AS NADINE AND LAWRENCE are being led away by a burly guard, they're both thinking, At least we're away from the terrace. There was definitely no escape with so many people around. But, now what?

The three of them cross the kitchen to the back stairs. Nadine spots a liquor cabinet and shouts, "My husband can't go another step without a drink."

On cue, Lawrence falters and collapses against a table. The guard, very annoyed, says, "Okay, get him some water."

Nadine shouts, "No! I'm a doctor! No water! It has to be alcohol. The purer the better. He's got esophageal immotility!"

The guard is confused. Nadine rummages through the liquor and pulls out Armagnac, Grand Marnier and Irish whiskey. She pours them all into a very large glass. "It just has to coagulate."

Lawrence wheezes. The guard asks, "How long is this going to take?"

"Just a moment...While we're waiting, would you be so kind as to give an old lady a cigarette?"

The guard replies, "I don't smoke."

Nadine is surprised and speechless. Bad guys always smoke!

Lawrence picks up the slack. He stammers and stutters but says, "We have to heat up the drink. Quick!"

He then grabs his heart and starts moaning.

Nadine acts as though she just was hit by lightning. "Of course, it won't coagulate without heat!"

She immediately rummages around the gas stove until she finds a box of matches.

The guard looks at Lawrence moaning and says, "Hurry up then! Let's get this over with."

Nadine finds some matches, brings the glass full of liquids next to her and turns on the gas stove. She then lights the match and throws it into the glass causing it to burst into flames. She throws it into the face of the guard who screams in pain.

Lawrence and Nadine rush out looking for Sabrina Rose... while silently praying that Monique is still alive.

44

DIMITRA COOLY SITS with her legs spread wide across the back of a chair facing Sabrina Rose and Monique. A gun dangles from her hand. The silence in the room is broken by sand blowing against the window. The amount of sand increases by the minute.

Her phone rings. She orders Monique to shut the window and then answers the phone. Dimitra listens as Dalakos tells her that the money will soon come through. She is instructed to keep an eye on Monique and Sabrina Rose until he arrives. He ends the conversation by saying, "As promised, you can have the honor to kill them both, but I want to be there to enjoy it."

Dimitra hangs up and smiles. She knows she can't kill her prisoners yet but that won't stop her from having some fun.

She asks Monique, "I'll give you a choice. Who do you want me to kill first, you or your daughter?"

Monique looks desperately around the room. For some kind of escape, for some kind of weapon but there are no weapons and certainly no escape.

Monique stalls for time. Just have to keep her talking. "Kill me. But don't kill my daughter, I beg of you." Sabrina Rose begins to whimper.

Dimitra is clearly enjoying this moment. She says, "Maybe you didn't hear the question. I said..."

Monique says, "I...I...Kill me first!"

Monique stands up and puts Sabrina Rose behind her. Dimitra is enjoying every moment. "Just as I thought you would say."

She too gets up and crosses the room toward them. "Get out of the way. I want you to watch your daughter die."

Sabrina Rose clutches her mother and screams, "No!"

Monique gets on her knees and wraps her arms around Dimitra's legs. She pleads, "Please don't. Please!"

While on her knees, Monique slips off one of her high heels.

Dimitra laughs and says, "Get up. I want you to watch. Like I had to watch you and Christopher."

Just the thought of Monique and Christopher puts her into a rage. She pulls Monique by the hair and shouts, "I said get up!"

The moment Dimitra pulls her hair, Monique screams to her daughter, "Run for the door!"

Sabrina Rose makes a dash for the door. Dimitra points the gun at her just as she gets there. Sabrina Rose turns the door knob and just as Dimitra pulls the trigger, Monique slams the heel into Dimitra's wrist.

The force of a mother protecting her child. A force she didn't know she had. The gun goes off as Dimitra drops the gun to the floor. The bullet hits the wall. Sabrina Rose gets safely out the door.

Monique screams to Sabrina Rose, "Wait for me at the bottom of the stairs on the ground floor!"

Sabrina Rose doesn't hesitate, she heads for the stairs. Dimitra and Monique face each other. Neither one says a word.

Dimitra is clearly in pain, blood spurting from her wrist.

They both dive for the gun but Monique gets there first.

Monique points the gun at her and Dimitra freezes. Dimitra says, "You don't have the nerve!"

Monique doesn't bother answering. She thinks, How hard can it be to fire a gun? It's gotta be just like plug 'n play...point and pull. Well, only one way to find out.

In the background, Dimitra has changed her tune. "I was forced into all this by Christopher against my will but the two of us together could stop him! Yes, we could kill him!"

Monique barely hears her. Without a word, she fires a shot into Dimitra's chest. Monique is pleased that it wasn't complicated at all.

Dimitra collapses to the floor. Monique doesn't want to use all her bullets.

She puts the gun to Dimitra's heart and fires. After making sure she's dead, she kicks off her other heel and rushes out the door.

45

YOU NEVER KNOW how loud a gunshot is until you've actually fired one. Nadine and Lawrence hear the shots and run towards the sound. They get to the floor just as the door to the stairs closes.

They rush into the dressing room, see Dimitra lying in a pool of blood and immediately head for the stairs.

The sound of the bullets is also heard on the roof top terrace. The terrorists' bodyguards draw their guns and face each other. There is no honor amongst thieves, only suspicion. Dalakos takes three of his men and runs out of the room in the direction of the gun shots.

He throws open the door to the dressing room and finds Dimitra lying in a pool of blood and very much dead. Dalakos follows the trail of blood to the stairwell.

He thinks, What's done is done. The money should be coming through any time now. I can't just disappear before it does.

He orders the three men to find Monique and Sabrina Rose but not to harm them. The thought of torturing Sabrina Rose to death while her mother watches puts a smile on his face.

Dalakos calmly walks back onto the Terrace. Tension fills the air. Guns are out and it looks like things could explode at any second.

He coolly announces, "Nothing to worry about. It seems that Monique Williams killed herself...three bullets to the head!"

Everyone laughs and then laughs some more. The laughter of relief, of release. The terrorists retake their seats followed by their bodyguards who slowly put their guns away.

46

MONIQUE RUSHES DOWN the stairs and finds Sabrina Rose cowering in the stairwell by the ground floor. They fly into each other's arms.

They hear heavy footsteps coming down the stairs. Monique wonders if she should go out through the lobby or head for the underground parking. She looks back upstairs and sees that she's left a trail of bloody footprints behind her.

Monique reaches under her dress and pulls off her blood-stained stockings. She opens the door to the hotel lobby and throws the stockings across the floor. The footsteps get louder. Monique takes Sabrina Rose and they rush down to the underground garage.

They speed past the parked cars to the ramp that hopefully will get them out of there. But there's an armed guard blocking the exit. Monique puts her hand over Sabrina Rose's mouth and backtracks.

Dalakos' men reach the ground floor and see a trail of blood leading out into the lobby. They scramble into the lobby and look desperately for Sabrina Rose and Monique just in time to spot a cleaning woman carrying blood-soaked stockings.

Underground, Monique tells Sabrina Rose, "Stand on the other side of that pillar."

Sabrina Rose doesn't want to leave her mother. Monique takes her in her arms and quietly says, "Trust me. You have to trust me. Now go on."

Sabrina Rose reluctantly heads for the pillar. Monique points her gun at the gas tank of the car closest to the stairwell door. She fires and waits for an explosion. But unlike in the movies, all she gets is a steady stream of gasoline pouring out of the car.

Monique frantically tries the doors of the cars in the garage. Locked.

She hears footsteps coming towards the door to the garage. She only has one bullet left. She points it towards the door and waits.

Sabrina Rose runs towards her mother waving a broom like a crazy little witch. Monique sees her coming and shouts, "What are you doing? I told you to stay there!"

Sabrina Rose runs right past her and slams the broom onto the concrete floor. "There was a spider coming to get you. He was this close!"

She lifts up the broom and there is a big black crushed scorpion. "I couldn't get anything out of my mouth. I couldn't speak!"

Monique says, "Thanks, sweetheart. Now, get over behind that pillar."

Before Sabrina Rose can move, the door opens and just as Monique is about to fire she sees that it's Lawrence and Nadine. She nearly collapses thinking she almost shot them but quickly regains her wits.

She shouts to them, "Do you have any matches?"

Upstairs, Dalakos' men notice that there is no more trail of blood. They decide to split up and two of them head back for the stairs to the underground garage.

47

UP ON THE roof top terrace, Dalakos gets a phone call. He listens and then announces, "The money has come through. In exactly one hour, Washington, D.C. will be Lazered!"

The assembled terrorists applaud.

Dalakos presses a button and a big screen comes down. "I have alerted the media that something big is going to happen around the White House in one hour. Little do they know that they will be rushing to film their own deaths. We can all watch it together on CNN! Until then, enjoy the party!"

Dalakos gets a standing ovation. Their applause washes over him like a cool refreshing breeze on a hot humid day. As a sure sign the Gods are smiling upon him, the wind picks up dramatically and blows across the roof top terrace.

48

LAWRENCE'S VOICE is almost a whisper as he looks directly at Monique. "Okay, we stick with your plan. We set off the explosion as a distraction. You run and tell the guard that there are men killing each other down here. He'll go get help or he'll come down himself. Either way, the three of you will be able to get past him."

Monique asks, "Where will you be?"

"Someone has to light the fireworks and stay down here making noise. Now get going! All of you!"

Monique doesn't hesitate. She grabs Sabrina Rose and heads towards the ramp that will take them outside. She looks back, sees that Nadine isn't with her and shouts, "Come on!"

Nadine's voice is firm. "No, I'm staying here with my husband. You two go on ahead."

Monique doesn't wait a second. She takes Sabrina Rose and heads up the ramp.

Lawrence looks at his wife and says, "I love you, baby, but I sure wish you had gone with them."

"We would've only slowed them down. Now, shut up and pass me the matches."

Lawrence lights a match and hands the box to Nadine. She lights a match and heads to the other pool of gas. They both drop the matches at the same time. They come together behind a pillar and wrap their arms around each other. At that moment, the stairwell door opens...just as the car explodes. The screams of two of Dalakos' men can be heard above the sound of the burning car.

Monique and Sabrina Rose reach the top of the ramp and scream, "Help! Help! They're killing each other down there!"

Down in the garage, the explosion is mixed with Dalakos' men screaming and Lawrence and Nadine improvising a war of words. Lawrence shouts, "I'll kill you DALAKOS!"

Nadine shouts back, "KILL DALAKOS!"

The armed guard hears Dalakos' name and makes his way down into the garage without giving Monique and Sabrina Rose a second thought.

Out in the sand swept air, Sabrina Rose and Monique rush to get as far away from the garage as possible.

From behind, they hear, "Stop!" It's the third of Dalakos' men. He has come out from the lobby and is chasing them. Monique and Sabrina Rose continue running. Monique shouts, "Don't look back!"

But, the two of them are no match for the man. It's just a matter of time before he catches them. Then, from behind they hear what sounds like a horse. They don't dare look back.

They continue running for their lives.

The sound of the horse gets closer. The guard turns. The last thing he ever hears is a horse coming at him. The last thing he ever sees is Kidd's sword coming down to cut off his head.

Kidd has to shout to be heard over the wind. "Monique wait! I'm here to help you!"

Monique and Sabrina Rose continue running. Kidd rides past them and turns, blocking their way. Monique and Sabrina Rose stop, exhausted, out of breath. Monique takes Sabrina Rose in her arms and looks up at the man on horseback. She sees a black man on horseback with a sword at his side.

Kidd notices Monique staring at his sword and immediately heaves it behind him. Kidd jumps off his horse and faces Monique and Sabrina Rose. "Monique, I'm here to help you."

Monique looks at Kidd and says, "Sabrina Rose, I want you to meet the man who is here to help us. I want you to meet Mr. Kidd Black."

Sabrina Rose says, "Hello, Mr. Kidd Black, my name is Ms. Sabrina Rose Williams."

Kidd puts out his hand and says, "A pleasure to meet you. A real pleasure."

They shake hands and Kidd turns to Monique. They stand there looking at each other. Monique is exhausted and near tears. After all the stress she's been through, she finds herself face to face with Kidd Black. Silence.

Sabrina Rose says, "Say something, mommy."

Monique says, "I can't. I can't. I can't believe it."

At that, Monique falls into Kidd's arms and begins to cry. Kidd holds her. He holds her like he'll never let her go. Sabrina Rose looks on curiously. Who is this man? Why is my mother crying?

Ike rides up to them with Nadine and Lawrence on his horse. He coughs and says, "We'll have plenty of time for all this later. Now we've got a rendezvous point to get to."

Kidd and Monique don't move. Ike continues, "We've got to get as far away from here as possible."

Nadine says, "We're running out of time."

At the sound of her voice, Monique and Kidd look up. Monique asks, "You're alive? You're alive!"

Nadine says, "Yes, this nice man came down into the garage at just the right moment. As they say, we thought we were goners."

Lawrence adds, "But, here we are!"

Ike says, "I'll take Mrs. Williams and Sabrina Rose on my horse and you take your parents on yours."

Kidd savors the last moment of his embrace with Monique. He reluctantly pulls away and says, "No. I'm going back to take care of Dalakos. No mistakes. I want to see it for myself."

Ike thinks about trying to stop him but figures it's no use. "Okay...But, they'll be here in an hour. An hour maximum!"

Monique says, "Who? What are you talking about?"

Kidd ignores her and says, "If they come. I'm going back. Put my parents and the girl on Chataqua. You and Monique will have to walk...There's an oasis due west from here. Wait for me."

He looks into Monique's eyes and says, "I promise I'll be there."

Lawrence says, "My son never went back on a promise in his life. Now, let's get going!"

Monique looks out at the ominous desert and asks, "We're going out there?"

Ike says, "Look on the bright side. At least we can be sure no one will follow us."

Kidd says, "These storms can't last forever. I'll find you with the GPS."

Ike knows Sabrina Rose has been through a lot. He tries to comfort her by saying, "Don't worry, I'll get a message to your Dad. He has GPS, too."

Sabrina Rose says, "Duuhh, my daddy invented GPS." Ike says to Monique, "Charming kid you have there." Monique says, "Time for us to get out of here."

Kidd picks up his sword and sheathes it. Ike dismounts and says, "Kidd, take Chataqua."

Before Kidd can protest, Ike continues. "He's faster and smarter than the horse you've got. Plus, Chataqua isn't used to being a pack horse."

Kidd nods his head and mounts Chataqua. Ike lifts Sabrina Rose up onto Scheherazade and says, "Here we go."

Monique stares at Kidd who stares right back. Once Sabrina Rose is on the horse, Ike says, "Okay, Mrs. Black, you're next."

Nadine is helped up on the horse. She looks down at Kidd and says, "For all the good it'll do, I have to say it...be careful!"

Kidd smiles and says, "Careful is my middle name, mom."

Ike boosts Lawrence onto the horse and gets ready to leave when he notices Monique hasn't moved.

Monique is lost. Lost in the endless blue eyes that she's never forgotten. She can't bear to leave him. She's lost in a spell, a spell broken by her daughter's voice. "Mom, let's go."

Monique quickly turns away and stands next to the horse. Ike says to Kidd. "One hour maximum."

On foot, Ike leads the horse out towards the desert with Monique walking next to him. Kidd doesn't wait for them to get out of sight. He says, "Come on, Chataqua, we've got a date and we can't be late."

He pulls once on the reins and Chataqua immediately takes him flying across the desert.

49

UP ON THE terrace, the mood has gone from uneasy to panic. Explosions rip through the underground garage. The fire that Monique had started had now spread to the other limousines. And, many of them were filled with various types of explosives. Just in case. This crowd knows what their fellow terrorists are capable of. They don't trust anyone.

Dalakos gets word that Monique, Sabrina Rose and Kidd's parents were rescued by two very unusual Bedouins. A black one and a white one. He knows he has to get out of the hotel.

But, smoke billows up towards them. The ground floor is engulfed in flames. The elevators are out. The electricity is out. They're all going to have to make a choice. Try the stairs, six flights down, in the hope that they can get through the fire and smoke or stay on the roof and wait for help.

Each terrorist makes his own calculations. How long will it take for help to come? Help in the guise of a helicopter. What type of helicopters are around here? Where are the nearest ones? How many of them can they take at once?

Dalakos knows what they're thinking. If there's only room for one person on a helicopter, they might have to kill the others. He also knows that they'll stay on the rooftop terrace. Terrorists are cowards at heart. They attack the weak, the defenseless. Which is why I was born to lead. Born for greatness. I choose the hard way. I attack the strong.

Dalakos watches smugly as his guests huddle in fear on the terrace. He calls two of his men and says, "Follow me."

50

DEVON, BARRY AND BREWER arrive at the SCC. Devon's phone buzzes. He tells Barry and Brewer to go on ahead. As they walk towards the door, Devon reads the text message from Caroline. Expect the unexpected.

Devon sighs and thinks, Easy to say, tough to do. He downloads the photo she sent.

Brewer says, "When all this is over, we're going to have the biggest barbecue since Mrs. O'Leary's cow burned Chicago. Barry Riley, you ever had barbecued camel?"

Barry says, "Camel? You humping me?"

Brewer guffaws. "Humping me? Now, that's funny."

They come up to the retinal I.D. security system. Brewer is still laughing when he puts his eye up to it. He stops laughing and gasps. "It doesn't work."

Barry says, "Is this a joke?"

Brewer tries again. "It doesn't work. We can't get in!"

Devon comes up behind them. "I suggest you find a way to get it to work."

Brewer says, "Devon, this is crazy. Someone must've tampered with it. I've tried it twice. We can't get in. It could take a day to troubleshoot this."

Devon moves closer to Brewer and his tone of voice is cold and threatening. "I said I suggest you find a way to get it to work, Valery."

Barry thinks he's hearing things. Valerie?

Brewer smiles but his eyes are looking for an escape. He says, "I don't..."

Devon cuts him off. "Valery Bassilov. Doesn't sound like the name of a good ole' boy born and bred in Texas, does it Barry?"

Before Barry can say anything, Devon continues. "Born in Siberia but bred by the Soviet Union as a mole to be implanted in the US."

Barry says, not the least bit convinced, "The Soviet Union? Huh?"

Devon says, "Yeah, I imagine they pulled a few strings for you but you did most of the work yourself. Here's a photo of a Young Pioneer in the USSR. Look familiar?"

Devon shows it to Brewer who doesn't look at it. His eyes are focused on Devon who continues, "The Wonder Boy. But, tell me, Valery, what happened to you when the Wall came tumbling down and with it the Evil Empire?"

Brewer's shoulders sag. He leans against the door and says, "I drifted. I was lost. My dream of helping the Revolution went down with that Wall. Then, I got a new cause. A new way to make the Revolution happen."

Devon looks like he just ate some spoiled meat. "But, Dalakos? The murderer?"

Brewer says, "One man's terrorist is another man's Freedom Fighter."

Devon is disgusted. "Talking time's over. Now, open that door."

Brewer says, "I can't do it. I changed the retinal I.D. code."

Devon puts a grip on Brewer's cheeks and pulls him close. "Don't fuck with me! I know how these systems work. You have to be here to do that and you were with us the whole time. Now open it!"

Brewer is surprisingly cool, "It doesn't work! And, by the time you get it open, it'll be too late."

Devon stares into Brewer's eyes. He smells the bittersweet taste of almonds right before Brewer's body starts to shake. Devon thinks, Almonds, contortions. He's taken cyanide!

Devon screams, "He's taken cyanide! What kind of people are we dealing with here?"

Brewer grabs his stomach and his head tilts back. That's when Devon spots Brewer's contact lenses. Contact lenses that blocked the retinal I.D. He rubs his finger across Brewer's eye, knocking the lens to the side.

Brewer realizes what's going on and shuts his eyes. Devon forces him up against the retinal I.D. He shouts to Barry, "Kick him in the balls! Hurry!"

Barry doesn't hesitate. He gets in position and kicks Brewer right in the balls. Brewer's eyes pop open and the door clicks. Brewer collapses and Devon lets his body drop and then takes a step towards the door.

Barry, ever the doctor, reaches for Brewer's pulse. "Classic case of Black's crack in the plaque."

Devon stops and asks, "What're you talking about?"

"Heart attack. A lot of what we know about heart attacks comes from Kidd's Uncle Asher, circa 1975. Look it up if you don't believe me."

Devon looks at him blankly and takes a step inside the SCC. Barry calls out after him, "Never heard of Dr. Asher Black?

What did they teach you at Harvard anyway?"

51

DALAKOS GLANCES AT the elevator. Smoke is beginning to come up through it. Only a suicidal maniac would try an elevator in a fire. I might know a bunch of them, but I'm not one.

He puts his hand on the door to the stairwell but it's already hot to the touch. The fire is moving faster than he thought. He rushes to the service stairs, opens up the door and smoke wafts up at him. He rushes to the toilet, grabs a paper towel, soaks it in water, throws it over his face and tries the stairs again. He gets face down on the ground and starts crawling through the smoke down the stairs. He's not the least bit surprised to see that his guards haven't followed him.

He makes it to the fourth floor gasping for air. He kicks open a door and staggers to a window. He throws a TV through it and sucks in the air. He looks down to see the fire is burning through the first two floors. At that moment, a group of firemen are getting a safety net together for some people to jump from the third floor.

Dalakos takes a towel from the bathroom, fills it with water and wraps it around his face. Back through the smoke he works his way blindly down the stairs to the third floor. He runs down the hallway to the room where he saw the people waiting to jump. He bangs on the door, pleading to have it opened. Immediately, someone opens the door. He hurries in and shuts the door behind him.

There are two families of Saudis there. Two sets of parents and four young kids. Terrified. It's a race against time. Will the firemen be in place before the smoke and flames reach their room?

Dalakos calculates. There might not be time for all of us to get out. Maybe yes, maybe no. More smoke comes in through the door. Dalakos coolly takes out his gun and puts a bullet through the heads of both fathers. The women scream and rush to protect their hysterical children.

Without saying a word, Dalakos goes to the window and waits for the firemen to get in place. They signal to him that it's okay to jump.

Kidd too is surveying the scene. He spots people on the roof frantically waving down to the street for help. He zooms in and recognizes some of them as the terrorists he saw coming into the airport. He doesn't see Dalakos but assumes he's with them.

His attention is drawn to the third floor as a man jumps to safety. Bulls eye. Dalakos! Two of his men come rushing up to him. He gasps for air but is steady.

The firemen wait for more people to jump but all they see is smoke billowing out of the room.

Dalakos staggers into a nearby bungalow. The two men follow him. Kidd is disgusted when he sees three bodies dumped outside the door. Dalakos had killed everyone inside. They were clearly in his way.

Dalakos' men take position in front of the bungalow. The wind picks up and visibility is limited to ten yards.

Inside, Dalakos throws some water on his face and then picks up a phone. "Prince, I want the desert scoured inch by inch. Monique Williams and her daughter have escaped!"

He listens for a moment and then screams, "I don't give a fuck that you don't want to get involved. Make your choice. Us or them! Right now!"

He listens for a split second and says, "That's better. Get everyone out there!" The storm takes a sudden turn for the worse. Barely able to see in front of him, Kidd works his way slowly down the windswept hill and then puts Chataqua into a gallop. They approach Dalakos' bungalow and jump the fence. One stunned guard dies frozen in fear, throat slashed. Chataqua never slows down as Kidd has him jump the fence behind the bungalow. One down, two to go.

The remaining guard desperately bangs on the bungalow door pleading with Dalakos to let him in. Dalakos asks himself, Do I want that coward in here with me or not? He quickly makes a decision. He opens the door, shoots the man, takes his gun and slams the door shut.

Chataqua and Kidd come back over the fence and see that there are now two dead guards. Kidd dismounts and gropes his way towards the dead guards. He checks the one that Dalakos shot and sees that his gun isn't there. He crawls towards the one he had killed and takes his gun. A Beretta, eight bullets.

Kidd walks Chataqua behind the bungalow and has him lie down against the wall to protect him against the storm. He takes out his sword and goes to the front of the bungalow. He then smashes in the front windows allowing the wind to whip sand into it. Immediately, bullets come flying towards him but he's already at the side of the bungalow.

Kidd thinks, I know how many bullets I have but I have no idea how many he has. For all I know, he could keep on spraying those windows all night. If I can get up on the roof, I might find another way in.

Kidd searches the side of the house for a fissure, a crack that will allow him to get a grip to scale the wall. He spots a slightly dark spot caused by a small leak from the water pipes. He thrusts his hand over it and gets his grip. He starts climbing.

Kidd gets one hand on the roof and then another. He pulls himself up and comes face to face with a Widowmaker Scorpion. Kidd freezes.

The scorpion stops. After what seems like an eternity, it continues across the roof, heading right for Kidd's hand. Kidd pulls his hand away and hangs by his other hand. Using just one hand, he pulls himself up on the roof. The real Spiderman.

Once on the roof, Kidd puts some distance between him and the Widowmaker. He then looks for a way into the bungalow. Nothing.

He then hears bullets being fired at the front windows from inside the bungalow.

Kidd thinks, Clearly, Dalakos has ammunition to spare. But why shoot at the windows. Unless he's planning on making a break for it...through the back door!

Kidd rushes across the roof to the back of the bungalow. He looks down and there's Dalakos pulling up Chataqua. Kidd takes aim but Chataqua is between him and Dalakos. He can't risk a shot, not in this weather.

Kidd leaps from the roof and lands on Dalakos. The two of them roll off the horse onto the ground. Kidd puts his gun to Dalakos' head and pulls the trigger. Nothing! The sand has jammed it. Dalakos grabs for his own gun, but Kidd slams into him and the gun drops to the ground.

Dalakos barely watches the gun disappear into the sand. With his left hand, he grabs Kidd's ankle and uses his own momentum against him. He spins Kidd around and jumps on his back, knocking him to the ground.

This is no Hollywood fight. No time for witty conversation, just a fight to the finish. Dalakos pins Kidd down and uses his legs to spread-eagle him. He reaches under Kidd's arms and puts him in a hold he can't get out of. He's got him half-nelsoned and half-chicken winged.

Dalakos moves in for the kill. He slides his thumbs around Kidd's neck and starts to squeeze. In doing so, he turns Kidd's head to the side.

Kidd spots a Widowmaker against the wall of the bungalow.

It's a race against time and Kidd's time is running out fast. He pushes from his legs and inches his way towards the wall.

But, even the strongest flame, when denied oxygen is doomed to go out. Dalakos leans forward putting more pressure on Kidd's neck. This gives Kidd a chance to move faster along the sand.

Dalakos can't see anything with his head buried in Kidd's back. Kidd has maneuvered Dalakos' arm next to the Widowmaker but the Widowmaker seems totally oblivious. Kidd's mouth is dry but he forces himself to cough up some saliva.

He spits at the Widowmaker who lashes out and bites Dalakos' arm. Dalakos experiences intense pain and loosens his grip for a split second but it's still too strong for Kidd to get free. But, he's able to grab a breath.

Dalakos renews the pressure on Kidd's neck. Dalakos' heart, pumped with adrenaline, beats wildly. Kidd is fading as the poison flies through Dalakos' system. Just as Kidd's lights are about to go out, Dalakos flinches. He rolls off Kidd and his muscles contract as his mind clouds and he begins to salivate and sweat profusely. His eyes tear, his pupils dilate and his vision becomes impaired. His eyeballs pulsate and he begins to vomit blood.

Kidd gasps for air and forces himself to get up. He stands over Dalakos who looks up at him with fear and hatred. Then Dalakos forces a contorted smile and gasps, "You're too late. Too late. Too late."

He then starts convulsing, goes into respiratory paralysis and dies.

Kidd learned his lesson from Ike. He takes the sword and stabs Dalakos three times in the heart. Once to kill him, once to be sure, and once for all the innocent people Dalakos murdered.

52

MICHAEL DOWD is bored. The CNN news room had received a call that there would be something big going down at 1500 Pennsylvania Avenue, just outside the White House security perimeter. So, here he was, waiting with his crew and then waiting some more.

Michael shakes his head and thinks, Like Christopher Dalakos himself would phone us to say that there was going to be an attack...And then rumors start flying that Amanda Mason is taking a "leave of absence".

Michael sighs. Amanda Mason taking a leave of absence. Now that's a story I should be following instead of this waste of time.

He looks over at the FBI guys. They've decided to block off the street. Uniformed DC cops move into action. Another traffic jam in the Great War Against Terror. Well, at least we have something to film.

Michael signals to his crew. "Let's do it."

They lethargically get up and get into place. Michael checks himself in a mirror. Back when I had a career, I had a cute young woman to do my make-up for me. Now, it's do it yourself. Kind of like my sex life.

The only thing that makes me feel any better is that those jokers from Fox and Al-jazeera are here too. I'm not the only sucker around here.

The crew is in place. Michael says in his most ironic voice, "The 'terrorist attack' is scheduled to start at six on the dot. So, let's start with some shots of the cops causing yet another traffic jam and then we'll come back live to me at six."

53

DEVON IS FRANTIC.. The supercomputer has been overridden. He has no control over it whatsoever. Barry just stands aside. He knows there's nothing he can do. Devon says, mostly to himself, "There has to be a Wi-Fi signal here somewhere. But where?"

Barry hesitates and then suggests, "Maybe we could block off the windows so it can't get out."

Devon says, "That's the beauty of Wi-Fi. It goes through walls. Where the hell is it?"

Devon stares at the computer screen of the supercomputer. "The lazer has been activated!"

Barry says, "Do something!" Devon says, "Fuck you!"

Barry says, "Pull out the plug!"

Devon shouts back, "You idiot! Supercomputers have internal backup battery power!"

Devon watches helplessly as the lazer moves into position. Over Washington!

Barry says, "Does Wi-Fi go underground?"

Devon says, "It depends. If there's an antenna above ground to catch the signal."

Barry says, "I tried Wi-Fi. Didn't always work." Devon says, "What's your point?"

Before Barry can answer, Devon has a moment of recognition. Maybe there is no Wi-Fi. Maybe there's a cable! Devon shouts, "Barry, you're a genius!"

Barry has that surprised look of someone who's totally confused. Devon gets on his hands and knees and says, "If there's a direct link to the overriding computer, it's got to start here."

Barry says, "It's got to be drilled right through the floor. We'll never get to it from here!"

Devon says, "Right. Let's get down to the garage."

54

THE CHAMELEON LOOKS at a security camera screen and sees Barry and Devon rushing into the underground garage. He sets the Lazer in motion, grabs a gun and rushes out of the bunker.

Back at the roof of the Banquet Center, things have calmed down. The fire still rages but the Prince is sending a fleet of helicopters to rescue the guests. One of the terrorists is on the phone and shouts, "CNN is on the air, LIVE! Oh, what I would give for a TV set now."

A man in traditional Arab dress looks out across the desert and quietly says, "This is no ordinary storm."

At that moment, Michael Dowd is ready to go live on CNN. How the hell am I going to fill two minutes with this story? There's nothing. Nothing. I got thirty seconds at best.

He gets the signal and puts on his game face. "It's another tense day here in Washington. Homeland Security has received a tip that something big is going to happen right here at 1500 Pennsylvania Avenue.

That's right, one block from the White House. The D.C. Police have blocked all traffic here. So, if you're a government worker heading home, avoid this part of town at any cost. The FBI is here so it could mean there's something to this tip."

Michael walks over to an FBI agent and asks, "Hi, Michael Dowd from CNN, is there anything you can tell us?"

The FBI agent says, "No," and walks away.

Michael tries not to look too chagrined. "Now, that could be a no or a no. As we've all learned, 'no' can mean a lot of things."

Michael thinks, Jesus, I'm blabbering.

Just then, the Lazer beam bursts through the sky and explodes right on Pennsylvania Avenue. Bulls eye.

People start screaming. Michael shouts, "Get a shot of that! Get a shot of that!"

The camera zooms in on the Lazer as it slowly works its way down the now-empty Pennsylvania Avenue.

"There's a beam, a death beam working its way toward the White House. This place is absolute chaos! Someone warn the President! Someone warn the President!"

55

DEVON AND BARRY run into the dark garage and turn on the lights. Most of the bulbs are out but in the dim light they stare up at the ceiling. They walk to just below where they think the supercomputer must be.

Devon shouts, "There's nothing! Nothing here!"

Barry jumps up on a car and puts his fist through the low ceiling. "It's a fake ceiling. There's a cable up here! Let's rip it out!"

Devon jumps up on the car and stands next to him. "Careful, there's a lot of juice running through it."

The unforgettable voice of the Chameleon comes across the length of the garage. "Careful indeed my friends. Move away from that cable or you're both dead."

Devon whispers to Barry, "Give me a hand up and then get the lights!"

Instantly, Barry boosts Devon up into the false ceiling. The Chameleon comes running towards them from across the garage. Once Devon is up, Barry jumps off the car and races towards the light switch. The Chameleon shoots and misses but Barry doesn't slow down.

Devon quickly crawls through the false ceiling. He supports himself with the metal framework that holds the ceiling in place and follows the cable. When he hears the Chameleon coming towards him, he freezes. Just then, Barry gets to the lights and shuts them off. Darkness.

Barry peers through the darkness trying to see where the Chameleon is. But, if he finds him, what's he going to do? He needs a weapon. Something.

The Chameleon stares at the ceiling listening for a sound. He has seven bullets in his Beretta.

In the darkness, Devon can hear the humming of the cable. Devon puts his hands on it. Even through the insulation, he can feel the power running through it. Devon takes a deep breath and clutches the cable. He gets a good grip on it and gets ready to pull it.

Barry also breathes deeply and gets ready to rush the Chameleon. He hopes this will give Devon enough time to rip out the cable.

56

MICHAEL DOWD CONTINUES to broadcast. "The beam is heading right for the White House! Someone do something! Oh, my God! It's going to be there in a matter of seconds! Has someone called the President Evacuate the White House! Evacuate the White House! Evacuate the White House!"

57

THE CHAMELEON HEARS a rustling in the ceiling. He gets under it and aims his gun. He turns as he hears Barry scream. As the Chameleon shoots into the darkness, Barry instinctively dives to the ground. The bullets fly past him.

Knowing it's now or never, Devon grabs the cable and screams as the power rips through his body. The Chameleon hears Devon scream and turns his gun up towards him. As he's about to shoot, Barry slams into him. The bullet is way off target.

The two of them go flying onto the hood of a nearby car.

Barry gropes desperately for the Chameleon's gun. He finds it and tries to force it from his hand but can't. The Chameleon rolls him over on the hood and starts forcing the gun towards Barry. Barry tries to kick the Chameleon but they're too close for it to have any effect. The gun slowly works its way towards Barry.

Barry reaches back with his right hand and grabs onto a windshield wiper. Just as the Chameleon's gun is almost pointed at his head, Barry rips out the windshield wiper and shoves it into the Chameleon's mouth.

The Chameleon drops the gun as he screams. Barry doesn't let up. He forces the wiper down the Chameleon's throat until he gags. Barry gets behind him and bangs his head against the hood of the car. The Chameleon's body goes limp. Barry reaches along the floor until he finds the Beretta. He puts it to the Chameleon's head and pulls the trigger.

Then, just to be sure, he pulls it again.

58

MICHAEL DOWD CONTINUES on CNN. "The Death Beam stopped! It just stopped! Who knows how and who knows why and who cares! It stopped! I repeat, it stopped!!!"

Behind him, a crowd of people can be heard cheering wildly. Michael shouts to the cameraman, "Get a shot of these people!

Get a shot of the happiest people on the planet! There's nothing better than staring into the face of death and coming out smiling!"

59

BARRY TURNS ON the garage lights and rushes back to find Devon. He glances at the distorted body of the Chameleon just to make sure that he's dead. Barry jumps up on the car and works his way into the false ceiling. He finds Devon's limp body and drags it out towards the car. When he gets it above the car, Barry slides down and then lowers Devon onto the hood.

He doesn't even bother to feel for a pulse. He tilts Devon's head back and breathes into his mouth. Rhythmically, one breath after another he tries to revive him. Devon twitches. A sign of life? Barry pounds on Devon's heart. He pounds again. More mouth to mouth. More pounding. Finally, Devon coughs. Barry turns him over as he throws up.

60

UP ON THE ROOFTOP TERRACE of the Hotel, the terrorists are terrorized. Where are the Prince's helicopters? Unfortunately for them, they were grounded by the sandstorm. So, they watch in horror as the flames reach the fifth floor.

The firemen take shelter from the storm. For the terrorists, there's no way out, except for a miracle. Those of them who think of themselves as religious, pray. Those who want nothing to do with religion, they too pray.

Then like an answer to their prayers, the wind becomes even more ferocious. And, if there is a God in Heaven, He certainly speaks in strange ways. The gusts bring sand with them and the sand smothers the fire. When the smoke clears, the hotel isn't burning. The terrorists can escape!

They work their way carefully down the stairs heading towards their waiting limos. From there, the airport. They've had enough of Dalakos' hospitality.

61

BARRY CARRIES DEVON into Brewer's car and sets him in. Devon's conscious now but in no condition to drive. Barry rushes around to the driver's seat, gets in and starts the car. Then he laughs. He has no idea how to get to the meeting point to hook up with Ike, Monique and Sabrina Rose.

Devon pulls his portable phone out. His voice is weak but he says, "Pull out of the garage. Then just follow the GPS and it'll take us right there."

Devon sits back. He has a contented look on his face. The ordeal is over. Now, as they track the GPS which will take him back to his family, he leans back in the seat and closes his eyes.

Barry shouts, "Holy shit!"

Adrenaline rushes through Devon as his eyes jolt open. They've come out of the garage and the visibility is near zero. The sandstorm is whipping out of the desert blinding everything in its path.

62

KIDD IS IN no-man's land. Too far in the desert to turn back and the GPS has stopped working. There's nothing to do but have the horse lie down, nestle into him and wait for the signal to come back on. He tries to get Chataqua to lie down but he won't. He insists on going forward.

Kidd thinks, Maybe he smells something I don't. Either way, he's not stopping. It looks like I'm along for the ride.

Kidd huddles over Chataqua who inches his way across the sand.

At the airport, twelve private planes wait to take off. The terrorists are comfortable in their planes. They've gotten word that the Lazer didn't reach its target. But, they're just happy to be alive and tomorrow is another day. There will be other targets and other weapons.

63

DEVON CHECKS THE GPS on his portable phone. Nothing. He takes out his laptop and checks to see if there is another way to reach the satellite. The satellite is working fine but the GPS can't get to the cell phones. The network is either overloaded or has been damaged by the storm.

He sees a flashing light on his computer's desktop. It's the homing device. The signal is coming from the desert at the oasis where they're supposed to meet!

Devon doesn't know if that's a good sign or not. If somehow Monique or Ike has gotten hold of the homing device, then they're safe.

But, if Dalakos is there...He doesn't even want to finish the thought. Because at this time, Devon has no way of knowing that Dalakos is dead.

Devon's voice is surprisingly strong as he says, "We've got to get to that oasis!"

Barry looks at the wind swirling past them and says, "We'll never make it in this car. We won't get fifty feet."

Devon reaches into the laptop case and pulls out a pile of bills. "If we can't find camels here, we can't find them anywhere."

He puts the laptop into its case, opens the door and steps out into the sandstorm.

Barry reluctantly gets out thinking, Camels?

64

MONIQUE, SABRINA ROSE AND IKE huddle into Scheherazade. They're all thinking, We've been through so much. We can't die now. We can't!

Monique holds Sabrina Rose tight and shouts over the storm, "We're going to make it! We're going to make it!"

As though the storm hears her, the wind seems to die down just a little. Just enough to give them hope that this storm isn't going to last forever.

In fact, the screen at Command Central in Kuwait bears out what Monique is feeling. The storm is breaking up. This is the signal they're waiting for.

The General isn't too sure what the political repercussions are going to be from bombing Saudi Arabia but it gives the old soldier a thrill to give the go-ahead. He figures that the Saudis will never admit that they were bombed and something would be worked out like it's always been done before. But all the King's horses and all the King's men aren't going to be able to put that airport back together when his boys are through with it.

What the General doesn't know but will soon find out, the terrorists are all lined up like sitting ducks just waiting to be roasted.

65

THE STORM HAS passed. Ike, Monique, Sabrina Rose and Kidd's parents wait in the desert with Scheherazade. The horse is lying down and the five of them are huddled into her for warmth, Bedouin-style. All of them, including the horse, are passed out. Gone to the world.

Off to their left, Chataqua trots towards them. On their right, a camel carrying both Barry and Devon heads their way. The horse and camel arrive at almost the same time on either side of them as they sleep.

Battered and hurting but proud of a job well done, Kidd and Devon look over at each other. But, it's not over yet. There's one more thing to be decided. Without saying a word, Kidd painfully dismounts from Chataqua and Devon grimaces as he gingerly gets down from the camel.

Barry stays on the camel and watches.

Kidd and Devon nod to each other and walk over to where everyone is asleep. Devon is almost near tears when he sees his daughter. He wants to pick her up and hold her in his arms but decides to let her sleep.

In the distance, a helicopter is heard. Monique stirs in her sleep and holds Sabrina Rose tighter. Monique looks up and sees Kidd and Devon standing there looking down at them. Her eyes go from one to the other. The two men of her life. One, the man she married and the father of her daughter. The other, the phantom she's dreamed about for eighteen years.

Monique has learned a lot these last few days. A lot about herself and a lot about life. She knows they want her to choose. And, she's going to.

Kidd speaks first. For eighteen years her name was in his thoughts. He can't bear the thought of losing her again. But, deep in his heart, he knows he has no choice but to bear it.

He forces himself to speak. "You and Sabrina Rose are now safe and Devon is here for you."

Kidd's parents hear their son's voice but sense that this would be a great moment to pretend they're still asleep...which is exactly what they do.

Devon thought he didn't care about losing Monique after seeing the passageway at Mohonk...but he knows that she's the only woman he'll ever love. And, she's the mother of his Sabrina Rose. He whispers, "He's right. I'm here for you. I'm here for you and Sabrina Rose."

Monique swallows hard and forces herself to speak. She looks at Devon and says, "I know. Deep inside, I've always known."

The helicopter is clearly getting closer. It will be there any moment now. Monique gently awakens Sabrina Rose and says, "Honey, look who's here."

Sabrina Rose opens her eyes to see the greatest sight she's ever going to see in her entire life. She jumps up and rushes into her father's arms.

She can't stop shouting, "Daddy! Daddy!"

Devon starts to cry. Ike, who was pretending to be asleep, wipes a tear from his eye. Barry too sniffles as father and daughter are reunited.

Kidd's parents can't take it any longer and they too "wake up".

Monique gets up and walks over to Kidd. "Thank you. Thank you for saving my daughter's life and that of my husband. And thanks for giving me back my life. For bringing me back to life."

She looks into his blue eyes not knowing when she'll ever be this close to him again.

Her eyes say one thing, My heart wants to go with you more than anything in the world...but not if it means leaving Devon and Sabrina Rose. I'll never forget you. You'll be in my heart forever...but her voice says another thing: "Goodbye."

She kisses him on the cheek and walks over to Devon. Devon puts out his free hand and Monique takes it.

Kidd searches for something to say, but the helicopter landing saves him from trying to find the right words. He also knows it saves him from saying the wrong words. But the noise of the helicopter can't hide the fact that his blue eyes are screaming out in pain, I, too, will never forget you. You'll be in my heart forever…

An American Special Forces soldier in full battle gear jumps out of the helicopter and shouts, "Let's go!"

Devon looks at Kidd and says, "It's great to have you back. The best. The best there ever was, the best there'll ever be."

Devon turns to Barry and says, "Thanks for saving my life."

Barry shrugs and says, "Hey, don't worry about it, I give all my patients a lifetime guarantee."

Kidd's parents walk over to him and put their arms around him. Kidd's mother lets her tears fall as she says, "My boy. My boy is back!"

The soldier shouts, "Let's go, go, go!"

The helicopter motor revs and the sound becomes almost deafening. The soldier pulls Nadine and Lawrence away from Kidd and escorts them to the helicopter. Devon, Sabrina Rose, and Monique follow.

The soldier screams over to Ike, Barry and Kidd. "Come on, come on! Let's move it fellas!"

Ike shouts back. "I'm not leaving my horse here, young man. You'll have to go on without me."

Kidd shouts, "And I'm not leaving Ike or my horse here. You'll have to go on without me."

Barry shouts, "And I'm not leaving my, uh, camel. So, get the hell out of here!"

The soldier smiles, shakes his head and gets into the helicopter. It immediately takes off and soon disappears into the coming dawn.

The three of them silently watch as the helicopter carrying Devon, Monique, Sabrina Rose and Kidd's parents crosses the horizon.

Once the helicopter is out of sight, Kidd, Barry and Ike slowly set off.

Kidd asks, "Who says the hero always gets the girl, anyway?" Ike says, "Ah, women. Give me a good horse any day." He tenderly rubs a hand along Chataqua's neck.

Barry asks, "Easy for you guys to say, I'm the one on the camel!"

Kidd says, "That reminds me of a joke."

Barry says, "I thought you were through with telling jokes."

Kidd continues, "That was back when I was dead. So, if you don't mind, I was about to tell a joke."

Ike says, "Hey, let the guy tell his joke."

Kidd says, "Thanks...A camel walks into a bar and orders a glass of wine..."

Barry shakes his head and says, "You're not telling it right. You're telling it like a guy who hasn't told a joke in eighteen years!"

Kidd smiles and says, "Give me some time. Just give me some time."

Ike smiles and says, "Take all the time you want. We've got all the time in the world."

Barry smiles, too. "Yeah, all the time in the world." The three of them ride off into the rising desert sun.

...and so it begins.

Printed in the USA
LP2970JV

ISBN: 978-0-9839433-0-3

CPSIA information can be obtained at www.ICGtesting.com
Printed in the USA
BVOW08s0647060913

330349BV00001B/2/P

9 780983 943303